ZELFAR SERIES BOOK TWO

ZELFAR
MISSING

Ruth Colter

the publishing CIRCLE

admin@ThePublishingCircle.com
or
THE PUBLISHING CIRCLE
Regarding: Ruth Colter
Suite 310
Cheyenne, Wyoming 82001

The publisher is not responsible for the author's website, other mentioned websites, or content of any website that is not owned by the publisher.

ZELFAR – THE MISSING/RUTH COLTER
ISBN 978-1-947398-12-2
Printed in the United States of America

Book design by Michele Uplinger

ZELFAR
MISSING

Ruth Colter

I dedicate this book, in loving memory,
to my big sister and life-long friend,
Janet Eileen Dorris

And to my husband,
children, grandchildren,
great-grandchildren, and my siblings.

CHAPTER 1

"Zophie!" My husband grabs my arm, shouting over the spectators. "Can you believe it? We'll have enough energy to send a hundred space shuttles to the moon and worlds beyond."

That's one of the many things I love about Travis—his excitement over new possibilities. His expertise may be agrophysics, but his curiosity is infinite.

"If anyone's going to other worlds," says our teenage son, Zack, "it's gonna be me. It was my idea to isolate the power of zilimite, so I should get to be first to test it in the cosmos."

I laugh, reaching to pat his shoulder. With teenage agility he easily dodges my hand. I pull back my arm as my smile fades, with thoughts of one world where my son can't go. He doesn't know you don't need a space explorer to go to another world. I wish I could tell Zack about the portal to Oregon, a place in a country called the United States of America, a place I've secretly visited for nearly four years. I hate keeping secrets, especially from my son.

"Your attention, please!" Bayl, an elder in Zelfar, stands tall on his hoverdisc, and his voice booms through the zelcom on his wrist. Six thousand pairs of eyes, Zelfar's entire population, stare at him floating above our heads. Every one of Zelfar's inhabitants is assembled in this wide grassy meadow, eager to observe the outcome of months of elaborate experiments.

"What you are about to witness," Bayl says, "is proof of our ability to harness enormous power. You will see a spectacle of lime colored arcs streak across the sky when the combined force of zilimite and the large green diamond is channeled to six special energy-holding domes."

Bayl waves a bright yellow flag in a large sweep over his head, signaling to begin the event.

Three-year-old "K" tugs at her brother's pant leg, and Zack lifts her to perch on his shoulders. We gaze at the sky. A hush fills the air. Static-charged particles tickle my nose and my feet tingle as if the ground were humming.

"Oooh!" K squeals and points at the first brilliant arc. She claps her hands, and Zack pivots in a circle, giving her the full spectrum of the light show.

BOOM!

My ears ring, and the ground heaves, bringing gasps from the crowd. I grab Travis's arm and reach a hand toward K fearing Zack may drop her. Instead, he falls to one knee, gripping his little sister to his chest. She wails in protest.

Before I can take her, another explosion tumbles all of us to our hands and knees. Bayl yelps, and I gasp as his hoverdisc plummets to the ground, toppling him into the crowd.

Several blasts echo in succession, filling the air with sulfuric smells, and the light show stops. Travis stretches his arms outward, bringing our family into a tight huddle.

"What's happening, Dad?" Zack squats closer to his father, and K leaps into my arms.

"I don't know, son. Just stay low until the ground stops

moving."

The rumbling earth finally settles, and I rise slowly. My wobbly legs strain to keep me upright. The murmuring crowd stares at the sky, at the ground, at each other. Our world never quakes. The weather is always sunny and seventy degrees. Minor accidents are rare; major ones never occur at all.

I press my little girl's face into my shoulder and stare at the destruction. Health Dome, nearest the meadow, lies as a huge mound of rubble, leaving nothing but jagged chunks of its crystillium shell. A lump forms in my throat. As a health expert, I serve in the Health Dome. Nearby, one of the energy-holding domes has turned into a heap of yellowish-green sand.

"Vad, can you hear me?" My husband taps at his wrist and shouts into his zelcom. He taps it again. "Vad, answer me. Are you all right?"

"Yes, Travis, I am unharmed." Our android's voice is loud and clear. "Our homedome is intact, but communications have been disrupted. I altered the frequency in your zelcom to connect directly to me."

"Fire!" a man yells.

Fire? We haven't used fire for years.

"The forest is on fire!" A woman shouts.

Travis and I turn in the direction of the pointing fingers. In the distance, an orange glow pulses amid billows of dark purple smoke.

"The portal!" I scream, then clamp my hand over my mouth. With trembling fingers, I grip my husband's shirt. "What if we can't get to Krissie and Gram?" My grandmother raised me after I lost my parents when I was eleven. I can't bear the thought she might have to raise my daughter, too.

Travis shouts at his wrist. "Vad, bring our ionic wave detectors and meet us at Paradise Falls." My husband taps his zelcom again. "Enclosed sphere, four passengers."

He and I both shoot glances right and left. No hoverspheres or hoverdiscs, our primary modes of transportation, are in the air. The power surge must have taken out Transport Dome. Travis takes K and shouts, "We have to run for it."

I nudge my son, but he pulls back.

"Run where?" Zack asks, swiping at his scraggly orange bangs. "I have to see if Brita's okay."

"You can see your girlfriend later." I give his hand a firm tug, and we sprint toward the blazing forest.

My head pounds, not just from exertion, but from panic-driven questions. Did the earthquake destroy the portal? Will the fire keep us from getting to it? Will I ever see Gram and Krissie again?

Adrenaline sharpens my focus. I have to get through the portal, and I'm not leaving Zack behind this time. For more than three years, at the behest of the elders, I've kept the world beyond the portal a secret from Zack. I've hated every lie I've had to tell him about where I was going each time I went away.

At the edge of the woods, I pause, overwhelmed by the flames reaching high enough to lick the branches, jumping from one pine to another. Zelfar's safety plans don't cover forest fires.

Travis nudges my elbow. "We have to get to the portal."

"We can't just run into that!" I point at the raging flames and cough, covering my nose to withstand the stench of burning sap and scorched pine needles. My cheeks feel hot against my fingers.

Travis skirts along the edge of the tree line, trots a few yards, then stops. "There. There's a break. The falls are at the top of that rise. We should be able to make it there before the fire does."

"Wun, Daddy, wun." K bounces up and down in his arms.

Travis glances from K to me. "What am I doing?" he asks. "You stay here, and I'll go get Krissie and Gram."

My sweaty hair flips back and forth as I shake my head. "That's crazy. What if you get through the portal, and you can't get back, ever? We're going through *together.*"

"What's a portal? And who's Krissie?" Zack coughs and waves a hand in the direction of our community. "Don't you realize I need to go see what went wrong with the zilimite . . . and find Brita?"

"I'll explain everything when we get to Paradise Falls." Before I can say more, Vad appears next me.

I breathe easier, relieved. Vad is our best chance of getting to the portal before the fire reaches Paradise Falls.

Vad stands six feet tall, eye-to-eye with Travis. More than an android, he can feel, sense, and learn. Vad looks like a man, including his facial features and his zeltire, similar to what we all wear, of loose fitting pants and shirt.

"Oh, great," Zack sneers. "It's the robot who thinks he's human. If it can come, why can't I go get Brita?"

The explosion doesn't seem to have diminished Zack's long-standing conflict with Vad. I assume Zack is jealous of the time Travis devotes to his android, which he built five years ago. I've asked Zack why he dislikes Vad, but so far, Zack hasn't given me any clear reason.

Vad ignores Zack and says to Travis. "At the rate the fire is progressing, it will reach Paradise Falls in eighteen-point-two minutes. We must hurry."

"Hey, Zophie, Travis, wait up," a panting voice calls from behind.

"Clay," I say. When he stops next to me I add, "I'm glad you're okay." Clay is my best friend and colleague. He's here for the same reason we are—people we care about are on the other side of the portal. Clay is in love with an American doctor, whom he contends knows nothing of our world, except that our technology is far more advanced than her 1974 America. Secrets thrive on both sides of the portal.

Vad motions toward the approaching flames.

"Seventeen-point-two minutes."

My husband rubs his chin, his familiar gesture for decision making, and stares at the android. "Since you can't carry all five of us at once, Clay and I will head up the hill. You run Zophie and the children to the falls. Then come back for us."

"I'm not a child," Zack says. "I'm fifteen. I can stay with you and Clay."

Travis, for the first time, barks an order, "Go with Vad and your mother. Now!"

Thankfully, Zack offers no rebuttal. Instead, he shoots a quick glare at Vad, whose human-looking hands instantly transform into two large seats. Zack's lips purse as he hops into one of them. I sit in the other, K clutching tightly to my neck.

Vad's super-human legs race to the top of the hill. Sweat dots my uncovered arms. Thankfully, the air is cooler when we reach Paradise Falls.

Vad stops at the base of the waterfall and lowers us to the ground. With barely an audible click, his hands become human-like again.

I grab his arm when he starts to turn. "Vad, please get to them before the fire does." I can't bear the thought of being separated from Travis and Clay.

Vad hands me the two portal keys, a pair of earrings, and a belt. In a blur, he vanishes down the hill.

Zack thrusts his hands into his pockets. "So, are you gonna tell me what we're doing here?

I walk closer to Paradise Falls and sigh when the mist touches my face. I had hoped this moment would never come.

With practiced fingers, I put the earrings in place and pull gently on the small pyramids dangling from each lobe. The retractable chain hidden in the tiny triangles allows them to clasp together beneath my chin. The pyramids touch, dissolving the cloak over the portal. A shimmering light beckons through the waterfall.

Zack steps back. "Whoa."

CHAPTER 2

"How did you do that?" Zack walks closer to the falls.

I lead him behind the cascading water, and we stand in a large half-moon cave. Zack's wide eyes remind me of my first exposure to this cave nearly three years ago. I've protected Zack from the world beyond the portal where greed rules people's hearts. Zack has only known equal sharing among citizens. Hopefully, his glimpse of America will be brief, and we can return to Zelfar tomorrow.

Zack lowers K to the ground, and his mouth drops open as he peers beyond the shimmer into another dimly lit cavern. I unclasp my earrings, closing the portal, and the cave beyond disappears.

"What happened? Where'd it go?" Zack touches the glow, and his fingers stop at a solid rock surface.

I lay my hand gently on his shoulder. "What you just saw is a portal, a doorway to another world."

"Another world?" He breathes the question. "What's it like?"

"The waterfall and surrounding forest make that world seem

the same as ours. However, the weather is often cold and wet, and there are animals and bugs. You've never seen either, but both can hurt you. People look and talk like us, but they live in wooden structures and travel in noisy, stinky things called automobiles."

"Can we go there?" He rubs his hand over the rock wall. My negative portrayal of America hasn't curbed his curiosity.

"Yes, but there is something you need to know first."

He tightens his lips and squints at me.

"We have another home in that world, and Gram is there right now. So is your other sister."

"My what?" Zack shrugs my hand from his shoulder and steps back.

"You have two sisters. Their names are Kayla and Krissie. You know them as K, as does everyone in Zelfar, because the girls are never in Zelfar at the same time. They're identical twins, so they are easily assumed to be the same girl."

"You mean like two people who are the same?" He glances at K and back to me, splaying his hands wide. "How come you lied to me?"

"I'm sorry, Zack, but the portal had to be a secret."

"I'm family! You could have told me." Zack stomps a foot, scattering pebbles.

"No, Zackie!" K, sitting on the ground, lays her hands on the pebbles in front of her as if protecting them. Dust covers the ends of her pale pink sleeves.

Zack glares at me. "No one has two babies at the same time."

"I'm the first Zelfarian in decades to give birth to twins, because my protizine levels are high enough to sustain two babies." I point at the rock. "I found protizine in the world through there."

"You found the cure for newborn loss syndrome, and you didn't tell anybody?"

"I can't tell anyone. Not until we can make protizine in

Zelfar. I don't like having to take only one of your sisters at a time to Zelfar, and I wanted to tell you about them, but I never wanted you to have the burden of keeping such critical secrets. I thought we'd have been able to take honey to Zelfar long before this. The more time passed, the easier it became to continue deceiving everyone. I'm truly sorry, Zack. I should have stood up to Bayl when he refused to let me tell you. I should have trusted you with the truth."

"Yeah. You should have told me," he says, punching his thumb to his chest. "Nobody is gonna understand why you lied."

"Probably not, but I'm hoping you will once you see the extremely dangerous world on the other side of the portal. Then you'll know why Zelfarians can never know America exists."

I step toward Zack and stop when my nose wrinkles at the scent of fresh blood.

"Zophie, come quick!" Clay's deep voice rises above the roar of the tumbling water.

"Get K!" I shout to Zack and dash out of the cave.

"Travis!" I rush to my husband where he dangles in Vad's outstretched arms. Red splotches and rips in Travis's shirt and pants reveal minor cuts and scratches. He appears unconscious, but moans when Vad lays him on a large patch of grass.

"Travis!" I pat his cheek, and he moans again. I shout at Clay, "What happened?"

"A tree fell on him," Clay answers. "The fire came up behind us. I heard a loud crash and Travis yelled. He was pinned to the ground. I tried to pull him free or dig him out with my hands, but it was no use. Thank the cosmos, Vad showed up, threw the tree off Travis and scooped him up. I hopped on Vad's back."

Clay swipes the sweat on his forehead. "I'm sorry, Zophie. I can run faster than Travis. I should have dragged him with me."

"Don't blame yourself," I say. "Just help me determine the extent of his injuries."

"When I got to him, he was face down, and his legs were pinned. He was unconscious."

I run my fingers along Travis's lower limbs from ankle to knee, then touch his left thigh.

"Ohhh," Travis moans.

"Sweetheart," I touch his cheek. "Can you wiggle your toes?"

My husband clenches his jaw and takes a deep breath. That's a good sign.

"I can move my right ones, but not the left. I must have knocked the wind out of myself. I think I'm okay, except for my left leg." Travis grunts, trying to sit up. "You can patch me up when we get to the house."

I kneel next to my husband. "Your femoral shaft is broken. I can set it when we get to the house, but I can't heal it. If we go back to Health . . ." I stop myself. Zelfar's healing tube is in the pile of rubble that used to be Health Dome. I tuck my head, trying to hide my worry. I've never been unsure about how to cure a patient. Without the use of our advanced technology, I can only guess at the extent of Travis's injuries.

"We couldn't get back down the hill, anyway." Travis reaches for Vad. "If the portal still works, we should go through now."

"Wait!" Clay says. "We need to immobilize his leg to prevent further damage."

"I'll do it," Vad says and sprints into the brush. He returns with three thin tree limbs, whips off his shirt, and binds the sticks around Travis's leg.

"That feels better already." My husband gives a half-smile. "Now Vad can help me walk." Vad scoops Travis into his synthetic arms. "Or carry me."

I impulsively pick a handful of pine needles from my hip pocket. Like most Zelfarians, I always carry pine needles for when I need a moment of calmness and don't have access to a serenity simulator. Breathing pine scent is all the calm I'm going to get for now.

"Mommy." K, held tightly by her brother, wiggles her fingers toward me. Zack, silently watching from the edge of the falls, stares at his father. He releases his sister and slowly approaches Travis.

"Dad, your leg needs to be repaired." His voice trembles. "Shouldn't we go back to our homedome? Mom has healing stuff there."

"I'll be fine, son. If the portal is still intact, we'll come back to Zelfar tomorrow."

Zack turns his gaze to the waterfall. "The portal."

I pick up Kayla and we all follow Vad, carrying Travis, into the cave behind Paradise Falls. I connect the pyramids on my earrings. The shimmery portal appears, but when Zack tries to walk through, his toe thumps against an invisible barrier.

"Ow." He frowns, looking at me. "Is it broken?"

"You can see the portal when I open it," I explain, "but you cannot pass through without being in physical contact with a portal key. Since your dad will be touching Vad's, he won't need this." I extend the brown leather belt to Zack.

Zack wraps the belt around his waist, clicks the buckle in place, and says, "Can I go through now?"

I point at the raised bird in the center of the metal buckle. "Press on the wings with your index fingers."

Zack presses, the wings open, and a tiny pyramid appears.

"Press on the pyramid and you'll be able to walk through the shimmer."

I smell a hint of smoke and glance outside. The trees are blurred through the waterfall, but I see only green. No orange flames . . . yet. Vad presses the tips of his thumb and first finger together—his portal key—and touches them to Travis's side.

One after another, we walk through the glow.

CHAPTER 3

After disconnecting my portal key, I motion for Zack to do the same. His shoes grind on the mossy pebbles, and he looks back at the passageway, now a large gray rock.

"Are you sure we can get back?" Zack asks.

"I certainly hope so, sweetheart. Come on, we need to let Gram know what's happened."

"That portal thing is zap. I still can't believe you never told me about it—or about my other sister." Zack sneers at Vad. "*It* knew, didn't it?"

Vad walks out of the cave ahead of Zack. I wish Zack would tell me why he dislikes Vad. Whenever I've asked, he shrugs it off and calls Vad a "stupid robot." Now Zack's angry with me, too. In Zelfar, I could send Zack to a serenity orb to diffuse his anger. Here, he could stay mad at Vad and me forever.

I exit the cavern with my usual dread. I don't like this side of the portal with its lack of sunshine, pungent odors, and danger around every corner. I glance at the sky—cloudy, as usual, but at least I won't have to explain rain. In Zelfar, the nightly dews, heavier in the higher regions, form rivers and provide ample water to sustain life. Here, in Rainier, Oregon, water falls from the sky—a lot.

My precious Zelfar is burning to the ground, and I'm glad it's not raining in America. What's wrong with me?

"Why is it so cold?" Zack pats his arms.

"Temperatures here change with the time of year. It's early autumn now. Winter comes next, which is much colder. Our house is always warm, and we'll be there in a couple of minutes."

"What's a house?"

"This world's version of a homedome," Clay answers Zack.

We traverse the short bank and step onto the dirt path along Agate Creek. Vad's clone, standing on the path, says, "Hello."

"No!" Zack nearly stumbles, glaring between the two androids. "One wasn't bad enough? Now I have to put up with two talking homebots?"

The American Vad transforms his hands into chairs and says, "We're actually two of the same, Young Zack—one mind in two bodies."

Holding K, I sit in one of the seats, and Zack slumps into the other.

"I hate being called Young Zack, and you look stupid in that red plaid shirt. Can't you tell it's too small for you?"

Before I can chastise Zack's rudeness, a small web harness drops from the android's back, and he says to Clay, "Strap yourself in."

Vad, carrying Travis, follows swiftly behind his clone. The half mile is a short sprint for the androids, and soon we are in front of our American home deep in the woods near Agate Creek and at least a mile from our nearest neighbor.

The androids stroll across the lawn and stop on the cobblestone walkway that connects our house to the driveway.

"Zap! A square homedome with a triangle top?" Zack hops

from the clone's hand and runs up the wooden porch steps. He doesn't slow down, assuming the door will sense him and slide open like in Zelfar. His head thumps loudly against the solid oak door, and he rebounds backward, grabbing the rail to keep from falling into the azalea bushes.

Clay, Travis, and the two androids do a poor attempt to stifle their chuckles.

I set Kayla on the ground and rush to Zack's aid. "Are you okay, sweetheart?"

He avoids my outstretched hand and straightens himself, rubbing the small bump forming on his forehead.

The door creaks inward, and Gram peeks through the opening. "Did I hear someone bang on the door? Zack? What are you doing here?" She opens the door wide and moves a hand to her chest. "Travis, you're hurt! What in the world's going on?"

Without waiting for answers, my grandmother steps back, making room for us to enter. She closes the door behind Clay.

"Kwissie!" Kayla runs across the living orb, or "living room" as we call it here. I follow and place her inside the play enclosure with her sister. The twin toddlers immediately lunge for the same toy, giggling and rolling on the soft padded floor.

Zack stomps toward me, his spiky orange bangs appearing as if flames are shooting from his scalp. "If it weren't for the explosion, I still wouldn't know I had two sisters or where Gram's really been . . . *all along*. You shouldn't have lied to me!"

"Explosion?" Gram's face pales.

"It was scary," Zack says, walking toward his great-grandmother whom everyone in the family calls Gram. "There was the loudest boom, then the ground started shaking so hard we couldn't stand up."

Gram's small hands tremble, covering her gaping mouth.

"When they turned on the power to merge the zilimite with the green diamond, the energy-storage domes exploded." Zack scowls. "Instead of letting me figure out what went wrong, Mom rushed us here. I didn't even get to see Brita."

I give Zack a quick glance, and then say to Gram, "We didn't have time to assess all the damage, but we do know Health Dome was destroyed." I start toward the staircase. "I'll explain more after we take care of Travis."

"No Health Dome?" Gram looks at Travis, still perched in Vad's arms. "How badly is he hurt?"

"His leg is broken. Clay and I will do our best to set it."

"It'll be all right, dear," Gram says, and I'm not sure she's right this time, but her familiar words comfort me.

I give her a weak smile and say to Zack, "While I do what I can to heal your dad, try to figure out how to tell your sisters apart. I'm sure Gram will help."

Gram lays an arm across Zack's shoulders and turns him toward the play enclosure.

Clay and I follow Vad upstairs to our health room—our limited version of a healing orb. It doesn't have an instant healing tube, but it's still far better than anything American hospitals have to offer.

Vad walks to the center of the room and places Travis on the floating bed—a clear slab of crystillium, a Zelfarian mineral that looks like clear plastic in America. Travis and I agreed to limit the use of Zelfarian technology in this house. The floating bed was purposed for physical examination if Vad's healing skills ever became necessary, like when my twins were born.

I stand in front of a tall narrow cabinet and clench my teeth when Travis moans, straightening himself to lie flat on his back. Vad waves his hand, and Travis's skeletal image appears in the air.

My breath catches at the sight of so many bone fragments. "I've never set a broken bone before," I say to Clay, who stands at my side. "Have you?"

"I have, but it was many years ago, and it was a clean break." Clay studies the image. "Travis's leg appears to be shattered."

Shattered. I stare helplessly, wondering if Travis will ever walk again.

Vad tilts his head, scrutinizing the damaged femur.

"Vad? What are you thinking?" I ask.

"My ability to regenerate cell growth in humans continues to advance, but I have never attempted to restore bone." Vad moves around the bed, glancing intermittently between Travis and the skeletal image.

"Vad, you have to do something," I say. "I can't reset shattered bones."

"Zophie, wait." Clay touches my arm. "What if Vad makes it worse?"

"Worse than Travis living in a wheelchair? Vad has more knowledge than any health expert on Zelfar. Right now, I trust him more than I trust myself."

Vad nods as if to say my trust is well placed. "The broken femur continues to inflame the surrounding muscle and tissue. If I concentrate on mending that bone first, I should then be able to stimulate the regeneration of his cellular structure."

Travis peers anxiously at Vad. "Will I feel anything?"

"I will silence your awareness. You will feel nothing."

Travis looks to me, and I move closer, briefly touching his cheek. "You're going to be all right."

Vad places his palm on Travis's forehead. Travis's eyelids close, and his arms fall limp at his sides. American doctors use chemicals. Vad uses energy waves.

Vad's hands form a heart-shaped opening between his thumbs and forefingers. He moves his hands in a small circle above Travis's injured thigh, a beam of blue light streaming from his eyes and shining on Travis's leg. Inside our healing tubes, light beams stimulate the regeneration of cells, but I hadn't realized our android could mimic the process.

The projected image of the damaged leg goes from shattered to smooth, as if Travis were indeed inside a healing tube. Travis's leg looks normal—no swelling, no purple impressions. Vad rubs his hands together, then floats his palms above Travis's body from head to toe. I can't see the pulses of energy, but I know Vad is stimulating healing cells as he did for me after I gave birth to our twins. If Vad succeeds, Travis will have no residual effects from his injury.

Vad touches the tip of his finger to Travis's forehead.

Travis opens his eyes, wiggles his fingers and toes, and a grin spreads across his face. Sitting upright, he swings his legs over the side of the bed and rubs his thigh. "Way to go, Vad. Looks like the enhancements we recently made with your link to Health Dome gave you more healing ability than we'd hoped.

Our android simply smiles.

I rush to Travis, and he kisses me with the same fervor and relief that overwhelm me.

Clay slaps Vad's back. "If we end up being stuck here, I'm glad we have you. Can your double do the same thing?"

"Of course," Vad replies.

"Excellent," Clay says. "Good to know."

Travis hops to his feet. "I'll feel even better when I get cleaned up." He points from me to Clay. "You two don't look so fresh either."

Clay grasps Travis's hand. "Welcome back. I'll see you downstairs in a few minutes."

Happier than I've been all day, I walk with Travis down the hall to our master suite. We shower, don jeans and button-down shirts appropriate to this side of the portal and go downstairs.

From the hallway, I glance into the living room. Seeing the twins in their play area, Zack on the sofa, Gram in her favorite purple chair by the fire, and Clay on the bench under the picture window—everyone together for the first time ever—brings a smile to my face. I've waited so long for this.

"Dad! You're walking!" Zack lays his half-eaten cookie on the small side table and runs into the hall to Travis. "How'd you fix him so fast, Mom? Do we have an instant healing tube here, too?"

"Not exactly. Vad healed your dad."

"Vad?" Zack looks up at Vad. "Huh, well, thanks."

Zack expressing appreciation for Vad? That's a first. Maybe this incident will help him realize how valuable our android is to us.

American Vad joins us from the kitchen. Through their shared brain link, they reply in unison as if both were in the healing room, "My pleasure."

Zack glances between the two androids, shakes his head, and glares at me. "What else don't I know? How could you lie to me for so long? I should have been here with Gram and my sisters. It's not fair!"

Travis places a hand on Zack's shoulder. "You're right, son, it's not fair. Nothing about us being here is fair. We're living a double life, trying to protect you—to protect everyone in Zelfar. We're sorry we lied to you about where Gram has been. We know you've missed her." Travis glances toward the play area in the living room. "And we're sorry we didn't tell you about Kayla and Krissie. You can continue to hurt your mom and me by being angry and spiteful, but know that you're also hurting Gram and your sisters. Is that what you want?" Travis drops his hand and looks expectantly at Zack.

"No." Zack hangs his head. "I don't want to hurt Gram and my sisters." He looks up at his dad. "But I'm mad at you and Mom."

Gram walks from the living room and stands next to me. I expect her to say something to Zack, either consoling or advising. Instead, she takes my hand and leads me toward the sofa, and

Travis turns Zack toward the back door.

Gram opens her hand, motioning for me to sit. "Let Travis converse with Zack for now." She sits in her chair by the fire. The twins glance up from their play enclosure, then continue plunking discordant notes on a toy piano. I lower myself to the edge of the sofa cushion, keeping my ears tuned to Travis, wondering what novelties he plans to share with Zack.

"What's there to do here, Dad? Can we play bodyball?" Zack asks.

"No bodyball domes," Travis says, "but how would you like to see a car? It rolls on wheels on the ground and has to be driven by a person. It's like the real-life version of a virtual maneuvering game."

"Can I drive the car?" Zack asks. So much like his father.

Travis's voice trails out the back door. "No driving today, but after I show you the car, I'll show you how insects make food."

I barely hear Zack say, "What are insects?" before the back door bangs shut.

CHAPTER 4

Relieved that Zack is temporarily distracted from his anger, I relax into the sofa. Clay, sitting next to me, lifts his wrist, exposing his zelcom. We don't need the bulky turquoise telephone mounted to the wall in the kitchen, a common device in American homes. The phone is merely a prop to allay our American friends' suspicion. We can't reveal that our "watches" are portable phones that store all kinds of information.

"Clay. Wait." I grasp his arm. "Janet will insist on coming to see you, and I'd rather not have to introduce Zack to anyone. Hopefully, we can take him home tomorrow."

Clay tugs his sleeve back over his zelcom and stands. "Okay. I understand. Guess I'll go join the fun and watch Zack marvel over everything in the *barn*."

I grin at his emphasis on the word barn, knowing that it houses an elaborate Zelfarian-type laboratory instead of farm animals. I'd like to enjoy Zack's amazement, too, but at that moment, Kayla screams, "Mine!" and Krissie starts wailing.

I go to their play enclosure and lean over the three-foot high, clear plastic side, ready to reprimand Kayla for not sharing her toy drum. Remembering Kayla just had a traumatic experience in Zelfar, I decide to let her play by herself. I lift Krissie, who sniffles and lays her head on my shoulder.

We sit together on the sofa, and I rub her back, relieved we can all be together. I should be rushing to assist my fellow citizens in Zelfar, but right now, I feel grateful my family and my dearest friend are safe. I just hope Zack doesn't stay mad at me for too long.

Gram takes a sip of her tea and glances at me over the rim. "Do you think Zack will be able to remain silent about the portal?"

I turn to Gram and feel my jaw tighten. "I have to believe he can. I didn't have time to think about it. The forest was on fire, and we ran to get here while we still could. Since we don't know how vulnerable the portal is to quakes or fire, you can see why I had to bring Zack. I'm glad he finally knows he has two sisters. I hope he can forgive me for not telling him sooner."

Gram reaches forward and pats my knee. "You don't have to defend your actions, dear. You did what any mother would do. I know keeping the twins a secret from Zack has been a heavy burden. I, too, am glad you no longer have to carry it."

Vad walks into the room and says, "If Young Zack starts to tell anyone of the portal or of his twin sister, I can tap into his zelcom and interrupt his conversation."

I know by his loose hemp pants and shirt that this Vad is the original.

"No," I say, "Zack is already mad about not being trusted with our secrets. If he knew I'd given you permission to tap him, he'd hate me forever. There will be no spying."

I catch a slight upturn of Vad's mouth, sensing he would enjoy some control over Zack. Travis created Vad as an experimental model, unique in his ability to feel emotion. I wonder if it occurred to Travis that his android might become antagonistic.

Vad's loyalty to Travis and me is unquestionable. Yet he calls our son "Young Zack" when he knows Zack detests it. What is causing such friction between them?

A creak echoes from the hallway, and the back door bangs shut. "So, all we have to do is figure out how the bees make it?" I hear Zack say. "Why can't we just take some honey home with us and experiment with it there? We could all be eating honey now and get our protizine levels back up. I can't wait to tell Brita about this place. I could bring her back with me to get more honey."

"That sounds easy enough," Travis says, "except you can't tell Brita, and we can't take the honey home."

"Gram would you . . .?" I tip my head toward Krissie, dozing beside me.

Gram smiles and takes my place on the sofa. Krissie snuggles her cheek on Gram's leg with a contented sigh. I glance over at Kayla. Her head rests on a pillow with her arms tucked out of sight. I lay a blanket over her and walk quietly out of the living room.

I enter the kitchen to see Clay at the table munching an apple and Travis and Zack sitting at the counter. Zack swivels on his stool, and his lips tighten when he sees me.

"Why can't we say the honey came from here?" Zack asks.

Because no insects live in Zelfar; its inhabitants have never heard of honey. It took Travis more than a year to fully understand the differences between Zelfar's ecosystem and that of America. As he explains it, in Zelfar, all plants, including flowers, trees, and vegetables, are self-pollinators or cross-pollinators, while many plants on this side of the portal require the assistance of pollinating insects, such as honeybees.

"If we take honey to Zelfar," Travis explains, "our atmospheric sensors will identify it as a foreign substance, much like they do with meteors, and they'll trace the source to the portal. If the portal were no longer a secret . . . well, I know you can't understand this, but people in this world will hurt others to get what they want. Greedy people would destroy Zelfar."

Zack grips the edge of his stool. "But we need the honey. Mom said herself, that's why she had *two* healthy babies. Me and Brita just wanna have *one*."

My eyes go wide. Zack and his girlfriend are fifth-generation Zelfarians, which means they don't have enough protizine in their bodies to produce healthy infants. Besides that, they're too young to be making family plans.

Travis places a hand on Zack's shoulder. "You and Brita are only fifteen. I promise I'll get this worked out before you two are ready to have children . . . when you're adults."

Maybe I was wrong to let the elders convince me we have time to come up with the protizine solution. Third and fourth generations can still populate Zelfar with healthy babies, but Zack and Brita are talking about my grandchild.

"Travis," I say, perching on the stool next to him, "after today's catastrophe, perhaps exposing the portal isn't so bad. We could take honey and both of our girls home."

Travis rubs his chin. "I don't know. The risk of war between Zelfar and America is huge."

"What's war?" Zack asks.

Clay wraps his apple core in a napkin and says, "Short definition—war is when people fight and kill each other."

Zack snaps his head to look at Clay. "What does kill mean?"

"Causing someone to transcend," I say.

"On purpose?"

"Yes, son, on purpose."

Zack huffs. "Well, we wouldn't let anyone do that in Zelfar. We'd *kill* them first."

Oh my! Zack thinks he's capable making someone transcend? Cleary, the portal needs to remain a secret.

"Forget about war." I rise and stand next to Zack. "I'll talk to Bayl about taking honey to Zelfar. In the meantime, wouldn't you like to spend some time with both of your sisters together?"

"I guess so." Zack hops from his stool. "I still can't tell them apart."

I follow Zack to the living room, and when we enter, he pinches his nose and says, "Pew!"

Gram scoops a whimpering Krissie into her arms. "It's all right, sweetie. Accidents happen."

I pick up Kayla and follow Gram upstairs to the girl's bedroom. Pulling two teal dresses from the small closet and handing one to Gram, I say, "Zack wants to know how to identify each twin. Let's make it fun."

Gram smiles. We put the girls in matching outfits and return to the living room. When we stand them together in the center of the room, they squeal and run to their brother, sitting on the sofa. Zack laughs and lifts them onto his thighs. His brow wrinkles as he studies each one.

"Kayla?"

Two little blonde heads turn, and four brown eyes sparkle up at their brother.

"Don't they know their names?"

"I think they are responding to your voice. But yes, they know their names. In Zelfar, they answer to K, because the girls are never in Zelfar together, and everyone assumes K is one child." I perch on the arm of the sofa. "They take turns going with me to Zelfar."

Zack turns to Gram in her purple overstuffed chair. "How do you tell them apart?"

"Think about your experiences with them, dear. Although the girls are more similar than different, their personalities are unique."

Zack's face brightens, and he smiles at Gram. "That's why I thought there might be something wrong with K. One day she's all bubbly and trying to do everything herself, then the next day, she's all timid and wants me to do everything for her. Kayla was with us at the experiment today, and she's the independent one. The explosions probably would have made Krissie cry."

"Very good," I say. "You're exactly right."

One of the twins hops up and down, encouraging Zack to bounce her. He steadies her with his hand. "Hello, Kayla."

She giggles. "Bounce me."

* * *

Shortly after dinner, Clay retires to his room to call Janet, promising he'll tell her he can't see her tonight, but that he'll call her again tomorrow. Travis and I sit together on the sofa and watch our three children playing in front of the fireplace. I smile at Zack stacking wooden blocks and each twin taking her turn at toppling the tower. I want to throw my arms around all three of them. But Zack might push me away.

When Kayla rubs her eyes, I pick her up and say, "Zack, would you bring Krissie and help me tuck them into bed?"

His shoulders slump, and I anticipate him saying no. But Krissie wraps her arms around his neck and says, "Kissie wanna story."

Zack chuckles. He stands, lifts Krissie, and follows me upstairs to their room. When Zack sets Krissie on the floor, she runs to her bed.

"Kissie." She points at the block letters painted on the wooden footboard of the double bed. "That's me." Zack kneels beside her.

"And someday you'll be able to pronounce the *r*." Zack looks up at me. "Ha. Now I know why K sometimes omits *r*'s and other times replaces them with a *w*."

"That's my name." Kayla yanks at his shirtsleeve, pointing at the other side of the footboard.

When the girls are in their pajamas, Zack lays with them on their pink floral comforter. In unison, the twins chant, "Story, story." Zack props himself between them and taps his zelcom. He glares at his wrist and taps again. The girls laugh and tap repeatedly on their zelcoms.

I take a book from the bottom shelf of the nightstand and extend it to Zack. "Zelcoms don't project on this side of the portal. You have to read with books."

Zack rubs his hands over the shiny cover, opens to the first page, and reads aloud, "Once upon a time . . ."

Kayla and Krissie lay their heads against Zack's arms. I sit on the padded bench at one end of the dresser and listen contentedly. If only they could be together every night.

By the time Zack is half-way through the book, the girls are sound asleep. He eases himself off the bed, and I tuck the covers around each twin. I turn off the light, and we exit, leaving the door ajar.

Zack moves closer to me and whispers, "I'm gonna figure out how the bees make honey so we can take both of my sisters to Zelfar at the same time."

I wonder how much of our precious Zelfar is still there.

When we start downstairs, Zack says, "Brita is gonna zap when she finds out K is two people."

CHAPTER 5

Shortly before eight a.m., I walk down the creaky stairs and hear Gram's cheerful voice. "Good morning, dear."

I peer over the rail and see no one in the hall below.

"In here," Gram calls.

Two toddler voices echo, "In here, in here."

I chuckle and find the three of them in Gram's art studio—the spare room behind the stairwell—sitting in chairs in front of wooden easels. Gram, in her favorite long-tailed paint shirt, looks up from helping Kayla dab green paint on her canvas.

"Where is everyone?" I ask.

"Vad, Travis, and Clay have gone to check on the portal," Gram says. "We've already eaten, dear. Go get yourself some breakfast."

I give Gram and each twin a kiss on the tops of their heads. Gram must have let the twins use her shampoo again. All three smell of strawberries.

I walk toward the scent of fresh orange juice and overhear Zack and one of the androids talking in the kitchen. I slow my steps and edge silently along the hallway, stopping a couple of feet from the doorway.

"You do realize you're just a clone, don't you? You're not actually Vad." The condescension in Zack's voice is all too familiar.

"I'm Vad, and he is me," American Vad replies.

"No, you're not. Just think about it. When Vad's in Zelfar and out of sync range, don't you think for yourself? You decide what you do, and how you feel about things. Right? Do those feelings change after Vad syncs up with you?"

"They merge with Vad's and become our shared feelings, our shared memories. We have the same brain."

"See? You called him Vad. That means you see him as someone other than you."

I envision a big grin on my son's face.

"You don't actually have the same brain—you have a duplicate brain. Yours is programmed to grow both intellectually and emotionally, like Vad's. You live in different places, so how can you grow the same? Haven't you noticed you use contractions, and Vad doesn't? That's a big difference right there. Don't you wanna be your own man?"

"My own man? I'm an android. My purpose is to serve your family, Young Zack."

I grin at Zack's loud sigh.

"Listen. You're different. You should have a different name. How about I call you Young Vad? The other Vad was first, so you are younger."

"I don't like that name." The android's voice sounds dejected. I can almost see him pouting.

A chair scrapes on the hardwood floor.

"Then maybe you know how I feel. How about you don't call me Young Zack, and I won't call you Young Vad?"

"Agreed. Perhaps you're right, Zack. If Vad and I are going to be here at the same time, I would like to have my own moniker."

"Now you're computing. Know any names you like?"

"Einstein. I should like to be called Einstein." The android's response is so spontaneous, I wonder if he's thought about his own identity before this conversation.

"Einstein it is," Zack says.

I enter the kitchen, inhaling the tangy scent of oranges. When Zack sees me, he walks to the nook and scoots around the table, sitting in the chair farthest from me. I understand his anger at my betrayal, but it hurts.

Vad's clone pours a glass of juice and extends it to me.

"Mmm. Thank you, Vad."

Zack thumps his knee against the underside of the polished wood table. "Portal Vad decided he wants to be called Einstein."

I smile as if I'm hearing the name for the first time. "Einstein was a genius in this world, as are you, Vad."

"Please, Mom. Call him Einstein. One Vad is enough."

"Einstein, may I please have a cranberry muffin?"

Einstein smiles and removes a tray of muffins from the oven that looks American, but uses Zelfarian airwave technology to heat and cook food. He places a muffin on a plate and sets it on the counter for me.

I eat a bite of muffin and walk toward Zack. "How'd you sleep?"

He shrugs, staring through the window. "I heard weird noises outside."

I start to explain birds, wind, and creaking branches, but our attention turns to the squeak of the front door followed by voices.

"Dad's back!" Zack hops from his stool and runs out of the kitchen.

I hurry into the hall and stop short when I see Bayl standing next to Clay in the entryway. The elder's usual beige pants and shirt hang loose, like he's lost weight since yesterday. Guilt twinges my chest, as I realize that in my haste to save my family after the explosion, I didn't check on Bayl.

"Hello Bayl," I say, walking toward him. "I'm glad to see you weren't hurt when you fell from the hoverdisc."

Bayl dips his chin, as hairless as his scalp.

Travis opens his arms in a sweeping motion toward the living room. "Let's all go in there to talk about the situation in Zelfar."

Vad and Clay lead the way, followed by Bayl and Zack.

"Einstein," I say, as he enters the hall from the kitchen. "Gram is in her studio with the twins. Tell her Bayl is here, and please keep the girls occupied for a while."

"Yes, Zophie."

Travis watches American Vad walk away and looks at me. "Einstein?"

"I'll explain later. Right now, I want to know if we can take Zack home."

Travis and I enter the living room, and Zack sidles next to Travis. "Even if you take me home, I'm gonna come back with you next time. Right, Dad?"

Travis leans toward Zack's ear. "Let's hear what Bayl has to say before we talk about coming back."

Zack gives a little huff and walks over to the bench seat under the big window. Travis and I sit on the sofa, with Vad standing behind us, and Clay by the fireplace.

Gram enters the room, wiping her dainty hands on a paint-stained cloth, and walks directly to her favorite stuffed chair. She sits facing Bayl. "What's happening at home?"

Bayl sits with his back as straight as his wooden chair. "Much of Zelfar is in ruins. Three of our major service domes were completely destroyed—Health, Energy, and Transportation."

Travis taps the arm of the sofa. "What about Agriculture and Robotics?"

"I do not have a full assessment of those domes."

"Were the homedomes spared from the explosions?" I ask.

"Homedomes appear to be intact."

"Homedomes," Travis explains, "are powered by subcentric green diamonds, independent of Energy Dome, so they should all have power."

"And there is debris everywhere." Bayl rubs a hand down his shirt sleeve. "My walk to the portal was precarious."

I peer anxiously at Clay. He returns a worried glance. "What about injuries?" we ask in unison.

"Sadly, Gina and Phil transcended while extinguishing the forest fires."

I gulp, clutching my throat with one hand and Travis's thigh with the other.

Gram gasps. "No! Not Gina." She leans back, and tears flow freely down her cheeks. Gina was Gram's best friend and the council expert who represented Serenity and Personal Growth.

I go to my grandmother and pull her into my arms. She sobs on my shoulder, and after a moment, I kiss her cheek and return to the sofa.

Bayl looks at Clay. "I do not know the extent of physical injuries, but Quaid's granddaughter has been unconscious since the explosions."

Zack jumps to his feet. "Brita? What happened to her?"

"The blast knocked her from her hoverdisc. She hit her head on a large stone when she fell," Bayl answers in his typical monotone, relaying facts.

"Mom! See?" Zack's eyes redden and his voice cracks. "I told you I needed to go check on her yesterday. I have to go see her—now."

I lift my hand to stop him. "We'll make plans to leave as soon as Bayl finishes his report."

Zack picks up a cushion that had fallen, slaps it back on the bench, and plops down.

Bayl rises and walks to the fireplace. With his hands cupped behind him, he faces Travis and me. "Morale is extremely low. Many were hoping we would find a source for protizine out there in the stars. Now they see little reason to rebuild."

Hopelessness. I know that feeling every time I must leave one of my little girls behind. "Can't the Zelfar Foundation Team pull the community together?" I ask.

"I tried to call a council meeting this morning, but without zelcoms and hovertransports, there is no easy way to communicate. I hoped you and Travis might have a breakthrough with the honey, because the cure for newborn loss syndrome would certainly provide community-wide incentive to rebuild our service domes."

Travis shakes his head. "We're close, but no breakthrough yet."

Gram sweeps her hair over one shoulder and looks up at Bayl. "What is the condition of our serenity orbs?"

Bayl lowers his eyes to Gram. "Only a handful remain, and the walk to get to them is long and hazardous."

Gram is the only person in Zelfar more highly regarded than Bayl and Quaid. Her father, when he was a professor at a college in 1850 Portland, Oregon, invented a device that detected the portal. He took selected scientists and their families through the portal and founded Zelfar 125 years ago. When Gram retired from the council, she appointed Bayl to take her position, both as council member and as elder alongside Quaid.

Gram pushes up her sleeves. "I will need to consider an alternative." Poor Gram. Long before I was born, Gram developed tranquility inducing techniques and created serenity orbs where people could use serenity simulators. Now, she'll have to see her serenity orbs in ruin, and she doesn't have Gina to help restore them.

Bayl ambles back to his chair and sits stiffly.

I clear my throat. "Bayl, what if we took a sample of honey to Zelfar? We could say it has protizine, but that we have to do more experiments before we can produce enough for everyone." I rub my hands on my legs and talk faster. "I can take both girls home and show people how honey enabled me to have two babies, not just one."

Bayl's chest heaves, but before he can speak, Zack jumps up, his eyes sparkling.

"Yeah! And me and Brita will help spread the word. We'll tell everyone in our generation we don't have to worry about not having our own families. And with zilimite energy, we can build everything better than it was."

Gram looks at Zack and says under her breath, "Oh dear."

Bayl thrusts upward, nearly toppling his chair. "No!"

My body jolts, shocked at Bayl's uncharacteristic reaction. Zack scowls and sits stone still. Travis presses his hand on my thigh, and Vad steps to the end of the sofa between Bayl and me.

Bayl widens his stance. "We will not, under any circumstances, expose the portal."

Zack hops off the bench again. "Who cares if people know about the portal?"

"Zack!" Travis points a finger. "Sit down. Do not rebuke our elder."

Zack plops back onto the bench and folds his arms in a sulk.

Bayl sits, setting his eyes on me, and says firmly, "Right now, people trust you, Zophie, and they are happy you had a healthy baby. If you show them you had two babies when many of them could not have any, they will not only demand to know how that was possible, they will be livid you kept this a secret, that you have been fooling everyone . . . for three years." He glances from me to Travis. "Neither of you would be free of suspicion. You would be followed everywhere. And so would your children. Your access to the portal, and thereby your ability to work here to perfect the synthetic honey formula, would be in jeopardy."

My jaw tightens. I want to lash out at Bayl, but I know he's right.

Bayl relaxes his shoulders and continues. "When you see the destruction in Zelfar, you will understand why everyone would flee to America, especially if they knew the cure for newborn loss syndrome is found here. Exposing the portal would most certainly end our world."

I cringe at the thought of losing Zelfar. This crazy double life I've led for the past three years has preserved the sanctity of my real world by keeping the portal a secret. Have I done the right thing by not sharing the cure, not trusting my community with the truth?

Travis slaps his knees lightly. "How do we inspire people to rebuild?"

Bayl looks at me, and his eyes soften. "Zophie, you can restore hope. The community has looked up to you to cure newborn loss syndrome. You need to remind them that women of your generation and older can still bear healthy children, and our young people need only be patient a while longer. Tell them you are certain you will have the cure before long. The community must focus on rebuilding while you complete your mission."

My face heats with the thought of me alone trying to inspire six-thousand people who see their world as doomed. Gram rises and comes to sit close to me on the sofa. She puts a comforting hand on mine and looks at Bayl.

"I would hope our community is not capable of the resentful actions you foresee," she says, "but without serenity orbs, I can't say jealousy won't occur. You've made your point. Zophie and her family will continue splitting their time between worlds. When Travis is able to make synthetic honey in Zelfar, they will return home at that time, all of them, regardless of suspicion. For the immediate situation, I agree with you. My granddaughter is the voice of hope."

Gram cups my chin, and her hazel eyes meet mine. "Instilling hope is a gift you were given to share with others, dear. Your enormous personal sacrifices these past three years are proof of your strength and unwavering belief in Zelfar. Use your gifts now to help your fellow citizens."

Gram's guiding words focus my intention, as they have since I was young. I have a responsibility to use my talents to reunify our community during this crisis. I will help those facing despair, as well as the injured.

I glance at Zack's worried face. I need to tend to Brita and secure Zelfar's future for them.

I squeeze Gram's fingertips. "I'll do whatever I can." Brave words for someone who has the cure for newborn loss syndrome, yet allows the elders to stop her from using it.

Gram pats my hand. "I love you, dear."

"I love you, too, Gram."

Travis folds my fingers into his strong palms. "We'll do this together." His reassurance makes me eager to return to our real home. He stands and says, "This is a new beginning for Zelfar. Let's get started."

Bayl rises. "We will assemble the foundation team to get a full report of the damage. Then Zophie will address our community."

Clay moves from his stance by the fireplace and stands next to me. "First thing we need to do is tend the injured. We can use my homedome." He glances at Vad. "I'm sure we can use his talents."

Vad smiles, nodding to Clay and me.

Bayl walks out of the living room, followed by Travis, Zack, and Vad. Gram exits to her room to change into zeltire. I walk with Clay into the hall.

"Did you get a chance to talk to Janet this morning?" I ask.

"Yes, and I'm glad I convinced her not to come see me."

Clay raises an eyebrow toward Bayl. "She might have been here in the middle of all this. That would have required some tough explaining."

"Speaking of tough explaining, I have to get one of the girls ready to go." I walk into Gram's studio as Krissie and Kayla remove their paint shirts. I smile when I see Kayla is wearing a hemp playsuit—typical zeltire for a Zelfarian toddler. Gram knew I'd need to bring Kayla to Zelfar today.

I should be taking Krissie. But Kayla has already experienced the destruction, and Krissie takes extra time and patience, which I won't have today. I lift Krissie, kiss her, and squeeze her to my heart. I hate leaving either of our girls behind. And Krissie won't have Gram this time. Only Einstein. Even with caring emotions, he's still an android.

I whisper in Krissie's ear, "I have to go help some people. You're going to stay here with Vad, I mean Einstein. We're going to call the Vad that lives here Einstein from now on."

Krissie ignores my comment about American Vad's new name, clenches her arms around my neck, and wails. "No, Mommy. It's my turn."

Kayla clings to my knees, crying. "I want Kwissie to go, too."

"Einstein," I choke out. "Take Krissie."

Krissie grips my shirt sleeve, flailing her legs as Einstein pulls her from me. With sad eyes, the android hugs my child to his chest.

I rub Krissie's back. "I'm sorry, baby. Mommy is so sorry."

I grab Kayla and walk into the hallway. Travis sees me and comes over to kiss my tear-soaked cheek. "I'll take Kayla. You walk with Gram."

Kayla hangs onto Travis's shirt, bunching the loose fabric in her little fingers.

"It's unfair we have to choose which one to take with us." I sniffle and grab a handful of tissues from the box on the hall table.

Gram walks from her bedroom, her loose pantsuit flowing in a swirl of yellows, greens, and blues. Most Zelfarians choose zeltire of solid colors, but Gram's outfits are always two or more hues of the rainbow. Krissie gets her flare for color from Gram.

Gram and I hurry outside to follow the others across the lawn and onto the path into the woods.

"Ouch!" Zack stops suddenly and slaps the underside of his wrist. "I think an insect just bit me. Look!" He opens his hand, displaying a flat mosquito and a tiny splotch of blood.

Vad halts when Gram and I stop next to Zack. Clay grins, winks at me, and walks on with Travis.

I bend down and scoop a dab of mud with my fingertip and hold it toward Zack. "Here, this will keep the bite from itching."

Zack jerks his wrist away. "Mud?"

"Or Vad could heal your bite," I say.

Zack huffs, wipes the mud from my finger to his, and glares at me. "You should have brought me here a long time ago. I would have known about insects and my sisters. I bet Dad and I would've even solved the honey thing by now. Then Krissie wouldn't have to stay here all alone with Vad's clone." He turns and jogs to catch up with Travis.

Gram and I enter the cave behind Agate Falls with Vad on our heels. The back of Bayl's bald head vanishes into the glow. I clasp the pyramids of my earrings under my chin and take Kayla from Travis.

Clay pulls his portal-key ink pen from his shirt pocket and clicks the pen's top, activating the miniature pyramid inside the silver-tone barrel. He says to Travis, "Vad can bring my pen back for Zack."

Travis nods to Vad, and the android follows Clay through the portal. Immediately, Vad returns with Clay's pen and extends it to Zack. Zack grins, wraps his fingers around the portal key, and walks into the glow after Travis. I clasp Kayla's fingers around the miniature pyramids under my chin and step into Zelfar.

CHAPTER 6

Zack laughs, looking back at the portal. "Weirdest thing ever!"

Clay chuckles and holds his open palm toward Zack.

Zack twirls the pen in his fingertips and lays the portal key on Clay's hand. "Thanks."

Outside the cave, Zack walks up to Travis. "Dad, I gotta get one of those portal-key things." Zack points excitedly at Clay's pen. Travis and Bayl reply in unison with a sharp shake of their heads. Losing his grin, Zack shoves his hands into his pockets.

Travis lays a sympathetic hand on Zack's shoulder. "Do you think you can ride on Vad's back?"

Zack perks up. "Sure. Beats sitting on its hand."

Vad turns his back toward Zack, and Zack straps himself into the harness seat. Gram takes Kayla from me and sits in one of Vad's hand-chairs.

"I'll meet you at your homedome as soon as I can," I say to Clay, giving him a quick hug.

"Hope to the cosmos our homedomes have power." Clay pecks my cheek, and I slide onto Vad's empty hand-chair.

"Vad," Travis says. "Take them home and hurry back for Clay, Bayl, and me." He gives me a kiss and says, "See you soon."

Vad dashes down the hill, dodging scorched trees and charred stumps. I hold my nose until the ashy stench becomes fainter amid the circles of homedomes, which have come to remind me of the clusters of cul-de-sacs I've seen in America. The colorful crystillium shells indicate our homes have power. Our android stops first at Gram's dome which is beautifully striped like a radiant rainbow.

Gram hands Kayla to me and says, "I'll see you at the council meeting."

Vad continues around two more circles of domes and sets Zack, Kayla, and me on the ground-level platform outside our dome. I look past the flowers and bushes that surround our platform and glance next door at Brita's homedome. A layer of fine ash coats the curved surface, making Brita's dome appear a dusty cobalt instead of its usual bright blue.

"I must retrieve Travis, Clay, and Bayl," Vad says.

"Yes, go," I reply.

Vad zooms away, and Zack approaches the door to our home. It slides open, allowing Zack to enter. Kayla and I follow him into our dome.

Zack vanishes around the curve in the center corridor that leads to his sleeping orb. Kayla starts to run after him, but I grasp her hand.

"Let's check each orb to make sure everything is okay.

Kayla nods and walks with me. We pass the cooking orb and dining orb. Both appear intact. When we enter Kayla's sleeping orb, she runs to her small oval bed, which floats six inches off the floor. She pats the bright pink coverlet. Next, she runs to her toy tube and yanks a cloth doll from the top. She kisses the doll's cheek and smiles at me.

"My orb's okay," she says.

Zack raps his knuckles on the wall inside Kayla's doorway. Kayla lays her doll on the bed and runs to her brother. He laughs as he grabs her up and swings her around. When he sets her down, she continues to spin, holding out her arms, staggering and laughing.

Zack runs a comb through his unruly bangs. "I'm going over to Brita's."

I want to see Brita, too, but I don't want to intrude with a toddler. I consider asking Zack to wait for Vad to return, but I see in his eyes that he needs to see her now to know if she's conscious yet.

"If she's awake, please bring her over," I say, knowing she probably isn't or she would already have come to see Zack.

Zack shoves the comb into his pocket and walks out of the orb.

I grab Kayla to keep her from following her brother. "Get your doll and let's rock her."

We sit in the living orb in the rocker Gram gave me shortly after Travis and I united. I breathe in the strawberry scent of Kayla's hair, and for a brief moment, forget the destruction outside.

"Hi, Daddy," Kayla says, and I look up into Travis's smiling face, with Vad standing behind him.

"It's nice to see you relaxed for the moment." Travis gives me a long kiss and gently rubs Kayla's cheek.

Why can't we have more of these moments? I barely remember how serene our lives were before newborn loss syndrome and our race to find the cure. Serenity aside, if it weren't for my search for protizine, my girls would never have been born. The portal somehow deactivated my ovarian chip, and I became pregnant with my precious twins. Kayla and Krissie have made our complicated lives worth every minute.

"I'm going to assess the damage to Agriculture Dome," Travis says. "Vad is all yours."

Kayla, Vad, and I walk outside with Travis. Zack approaches from the direction of Brita's dome, and Travis sprints toward his service dome.

"Zackie!" Kayla runs to Zack and grabs his knees, but his shoulders hunch, and he doesn't offer to pick her up.

"I wanna fly with you." Kayla tugs on his pant leg.

Zack squats eye-to-eye with his little sister. "The hoverdiscs can't fly anymore, K. Besides, I don't feel like flying."

Kayla turns and runs to Vad. "Swing me, pwease." He lifts her, sits her in the nook of his elbow, and gently swings his arm.

"Is Brita still unconscious?" I ask.

Zack nods, gazing at his feet.

"I'd like to see her. Do you want to come with me?"

He lifts his head, his eyes red and puffy. "Yeah. If anyone can help Brita, you can."

His confidence in me gives me hope. If I can heal Brita, not only will we have one of our favorite girls back in our lives, but Zack might forgive me.

"Vad," I say. "Please tot-watch Kayla while Zack and I go to Brita's."

Vad says to Kayla, "I will help you build a bell tower taller than the sofa."

"No. *I* will help *you.*" Kayla's voice fades as they enter our homedome.

When Zack and I approach Brita's dome, the doorway slides open, and Elka reaches her long arms toward me.

"Zophie! You're here." Her brown eyes glisten amid dark rings. She grasps my hand and pulls me inside. "You have to help Brita. Please wake her up."

At five foot ten, Elka is tall for a woman, and Emery, Brita's dad, at seven feet, towers over almost everyone. Emery tips his head to me.

"Hello, Emery," I manage to say, struggling to maintain my balance with each anxious tug from Elka's strong fingers.

Once we're in Brita's sleeping orb, Elka releases my hand and weeps, gazing at Brita, who lies still. Unnervingly still. Brita's orange bangs hang loosely over her dry forehead. If she were awake, I'm sure she and Zack would be wearing a new hair color by now. I long for that sparkle in their eyes when they show off their latest hair art.

Zack walks to Brita's curio shelves and grasps the small stuffed doll he gave Brita when they were six. She had thanked him with a kiss. Zack lays the doll inside Brita's elbow and says, "Mom's here, Brita. She's going to heal you."

Zack backs away, and I'd give almost anything to erase the pain in his eyes. I hope I can do what he believes I can.

I check Brita's pulse—slow, but not alarming. Her breaths are steady, but short. I gently lift each eyelid—her pupils are nonreactive. I tap her knees and elbows—no response. Without health scanners, I can perform no further analysis.

I gaze at Brita's parents. "Would you mind if my android does a quick scan of Brita?"

Zack slaps his hands together with one loud clap. "Yeah! Vad can heal her like he did Dad!"

"Travis was hurt?" Emery looks at me.

"Only his leg, and Vad was able to fix it."

Elka's voice quivers. "Vad?"

"Vad is a unique android," I say.

Emery and Elka clutch hands, and Emery says, "We'll try anything to bring our daughter back."

Zack lays his hand over Brita's and says, "My android is gonna fix you."

I lift my wrist, hoping Zack is right. "Vad, please come over to Brita's homedome."

Emery hastens to greet Vad, and Elka stares wide-eyed at

my wrist.

"Your zelcom works?" she asks.

"Only for our android." I tuck my wrist behind me, feeling oddly guilty for having the only android like Vad.

"How is that possible?" Elka asks. "My zelcom won't work for my homebot."

How can I explain something I don't fully understand?

"It's because Dad combined our dome's intelligence with our homebot and made an android. Vad's an experiment," Zack explains. "He's a simulated brain in human form. You'll see. He's not a regular homebot."

Vad, carrying Kayla, enters Brita's sleeping orb with Emery behind them.

Vad stops in front of me, and Kayla shakes her hand at Brita.

"Bwita!" Kayla pats Vad's cheek. "Why is Bwita sleeping?"

Before Vad can reply, I say to him, "I want you to heal whatever injury is keeping Brita from waking up."

Vad hands Kayla to me, and I lower her into the large chair near Brita's bed. I sit on the overstuffed arm and keep one hand on Kayla. Elka and Emery huddle at the end of Brita's bed, staring at Vad.

Zack plucks the doll from inside Brita's elbow and steps back. His knuckles whiten as he squeezes the doll, and he shifts his weight from one foot to the other.

Vad moves slowly, rotating his hands over Brita, like he did with Travis. Tense seconds pass before Vad stands stiffly and drops his hands to his sides. "Brita's brain waves are in an interrupted state. Her thalamic pathway is not receiving consistent sensory input. Her body requires nourishment. Her lungs require increased oxygenation." Vad's face shows no emotion, as if feelings were never programmed into his synthetic mind.

"We don't care what's wrong, Vad." Zack's chin trembles. "Just fix her!"

Kayla whimpers and tugs on my hand. "Mommy, Zackie's hurting Bwita's doll. Can I hold her?"

Zack stomps around Brita's bed and stops in front of Kayla. His breath catches, and he drops the stuffed doll in Kayla's lap. She hugs the doll to her cheek.

I glance from Zack to Vad. If Vad could heal Brita, he would have. Dreading the answer, I ask, "If we feed her and increase her oxygen levels, can you restore her brain waves and sensory input?"

Vad replies with a single, devastating word. "No."

"You have to fix her . . . you stupid robot!" Sobs overtake Zack, and he collapses on the edge of Brita's bed.

"I wish I could, Zack." Vad's body slumps in grief. "I wish I could."

Zack glares at Vad. "I hate you. Get out of here!" Zack points to the door.

Vad's sad gaze meets mine. I give him an affirmative blink, and he exits with the wilted shoulders of a man in despair.

"What do we do now?" Emery's husky voice cracks.

"Your android said she needs nourishment, but Brita can't eat." Elka sniffles. "Does that mean we're going to lose her?"

I pick up Kayla and step closer to Brita's parents. "I'm setting up a temporary Health Dome today. If I can prepare a special orb for Brita, will you let Vad take her there?"

A spark of hope glints in Elka's swollen eyes. She glances at her husband, and together they say, "Yes." Elka adds, "We'll do anything."

When I try to take Brita's doll from Kayla, she tightens her grip and grimaces at Zack.

Elka rubs Kayla's back. "K can tot-watch the doll until Brita wakes up."

"I'll do everything I possibly can for Brita," I say. "She's a part of our family, too."

"Come on, Zackie," Kayla says, curling her fingers, urging him to follow us out of Brita's orb.

Zack shoves his hands into his pockets and walks sullenly behind us. Elka and Emery lead us outside where Vad is waiting on their oval platform.

"Toss pine," Elka and Emery say, and amble back inside their homedome.

I lower Kayla to her feet and reach out to Zack. "I'm sorry we couldn't wake Brita."

Zack glares through red eyes and pulls away. "I should have known I couldn't trust you . . . or that stupid robot."

Tears of rejection sting my eyes and stream down my face. How can I heal others' despair when I can't heal my own?

"I'm going to Sheldon's." Zack starts to walk away.

"No," I say before he takes a step. "Again, I'm sorry, but you must tot-watch Kayla while Clay and I set up a temporary health dome."

"Isn't that part of its job?" Zack flicks his hand at Vad.

"Vad has to take me to Clay's and then to collect the injured."

Kayla runs to Zack. He frowns, but obligingly picks up his little sister and walks toward our dome.

"Are you ready to go to Clay's?" Vad asks.

I wipe my cheeks with my palms. "Give me ten minutes."

CHAPTER 7

Inside our unity orb, I take a quick sonic shower and don clean zeltire of yellow pull-on pants and a lighter yellow cotton shirt. Before leaving the orb, I wrap a red band around my forearm to designate I'm serving as a health expert today.

As soon as I walk outside, Vad's hand transforms, and I scoot into the curved seat. Vad covers the mile and a half from my home to Clay's in what feels like seconds.

Clay walks out of his bright yellow dome, wearing a red armband and wiping his forehead with a white cloth. "Welcome," he says.

I grin. "How long has it been since you worked up a sweat? Anything left for us to do?"

"My homebot did the heavy lifting. Come in. I'll show you what I've prepared." He tugs playfully at my sleeve. "Did you dress like my homebot on purpose?"

I poke his rib. "I didn't know your dome would be yellow today instead of its usual green."

We walk on shiny floors and breathe the clean scent of

pine. The entry and wide circular hallway have been cleared of furniture. Clay leads us to the center of the dome, his thirty-foot living orb. With two sofas and several chairs, the orb looks similar to a waiting area in the American hospital where Clay's girlfriend works.

"I figure this is where we'll treat minor injuries." Clay shoves the cloth into the hip pocket of his tunic. My eyes follow his gaze to trays of disinfectant, wraps, and tape on a long narrow table.

"And for serious injuries?" I ask.

"We'll use my two spare sleeping orbs for those who need beds until Vad can do his healing thing with them. And since we don't know how many we have to treat, let's get started." Clay rubs his hands together and grins expectantly at me.

"Vivacity times two!" He and I shout in unison, clapping one another's palms in one loud smack on the word "two." We laugh like we have for two decades, ever since we created our unique pep-gesture during a tutor session in advanced health studies.

"Vad," I say. "We're ready."

Moving swiftly, Vad transports one patient after another. Clay and I clean and wrap minor wounds on fifty-some citizens. Our bandages and antiseptics dwindle, and my mind flashes to the overstocked supply closets in Janet's American hospital.

Finally, Vad walks into the center orb, sets a tall woman on the sofa, and announces, "Oak is the last of the injured."

My ears perk up at her name, and Clay runs to his sister. "Oak! Where are you hurt?"

"Don't boil your beaker, Clay. It's just my wrist."

I step closer to Clay and nudge him with my shoulder. "Let me tend to Oak. You get Vad started in the healing orb. Okay?"

Clay sighs, motions for Vad to follow, and exits the orb.

I sit on the footstool in front of Oak and take her bruised wrist gently in my fingers.

"I didn't expect to see you serving today, Zophie," she says.

"You should be at home tending your little one."

"Zack is tot-watching K today. I'm needed here." I press lightly on her wrist, and her eyes wince. "I think your wrist is badly sprained. But before I wrap it, I'll have Vad check it to be sure. Stay here, and he'll be with you shortly."

Vad heals at least twenty broken bones, including Oak's wrist. Clay had hovered over his sister while Vad healed her. I probably would do the same if I had siblings.

The despair Bayl spoke of earlier has not been apparent in the people I've treated today. Everyone has been deeply appreciative, especially those made whole by Vad. Every person left smiling.

When the last patient leaves, Clay's yellow homebot clears remnants of soiled bandages and begins sanitizing the dome.

Clay plops onto one of the small sofas. "I don't know about you, Zophie, but this is the most exhausted and the most exhilarated I've ever felt."

"I know what you mean." I let myself fall into the soft chair beside him. "We made a huge difference today, and we did it with our own hands, no technology—well, except for Vad."

"Yeah, like before the healing tube when we had to do compositional healing once in a while." He chuckles at the memory. "Got time for a refreshment before you head home?"

"Yes, please." I place my hand over his fingers. "I miss this, you and me."

"Me, too."

I drop my head back on the chair, tired but happy.

"Dome," Clay says. "Two iced cooiberry juices and some quinoa cookies to the living orb."

After a few sips of juice and half a cookie, I say to Clay, "Now we need to tend to Brita. Vad couldn't wake her. I'm hoping we can set up a health orb for her here."

Clay sets his glass on the table. "Unconscious . . . can't feed herself. Probably needs oxygen. . ."

I picture Brita lying so frighteningly still. "How are we going to get her the things she needs to survive? I wish we had a neo-tube big enough to fit a teenager."

Clay jolts up. "That's exactly what we need. Marc can help us set up a large incubator—a health tube. That is—if he's willing. I'm surprised he wasn't here helping us today."

The thought of Marc makes my stomach hurt. He probably stayed home today because he doesn't want to see me. I doubt he'll ever forgive me for not being here to try to save his newborn. I wish I could tell him I was in America searching for a cure to save his baby. If we had discovered protizine in honey before his baby died, I would have snuck some honey to him, regardless of what the elders said. I understand if Marc can't be around me, but he's the expert who can construct a tube that could sustain Brita's life.

"I'll go see if Marc's home." I sigh and stand.

Clay stretches his long arms over his head. "I'll rest until you get back."

The fifteen-minute walk from Clay's dome to Marc's seems like five, my nerves edgier with each step. I break a couple of pine needles and breathe the fresh scent. With many of our serenity orbs destroyed, I suspect others are doing the same thing.

When I see Marc sitting on a bench outside his dome, its dull-green hue blending with the shrubs around it, I put on a pleasant face and plod forward. He jumps up and glares with cold blue eyes.

"What do you want, Zophie?"

Swallowing hard and reminding myself I'm here for Brita, I meet his glare and say, "Marc, have you heard about the girl who is unconscious?"

"What are you talking about?" His shoulders relax a little.

"A teenager, Brita, fell from her hoverdisc during the explosions yesterday. She hit her head and is still unconscious.

Clay thinks you can design something like a neo-tube for her. Will you try?"

"Of course." Marc takes a step toward the entrance of his dome. When it slides open, he shouts, "Darcy! A girl's unconscious. I'm going to help."

After a muffled response from inside, Marc says loudly, "I'll explain when I get back. See you later." Before his dome seals itself, I get a whiff of the unpleasant odor of old food.

"Is your homebot malfunctioning?" I rub my nose.

"Forget about my homebot. Take me to Brita."

When we arrive at Clay's, he leads Marc to the one orb we hadn't used earlier—the birthing orb. Marc studies the neo-tube floating in the center of the orb. He then instructs Vad and Clay's homebot on the process of replicating the clear crystillium life-support chamber on a larger scale.

Vad scurries away to get the necessary amounts of crystillium and hardening agent. He returns and, in less time than I thought possible, a health tube is ready for Brita in one of Clay's spare sleeping orbs. Vad rushes off again and moments later, hastens into the orb carrying Brita's limp body. Her white pant legs cover her feet, and her long straight hair drapes over Vad's arms.

Marc raises the top section of the tube and Vad carefully places Brita inside. Brita's body sinks slightly into the clear gel bed. Marc lowers the top and the tube closes with a slight hush.

Vad waves his hands above the tube, and a puff of orange fog fills Brita's chamber. The fog slowly dissipates, and the round ends of the tube glow green—the most beautiful shade of lime I've ever seen.

"The oxygen and biological infusions will keep her body healthy," Marc says, swiping at his cheeks and eyeing Brita with compassion as if she were a newborn.

I take a few pine needles from my pocket and cup them under my nose. If I knew more about brain function, maybe I could adjust this health tube to awaken Brita's mind.

"I must program your homebot to maintain the infusion levels," Vad tells Clay.

"Is it going to be like Einstein when you're done?" Clay covers his mouth, and my eyes go wide, waiting for Marc's reaction.

"Who's Einstein?" Marc asks.

"It's a story character Zack made up," I blurt.

Clay chuckles, either at my discomfort or at my ability to lie so quickly.

"Your homebot will administer Brita's nutrients," Vad says.

"So, Marc and I don't have to do anything?" Clay puts a hand on the health tube and peers at Brita.

"Precisely," Vad says.

Marc snorts. "I'm not leaving this girl's care to a homebot." Marc turns to Clay. "I'll be here to check on her every day."

Clay nods and presses fingers to his smiling lips.

"Elka and Emery have arrived on the front platform." The words emanate from Clay's homedome, and Clay walks out of the orb.

"Thank you, Marc." I step toward him.

Marc backs away. "You don't have to thank me. I'm not doing this for you."

Elka and Emery rush into the orb, and Marc turns his attention to them.

"Come on." Clay nudges my elbow, and I follow him out of the orb, motioning for Vad to come with me. Outside on the platform, Clay says, "Give Marc some time, Zophie. He's still hurting."

I breathe a heavy sigh. "I'll never be able to ease his pain and tell him where I was instead of being in the delivery orb with him and Darcy."

Clay wraps his arms around me to comfort me. "I know. I hate keeping secrets, too."

"Thank you for giving up your homedome."

"I'll see you at the community meeting tomorrow," Clay says, kissing my cheek.

"The meeting!" I'd forgotten about the next hurdle—addressing the community to somehow restore hope.

Clay pulls a handful of pine needles from his pocket and drizzles them over my head. "Stay calm."

I chuckle, shake the needles from my hair, and perch on Vad's hand-chair. Vad sprints in the direction of Loop Four, Circle Elm.

When I walk into my homedome, the chatter of familiar voices leads me to the cooking orb where Kayla is happily perched in a small floating chair with crumbled cookies on the tray in front of her. I'm so glad we still have power.

Sheldon, Zack's best friend other than Brita, sits at the counter with Zack on the stool next to him.

"Mom, good, you're back." Zack's eyes dart to our android and back to me. "Can we borrow Vad?"

"Why do you two need Vad?"

Sheldon blurts, "We have to find my uncle."

Zack jabs his elbow into Sheldon's ribs.

"Rudy's been gone for four years," I say. "Why the urgency to find him now?"

"Maybe he got hurt in the explosions." Zack hops from his stool. "Maybe he's trying to get back. We wanna go look for him.

No matter how I say no, he isn't going to like it. "Vad has to bring Bayl over here so we can prepare for the community meeting tomorrow. And until we know the full impact of yesterday's explosions, I don't want you two searching for Rudy, with or without an android."

Zack's jaw tightens, and he looks at Sheldon. Sheldon grabs a cookie and hops from his stool.

"That obnoxious robot won't do what I tell him, anyway." Zack narrows his eyes at Vad, and the boys leave the orb.

"Thank you for watching your sister," I yell after them, but my gratitude goes unacknowledged, perhaps unheard. I feel like I can't do anything right by Zack lately, and we're getting further and further apart.

Almost two hours later, Bayl still hasn't arrived. My nose catches a smoky odor, and I look toward the doorway from the living orb. Zack walks in, his shirt streaked with smudges, and he slouches onto the sofa.

"Zackie!" Kayla jumps from my lap and runs to him.

"You won't believe the ashy mess at what used to be Energy Dome," Zack says, lifting Kayla to sit on his knee, making me wish Krissie were here, too. "When the scientists start working on the power sources again, they hafta let me help figure out what went wrong. I know as much about zilimite as any of them."

I smile. Zack is talking to me like he used to before this whole mess. "I think they would be wise to take advantage of your expertise."

"Mom," he says softly. "I know it's not your fault you can't fix Brita, but I still hate it that you kept all those secrets from me."

I touch his hand and thank the cosmos when he doesn't withdraw.

Vad enters the living orb—alone.

"Where's Bayl?" I ask.

"Bayl said to tell you he will see you at nine o'clock tomorrow morning at History Dome. The council will assemble at that time."

My mouth goes dry. I really wanted to feel more prepared before addressing the whole community.

Zack rolls his eyes and stands, dangling Kayla over one arm like a large rag doll. "What took you so long to do nothing?" Without waiting for a reply, Zack swings Kayla onto his back and marches out of the orb.

I would ask Vad for more explanation, but the message

sounded like Bayl's own words.

Why can Travis build a complex homebot, but he still can't make synthetic honey? If we had the antidote for infant loss syndrome, rallying the community to rebuild would be easy. I wish I knew what to say to my fellow citizens tomorrow.

CHAPTER 8

This is it, the day I have to address all of Zelfar. I barely slept, and now I can't eat.

Travis walks into the cooking orb, and Kayla squeals, "Daddy!"

She waves a grape in the air, and I wish Krissie were having breakfast with us, too.

"Just a minute, cutie," Travis tells Kayla. He sits on the stool next to me and rubs a hand between my shoulder blades. "Worried about your speech today?"

I must look as tense as I feel. "I have to inspire everyone to believe in our future."

"You'll do fine, my love. Everyone wants to have hope. Just give them some words of encouragement." Travis accepts a mug of steaming coffee from Vad and brings the rim to his lips.

"Ow! Vad, too hot!" Travis waggles his tongue and shakes a disapproving finger.

Kayla mimics with her finger. "Too hot, Vad."

I chuckle and think how Zack would enjoy seeing Vad get

into trouble.

I gaze at the green numbers in the curved wall above the door, and my pulse quickens with each second blinking closer to nine o'clock.

Zack pokes his head in the open doorway. "I'm going to Sheldon's, okay?"

"No." I slide from the stool. "You're coming to the council meeting with us this morning."

"I've never had to go before."

"You said you want to help figure out what went wrong with the zilimite, right?" This distraction will be the perfect thing to keep his mind off going back through the portal.

"Yeah, but—"

"Sounds like your mom's made up her mind." Travis sets his coffee mug on the counter. "You're coming with us."

"Why does it feel like I never get a choice anymore?" Zack shoves his hands into his pockets and retreats into the hall.

I should trust Zack's intelligence and encourage him to follow his instincts, like Gram did for me when I was fifteen, but I must be careful now that he knows about the portal.

A few moments later, Vad sets us on the platform outside History Dome. Rather than being near the lake like most of our service domes, History Dome sits at the end of the clearing closest to the mountains and forest. I wonder if the closer proximity to Paradise Falls made Gram choose to build her secret archive orb under this dome where she hides her father's journal and the items he and she used on their undisclosed trips to America.

Travis puts Kayla in Vad's arm and says, "Tot-watch Kayla, and stay close to the exit."

Vad nods.

Zack walks into the dome, and I ask Travis, "Close to the exit?"

"I just like knowing Vad's close by."

I agree. If it weren't for our androids, our double life would be impossible.

We enter the dome and see Bayl standing next to Zack.

"Good morning Zophie, Travis," Bayl says. "Is it your intention to include Zack in the council meeting?"

"Yes," Travis answers. As a council member, Travis may invite guests to join the meeting.

"Very well." Bayl leads us down the corridor, and I look longingly at the serenity orb when we pass by. I sigh, wishing we had time for a few minutes of serenity simulation. When we reach the conference orb, Bayl waves his hand, and the door slides open. He motions for us to enter ahead of him, and he walks away.

A moment later, Bayl, carrying a chair, joins us in the conference orb. Travis takes the chair from Bayl and places it next to mine. Zack sits between Travis and me. One chair remains vacant. At least we weren't the last to arrive. The council, officially known as the Zelfar Foundation Team, consists of eight members, each representing two areas of expertise. Zack and I are the only guests today.

Bayl stands stiffly with his hands behind him and says, "As many of you do not remember a time before hoverspheres, I thank you for overcoming the difficulty in attending today."

Why would Bayl start the meeting without everyone present? Oh. Gina is the absent member. The realization weighs heavily on my chest. Poor Gram. Gina's transcending would be like me losing Clay. I shiver at the thought.

Without explaining Zack's presence, Bayl asks Quaid for an update. Zack swivels a little in his chair and glances around the table. I should have told him what to expect at a council meeting. Zack may not know everyone, but their reports should hold his interest. At least he knows that areas of expertise are denoted by their different colored arm bands.

Quaid stands and clears his throat. "Water Dome was

unharmed, but as y'all know, Energy Dome is gone." His drawl, one of a kind in Zelfar, sounds like the cowboys on American television. According to Gram, as a young child, Quaid developed the accent by emulating his grandfather, one of Zelfar's original inhabitants. "Anythin' that got power from Energy Dome is inactive, including the bodyball domes. But thank the cosmos, our homedomes use their own green diamonds and all have power."

Zack sits on the edge of his chair, drumming his fingers on the table.

"You got a question, Zackie boy?" Quaid asks.

"Do you mean we can't play bodyball? None of the five domes has its own power source?"

"That's right."

"We have infinite zilimite and green diamonds." Zack wrinkles his brow. "Can't we put a power source in at least one of the bodyball domes?"

I really wish I'd coached Zack on council protocol.

"Wish it was that easy." Quaid half-frowns. "One thing for sure, we won't be mixin' green diamonds and zilimite until we know what went wrong last time. How'd you like to be on the team figurin' that out and helpin' us build a new energy dome?"

"Yeah!" Zack beams, and Quaid sits.

I don't know if Quaid putting Zack on the energy team was deliberate to keep Zack on this side of the portal, but I'm glad we brought Zack with us.

The corners of Bayl's mouth turn up slightly, and he gives Oak a quick nod. Did Bayl just smile at her? He never smiles.

Oak rises, standing nearly six feet tall. "Architecture Dome appears intact, but its power came from Energy Dome, so, like Quaid said, it's inactive. Transportation Dome is a pile of rubble along with every hoversphere and all but one hoverdisc. We have ample crystillium to rebuild domes and transports, but don't expect immediate recovery."

"So, we have to *walk* everywhere?" Zack blurts. "Uh, sorry. I, uh, sorry." Zack sinks into his chair under Bayl's frown. Travis hides a grin.

"No, Zack, we don't," Oak says. "We will reactivate the old magnetic lanes and distribute magnadiscs, at least one per family. That'll get people to and from their service areas and homedomes—not as fast as a hoverdisc, but certainly faster than walking." She sits.

Zack pokes my arm and mouths. "Magnadiscs!"

I wink. Zack has never ridden magnadiscs, nor have I. They were replaced by hoverdiscs before either of us was born, but we learned about them in history studies. The discs were round with a T-bar handle, and they floated two inches off the ground along magnetic lanes. I may stick to Vad for transportation.

All heads turn to Clay as he stands. He's the newest council member, appointed after the previous health expert resigned last year. "Health Dome is unsalvageable, including the instant healing tube and all the healthbots. Yesterday, Zophie and I set up a temporary health center in my homedome. If it weren't for the healing abilities of Travis's android, we would still be setting bones and suturing wounds. I'll lead a team to set up more health centers in the homedome loops, including temporary birthing centers."

Faces brighten with Clay's reminder that third and fourth generation women are still bearing healthy infants. I don't know why, but living in Zelfar has expanded our longevity by several decades over our American counterparts. Even so, our extinction is inevitable if Travis and I can't bring the protizine cure to Zelfar.

I grip the sides of my chair, wishing I could say how close we are to ending newborn loss syndrome. Bayl narrows his eyes at me as if he senses my urge, warning me to stay quiet.

Lena reports that Robotics Dome has no power, and

Communications Dome is destroyed. Everyone around the table glances at their zelcoms and agrees restoring communication must take priority.

Travis stands next and twists his green and blue armbands higher on his bicep. "Our gem and mineral mines are intact. Agriculture Dome sustained moderate damage from airborne debris, but two of our largest orchards were destroyed by fire, and a third of our crops are dusted with ash. We won't starve, but there won't be as much variety for a while." The curved walls seem to close in, and Travis sits.

At that moment, the door to the conference orb slides open, and Gram strides in with her usual confidence—petite, yet strong. Her silvery blonde tresses are pulled to one side, and two narrow bands—purple and lavender—circle her upper arm.

Bayl stands. "Sadly, as most of you know, we lost Gina in yesterday's tragedy. Please welcome Lilly back to the council to represent Serenity and Personal Growth. Lilly has graciously agreed to fill Gina's position until she names someone else for the role."

My grandmother served on the Zelfar Foundation Team for more than five decades. When she retired from the council, about the time I was born, she passed her elder position to Bayl and gave him access to the secrets she'd been protecting—the archive orb she built, her father's journal, and portal keys to America.

When my great-grandfather, Ozell Farlum, retired from the council, he appointed his daughter, Lilly, to be the council's first elder and her colleague, Quaid, to be the second. Both would serve as elders as long as they chose.

Quaid smiles broadly when he catches Gram's eye. Fine lines lightly define Quaid's cheeks, the only sign of having celebrated his centennial birthday.

"Only a third of our serenity orbs remain intact," Gram says. "Without hoverspheres, our ability to get to them is limited. We cannot let the current despair override our focus on serenity. We must set up lounges and serenity simulators in vacant homedomes where they are easily accessible. As soon as possible."

Quaid raises his hand. "I'll help ya find volunteers, Lilly."

Gram smiles. "Thank you."

"In addition to serenity orbs," Bayl says, "we must rally people to rebuild our community. This requires reaching everyone with the same message. Lena, do we have any mass communication abilities at all?"

Lena's thin lips turn down. "Sorry, no."

Travis says, "My android has the ability to amplify his voice, and I think he can amplify someone else's."

"Can Vad come here now?" Bayl asks.

Travis lifts his wrist. "Vad, bring Kayla and come to conference orb one."

"Kayla?" Oak asks. "I thought your daughter's name is K."

"It is." Travis chuckles. "She likes to pretend she's Kayla. Guess she has me pretending, too."

I cross my arms and shrink into my chair, hoping no one asks more questions. This double life is getting too hard.

Bayl waves his hand, and the door slides apart, allowing Vad to enter.

Kayla squeals, "Mommy," and reaches for me.

I lean to Zack and whisper, "Would you entertain K in the corridor for a couple of minutes? We'll be right out."

Zack takes Kayla and exits the orb. When the doorway slides closed, Bayl says to Vad, "We would like to test to see if you can amplify a person's voice." Bayl waves a hand toward me. "Zophie?"

I gulp. I'd thought Vad would be testing Bayl's voice. And maybe I hoped to get out of addressing the community.

Vad grasps my fingers with one hand, and with the other, touches his diaphragm. "Speak," he says.

I choke back a giggle. That's how my American friend commands her little white dog to bark. "What shall I say?" My voice comes out so loud that the council members cover their ears with their hands.

"Excellent!" Travis claps.

I yank my hand from Vad's.

"Community meeting today, three o'clock," Bayl says. "Gather everyone to the clearing." Bayl waves his hand to open the door.

We step into the corridor and Zack asks, "Is the community meeting happening today?"

"Yes, in the clearing at three," I say, taking Kayla's hand.

"I'll go get Sheldon. See ya there, okay?" Zack dashes out of sight before I can thank him for tot-watching. What if he isn't strong enough to resist telling Sheldon about the portal?

Gram exits the orb with Quaid. "I'll see you at the clearing, dear."

"Okay, toss pine," I say and walk to the exit with Travis, Vad, and Kayla.

Outside, Travis takes my hand and says, "I'm going to start spreading the word about the meeting. Vad will take you and K home." He kisses my fingers.

"I go with Daddy." Kayla reaches her hands toward Travis.

"I'll see you at two thirty," Travis tells Kayla and puts his lips to her fingers, pretending to nibble them.

Kayla jerks her hand back and says, "Two thirty!"

Vad hurries Kayla and me to our dome and then zooms away to help Travis.

I sit with Kayla while she naps on the sofa beside me. My eyelids get heavy, and sometime later, I feel Kayla's little hands pat my cheeks.

"Mommy, wake up. I hungwy." She presses her nose to mine.

I laugh, grasp her fingers and carry her to the cooking orb

where several clear storage cylinders float along the curved walls. I'm no android, but I can make a sandwich.

Kayla eagerly accepts the peanut butter and jelly sandwich and takes a big bite.

"Sweetheart?" Travis's voice echoes from the center corridor.

"In the kitchen, I mean cooking orb." Oh my. My two worlds are starting to blur.

"We need to get to the clearing. People are gathering now." Travis enters the orb and grimaces at the sight of his gooey-faced three-year-old.

"I'll be ready shortly." I walk out of the orb, leaving toddler cleanup to Travis.

In our unity orb, I don fresh zeltire—a cheery yellow and pink tunic and white pants—trying to steady my trembling hands, still unsure how to lighten the strife people feel right now.

I hurry outside where Travis sits in one of Vad's hand-chairs, holding Kayla. When I'm seated, Travis says, "Let's go, Vad."

Whoosh. My legs swing freely as our android sprints to the clearing. Murmurs grow louder when we approach the crowd, and an unfamiliar tension fills the air. Vad stops at the bottom of a staircase leading to a crude wooden platform constructed for the occasion.

Travis holds Kayla and nods for me to climb the stairs. On weak legs, I slowly ascend the creaky steps. I'd give a green diamond for a floating hoverdisc right now. On the platform, Bayl stands near the rail with Gram and Quaid. Vad walks close to me, and Travis, still holding Kayla, stops next to Vad.

I gaze out at my fellow citizens, and the din lowers to a hum. Everyone appears to be here, eerily similar to the crowd of two days ago. The stressed brows indicate today's atmosphere is one of despair, not excitement.

I take a deep breath, and Vad wraps his human-like fingers around my hand.

"Hello, everyone." My voice resonates throughout the clearing, and wide eyes stare up at me. "I have encouraging news about the reconstruction of our domes."

A male voice yells, "Reconstruction! What's the use?" I spot Marc's blonde hair a few heads deep from where I stand.

"Yeah, what's the use of rebuilding for a future with no one in it?" Darcy, his wife, shouts next to him.

The absurdity of the question raises the hair on my arms. "I'll tell you the use!" My voice booms. "We are not extinct! Healthy babies are still being born. Don't we owe them a future?"

I swipe outward with one hand. "And what about us? I have a long life ahead of me. My son is fifteen and my daughter . . . er is two." Thank the serene cosmos I caught myself before making *daughter* plural. "Zelfarian children of today will be here creating things for many decades. Look what we've accomplished in the last hundred years. As scientists and inventors, imagine what we can do in the next century? And furthermore, I guarantee I will find the cure for newborn loss syndrome."

Heads nod and eyes shine brighter. Hope seems to spread throughout the gathering. If only I could tell them we already have the cure, that we're just figuring out how to produce it here.

I bring up, name by name, the ancestors of those who are here and discuss the contributions they've made to our growth, then talk about the growth we've seen due to those present. I can see the impact on each face as they realize the importance of each person and their contributions. Before I can name anyone else in the crowd, smiles replace the fear and someone from the middle of the crowd, shouts, "Rebuild now!"

As the crowd energy builds, I drop the rest of my speech and say, "We have resources, like crystillium and green diamonds, and we know how to use them." My open palm shoots above my head. "Let's all agree to rebuild now!"

Wide smiles greet me from those nearest the platform.

Hundreds of palms thrust into the air, mirroring mine, and a chant begins, "Rebuild now! Rebuild now!" Soon thousands of palms shake at the sky, and voices resound in the clearing, "Rebuild now! Rebuild now!"

Happy tears fill my eyes, my fingers still pointed toward the sun. Travis steps next to me, holding his free palm in the air and our daughter in his other arm. Gram and Quaid lift their palms skyward.

Kayla waves her hands and starts clapping. Bayl claps, too, in rhythm to the chant. Like ripples across the lake, row after row of hands clap with renewed enthusiasm. Travis taps Vad's hand and our android wraps Travis's fingers in his.

"Let's all go to our service areas and work together to rebuild now!" Travis's voice echoes over the rhythmic clap. He pulls a large handful of pine needles from his pocket and opens his palm to Kayla. She grasps as many needles as she can hold, and together, they lob pine needles into the air.

The crowd disperses with people chattering with excitement. This is the Zelfar community I love—everyone pulling together to make life better for all. But if my fellow citizens learn of my deceit, they will never trust me again.

When we descend the stairs, Travis says, "Great remark about our resources. I'm surprised Zack didn't shout out something about zilimite."

I glance outward, hoping to see my son making his way toward me. "I didn't see Zack in the crowd. Did you?"

"No, but where else would he be?"

CHAPTER 9

Where else would Zack be? Travis's question haunts me as I pull Kayla from his arms and make my way through the thinning crowd as I look for Zack.

"Great speech, Zophie," says Sheldon's dad. Perfect.

"Thank you, Greg." I glance over his shoulder. "Are the boys with you?"

"No. I haven't seen them since this morning." Greg crosses his arms. "They said they'd meet me here. Guess time got away from them."

Greg might as well have said, "Boys will be boys," like I've heard on American television. I know Zack will be Zack, but he wouldn't have missed my speech, unless . . .

My heart races, and I struggle to keep my voice even. "Did they say where they were going?"

"Sheldon said something about looking for Rudy on Crescent Peak where Rudy used to take him camping."

"I wanna go camping." Kayla pats my cheek.

"How long ago was that?" I keep my gaze on Greg and

struggle to keep my mind from zapping.

"About three hours, I guess."

Three hours. Okay. Zack could have miscalculated how long it would take to walk six or eight miles. I scrape my fingers through my hair. What if they're lost?

"Zophie, is something wrong?"

Kayla wiggles, and I set her on the ground, keeping a firm grasp on her hand.

"I just wish our zelcoms worked," I say to Greg. "If Zack shows up at your dome, will you send him home?"

"Sure. You do the same with Sheldon."

As Greg walks off, Kayla asks, "Can we go camping?"

"Let's go ask Daddy. Shall we run?"

We sprint as fast her little legs can move back to the site of the elevated platform. As we approach, Vad places a long plank on a neat stack, and Travis lobs a hammering tool onto the ground.

"What's wrong?" Travis wipes his hands on his pant legs and steps closer.

"We wanna go camping." Kayla drops my hand and runs to Travis.

"Camping?" Travis lifts an eyebrow.

"Greg just told me Zack and Sheldon went looking for Rudy about three hours ago. On Crescent Peak. The boys were supposed to meet Greg here, but they didn't show up."

"I thought they had forgotten about Rudy." Travis rubs his chin in his usual pensive gesture. "Regardless, Zack wouldn't intentionally miss the gathering."

"I know, but yesterday Zack wanted to borrow Vad to help search for Rudy. He thought the explosions and ground quake might bring Rudy out of hiding or that Rudy could be injured. Maybe I should have let Vad help them. Now Zack and Sheldon are probably lost like Rudy." I swallow hard, trapping my emotions in my throat.

"You did the right thing, but let's not assume they're lost. They're walking, so they can't have gone too far." Travis kisses my forehead and adds softly, "Don't worry, my love. Vad and I will find the boys. See you at home."

Travis sits on Vad's hand-chair, and they become a blur moving toward the mountains.

"Mommy." Kayla taps my leg. "I wanna go camping."

"We can't go camping today, sweetie." I heft Kayla onto my back. "Let's walk around for a while."

Kayla wraps her legs around my waist. I scan the area, half hoping to see Gram. She'd be able to calm my nerves, but she'd be no help in finding Zack.

I walk briskly across the grassy clearing and down the wide ash-covered corridor, winding among the service domes. My chest tightens when I stop at the mound of rubble that used to be Transportation Dome, where charred maple branches lie amidst indiscernible chunks of crystillium.

Panting from exertion and worry, I lower Kayla to her feet and take her hand.

We skirt among the citizens cleaning up the site, looking for one in particular. I breathe a little easier when I see Owen's big brawny hands easily sort and toss debris onto several small piles. A large man, tall, with well-defined muscles, Owen reminds me of Popeye in American cartoons, or maybe Paul Bunyan.

In an American adventure show, he would be known as Owen, the Explorer. In Zelfar, he's our expert on the outer regions.

"Hi, Owen. May I interrupt you for a minute?"

Owen stands and sweeps red hair from his forehead. "Sure, Zophie. Mighty fine speech you gave. If you're here to give an individual pep talk, you can skip me. I'm excited to rebuild."

"Thank you, but that's not why I'm here. Have you ever explored around Crescent Peak?"

"Dozens of times. Stood on top of that mountain more than

once. You planning a camping trip?"

"I wanna go camping." Kayla jerks my hand, and I pat hers.

Owen takes a cloth from his pocket and wipes some of the grime from his face. Lighter splotches emerge among dark smudges, and the curly hairs of his short, red beard clump together.

My instinct is to take the cloth and help wipe the smudges. Instead I blurt, "Zack and Sheldon are missing."

"Missing?" He spits the word like it tastes bad on his tongue. "For how long?"

"Three hours."

"And you think they're on Crescent Peak?"

"Yes."

"I'll get my gear. Wait here."

Before I can stop him, Owen tosses the soiled cloth into a bin and sprints away.

I wait a few minutes and then Owen rushes toward me, outfitted in full mountain-climbing zeltire and bulging backpack.

"Owen, I wasn't asking you to go look for them. I just wanted to know more about the area. Travis and our android are already searching."

"I know Crescent Peak. If the boys are up there, I'll find them."

I've only camped around Crescent Peak one time, but, impulsively I say, "I want to go with you."

"What about your little girl?"

"I can take K to Gram's."

Owen tilts his head and lifts an eyebrow.

I glance at my zeltire—lightweight tunic and pants, no boots, no backpack. I'm not dressed for hiking, but I don't care. I stick out my chin, daring him to tell me I can't go with him. What am I . . . a child?

Owen tightens his lips as if he's holding back a grin or, worse yet, a laugh.

"Zophie, I'll travel much faster by myself. And I bet I can track better than that robot of yours. I'll bring your son home. Purple homedome, right?"

I nod. Not just about our dome, but in agreement that I would slow him down. I wish his exploration hoversphere still worked. But even on foot, Owen knows the terrain.

"Thank you, Owen."

He dashes toward the mountains, and Kayla lifts her arms for me to pick her up. I carry her most of the way home, glad she's too young to understand the turmoil happening all around her. When our dome's entrance slides open, I'm surprised to see my grandmother inside.

"Gram, I thought you would still be busy setting up serenity simulators in the homedome loops."

Gram smiles. "Already done. I had lots of help."

"Did Zack come home yet?" Silly question, but I can hope.

"I haven't seen him since the council meeting."

That was hours ago. Too many hours ago.

"Zophie, dear, what's wrong?" Gram takes my fingers in hers.

I sigh heavily and gaze into her hazel eyes, which are clouded with concern. "Zack and Sheldon are lost."

"Oh dear." She pats my hand. "I assume Vad and Travis are looking for them, right?" Just like Gram—intuitive and calm.

I nod. "So is Owen."

"Well, then, they'll find the boys."

"They have to, Gram. Rudy's been missing for four years. I can't bear Zack being lost for one day."

"Mommy?" Kayla whimpers, hugging my knees. I paste on a smile.

"I bet my little girl is hungry." I pick her up and swing her in a circle. She giggles, and I stop with one twirl. My head feels dizzy enough.

Feeding Kayla and having a bite to eat myself sounds like a welcome distraction. Gram follows us into the cooking orb and insists on preparing our meal.

* * *

Two hours after Gram and Kayla have gone to bed, I still feel compelled to sit here at the counter and stare at the doorway. The digital time blurs to a solid green line. I rub at the tightness in my forehead. I've never known this kind of agony.

I tap my zelcom for the hundredth time. Why doesn't Vad answer? I wring my hands and glance toward the living room. The sofa would be more comfortable than this stool.

My ears perk. Did I hear something? I run to the door and hurry onto the outside platform where the faint glow from nearby domes barely cuts the darkness.

I shout into the void. "Zack? Is that you?" I shout again. "Travis?"

No one answers. My knees weaken, and I slump onto our outdoor bench. My son is lost . . . in the dark. My breath catches, thinking Travis might be lost as well. Did I send Owen into the depths of nowhere, too?

A soft sound brings me to my feet.

"Mom?" comes a familiar voice in the distance.

"Zack!" I lunge forward.

Zack sprints toward me. I throw my arms around his torso, and he engulfs me like he did when he would run into my open arms as a little boy. Zack holds me tight, pressing his chin into the hollow of my neck. My poor baby. He must have been frightened, too.

"I'm really sorry I missed your speech. We got lost."

"I'm just glad you're home."

Travis and Vad step from the darkness. Vad walks past me

and into our dome. I let go of Zack and leap into Travis's arms.

"You found our son!"

"I'm going to bed," Zack says as he starts inside.

"Wait." I release Travis and touch Zack's shoulder, scrutinizing him in the light of the doorway, frowning at his dirt-covered shirt. I gasp at the sight of dried blood on his pants.

"You're hurt!" I reach toward his leg.

"No, Mom, I'm okay. I had a little scrape on my shin, but Vad healed it."

I breathe easier. "All right, I'm glad Vad was there. A good sanitizing shower will clean up the dirt."

"Yeah. That'll feel good." Zack's shoulders droop with obvious exhaustion.

We step inside and Travis says, "Go on to bed, son. I'll tell your mom all about your rescue."

Zack kisses me on the cheek and ambles toward his sleeping orb.

"Rescue?" My stomach contracts.

Travis places his hand on my waist. "Everything is fine. Let me get cleaned up. Then I'll give you all the details."

I head towards our bed and crawl under the covers. Several anxious minutes later, I lift the blanket for Travis when he comes into the orb after his sonic shower. He slips into bed and reaches to pull me closer.

I resist his enticing spicy lime scent and move his hand aside. "The rescue?"

Travis chuckles and props himself on a pillow. "You know, if I hadn't been so scared for Zack, I'd say it was one of the best adventures of my life." His chuckle doesn't erase the words "scared for Zack."

"Hurry up and tell me what happened."

"Well, as soon as we hit the tree line, Vad found the boys' trail, or rather trails. The boys had split up, so Vad and I each took a trail. I took the one that looked easier to follow—wider, with fewer trees. After a couple of miles, the path narrowed again and led to a cliff. I stood on the edge of that ravine, wondering if, for the first time in my life, I might be lost, too. Had I found one of the boys, I'm not sure I could have led us out."

Travis lost? It was bad enough when that thought invaded my head earlier, but it's terrifying to believe Travis actually thinks that was possible.

Travis takes a deep breath and continues, "Then I heard someone call out to me. I could have kissed Owen when I saw him dressed head-to-toe in hiking gear."

"Owen led me back to the main trail, which he had no trouble following, even at dusk. We kept yelling for Zack, and my voice got so hoarse, I could barely talk. Finally, we heard Zack yell back. I have to tell you, I was so excited, I almost sprang into Gram's happy dance."

I smile, envisioning Travis in the middle of the forest with his arms in the air dancing in little circles.

"Turns out, Zack was stuck, hanging over a branch on the underside of a sheer cliff. He said he was standing on a fallen tree, peering into the ravine, when a piece of bark broke under his foot, and he slipped. He grabbed onto a thick branch as he slid over the edge. The branch wedged itself in the dirt, pinning Zack between the branch and the rim. Zack said he was afraid if he tried to free himself, he'd fall. He was right to stay still. It was a good fifty-foot drop."

"Zack must have been so frightened." I sit up and hug a pillow to my chest. "How long . . . how long was he stuck like that?"

"He doesn't know, but Zack was sure glad when he heard us calling him. Owen pulled out a rope from his pack, and we were struggling to secure the rope around Zack's waist when Vad showed up carrying Sheldon. Vad said he had found Sheldon about the same time he heard Zack yell, so he scooped Sheldon onto one hand and ran toward Zack's voice.

I squeeze the pillow, anxious to hear what happened next.

"I pointed to the cliff. Vad put Sheldon down and peered over the edge. In two micro-seconds Vad knelt on the rim and reached downward. Branches cracked, and Zack flew up, hanging in Vad's grip above the ledge. Vad laid Zack on the ground, and Zack panted, shaking a little, with blood oozing from his shin. Then Zack went completely limp and stared into Vad's eyes."

I gasp. "Zack must have been in shock!" And he was bleeding!

"I don't know," Travis says. "But Zack and Vad locked gazes, communicating mind to mind. Zack didn't even balk when Vad said he was going to silence Zack's awareness—you know, put him to sleep, like Vad did with me when he healed my leg."

I nod. "Then what?"

"Then Vad moved his hands above Zack's body, and in seconds, Zack was healed—no scrapes, no more bleeding. Then Zack hopped to his feet, and do you know his first concern?"

"What?" I finally feel like smiling.

"He didn't want you to be scared when you saw his bloody pants."

I grimace at the memory. "He was right. His blood-stained pants were frightening. But was Zack grateful to Vad for saving him?"

"A mumbled, 'thanks,' was all Vad got from Zack."

I snuggle up to my husband. "Maybe you're the one we should thank. You built Vad."

Travis kisses my forehead. "I'm glad I did."

I'm glad, too. Maybe Owen can out-track Vad, I don't know, but when it comes to speed and strength, and now instant healing, Vad is the one to have around.

"It'll be nice when we can have both of our androids here in Zelfar," I say.

"Maybe that will happen with the next batch of synthetic

honey. Both androids and all three of our children home with us in Zelfar." Travis sighs and lays his head on the pillow. "What a comforting thought."

"Thank you for bringing our son home safely tonight." I press my head into Travis's shoulder and close my eyes. No Zelfarians in America . . . Krissie and Kayla both in my arms . . . honey in Zelfar . . . no one questioning the rebuild, not even Marc. Poor Marc and Darcy. I would give them the first dose of honey.

CHAPTER 10

I sit on the sofa, sipping my morning coffee while Kayla rocks back and forth in her small chair next to me, humming to her doll. Travis and Zack went to the site of Energy Dome. Vad is transporting Gram home and should be back any moment to take me to see Brita.

When Vad arrives, I pick up Kayla, and our android transports us to Clay's homedome.

"Hi Zophie." Clay greets us at the door. We follow him to Brita's orb where she lies unconscious in her health tube.

I set Kayla on the floor, and Clay's homebot gives her a stem of grapes. She sits on a rug next to the wall and shoves a purple grape into her mouth.

I stare at Brita's unresponsive body. "I wish we knew more about her brain injury."

"I've heard Janet speak of coma patients," Clay says. "That's what they call people in prolonged states of unconsciousness." He leans to my ear as if his homebot might divulge our secret. "When are we going back to America? Janet might have knowledge we can use."

"Maybe today," I reply. "Another reason I came to see Brita is to get a few cc's of her blood. When Travis has a new batch of synthetic honey for me to test, I'd like to use Brita's DNA. I'll have Vad extract a sample from her now, and we can go to America this afternoon."

"I'll entertain K." Clay picks up Kayla and walks out of the orb, instructing his homebot to follow.

"Vad." I glance up at him. "Can you extract thirty cc's of blood from Brita without compromising the ecosystem of her tube?"

"Affirmative." Vad lifts the bottom of his shirt, and when he presses a fingertip to his side, a three-inch section of his synthetic skin slides upward like a miniature window. Vad withdraws a vial about the size of his little finger and steps to the foot of Brita's health tube. He raises the top portion, touches the vial to the pad of Brita's big toe, and almost instantly, bright red blood fills the vial. Then he holds his finger to the wound. By the time he removes his hand from the tube, the wound is healed. Vad inserts the vial into the open slot on his side, lets his shirt fall back into place, and reseals the health tube.

DNA samples for testing each new batch of honey are usually difficult to obtain. Brita's will be the first live blood sample. With every failed test, Travis assures me the next batch will be the one that saves our infants.

When Vad and I walk into the living orb, Kayla eats the last grape and holds her arms up to me. I lift her, and we exit the dome with Clay.

"Be at our homedome by three o'clock," I say and slide into Vad's hand-chair.

"See you soon." Clay turns to his dome and Vad takes us to ours.

Kayla runs inside, and I hurry after her to the living orb where we find Travis reclining in his favorite chair. I lean in to give him a kiss, and he pulls me onto his lap. He presses his lips against mine, and we kiss until Kayla wiggles her way up Travis's leg.

"Where's Kwissie?" she asks.

Travis chuckles. I gasp. How can we teach a three-year-old to keep a secret?

"Krissie is waiting for us." I gently tickle her ribs. "Shall we have Vad take us to her?"

"Yes!" Kayla squeals.

"We just launched the rebuild efforts," Travis says. "Don't you think we'll be missed?"

"Without zelcoms, we'd be hard to find anyway. And I miss Krissie. Besides, I have a new DNA sample to preserve for the next test."

"I wanna see Kwissie." Kayla pats my leg.

"Vad? Zack?" Travis calls out. "Come on. We're leaving for a day or two." He touches a dot on the side of his chair and the adjustable seat raises, bringing us to our feet.

Zack appears in the arched doorway. "I wanna stay here. I didn't get to see Brita today."

"Sorry, sweetheart. You can't stay here by yourself."

"Why not? I'm perfectly capable of taking care of myself."

I lift an eyebrow.

"I promise I won't go looking for Rudy."

"I just came from Clay's. Brita is the same."

"You know, Zack," Travis says, "I've been thinking about testing your theory of enzymes and the bees' regurgitation process. I could use your help in setting up the equipment. 'Course, we'll probably need to drive the car to Portland to get some new canisters."

"The car?" Zack's eyes brighten. Travis knows his son well. I don't like the idea of exposing Zack to Portland, but Travis and I can have that discussion once we get through the portal.

"Clay is here." Vad's voice reverberates from my zelcom.

Kayla runs ahead of me, past Vad in the curved corridor, and beats us to the door. "Wanna go see Kwissie?" she says to Clay.

Clay chuckles and walks inside. "I'm glad I'm early, Zophie. You said three o'clock."

"Three o'clock for what?" Travis asks.

"A ride to Paradise Falls." Clay pats his silver ink pen clipped to his shirt pocket.

Travis places his hand on Clay's shoulder. "You miss your girlfriend, and we miss Krissie. Wait here. I'll send Vad back for you.

* * *

"Mommy!" Krissie yells and runs down the porch steps. I sweep her up in my arms.

"I missed you so much!" I smack kisses all over her face and she giggles.

"Let's go play," Kayla says. Krissie wiggles out of my arms and the girls run into the house together. Travis, Zack, and I follow close behind.

When Clay arrives a while later, I meet him at the front door. He wipes his tongue with the back of his hand and I lift an inquisitive brow.

"I don't think I'll ever get used to your android open-air transport," he says. "Especially here. I think I ate a few bugs."

"Lunch is ready . . . if you haven't filled up on bugs."

Clay chuckles. "I'll be there in a minute, after I call Janet." He lifts his arm, exposing his zelcom.

I smile, let Clay pass, and look at Vad, standing outside. Vad pats his side and proceeds toward the lab. Brita's blood will need safe storage until Travis's next batch of synthetic honey is ready for testing. Since Gram is in Zelfar, Vad will return to be available for her.

I close the front door and walk to the kitchen.

The twins sit in their highchairs eating vegetable soup, while Einstein places steaming bowls in front of Travis and Zack, both sitting at the table.

"Would you like soup, Zophie?" Einstein asks. "Krissie and I made it this morning."

"I got to plop the mushshooms in the pot," Krissie says between bites.

"Oh, then I definitely have to try some." I smile, happy to be with her.

Zack turns to Travis. "I really get to ride in the car and go to the city?" Zack's excitement usually makes me smile, but not this time. I want Zack's exposure to this world limited to this property.

"I'm not sure taking Zack into the city is wise." I take a seat next to Travis.

Travis pats the back of my hand. "I want Zack to help us choose the new equipment. This could be the breakthrough we're looking for. We'll be fine."

"You don't know the sting of a bullet," I say, remembering the pain of being shot in downtown Portland four years ago when my purse was stolen.

"What's a bullet?" Zack asks.

"It's something on this side of the portal that can end life," I answer, and turn to Travis. "All the serenity orbs in Zelfar couldn't give me peace if something were to happen to you or Zack in this dangerous world. I'd never forgive myself for bringing you here."

"Sweetheart, we'll be careful." Travis moves his hand to my knee. "We'll be fine. I promise."

Zack pleads like he did as a little boy. "Please, Mom. I wanna go to Portland."

Finally, against my better judgment, I relent. "Okay." I point a stern finger at Zack. "You have to stay close to your dad and me and do exactly as we say." Why must I continually risk my family to save Zelfar?

Zack grins. "Thanks, Mom. I will."

Clay walks into the kitchen and sits next to Zack. "I just talked to Janet. She's busy at her new clinic and can't get away right now." Clay smiles when Einstein offers him a bowl of soup.

Travis takes a sip of tea and says to Clay, "We'll be heading into Portland after lunch. Do you want us to drop you off at her clinic?"

"Yes. Thank you."

I love Clay. We've been close since before I knew Travis, and I'm glad he's found a girlfriend. I just wish she was from our world. Once we can make synthetic honey in Zelfar, we'll close off the portal, and Clay will be forced to make an impossible choice—Zelfar or Janet. If he were to make that choice today, Janet might win.

After lunch, Clay says, "I'll go change into those uncomfortable blue jeans and see if I can find something to fit Zack." Clay waves at Zack to follow and they leave the kitchen.

When Travis and I enter our master suite, he closes the door and says, "I'll get the stunners." He walks to a tall mahogany bookcase. When he taps his zelcom the middle shelf slides away, revealing an opaque crystillium dome about thirty inches in height and width. Travis taps his zelcom again and an opening appears as if it were a miniature homedome with a sliding doorway. The *safe*, as Americans would call it, contains a small fortune in one-hundred-dollar bills and our two stunners.

Travis sighs. "I wish we didn't need these." He passes one of the small devices to me.

"I know." I glance at the stunner, hoping I'll never have to use it.

Bayl invented stunners for our protection after I was shot

by a thug on my first trip here. "Immobilizer" would be a better name because the light beam emitted by the device temporarily immobilizes people or animals, making movement impossible for sixty seconds. The stunners are small cylinders slightly larger than a man's middle finger, easily hidden in a pocket, and we never go into town without them.

I slip on a pair of flared blue jeans and a thick gray sweater. The sweater's warmth is the only thing that feels good about this trip. I don a tan raincoat and put the stunner into my pocket.

Clad in denim jackets, Travis and Zack walk down the hall toward the back door with Clay close behind. I hear Zack ask, "Can I drive?"

I gaze at Einstein and our twins stacking blocks in the living room. Einstein takes turns lifting them, so the girls can add blocks higher than they can reach. I consider staying home, but the agony of worrying about Travis and Zack compels me to accompany them. I slip quietly out the back door.

Travis backs our Jeep out of the garage and up the graveled driveway. Soon we are on the black surface of Highway 30, where the motor and tires compete for the loudest hum. I rub my nose to ward off the scent of wet leaves in yellow and brown clumps on the side of the road.

"Why can't I drive?" Zack leans toward the front seat.

"You don't have a license, son." Travis negotiates a quick pass of a slower vehicle. "America has a lot of rules about driving—and almost everything else. Besides, you don't have any reason to go to town without me."

"But I wanna drive a car, Dad. I don't care about going anywhere."

"Tell you what," Travis glances quickly to Zack and back to the road. "I'll let you drive on the road by our house."

"Okay." Zack leans back and crosses his arms. "How about when we get back today?"

"After we buy the new equipment, I think we'll be busy setting up the lab."

"Buying things sounds weird." Zack tugs on the seatbelt across his lap. "Money is confusing, and where does the money come from anyway?"

I gaze over my shoulder at Zack. "Governments manufacture money and people receive money for services they perform. If they don't serve, I'm not sure where they get money."

"Doesn't everybody wanna serve?"

"According to Janet," Clay says, "some people are too ill to serve so the government gives them money. There are millions of people in this world and many governments with different sets of rules. Their monetary systems are far too complicated for anyone to fully understand. Just be glad our society is much simpler."

"How did you get money, Dad? Did you do some kind of service for the government?"

Travis laughs. "No, we do what we can to avoid the government."

I'm glad Travis didn't tell Zack about our jeweler contact who gives us large sums of paper money in exchange for raw diamonds, which are plentiful in Zelfar and worth many American dollars.

Travis slows our Jeep to the city speed limit and we wind through streets that get busier with cars and pedestrians. Zack stares out the side window and says, "Weird. This world is zap." His trip to Portland is adding to all the things he'll have to keep secret.

"There's Janet's clinic." Clay points to a brick, L-shaped building that covers half of the city block. Travis pulls into the parking lot and stops at the entrance. Clay opens his car door and steps out.

At the same time, Zack points and shouts, "There's Rudy!" With robotic speed, Zack unclips his seatbelt, jumps out of the car, and zips past Clay.

"Zack!" I run after him.

Zack yanks on the door to the clinic and rushes inside. By the time I reach him, he is standing face-to-face with a stout man dressed in black leather jacket and pants. "Rudy. It's me, Zack," he says.

The man stares blankly.

"Rudy, come on. I know it's you. I'm best friends with your nephew, Sheldon." Zack touches the stranger's sleeve.

The man pulls his arm away. "I don't know who you think I am, kid, but my name is Johnny Ford."

"What? No." Zack stares hard at the man's face. "You're Rudy."

"Look, kid." The man scratches his thick beard. "My name's not Rudy." He sticks his hand in the back pocket of his black pants, withdraws his wallet, and shows his driver's license to Zack. "See? Johnny Ford."

I don't know why I don't grab Zack and pull him away, or at least whip out my stunner. But the man seems familiar to me, too, though I barely knew Rudy. I peer over Zack's shoulder to see this man's name shown as Johnny Ford and he lives in Beaverton, Oregon.

"I don't understand." Zack reaches into his pants pocket and extends a small figurine carved from a green diamond. "Isn't this yours?"

I knew it was too risky bringing Zack to the city. No one here has ever seen a stone like our green diamonds. I reach to snatch the diamond from Zack's fingers, but he's already laying the figurine in the man's palm. Johnny twirls the stone between his fingers and folds his hand around the small carving.

"I knew it was you, Rudy." Zack beams with a victorious smile.

The man shakes his head. "No, it's not mine."

"But what you just did is what you always do when you hold

that figurine."

He shoves the carving back into Zack's hand. "I gotta go, kid. Doc hates it when I'm late."

Johnny turns, jerks open a door, and the door closes behind him. The black letters on the clear glass pane read: *Dr. Thomas L. Filmore, M.D., Psychiatry.*

I smell a faint hint of pine and notice two pine needles on the floor. Did they fall from Johnny's pocket?

"Ow!" Zack winces at Travis's grip on his shoulder.

I don't like what America is doing to my family. Emotions on this side of the portal are often overpowering, and we can't seem to replicate a serenity simulator that works like those in Zelfar.

Zack slumps, and my eyes follow the green diamond as he pushes it deep into his pocket. I hope this carving isn't the same one he saw at Brita's grandfather's homedome—the one that made Quaid upset when Zack touched it. I doubt Quaid would have given Zack permission to borrow it. And why does Zack have the figurine with him now?

Clay taps my shoulder. "I'll let you know when Janet can take me back to your house."

"Give Janet a hug for me."

Clay winks and walks toward the corridor marked *Pediatrics.*

I follow Travis and Zack back to our Jeep. Zack is still sullen when he gets in and clicks his safety belt.

Travis looks over his shoulder at Zack. "I know you're anxious to find Sheldon's uncle, and that man resembles Rudy, but we are the only Zelfarians here. Focus on helping me make honey so we can take your mom and sisters home for good. No more chasing after people who look familiar, okay?"

"Okay." Zack slumps into the seat.

Zack is acquiescing for now, but I know my son. He'll figure if we're here, someone else from our world could be here, too. Hopefully, the American store will distract him from thoughts of

Rudy. And distract me, too. That encounter with such a similar person bothers me as well.

CHAPTER 11

Travis parks the car in front of a huge concrete building where wide windows span several feet on either side of the entrance.

"Come on, son," Travis says. "Let me show you my favorite hardware store."

I follow Travis and Zack up and down the aisles, enjoying Zack's amazement at the tall racks of gadgets. Travis gets tubing and tools. When Zack sees the canisters he wants, he lifts his wrist, pauses, and looks at me.

"How do we call a servebot to get these down and take them to the house?"

My husband grins and leans toward Zack. "There are no bots of any kind here. I'll find someone to help."

Travis hails a store employee, who retrieves the cylinders and takes them to the checkout counter.

Zack silently observes as his dad extends paper money to the cashier who, in turn, hands Travis a paper receipt. The man asks if we want help loading our items into our vehicle.

Travis declines and pushes our cart out of the store. Once

everything is loaded, we head home.

During the ride, the conversation centers on Zack's idea for replicating the bees' process. He is still explaining his theories when we pull into our garage.

"Let us know when dinner's ready," Travis says. He and Zack each lift a large canister from the car and walk toward the lab.

My heart feels lighter now that we're back from Portland and Zack is thoroughly preoccupied with getting the next protizine experiment underway. When I enter the hall, the twins run from the living room and tug on my hands.

"Play find-me, Mommy," they say together.

I hang my coat on a wall hook and cover my eyes with my fingers. "Okay, I'm ready."

"Count to ten, Mommy," I hear Kayla say, followed by giggles and scampering footsteps.

We play until Einstein's voice emanates from my zelcom. "Dinner time."

"I'm going to go see if Daddy and Zack are ready to come in. You two go wash your hands and get into your highchairs, okay?"

"Me first," Kayla says and runs down the hall with Krissie at her heels.

Excited about the possibility of Zack's inspiration being the final clue to making honey, I grab my sweater and hurry out the back door. The dampness of the cool evening amplifies the scents of cedar and fir. I enter the dome within the barn. The bubble-like ceiling, rows of clear shelving, and numerous glass beakers give me the comfort of Zelfarian technology. If Americans were to see our lab, they'd think they'd fallen into a science fiction movie.

Zack carefully inserts a long copper tube into a crystillium pouch about the size of a stocking cap. Sweet, steamy odors make my mouth water.

"Is this part of your idea?" I ask.

"Oh, hi, Mom. I'm setting up a different simulation of the

regurgitation process, and yeah, this pouch is like a bee's stomach. I added a synthetic oral cavity to act as the bee's mouth, and now I'm recycling the fluid from stomach to mouth. Between my process and Dad's breakthrough with a new enzyme, we might have the answer."

I'm impressed with how quickly Zack has familiarized himself with bees and honey. I move closer to Travis and say, "New enzyme?"

"Glucose oxidase." Travis shoves his arm deep inside a round tank and his voice transitions to tutorbot mode. "When I finish setting up this bioreactor to grow aspergillus, I'll isolate the enzyme, which could take a few weeks. Then I'll add the glucose oxidase to Zack's regurgitation process and you can test the results."

After three years of disappointing outcomes, my agrophysicist husband remains optimistic. He sees the breakthrough for protizine in every batch of lab-made honey. I smile as if I understand his process. Enzymes are necessary in the human body, but until now, I've never been interested in how they occur in nature.

Travis extracts his arm from the bioreactor tank and wipes his hands on his apron. "I assume dinner's ready?"

"Yes. I could have called you, but I wanted to see my two favorite scientists in collaboration."

"Come join us anytime." Travis puts his hand on my waist, and we start toward the door. I jerk when my zelcom vibrates, sending tingles up my arm. In Zelfar, I would feel a faint pulse.

Travis chuckles. "Still not used to that, are you?"

"I don't think I'll ever get used to it."

I tap my zelcom. "Zophie?" It's Clay's voice.

"Hi, Clay."

"I've decided to stay with Janet tonight. She'll bring me back tomorrow evening."

I nod, forgetting he can't see me. "Okay," I shout at my wrist. "Ask her to allow time to visit. It'll be nice to see her again."

"Will do. Toss pine."

"Toss pine."

"You know you don't have to yell." Travis scoops my hand into his.

Metal clanks behind me and I turn to see Zack lay two rods on the bench. I glance at his pocket, wondering if he's still carrying the figurine, and decide to talk to him after dinner.

By the time we've finished eating and I get the twins to bed, Zack is gone.

"Did Zack already go to bed?" I ask Travis at the bottom of the stairs.

"Yes." Travis presses a hand at the small of my back. "Let's turn in, too."

I guess I can wait until morning to talk with Zack.

* * *

When I descend the stairs for breakfast, I'm met by two shrill toddler voices.

"Mommy!" the twins harmonize near the front door. Gram smiles at me and returns to buttoning Krissie's plaid jacket.

"Gram," I say. "When did you get here?"

"Early this morning."

Does that mean you've finished setting up convenient locations for serenity simulators?"

"Yes. The simulators lack the full ambience of serenity orbs, but people are using them."

"I'm glad you're here, but aren't you concerned people will look for you to lead the serenity reconstruction?"

"I left explicit instructions and I've been around a long time, dear, in and out of a lot of things. I doubt anyone will question my whereabouts."

I kiss my grandmother's cheek. I wish I felt as confident as she always seems to be. "Have you eaten yet?"

"Yes, and so have the girls. We were going outside to sit on the porch swing. Care to join us?"

"Sure, I'll grab something to eat and be right out—unless I see Zack. I need to talk to him."

"Okay, dear."

I walk into the kitchen. "Mmm, Vad, it smells so good in here."

Clad in his familiar light-blue zeltire, Vad sets a cinnamon roll and a cup of black coffee on the counter in front of me. I bite into the roll and lick the sugary frosting from my lips. Einstein, always wearing a plaid shirt and jeans, is our android here. Vad's presence reminds me things are not normal in Zelfar.

"Has Zack been down yet?"

"He, Travis, and my clone are in the laboratory."

"Your clone? You may call him Einstein, like we do."

"My clone knows he is me, but he now acts as if he is not. I do not understand why he protests when I call him Vad."

"Maybe it would help if you thought of him as your twin instead of your clone." I'm beginning to sound like Travis, reasoning with androids like they're human.

Vad stares straight ahead, processing. Then he says, "I will consider Einstein my twin from this point forward."

I smile and take a sip of coffee.

After finishing my breakfast, I walk into the hallway, torn between the lab and front porch. Should I talk to Zack now? What if I distract him in the middle of a breakthrough?

I hear giggles out front and decide to move in that direction. Gram scoots to one side of the porch swing, and I sit beside her. Krissie climbs onto my lap, and Kayla scrambles onto Gram's.

We swing silently for a moment. My eyes follow Gram's gaze

as she stares up at the clear blue sky. Brilliant rays of sunlight stream through the large tree branches, glistening off the few remaining yellow leaves.

"This is a beautiful place when it isn't raining," Gram says.

I burst into laughter. "How many days a year is that? Five?"

Gram laughs, too. The twins giggle with us and bounce up and down, threatening the strength of the wooden swing.

"Blue sky or not, I'd rather be in Zelfar," I say. "Gram. Do you know anything about psychiatry?"

The swing slows to a gentle sway, and my grandmother peers curiously at me over Kayla's shoulder. "Psychiatry? Where did you hear that word?"

"I saw a sign on one of the doors in Janet's new clinic. I was curious what kind of service a psychiatry physician would perform."

"They're called psychiatrists, dear. They treat mental illness. We don't need them in Zelfar, because we use serenity simulators. The neuron sensors in our serenity devices not only focus thoughts and produce calmness, but they also rebalance brain abnormalities."

My pulse quickens with an odd feeling of indignation.

"Do you mean that without serenity simulators we wouldn't think straight? Are we programmed like robots? Is that why I feel overly emotional on this side of the portal?"

Gram pats my hand. "Healing tubes keep the body healthy and serenity simulators keep the mind healthy. As a health expert, you know triggering cells in positive ways works for any part of the body, including the brain. Think of serenity orbs as healing tubes for the mind."

"Okay . . . I guess that makes sense. So, if someone here in America goes to see a psychiatrist, does that mean his or her mind isn't healthy?"

"Short answer—yes."

"Then how do their minds get healthy again?"

Gram's brow wrinkles. "My understanding is psychiatrists, over a period of time, have several talking sessions with their patients and often prescribe psychotropic drugs to help numb their patients' anxiety."

"Conversation and pills? That's it? No serenity technology? Why didn't you ever share some of your serenity expertise with the doctors here?"

"Mommy, are you mad at Gwam?" Kayla lifts her head from Gram's shoulder and Gram caresses her cheek.

"Remember, dear," Gram says to me in her usual calm tone, but with an edge of firmness, "I told you on your first trip here that when you were born, I stopped coming to America. As much as I wanted to make this world better, my efforts were futile. So, I concentrated on making Zelfar the best I could. And for that, I will not apologize."

I touch her hand. "I'm sorry, Gram. I'm grateful you have always been there for me. And I'm grateful you built the serenity orbs in Zelfar. Please forgive my outburst."

Gram smiles. "It's such a beautiful day. Let's take the girls for a walk." The swing wobbles as she stands and places Kayla on the porch.

"I wanna go walk." Krissie jumps off my lap and runs down the wooden steps.

If I had a serenity orb, that's where I would go right now. I can't believe I judged Gram for anything in America. I follow her and the twins toward the edge of the lawn.

The twins run and play on the path through the woods, but when it's time to turn back, both girls beg to be carried. I lift Krissie, and she lays her tired little head on my shoulder. Gram carries Kayla, and we stride across the lawn toward the house. My eyes pause momentarily on the barn. I need to find time to talk to Zack about that figurine.

CHAPTER 12

I awake to feel the twins snuggled quietly on either side of me. I had only intended to lie down with them for a minute, not take an afternoon nap. Without disturbing either child, I ease myself from their bed and make my way to the living room.

My husband, reclining in his brown chair, grins when he sees me. "Cute hair."

I smooth the top of my head. "Has Zack come in from the lab yet?"

"He and Einstein were running tests when I came in the house, which was probably about the time you started snoozing." His playful jab makes me smile.

Vad appears in the doorway. "Hank in two minutes."

Travis rises from his chair and peers curiously at Vad. "What did you say?"

We hear gravel crunch outside, and Vad walks toward the kitchen as Travis opens the front door. Our private detective friend, Hank, and his daughter, Janet, stand on the porch with Clay.

"How nice to see you," I say. "Please, come in."

Hank removes his brown fedora, hangs it on a wall hook, and unbuttons his long tan coat. "When Clay said he needed a ride, I offered to drive. Always a pleasure to see you guys, and Clay says we're invited to dinner."

"Of course you are." Travis shakes hands with Hank.

"Peanut!" I reach for the Maltese in Janet's arms. Peanut wiggles and springs from Janet to me. I snuggle the small fluffy dog to my cheek. "You smell so good. And look at this cute little purple bow."

I glance out the door, expecting to see the dog's owner, a tiny woman in a wheelchair.

"Oh . . . Grandma isn't here," Janet says sadly.

"I wanted to tell you in person." Hank looks down, exposing the bald spot on his head. "Mom has gone on to heaven."

Heaven. She has transcended, or "died," as Americans say.

Hank's sadness fills my eyes with tears. "What happened? I thought she was doing well."

"She was." Hank hangs his coat on the hook next to his hat. "Mom hasn't been in pain for a long time, ever since Clay started treating her with his miracle doctoring. She was even getting around pretty good without the wheelchair. Then, a few nights ago, she up and died in her sleep. I sure do miss her."

"I miss her." Janet dabs at her eyes, careful not to mar her perfect complexion with mascara. Her long auburn hair hangs in loose curls as if styled seconds ago. In her tight green capri pants, emerald sweater, and silk scarf, Janet looks like a cover model on an American magazine.

Clay wraps an arm around Janet's waist and gently leads her down the hallway. Watching them makes me almost wish he'd never met her—not only because of the risk if he tries to take her to Zelfar and her unknown biometric reading sets off alarms from Health Dome, but worse if he chooses to stay in America with her when Gram seals the portal.

I close the front door and turn to see Gram and the twins. Both girls hug my legs, and Gram takes Hank's hands.

"I'm sorry for your loss."

"Thank you, Lilly." Hank bends and hugs Gram. "I wish Mom had your secret for staying young."

He straightens, moving Gram to arm's length, and scrunches his bushy brow. "Mom said she first met you when she was seven, and you were a young adult. Now, if my powers of deductive reasoning serve me, you must be at least ninety years old. Yet, I swear I look older than you." Hank looks from Gram to me. "I really wish I knew where you guys come from. Do you have an anti-aging potion or something?"

Gram smiles warmly at Hank and pats the back of his hand. "You know if I'd had a potion, I'd have given it to Mary. I loved her, too."

My grandmother outlived her first American friend, and now that friend's daughter. I sometimes wish I knew why Zelfarians are healthier and live decades longer than Americans, but hopefully, that comparison will soon no longer matter. For now, I just hope we don't start aging prematurely, too.

"Arf, arf." Peanut wiggles, and I put her down. As soon as her paws touch the floor, she scurries into the living room, her nails clicking on the polished wood. The twins giggle and run after the small animal.

"Kids love dogs," Hank says. "I'm surprised your girls don't have one of their own."

"They wouldn't be able to take it with them when we go home," I say, without thinking.

Hank twists his mustache. "No pets allowed where you come from?"

I'm getting too comfortable around Hank. "I'll let you visit with Travis and Gram while I go help with dinner." I walk away before Hank can repeat his question. When I enter the kitchen, I see only Vad.

"Where's Einstein?" Zack is the one I want to see, but he's probably with Einstein, and Vad can sense Einstein's location.

"Clone and Zack on errand. Back for dinner. Cannot access clone's brain."

"Why are you talking funny, and what do you mean you can't access his brain?"

Vad doesn't answer, but he appears normal, placing a large baking dish in the mock oven and pressing a button on his zelcom. Still, if he's lost his connection to Einstein, something is wrong.

"Did you say Einstein and Zack are on an errand?" I place a hand on the counter.

Vad remains silent.

My legs feel weak, and I sag onto a stool. Zack has taken off without telling me . . . again! The dangers of a Zelfarian mountain are nothing compared to thugs with guns.

"Vad! Think harder. Where are Einstein and Zack?"

Vad says nothing, and the fragrance of Hank's musk cologne turns my head to the doorway.

"May I," Hank asks as he reaches for an oatmeal cookie from the plate on the counter.

I push the plate closer. He takes a cookie and consumes it in two bites.

"It's funny," Hank says, wiping crumbs from his mustache. "I never smell food cooking in your kitchen until the minute a meal is served. These must have just come straight from the oven." He pushes the plate away from him and sits on the stool next to me. "How long 'til dinner, Vad? And what's with the hippie clothes?"

"Fifteen minutes, ten seconds," Vad answers. At least he's talking now. Thankfully, he didn't respond to Hank's comment about his zeltire.

Hank chuckles. "Right down to the second, huh? So, where's your twin brother? I'm looking forward to meeting him."

Travis comes into the kitchen in time to answer Hank. "I'll go get Einstein."

Hank smirks. "Must be a smart guy with a name like that."

I stand and move close to Travis. "Vad says they're not in the barn—they're on an errand."

Travis purses his lips and glares at Vad. "Zack and Einstein are gone? Where'd they go?"

"Sync with clone's brain incomplete," Vad answers. "Do not have information on clone."

Hank laughs. "Good one, Vad. The guy's your twin—doesn't mean you can read his mind."

Travis feigns a laugh. "Yeah, brother, good one."

Hank believes the androids are Travis's twin brothers. Like Travis, they are six feet tall with dark hair and eyes. Hank assumes this is the Vad he knows, though Einstein is the android Hank usually sees.

Vad announces in his unsettling monotone, "Clone and boy have arrived."

"Okay, Vad, you can cut the robot voice." Hank laughs again. "You must've been born first. Poor Einstein, having to grow up being called your clone."

Gram enters with a toddler holding each hand just before Zack walks into the kitchen with Einstein at his heels.

"Zackie!" Kayla and Krissie start toward Zack, but Gram redirects them to their highchairs.

Zack stops short when he sees Hank. "Uh, hi."

Travis moves so fast, he's almost a blur, and he grabs Zack by the arm. I can't hear what Travis whispers in Zack's ear, but Zack nods once and drops his gaze to the floor.

I want to reprimand Zack, too, but out of deference to our guests, I control my temper. Temper? Since when do I have a temper?

Travis keeps a hand on Zack's shoulder and says, "Hank, I'd like you to meet our son, Zack."

"Hello, Zack," Hank says.

Before Hank can extend his hand, Travis moves Zack aside. Zack has never seen the handshake greeting. "Sweetheart," Travis says. "Would you mind serving dinner to our guests? I need to talk with my brothers. Go ahead and start without us." Travis motions for the two androids to follow him. "Excuse us, Hank."

Janet and Clay arrive and nearly bump into Travis on his way out.

Zack jumps back, pointing at the little white animal trailing after Janet. "What's that?"

"She won't hurt you," Janet says. "She's a people dog, and her name's Peanut."

"I wanna hold Peanut." Krissie reaches out her arms.

"After dinner," I say to Krissie.

Janet extends her hand to Zack. "I don't believe we've met," she says. "I'm Janet."

Zack reaches into his pocket, and I quickly step behind him, squeezing his arms to his sides before he can hand pine needles to her as he might do when meeting someone new in Zelfar. "Janet, this is our son, Zack. He needs to clean his hands before shaking with anyone."

Zack washes his hands at the sink and then sits at the table across from Hank. I haven't told Zack much about our American friends, except that they know nothing of where we come from. Hopefully, he won't slip secrets during dinner. I can't ask Zack now about why he left without permission, but after our guests leave, I'm going to have a serious talk with him.

"So, the unasked question in the room, Zack," Hank says bluntly, "is where did you and your uncle go this afternoon?"

Zack looks at me.

I pause at the oven and give him a slight nod, hoping he understands.

"We . . . um . . ." Zack starts, and Hank stares at him, scrutinizing.

"Were you and your Uncle Einstein out scouting for deer tracks again?" I ask, fumbling with an oven mitt.

"Here, let me help you serve dinner," Clay says, walking behind the counter. I hand him the other mitt and he takes the dish of noodles and broccoli casserole to the table.

"Gwam, I hungwy." Kayla raps her spoon on her tray.

Gram puts a small scoop of casserole onto two small plates for the girls. I set a bowl of green beans in the center of the table and wink at Zack. "Deer tracks?"

A grin spreads across his face. "Not deer—bear. Uncle Einstein and I followed some bear footprints in the mud because I wanted to see where the bear lives. Unfortunately, we didn't find the bear's dome, I mean house, and it got late, so we decided to give up for today."

My palms sweat in anticipation of Hank's response. Zack would make a terrible actor.

Hank rubs his mustache with his thumb and forefinger. "Didn't find its house, huh? Looking for a bear's den isn't the smartest thing to do." He keeps steady eyes on Zack's face. "Interesting how your feet stayed so clean, traipsing around in the mud."

"We left our dirty shoes in the barn," Zack rebuts instantly. "And my feet are under the table. How would you know they're not muddy?"

I sit in the chair next to Hank, cringing at Zack's disrespect, but I'm proud of his quick mind. Before I can interject, Hank winks at me, leans back in his chair, and says to Zack, "It's my job to notice details."

"Your job? What's a job?"

I turn away from our guests and widen my eyes at Zack.

Hank laughs. "You're fifteen and you don't know what a job is? It's what you do to make a living. 'Course with your folks being so well off you probably won't need a job until you're out of college. Anyway, I'm a private investigator. People pay me to find out stuff for them."

Zack lays his fork on his plate. "Stuff?"

"Mostly I work with lawyers trying to find evidence, but sometimes I help the police by digging into corners they can't. The law is a funny thing," Hank says. "Sometimes it hinders more than it helps, but I'd hate to see the chaos we'd live in without it. 'Course if you know how, there's often ways to get around it. When you're picking your career, you might consider being a lawyer. They make darn good money." Hank leans toward Zack, meeting his gaze. "Something else about lawyers you might identify with, son, is they're good at stretching the truth."

Clay passes a tray of honey biscuits. Zack grabs a biscuit, takes a bite, and says nothing.

Krissie yawns, and her spoon clunks to the floor. Kayla smashes her remaining noodles with her spoon.

"I'll get them into their pajamas," Gram says, laying her napkin on her plate. I help her lift the twins from their chairs and set them on the floor. Gram takes their hands and leads them out of the kitchen.

I return to my seat, glad Hank's conversation with Zack is over, but it reminded me how easily Hank overcomes obstacles in this world. Through his connections, Travis and I miraculously became American citizens with doctoral degrees. He helped us get this house, our car, and licenses to drive. Hank's expertise might be helpful on another matter.

"Thank you, Zophie, for a mighty fine dinner." Hank tips back in his chair, pats his slightly round belly, and glances at his bulky silver watch. "It looks like Travis's conversation with his brothers has turned into a full-length conference. Janet and I should be getting on home."

Clay and Janet stand and, along with Hank, head to the front door. I follow them and we all step onto the front porch.

The evening mist penetrates the thin fabric of my blouse. I rub my arms and wait for Clay and Janet to descend the steps and walk to the car, then I slip a small piece of paper into Hank's hand and whisper, "Please investigate this name for me."

Hank gives a quick tip of his fedora. "Say good-bye to Travis for me." He steps from the porch and I let a few pine needles fall at my feet, thanking the cosmos for such a unique friend. I only hope the same qualities I appreciate in Hank don't cause problems for us.

Before Hank steps from the lighted walkway to his car, he slides the note into his pocket.

CHAPTER 13

Clay hurries into the house with me, gives me a peck on the cheek, and says, "Goodnight, Zophie."

I grab a handful of pine needles from the bowl on the hall table and shove them into my pocket, glad Einstein keeps the bowl replenished.

I walk into the living room where Gram sits in the rocking chair, humming to Krissie, who's cuddled in her lap. Kayla rocks her doll in a small chair beside Gram.

"Gram, I need to—."

"I know, dear." Gram stands and sets Krissie on the floor. "You go talk to Zack. I'll put the girls to bed."

Kayla, clad in red pajamas, jumps up from her chair. "No! I want Mommy wead us a story."

I bend and say, "Gram will start a story for you, and I'll be up as soon as I talk to Zack. Okay?"

Kayla frowns and crosses her arms. "No."

"Zackie can come, too." Krissie says, stumbling on the bottom of her nightgown. I take Krissie's hand; Kayla resists as I take hers, and I walk with them to the bottom of the stairs.

"I'll be up soon." I bend and kiss Krissie's cheek.

"I love you," Krissie says and hugs my neck.

"I love you, too, Mommy." Kayla loses her frown and wraps her arms atop Krissie's, both girls squeezing my breath away.

"I love you both so much. Pick a good story for Gram."

"Come along, girls." Gram leads them up the stairs.

"Good night, babies." I hear Travis's voice before I see him on the top step.

"I'm not a baby." Two toddler voices echo behind him.

Travis descends the stairs with his two androids behind him and his stern expression tells me things are serious. I hope our androids aren't broken.

"Where's Zack?" he says.

"I'm in the cooking orb," Zack answers as if this house were our homedome.

I follow Travis and our androids into the kitchen. Zack begins to stand when he sees us.

"Stay seated," Travis orders.

Zack's eyes widen, and he drops back down. Travis walks to Zack's side of the table and sits stiffly on the edge of a chair. I sit opposite them. Vad and Einstein appear normal as they walk to the counter and stand silently, side by side.

"One more stunt like this, Zack," Travis says, "and you'll be spending all of your time in Zelfar with Vad as your tot-watcher. Your mother and I have enough to worry about without your irresponsible behavior. Your Rudy hunting stops now. Understood?"

Rudy hunting?

Zack hangs his head, nodding slightly.

Travis taps Zack's shoulder. "No head bobbing. I want to hear you promise not to go anywhere, here or in Zelfar, without your mom's or my permission."

Travis said what I had intended to say. Zack may be struggling for adolescent independence, but with upheaval at home and dangers in America, and for his safety and our sanity, he must communicate with us.

"I'm really sorry, Dad." Zack looks up, his brown eyes more serious than I've ever seen. "I promise."

"Okay, then." Travis heaves a worried sigh. "Before we get into your explanation for why you had Einstein take you into Portland, I want you to understand the impact of allowing Einstein to sever his link to Vad. I know the separation was his idea, but the disconnection caused a glitch that regressed their emotional development. Luckily, I was able to restore their link."

Travis presses an elbow on the table and leans toward Zack. "Listen carefully, because this is important. I plan to create a whole generation of androids like these two, and I need to study their evolution as a pair. Do not let either of them try to sever their tie again. I've given them the same instruction."

Zack and Travis turn their heads toward the androids. Vad and Einstein nod in unison.

"Okay, Dad." Zack fidgets with his shirttail and peers sheepishly at his father. "So, Einstein told you where we went?"

"Not verbally. I saw the replay."

I clasp my hands on the table. "So, where did you go?"

Zack leans back and crosses his arms. "I told Einstein to take me to Johnny Ford's house."

I gasp. "His *house*? We told you people here can be dangerous. And so you know, unlike in Zelfar, people here have two names. Ford is Johnny's second name. Now, how did you even know where he lives?"

"When Johnny showed me his driver's license," Zack begins slowly and accelerates, "I saw his address, and I was telling Einstein about it, and he said he could take me there and keep Vad from knowing. I didn't know it would cause a glitch, Dad, and

I'm sure Einstein didn't know either. Don't be mad at Einstein. He was just trying to help me like he always does, and he knew Vad wouldn't. And we really thought we'd be back before you missed us." Zack looks at me. "Mom, I think this man is really Rudy. I had to talk to him again."

I understand my son's drive to solve a mystery without concern for physical safety. I did the same when I first came through the portal in search of protizine.

"How did you get to his house?" I scoot forward. "Please don't say you had Einstein transport you. You must have noticed that people here don't run at high speed and carry others around."

"I know that. Einstein only carried me through the woods until we got to blocks of square homedomes . . . I mean houses. We saw a two-wheeled car sitting by a sidewalk. Einstein studied it for a minute, said the thing was a motorcycle, and that he could drive it. He straddled the machine, started its power, and told me to hop on behind him. Then we rolled all the way to Johnny's."

Travis stifles a grin, and I know he's curious about Einstein's experience with the motorcycle. Travis clears his throat and narrows his brow. "That was an extremely dangerous thing for you and Einstein to do."

I slap my hands on the table. "You stole a motorcycle!"

Zack wrinkles his forehead. "Stole?"

How do I explain this? "Zack, when you take something without the owner's permission, it's called stealing. The laws here forbid this. Where is the motorcycle now?"

Zack shrugs. "We put it back where we found it."

I stand, staring hard at Zack. "Never, ever, do anything like that again, or you could go to a place here they call jail, where they lock people in cages."

Zack's jaw drops. "Cages?"

"Yes. Cages."

"So what happened when you and Einstein got to Johnny's

house?" Travis asks.

"Well, at first Johnny was kinda mad, said I was harassing him, and he should call the police, whatever that means."

"Police are people who put those who break the laws in a cage," I say. "Then what happened?"

"Then he just stared at Einstein for a few seconds. I thought maybe Johnny recognized him, so I asked him if he remembered Vad. He said, 'No, kid, I don't remember anything.' "

I chuckle at Zack's imitation of Johnny's deep voice, and he smirks with satisfaction.

"Then Johnny's wife came to the door," Zack continues, "saying he must have been born in a barn. She asked me and Einstein to come inside to talk, so we did. Turns out Johnny has something called amnesia, which he said made him lose his memory. I showed him the female figurine again, but he didn't want to hold it. He doesn't seem to want to remember, but he sure sounded like the Rudy I knew in Zelfar, complaining about how he hated going to service domes and not having a wife. Except here he complains about the rain and not having money. At least in this world he has a wife. I'm not gonna bother him anymore. I just don't know what to tell Sheldon."

"You won't tell Sheldon anything!" Travis and I shout in unison.

"Zack," I say, lowering my voice. "Even though you found a couple of similarities between Johnny and Rudy, they can't be the same person." I tap my fingers on my thigh, wondering if I'm trying to convince Zack or myself.

"The portal must remain a secret," Travis says, sitting straighter in his chair. "We brought you here after the explosions, without the elders' permission, because we had to ensure your safety. But we also thought we could trust you to keep the same secrets we're keeping. Can we trust you, Zack?"

Zack's eyes dart from me to his father. "You can trust me. I won't tell anyone anything."

"What about the figurine?" I ask. "Does it belong to Quaid?"

"Yeah," Zack says. "A couple of days before the explosion, I asked Brita to borrow the carving from her grandfather. I watched Rudy laser carve the green diamond into that figurine, so, unless he gave it to Quaid, it belongs to Rudy. I thought if Sheldon and I found Rudy, the figurine might make him want to come home."

"You and Sheldon planned a search even before the explosion gave you a new excuse," I say, and he lowers his eyes. "Why was the carving in your jean's pocket?"

Zack scratches at the edge of the table. "I've been carrying it with me everywhere 'cause it reminds me of Brita. And I'll have it to give back to her when she wakes up."

"Give the figurine to me." I put out my hand. "I'll return it to Quaid."

He slowly withdraws the green diamond from his pocket and lays it in my hand. "Can I go to bed now?"

Travis and I nod, and Zack sulks away. I wish I could let him keep the figurine.

Einstein places a plate with tonight's dinner in front of Travis.

I kiss Travis and say, "I think I'll head upstairs, too." I need to lock this diamond away with the stunners until I can return it to Quaid.

From the hallway, I notice Gram sitting alone in the living room. When I join her, she lifts her eyes to the oak-framed canvas above our large stone fireplace.

"I remember painting that picture shortly after my first trip to America more than seven decades ago," she says. Her nostalgic tone betrays a bit of longing. "The experience is still so vivid in my memory. That deer hidden in the shadows of the trees startled me so much, my dad offered to take me back to Zelfar. I'm glad I didn't let him. True, this world is full of chaos, but there are wonderful people here as well who want serenity as much as we do."

I walk over and sit next to the fire. "Gram, aren't you anxious to seal off the portal again and stop sneaking between worlds?"

Gram exhales, and I assume she's going to agree, but instead she asks, "What's that?"

I follow her gaze and open my hand, giving her a full view of the figurine. "A green diamond carving that I need to return to Quaid."

"Did Quaid do the carving?" Gram's tone is calm, but knowing her well, I notice the slight tension in her jaw.

"Zack says Rudy did the carving, but the figurine was in Quaid's possession."

"Interesting." Gram gets up from her purple chair. "I'm tired, dear. I'll see you in the morning." From the doorway, she looks back at me and says, "Closing off the portal as soon as we can is best for all, dear," She walks away, her strawberry scent fading into the hall.

"... is best for all, dear." I've heard those exact words several times. They always mean one thing—Gram knows something I don't.

CHAPTER 14

I hate when Gram keeps things from me. Wondering what she's not telling me kept me from a restful night's sleep. Hopefully, Quaid will give me some answers when I return the green diamond today. After dressing in zeltire, I walk to the girls' bedroom to find the room empty, bed made.

Assuming the twins are having breakfast, I head toward the kitchen. At the bottom of the stairs, voices emit from Gram's art studio behind the stairway. Krissie and Kayla are arguing over paint brushes and Gram, in a calm tone is settling the conflict. They've no doubt already eaten, so I proceed to the kitchen without disturbing them.

Zack, sitting on a stool with his back to the door, doesn't turn when I enter. He says to Vad, who stands on the opposite side of the counter, "You can go back to Zelfar. Me and Einstein don't need you here."

Since Zack met Einstein, his disrespect for Vad has gotten worse. Vad saving Zack's life seems to have changed nothing. Not only that, Zack sounds like he thinks he belongs here, which he doesn't—and he won't—ever.

"Good morning, Zophie," Vad says.

"Good morning, Vad." I sit on the stool next to Zack. "I'll need you to take Zack, Krissie, and me to Zelfar in a little while."

Zack hops up. "But I wanna stay here."

When I brought Zack through the portal, I didn't think I'd ever have to pressure him to return to his world. "Don't you want to see how Brita is doing? Tutor sessions are supposed to resume today, too. You and Krissie need to be there."

Zack shoves his hands into his pockets and nods. "Yeah, Brita's probably awake and wondering where I am. Sure wish I could bring her here."

I grip his arm. "You cannot consider bringing anyone here. Do you understand?"

"I said I *wish* I could." He slides from my grasp. "Why don't you trust me?"

"I do, but the portal will *always* have to be secret." I wish I could hug away the hurt in his eyes.

"No, you don't, or you would have told me about the portal years ago."

"I didn't want you to have to carry this burden." I frown at his plaid shirt and blue jeans, which are way too similar to Einstein's attire. "I don't want to argue, Zack. Go change into zeltire. We're leaving in a few minutes."

Zack huffs out of the kitchen.

After a quick breakfast, I go to the lab to inform Travis of my plans. When I enter the lab, Travis and Clay look up from a nearby worktable.

"Sorry to interrupt you two, but I'm leaving for Zelfar in a few minutes. I'm taking Zack and Krissie. Do either of you want to join us?"

Travis points at a two-gallon canister. "Not me. This batch will be ready for you to test in a couple of days. When are you coming back?"

"Tomorrow or the next day."

Clay puts a gloved hand inside a container. "I'm sharing an idea with Travis. Would you send Vad back for me this afternoon?"

"Sure. I love you both."

"We love you, too," they harmonize.

"Toss pine," the three of us say together, and I run through a light mist back to the house.

"Gram?" I call from the hallway. I smile at Vad who's waiting by the front door.

"In the living room, dear."

Kayla, dressed exactly like Krissie in an aqua jumpsuit, grabs my legs. "I'm going, too, Mommy!"

"Did you override Bayl's decision?" I lift an eyebrow to Gram.

"No, dear. Dressing Kayla in zeltire was the only way to stop her tears."

I bend and wrap Kayla in my arms. "It's Krissie's turn, sweetheart."

Her tears wet my shoulder.

"Why can't Kayla come with us?" Krissie whimpers, tugging on my shirt.

"I'll stay here with Kayla," Gram says. "I'd like to visit Quaid with you, but I'll see him in a couple of days. Come here, dear." Gram lifts Kayla and carries her into the hall. "Let's go paint a picture for Daddy."

Zack rises from the sofa and picks up Krissie. "It's not fair we have to leave one of them here, but don't you think we should take Kayla 'cause she's already seen the mess?"

"Krissie needs to see that the mess happened. Reconstruction is progressing and with tutor domes reopening, things will seem more normal. Krissie will be fine."

When we reach Agate Falls, Vad sets us down inside the American cavern. I pause before activating my portal key.

"How are you feeling today, Vad?"

"I am fine, Zophie. Why do you ask?"

"Just making sure you're yourself again." I can't assume the glitch that reversed his advanced programming won't happen again. And without Travis . . .

Zack sneers. "Oh, he's himself, all right."

Vad's lips turn down, imitating Zack's snarl. "I imagine you preferred me as a simple robot, Young Zack."

"Stop it, you two," I say.

"Stop it, you two," Krissie waves her finger between Zack and Vad.

I'd laugh if this weren't so serious. I point a stern finger first at Zack and then at Vad. "This callousness between you two is growing and I'm ending it right now. Every time I chastise you about being nicer, it only lasts a while, then you're back to this kind of behavior. I want a solid answer this time. Why are you two so spiteful to each other?"

Zack and Vad narrow their eyes at one another.

"I know you have never liked Vad," I say to Zack. "But you're friends with Einstein. Why can't you be friends with Vad, too?"

"I'm f'ends with Vad," Krissie says. She drops my hand and reaches for Zack's, but he folds his arms and tightens his lips—a common gesture when he doesn't get his way.

"Einstein has never made me a prisoner in my own homedome," Zack says. "Einstein treats me with respect. A robot is not supposed to tell me what to do. I'm not a child."

I stifle a smile.

"I merely watched Zack as Travis instructed," Vad says. "Zack tried to leave the homedome, forcing me to deny him access to the outside."

Zack's jaw tenses. He reaches for his belt buckle and takes a step toward the portal.

"Wait a minute." I grip Zack's sleeve.

"Wait a minute, Zackie." Krissie grabs his pant leg.

"I remember that day," I say. "When we got home, you were crying, saying Dad's new homedome intelligence wouldn't let you go to Brita's. You were only ten years old."

"Yeah, and Dad said our homedome was programmed to do what *we* said. I wasn't supposed to have to do what *it* said." He flips a thumb at Vad.

"But he simply obeyed your father's orders." Zack's eyes fill with hurt, so I add in a softer tone, "I understand your resentment, but that was a long time ago. Vad didn't have emotions back then."

"I'm old enough now for Vad to do what I tell him, but he still treats me like I'm ten. And now that he *has* emotions, I think he enjoys making me mad." Zack glares at the android as if daring Vad to deny it.

Vad half-smiles and says nothing. No wonder their bantering has never ceased for long. They both enjoy it.

Krissie scurries over to Vad and taps his knee. "Don't make Zackie mad."

Vad gazes down at Krissie, loses the smile, and lifts his gaze to me.

"She's right, Vad," I say. "You must treat Zack with respect, and that includes no longer calling him Young Zack. Understood?"

"Yes, Zophie."

"And Zack." I step between him and the portal. "You have to treat Vad with more respect as well. Be grateful he saved your life." I glance between Zack and Vad. "You will both make an effort to improve your relationship going forward. Agreed?"

"Okay, Mom."

"Yes, Zophie."

"Yes, Mommy." Krissie runs to me and I lift her to my hip.

"You can go through now." I nod to Zack. He activates his belt buckle and walks through the shimmering light.

Vad touches the tips of his thumb and forefinger together

and follows Zack through the glow.

I connect the pyramids on my earrings and carry Krissie through the portal, satisfied Vad has no lingering glitches, and hopeful that the dissidence between Zack and our android will finally end.

CHAPTER 15

We exit the cave behind Paradise Falls. I draw in my usual deep breath. Vad bows, offering one of his hand-chairs to Zack.

"You're not fooling me," Zack says under his breath, as he slides into the seat.

"Vad," I say. "Sarcastic gestures do not show respect."

Zack scowls. "Maybe if the robot-with-emotions used serenity orbs, he wouldn't be so sarcastic."

Vad tilts his head. "Perhaps I would benefit from a serenity simulator. I would like to calm the pain I feel from losing Hil. I hope she awakens with the reconstruction of Health Dome." Hil is short for health intelligence logic—the simulated intelligence of Health Dome.

Zack's eyes soften, and he peers at Vad. "Like Brita."

Vad transports us to Energy Tutor Dome. "Have fun today," I say to Zack, as he hops from Vad's hand.

"Actually, I will, 'cause I think I know what went wrong with the zilimite. They underestimated the exothermic chemical reactions of zilimite powder and used too much water." Zack waves at a friend near the dome's entrance and adds, "I wish Brita could be here."

I wish that, too. But if she were, Zack would have to fight his urge to tell her our secret. If I were Zack, I'm sure I would tell Brita everything.

"Toss pine, son."

"Toss pine," Krissie yells, and Vad runs us to Toddler Tutor Dome.

Krissie whines less than usual when she takes the tutorbot's hand and walks toward the dome. I tell Vad to take me to Quaid's.

The entrance to Quaid's dome slides open. Quaid stands inside, smiling. "Hello, Zophie, come on in."

I sit on the sofa across from him, averting my eyes from his exposed chest. Quaid chuckles and buttons his shirt.

"Sorry 'bout that. Wasn't expectin' company."

"Would you like a beverage?" says the voice of Quaid's dome.

"Bring two iced raspberry teas," Quaid answers.

Quaid's homebot, chestnut brown to match the hue of the dome, sets a frosty glass on the end table next to me. The bot extends the other glass to Quaid and walks away.

"How you comin' on the cure for our babies?" Quaid takes a sip of his tea.

"We think we're close. Hopefully, anytime now."

"Well, then, what brings you all the way out here? It ain't like my homedome is clustered with the rest of 'em."

I open my palm to reveal the small figurine. "I came to return this."

Quaid frowns, snatches the green diamond from my hand, and shoves the stone into his pocket. "I loaned this carving to Brita. How'd you get it? Oh, let me guess. She gave the figurine ta Zack, and he gave it ta you, 'cause of course, he can't give the carving back to her. She's still asleep."

I nod, my throat constricting with grief. "Did Rudy help you carve the figurine?"

"What makes you ask that?" Quaid's knuckles whiten around his glass.

"Remember, about three years ago, when I asked you and Bayl if you knew what had happened to a person who was missing? I'm raising the question again, because I saw a man in America who looks like he could be Rudy."

Quaid's face goes as pale as his knuckles. "Why would I know anything 'bout familiar lookin' folks?"

"Because you helped Gram build the underground archive orb to hide our world's history. You know more about Zelfar and the portal than anyone. Is it possible Rudy went to America?"

Quaid clears his throat and looks away. "Anythin's possible. Did you talk to him?"

"Yes, but he has a condition called amnesia, which means he can't remember his past. He says his name is Johnny Ford."

"Johnny Ford, huh? Can't remember nothin', huh?" The elder smirks, faint, but unmistakable. He sips his tea and the smirk turns to a smile, which seems to extend around the rim of his glass.

"Even holding the figurine didn't jog his memory," I say.

Quaid narrows his eyes at me, smile gone. "You showed an American a green diamond?"

My face heats with the implication of risk to our world. "Y . . . yes. Since Rudy carved a female figurine just like that one . . . I thought he might recognize it. But the man seemed to have no recollection of the carving or have an understanding of the diamond."

"Well, there ya go." Quaid sets his glass on the table and relaxes into his chair. "He's obviously not Rudy. Besides, folks from Zelfar don't get, what'd ya call it . . . amnesia? I'm sure Rudy's still out there explorin' somewhere. He wasn't happy anyway. Probably wanted to be left alone."

"How do you know he wasn't happy?" I study Quaid's reaction, unable to shake the feeling he's hiding something.

Quaid scoots forward. "Anybody who knew Rudy will tell ya he was always snivelin' about somethin'."

I scoot, too, mirroring Quaid. "Do you think it's possible Rudy found the portal?"

"Like I said, anythin's possible, but I don't see how anyone could find the portal, and if they did, where would they get a key?" Quaid's voice rises an octave. "I'm tellin' ya, Zophie, this Johnny Ford person's not Rudy."

Frustrated, I twist the ends of my hair, feeling no closer to the truth than before.

"Instead of worryin' 'bout some amnesia guy in America," Quaid says, "you might wanna go check on some trouble brewin' right here at home."

"What kind of trouble?" I ask, in case this isn't a ploy to change the subject.

"Marc was at the construction site fer Energy Dome yesterday, and he was tellin' people not to bother servin' 'cause their efforts was futile without another generation of kids to be buildin' for."

"Did anyone listen to him?" How can Marc want to spread his despair to the entire community?

"I ain't sure, but wouldn't hurt fer ya to go talk some negativity out of him."

Quaid stands. "Thanks for returnin' my little carvin'. Say hi to Travis for me. We're all countin' on you two ta find that cure. I'll let ya get back to it."

I exit Quaid's homedome and turn to say, "Toss pine," but the door slides shut.

The only thing that will change Marc's attitude is to give him and Darcy honey. Until then, I hope Marc's undermining efforts won't delay reconstruction.

"Vad, please take me to History Dome."

When we arrive, Vad connects telepathically to the dome's intelligence system. "Bayl is in conference orb three."

"Thanks, Vad. Wait for me here, please."

If Zack hadn't approached Johnny, thinking he was Rudy, and if I didn't think Zack could be right, I might not be so adamant about getting the truth from the elders. When I had questioned them about Rudy not long after he had disappeared, my intuition told me they were withholding information. When Zack's interest in Rudy's whereabouts finally waned, I dropped the subject. But that's when I assumed Rudy was in Zelfar. If Rudy is trapped with amnesia in a strange world, I want to bring him home before Gram seals the portal. Zelfarians don't belong in America.

Bayl stands when I approach and motions for me to sit at the round table. "Hello, Zophie. Have you come to tell me about a breakthrough with the honey?"

"Travis is working diligently, but that's not why I'm here."

The elder clasps his hands and rests them on the table. "I see. Then perhaps you are here because of Marc's attempts to thwart reconstruction and you are interested in counteracting his endeavors?"

I copy Bayl, clasping my hands on the table. Mirroring body language to put others at ease is something Gram taught me.

"I'll do what I can to boost morale, but I'm here to ask about Rudy."

Bayl leans back in the large swivel chair. "People, especially those who lost babies, are supporting Marc. You'd do better to focus on Zelfar's reconstruction."

My ears heat with rising frustration. "Please tell me what you know about Rudy."

Bayl straightens, locking his eyes with mine. "There is nothing I can tell you about Rudy."

I jump to my feet and slap the table. "You mean nothing you

want to tell me. You and Quaid must know something about Rudy's disappearance."

Bayl maintains his robotic composure and points at my chair. "Zophie, please, sit down. Such an outburst is not like you."

I remain standing and consciously lower my tone. "Living in two worlds and keeping one of my daughters a secret is not like me, either. You trust me with the portal and expect me to save our world. I deserve the respect of knowing the truth about Rudy."

"The truth is Rudy was not a happy man. He probably wanted solitude."

I hate keeping secrets, but I hate even more when secrets are kept from me.

I open my mouth, but Bayl speaks first. "Why is Rudy suddenly so important to you?"

The question surprises me. "Because my son keeps chasing a man in America who looks like Rudy."

Bayl runs both hands down his clean-shaven face, smoothing the fine lines and erasing any thought he could be a robot. "That is preposterous. Have you spoken to the man?"

"He can't remember his past, but isn't it possible Rudy could be in America?"

"No. That is not possible. No one else knows of the portal, and Zelfarians do not lose their memories."

He's practically mirroring Quaid. Again, I'm no closer to the truth.

Bayl rises quickly, and the door slides open. "You should concentrate on finding the cure for newborn loss syndrome and forget about Rudy." He points a finger at me and adds, "We worry Americans could corrupt our world, yet Marc, one of our own, is causing discord this very moment. He must be stopped." Bayl walks out of the orb, and the door closes behind him.

Alone at the large conference table, I stare at the doorway. Is

Bayl right? Has meeting Johnny Ford distracted me from saving Zelfar? But how does Bayl expect me to stop Marc?

I rise slowly, cross my trembling arms, and walk to the serenity orb near the exit. As questions swirl, I choose a green lounge chair to lie down, grasp the serenity simulator, and position the mask above my face.

Would all of us behave like Marc and Darcy if, like them, we stopped using serenity simulators? Will Travis develop a cure in time for Zack and Brita to start a family? Should I forget about Rudy?

A wave of calm washes over me, as the unanswered questions drift to the back of my mind. The scent of fresh roses instills a sense of well-being, and life is, once again, sane.

* * *

The next two days pass quickly. Clay and I prepare the new birthing orb in his homedome to deliver the next infant, due in two weeks. We expect the baby will be fine because the parents are fourth generation Zelfarians with low, but acceptable, levels of protizine. A healthy new baby should bolster the commitment to rebuilding our city.

Thankfully, few people heed Marc's rants against rebuilding. The fact that Marc's campaign is less compelling than Quaid and Bayl want me to believe convinces me the two elders are trying to distract me from questions around Rudy's disappearance.

I'm glad I don't have to hide my double life from Clay. I've enjoyed talking and laughing with him again. But with the immediate health concerns of Zelfarians under control, I'm eager to return to the rest of my family—and to find out what Hank has learned about Johnny Ford.

"Zackie! Wanna go see Kayla?" Krissie squeals when Zack joins us on the platform outside our dome.

"Can we go see Brita first?" Zack asks, watching Vad's hands transform.

"Of course," I reply. "Vad, please take us to Clay's homedome." Zack can visit his girlfriend, and I can see if Clay still wants to go back to America with us today.

Zack proceeds to Brita's orb, and Vad, taking Krissie's hand, follows me into the living orb where I expect to find Clay.

Krissie pulls her fingers from Vad's and runs to the toy tube at the end of the sofa.

"Hello, Zophie," Elka says, ambling into the orb. "I'm giving Zack a few minutes alone with Brita."

Elka's eyes sag with the exhaustion and worry of a mother who yearns for her child to make the slightest movement, to show some sign of life. Slowly, she lowers herself into the stuffed chair nearest the arched doorway.

I do my best to swallow past the lump in my throat and ask, "Is Clay here?"

Elka leans her head back. "I haven't seen him today."

"Vad," I say. "Please tot-watch Krissie while I check on Brita."

When I enter Brita's healing orb, Zack wipes his cheek with his sleeve and I find myself dabbing my eyes as well. As a health expert, I can look at Brita and keep my emotions from surfacing. But I can't control my tears for the girl who feels like a daughter. I can only imagine Zack's grief, seeing his girlfriend lying motionless, day after day. If I knew how to wake her, I'd gladly risk our secrets in exchange for her health and his happiness.

The ends of Brita's health tube glow green. At least we know her body continues to function while the neurologists try to heal her. I've spoken to them and done some studying, but nothing we've tried has helped. Zack sprinkles a few pine needles on the floor under her tube and walks with me out of the orb.

When Krissie sees Zack and me, she tosses a doll into the toy tube and runs to Zack. He picks up his little sister and says,

"We'll wait outside."

"Elka," I say, "Brita's body is functioning well while the neurologists and I are working on how to help her. Please, don't lose hope."

She rises, forces a smile, and walks toward Brita's orb. Vad and I join Zack and Krissie outside. I regret missing Clay, but Vad can come back for him later.

At Paradise Falls, I activate my portal key with a mixture of anticipation and dread. The elders' efforts to distract me from Rudy only riddle me with more suspicion. Part of me hopes Hank has discovered useful information about Johnny Ford. But I worry we may uncover something so horrific, I'll wish I'd heeded the elders' advice.

CHAPTER 16

When we arrive at the house, Zack carries Krissie into the living room, and Kayla scrambles to greet them. Gram gives me a hug, grabs her sweater, and leads me outside to the porch swing.

"How was your visit with Quaid?" Gram asks as we swing slowly.

"Not as informative as I had hoped. Quaid insists he knows nothing of Rudy's disappearance." I stop swinging and face Gram. "Do you think he does?"

Gram shrugs and gives me an uncommon frown. "I'm not sure what Quaid knows, but I don't like the tension Rudy's whereabouts is causing you and your family. You have enough burden to carry, dear. I had hoped Quaid could explain the mystery of Rudy and dispel your concern."

"Is that why you're anxious to close the portal again, because you're worried about me?"

"I'm not *worried*, dear." Her emphasis on "worried" tells me otherwise.

Gram pats my hand. "I just want you to be happy and secure

in Zelfar. That's where you belong, not split between two worlds. I'm sorry I encouraged you to birth your twins here. I should have revealed the ugly secret about our community when you were pregnant, and let you live your life as you chose."

The ugly secret is why people in Zelfar don't have twins. I did, only because Clay refused to abort one of my fetuses, a despicable practice only he and the elders know about. They abort one fetus to save the other, but they don't give the parents a choice.

I squeeze Gram's fingers. "You mustn't feel guilty. I care too much about the future of Zelfar to have made a different choice. Besides, Travis is close to perfecting the synthetic honey formula. When he does, we'll be able to seal the portal again." I pat her hand. "It'll be all right."

Gram chuckles. "I love you, Zophie."

"I love you, too, Gram."

Travis rushes up the porch steps. "There you are, my beautiful wife. The days are too long when you're gone." He pulls me from the swing and presses his lips to mine.

Gram stands and walks past us. "I'll see you two inside."

Travis releases me, and his eyes are alive with excitement. "I had a breakthrough! You remember how I created sput by crossing the sweet potato and peanut plants? Well, I've been crossing the bushes and trees the honeybees prefer. The pollen produced by a hybrid of huckleberry and apple creates an enzyme rich in protizine. I think it's the answer to the synthetic process."

"That's incredible!" I kiss him again. "When can we tell everyone?"

"I have to do one more test."

My heart sinks. I've heard that before.

"I just need a couple of items from the electronics store in Portland, which I'll pick up tomorrow. I'll take Einstein and Zack. Do you want to come?"

"I thought we agreed to limit Zack's exposure to the city."

Travis kisses my head. "Zack will be fine." He takes my hand and leads me inside. We sit on the sofa and gaze at our children.

Zack tosses a sponge ball to his sisters, and I reign in anxious thoughts of him in Portland with Travis, who will be absorbed in American gadgets. I'll go with them. I want to see Hank anyway.

I press close to Travis. "Would you take me to Hank's and come back for me when you're finished at the store?"

"Hank's?" Travis asks.

"Yes. He's helping with me something."

"Something you want to tell me about?"

While Zack has his back to me, I whisper to Travis, "It has to do with Johnny Ford. I'll tell you more when I know more."

Travis leans to my ear. "I have to admit. I'm curious about that man, too." He laces my fingers in his. "We'll leave right after breakfast. Vad can stay here with Gram and the girls."

* * *

I stand by the front door, and Zack bounds toward me, looking eerily comfortable in a blue denim jacket and jeans. I reach to pat his hair, and Zack swiftly plops on a navy ball cap over the red swirls that stand in waves above his black and brown bangs. He darts out the front door and I follow, closing the door softly behind me.

The Jeep waits in the driveway with Travis at the wheel, the motor running, and Einstein holding the front passenger door open for me. I slide into my seat, and Zack hops in behind me. Preoccupied with thoughts of Quaid, Bayl, and Rudy, I'm surprised the drive goes by so quickly. I barely hear the conversations around me. If Johnny is actually Rudy, I intend to find out.

Travis stops in front of Hank's house, and I unlatch my seatbelt. Blowing a kiss to Travis, I hop out and walk to the porch to greet Hank. Inside, he hangs my coat in a small closet by the door and leads me down the hall toward the kitchen. When we pass his living room where papers lay in uneven piles on a table in front of the sofa, I wrinkle my nose at the scent I've come to know as old newspapers.

In the kitchen, Hank opens an oak cupboard, worn dark at the edges, and removes two ceramic mugs. He fills them with coffee—extra strong by the aroma—and hands one to me.

"Mm, smells wonderful." I wrap my hands loosely around the hot mug.

"Brewed to perfection." Hank takes a big swallow.

I sip slowly, trying to control my anticipation. Communication is extremely slow on this side of the portal. I hope Hank has been able to learn something about Johnny.

Hank walks to a small desk at one end of the counter, picks up a bulging manila folder, and tips his head for me to sit at the kitchen table.

"Johnny Ford, the mystery man." Hank drops the contents of the folder onto the table, spreading several sheets of scrawled notes before me. "Mr. Ford is a man of little history. No one seems to know who or where he was before 1970. I can tell you what he's been up to for the past four years, but his life before that is a mystery."

My heart pounds. Johnny's history began when Rudy disappeared.

Hank taps his finger on a photograph. "A cop found this man sitting on the steps outside the Portland police station and told him to go home. Johnny started blabbering nonsense and was taken to the hospital. Other than having no memory, the doctors said he was healthy."

Hank takes another gulp of coffee. "He was dubbed a John Doe and put in a psych ward. They circulated his picture for a few months, but no one claimed him. During treatment, they found he was good at wood carving, so they hooked him up with a job and released him. They've kept him under the care of a shrink."

"A shrink?" I ask.

"Yeah. You know, a psychiatrist, a head doctor."

"Like Dr. Thomas L. Filmore?"

"Yeah, exactly. You already know Filmore is Johnny's shrink?"

"His office is in Janet's clinic, which is where I met Johnny. Johnny was on his way to see Filmore, but that's all I know."

Hank points to a piece of paper imprinted with Dr. Filmore's name and office location. "Filmore's been treating Johnny since day one, so I did a little digging on the doc. Turns out, he has another amnesia patient named Amber." He twists his mustache and continues. "For now, I can tell you about Johnny's current life—married for two years, no kids, still employed by the same woodworking shop, and loves motorcycles." Hank leans toward me. "But somehow, I think you're more interested in Mr. Ford's unknown past."

I meet his gaze and nod.

"Well then, you're going to need this." He pulls a large gray envelope from the folder and slides it across the table.

I lift the top flap and remove an official-looking document—a diploma in psychiatry for Zophie Green. Staring at Hank's tan shirt and striped necktie, I can't help but admire his ability to skillfully maneuver in such a complicated world. Still . . .

"Why do you think I need to be perceived as a psychiatrist?"

"If you want inside information, you need to get on the inside. The rest of the documents in this folder are case histories for Johnny and Amber. I suggest you study them before you go see Filmore. As a colleague, you'll be able to pull more information out of him than I ever could as a PI."

My hands moisten as I hold the documents, and my stomach tightens. "What would I say?"

Hank grins. "Don't tell me a hot-shot doctor from some

hot-shot country is afraid of a little undercover work? With all the caginess about where you're really from, you must be good at making up stuff. You are a real doctor, so some of the same lingo must apply. I can take you to his office right now."

The same lingo—like Health Dome and healing tubes? I don't think so.

Hank's chair scrapes on the linoleum floor as he stands and looms over me. "Well?"

I swallow hard. "Okay." *Did I just say yes?*

"Good. Leave the papers there and come with me." *Does he mean now?*

Hank walks out of the kitchen and I follow. We enter a room off the hallway where a rectangular bed with brass rails sits in the center. A swirl-print quilt in a dizzying mix of rusty orange and olive green covers the bed. I take a step back and lean on the doorframe.

"Janet keeps extra clothes here for when she spends the night." Hank glances over his shoulder at me. "You're probably her size. I'm sure she's got something that'll make you look like a shrink."

Hank reaches into the long closet and I watch silently from the doorway, weighing whether posing as a psychiatrist would be an unnecessary risk. He chooses a black skirt and jacket, a white blouse, a pair of black leather shoes with three-inch heels, and a matching handbag. I start to retreat from the room, but Hank raises a bushy brow and says, "You want inside information or not?"

I step into the room, and Hank exits, closing the door behind him. I don Janet's clothes, all the while wondering if solving the mystery of Johnny Ford is worth the possible consequences on either side of the portal. The skirt is a bit tight, but under the jacket no one will notice. Thankfully, Janet and I wear the same shoe size. Staring at myself in the tall mirror on the closet door,

I'm surprised to see how American I look.

If Bayl and Quaid had been forthcoming, I wouldn't have to lie to learn the truth. I push my shoulder-length brown hair behind one ear and grab the black leather handbag.

Hank grins when I walk into the kitchen. "Dr. Green, how sharp you look today."

I smile weakly. He hands me the folder and I walk gingerly in Janet's high-heeled shoes with him out the front door. With each step closer to Hank's car, I want to tell him this is a mistake and turn around. But I sit on the passenger's seat instead. After transferring my wallet from my purse to Janet's, I lay the folder on my lap. The pages of notes taunt me, but Hank thinks I can consume their contents on the twenty-minute ride to Filmore's office. I'll have to read fast.

CHAPTER 17

When Hank pulls his car into the clinic parking lot, I'm still pouring over the pages, trying desperately to memorize the unfamiliar medical terms. He turns off the motor and takes the folder from me.

"I think I've met Amber," I say.

"Interesting. When?"

"More than two years ago, she gave me a little card, see?" Without thinking, I tap my zelcom and show him the screen.

Amber's CRYSTAL WINDOW

Your portal to peaceful energy

Hank stares at my zelcom. "So, your fancy watch stores information, huh? Kinda reminds me of those new-fangled computers down at the police station, 'course your watch is a thousand times smaller."

Trying not to wince, I tug the sleeve of my borrowed jacket over my wrist. Bayl and Quaid would zap if they knew. "Do you think I'm ready to talk to Filmore?"

"First, you'll call him *Doctor Filmore,* and he'll call you

Doctor Green. There'll be a gal at a desk just inside the door to his office. She's his receptionist. You'll tell her you have a consulting session at . . ." Hank glances at the clock on the dashboard, ". . . one-thirty. She'll say you don't have an appointment, but you'll insist that your receptionist made this one. She'll wonder if she made the scheduling mistake. With any luck, Filmore will be in his office and she'll convince him to see you."

Hank points at the folder. "Don't let on you know anything about Filmore's patients. Just say you heard he's making strides with amnesia, and you have a couple of your own cases. Get him to help you."

Lure this doctor with cases I don't have?

"What if I slip and tell Dr. Filmore something I'm not supposed to know?" I ask, emphasizing his title. "What if he sends his cops after me?"

Hank laughs. "First, I doubt he has his own cops. But if he does, run like hell back to the car and I'll drive like hell to get us out of here."

Oh. Not funny. I should tell Hank to forget it, I know, but I step out of the car and adjust the borrowed skirt until the hem hangs below my knees. It's impossible to feel confident in constricting clothes and wobbly heels, but I hold my head high and enter the clinic. I feel like I did as a child going to my first tutor session—curious, and a little scared.

When I reach Filmore's office, I open the door and step inside, afraid if I hesitate, I won't go in at all. I clench my jaw and walk to the gray-haired woman seated behind a desk.

Hank anticipated the scenario with the receptionist as if it was a movie script. Within minutes, she escorts me into a square room and says, "Have a seat," waving an arm toward the green-and-gold-striped chair.

I rub my nose. *What is that awful smell?* Sweet and earthy, but I don't recognize it and I don't like it. Taking short breaths,

I glance from a wall filled with books, to a large clear case displaying multiple diplomas similar to my fake one, to the wall behind a massive desk where photographs hang in three columns. In each photograph, a different tall man shakes hands with the same short man.

The door opens, and the small man in the photos, barely five feet tall, enters. His large, black-rimmed glasses magnify his small eyes.

"Hello, Dr. Green," he says, in a surprisingly deep voice. "I apologize for the mix-up in our schedule. I can spare ten minutes before my next appointment." He sits at the huge desk and waves me to the chair opposite him. "Please have a seat and tell me what I can do for you."

"Thank you, Dr. Filmore. I'm curious about the work you're doing with amnesia patients. I have two perplexing cases and would appreciate any insights you can share." I smile, pleased with my confident tone.

Dr. Filmore doesn't smile. "Amnesia is tricky, isn't it? I don't know why we seem to have so many cases around here. Maybe the rain and gray skies make people want to forget who they are. Where did you say you're from, Dr. Green?"

"North. We get a lot of rain up there, too." I hope he doesn't ask for a specific location.

The little man folds his arms on the desk. "Tell me about your cases and I'll see if I can help."

"One female, one male. When I press them to recall details from their pasts, they get so anxious I have to end sessions early." I'm surprised how easily the lie comes out of my mouth.

The doctor adjusts his eyeglasses. "Have you tried hypnosis?"

"No," I answer slowly. "Have you found hypnosis beneficial?" I hope my response is sensible.

He gives me a quick look and I notice the hint of a smirk. "Using the subconscious mind to help memories surface can be quite effective," he says. "Unfortunately, I have a couple of patients who recite scenes from science fiction movies. Hypnosis can also be perplexing."

"What kind of science fiction movies?" My wrist vibrates and my arm flinches. Filmore doesn't seem to notice. Travis must be letting me know he's heading back.

"Whichever ones have flying spheres and domed cities."

Zap! "You have more than one patient with the same illusions?" I ask, straining to keep my voice even.

"Strange, isn't it?" Filmore glances at a large round clock above the door and stands. "Perhaps we can continue this discussion another time. My next patient is waiting."

"Thank you again for seeing me today, Dr. Filmore."

"Good day, Dr. Green. Please leave your card with my receptionist."

My card? I hurry past the receptionist's desk, rush out of the clinic, and stride briskly across the parking lot, hoping I don't sprain my ankle in these stilts for shoes. I hop into Hank's passenger seat, and he reaches for the key, glancing at the clinic entrance. "Do we need to make a run for it?"

I chuckle. "No."

I lean against the cushioned backrest, and Filmore's words echo in my head. "Flying spheres and domed cities." Science fiction to Filmore—Zelfar to me.

Fastening my seatbelt, I discreetly glance at my zelcom. No message. Interesting.

Hank looks over his shoulder and begins backing out of the parking space. "Tell me what happened with Filmore."

Zack's shrill voice blasts from my zelcom. "Dad, come quick! Something's wrong with Einstein!"

Hank jerks the car to a halt. "What the heck? Your watch talks, too?"

Ignoring Hank's observation, I uncover my zelcom and stare

at it.

"Where are you?" Travis's voice.

"The sign says *computers*," Zack answers.

"Call an ambulance!" yells an unfamiliar voice.

Zack must have his zelcom on full receive/send. I wish I could see images on this side of the portal.

Hank touches my hand. "Don't worry, Zophie. The ambulance will take Einstein to the hospital. We can meet them there."

I'm sure Hank is confused by the horrified look on my face. Tapping my zelcom, I shout, "Travis, you have to get to Einstein. The ambulance will take him to a hospital!"

My zelcom is silent.

"Travis! Travis! Did you hear me?"

No response.

"Is Einstein afraid of —?" Hank starts.

"Zophie, can you hear me?" Travis's loud whisper interrupts.

"Yes, and Hank can hear you, too."

"Oh, okay, well, um, Einstein's all right," Travis says. "We're leaving the store now. Are you ready to go home?"

"Yes." I've never been more ready to go home. "Hank and I will be at his house shortly."

"Okay, I'll pick you up there in a few minutes. Toss pine." I tap my zelcom and slide my sleeve over my wrist. My zelcom is again out of sight, but surely not out of Hank's mind.

Hank eases his car onto the street, and we ride in silence, eyes on the road ahead. Hank suddenly thumps his hand against the steering wheel and I jump. "You have a telephone on your wrist, for crying out loud! Do you know how much easier my life would be if I didn't have to hunt for a pay phone and worry about exact change every time I needed to call a client?"

I sit quietly and lower my head. There is no response I can give Hank to ease his frustration.

His tone turns suspicious. "Do you guys work for some secret government agency?"

"No, Hank. I promise you, we do not work for any government."

I shrink at the scowl on Hank's face and realize how much I depend on his friendship. I have to tell him something. "We're from a place where technology flourishes, and we have no government as you would know it."

Hank tosses his hat into the back seat and his eyes dart between me and the highway. "I've never heard of a place with no government. Where does *that* exist?"

My eyes meet his. "I can't tell you where, but what I say is true. We have a council that helps make community decisions, but basically everyone shares what they produce. We all have plenty of food and comfortable homes. We don't have what you know as crime, so we don't need law enforcement or government."

Hank scratches a thinning spot on the top of his head. "And you don't get old. Sounds like some kind of make-believe utopia. Is it in the mountains like Shangri-La?"

I can't tell if Hank is mocking me. "I don't know about Shangri-La, but our world is real."

"Well, if your world is so perfect, what are you guys doing here?"

"We have a serious problem our scientists have been unable to solve. A handful of us were sent here to find the solution. We wanted our presence to be discreet, and we never thought we would be here this long."

"Sent here, huh? Sounds a little science fictiony to me. Or I should say, science fishy. Why didn't you want Einstein to go to the hospital? Were you afraid word would get out you're here? Or because he bleeds green blood?"

"Green blood? What does that mean?"

"Nothing." Hank stops the car in his driveway and turns off the motor. With his hands still on the steering wheel, he sighs and looks at me. "Thank you for telling me a little something. Our families have been friends a long time and everyone I've met from wherever you call home seems like good people."

I reach into my borrowed handbag and remove my wallet. "How much do I owe you for investigating Johnny Ford?"

"Seventy-five."

I count out three hundred seventy-five and extend the cash to Hank.

He hesitates, and I nudge the money toward him. "Hank, please, it's nothing compared to everything you've done, and still do, for my family and me."

Finally, Hank opens his hand, and I place the bills on his palm. He shakes his head. "I can accept payment for services rendered, but that's a mighty steep tip, even if you do own a diamond mine."

"Please keep it."

Hank shrugs and pushes the folded money into his pocket. "Do you have enough information on Johnny, or do you want me to do more digging?"

"I would like to know more about Amber." I slip my wallet into my purse. "Are you familiar with the use of hypnosis in psychiatry?"

"I've seen shows where magicians hypnotize people and make them do weird things, but I don't know much about hypnotism and shrinks. But Janet might know something about hypnosis."

"Speaking of Janet, I'd better change out of her clothes. Travis should be here soon."

Hank unlocks his front door and tells me to go on inside while he puts the car in the garage. I quickly change back into my jeans and sweater and rejoin Hank outside on the sidewalk, just as Travis pulls up in our Jeep.

Zack hops out of the front seat. Hank comes up behind me, I assume to hold my car door, but instead, he playfully snatches

Zack's cap. Thick red curls on Zack's head spring free.

Hank waves Zack's baseball cap over his head and laughs. "Who the heck did that to your hair?"

"I did!" Zack reaches for his hat, which Hank pulls away two more times before handing over the cap. Zack plops it back on his head, hops into the back seat, and slams the car door.

"There's no explaining teens," Hank says.

"Thank you for all your help today," I say, and get into the car.

"Sure, anytime." Hank closes my door and waves goodbye.

Travis drives toward home, and I peer over my shoulder at our android, who sits quietly, staring out the side window.

"Is Einstein okay?" I ask, turning back to Travis.

"I underestimated the interconnection of American and Zelfarian technology. Next time I go into Portland, I'll purchase a computer so I can study its components. I'm curious to learn the circuitry that apparently can wreak havoc with my robot."

Travis glances at me and back at the road. "So, Hank heard us talking through your zelcom?"

"He and I were in his car when Zack's voice blared through."

Travis waits a few seconds. "And?"

"And Hank seemed jealous that I have a telephone on my wrist. He said he doesn't like having to hunt for pay phones when he's in his car."

"Car phones do exist here." Travis strums his fingers on the steering wheel. "They're rare, but perhaps we can purchase a car phone for Hank."

I gently bite my lip and gaze at Travis. "Do you think maybe we could give him a zelcom?"

Travis's mouth falls open. "No!" His voice rises two octaves.

CHAPTER 18

Today marks a whole month that I haven't been able to see Hank or Dr. Filmore to pursue proof that Rudy is from Zelfar, and to find Amber. Between Clay leading the reconstruction of Health Dome and Marc spending his time soothing his grieving wife, my focus needs to be here in Zelfar, supervising the temporary health dome and caring for Brita. Nothing the neurologists and I have tried has awoken Brita. My trips through the portal have been just long enough to let my daughters play together and to alternate their presence here.

Vad taps my shoulder and extends his hand-chair. "Health Dome?"

"Yes." I'm excited to see the new Health Dome, but more excited to see Clay. We've had very little time together, and I miss him.

Vad slows his pace when we approach Health Dome, and I stare in awe at the large curved structure, more majestic than ever, with rows of colored flowers along the bottom edge of the dome.

"Use crystillium to build that table and extend the length by two feet," Clay says to a construction bot.

"Hi," I say.

Clay turns and smiles. "Hey, Zophie. Ready for your guided tour and lunch in the new cafeterium?"

"If the inside is as finished as the outside, you'll have your homedome back soon."

"I think we should keep the mini health dome within the homedome loops." Clay leans to my ear. "I'd like my home to be closer to the forest anyway."

Clay taps his zelcom, and instead of a clear panel sliding to the side, a thin blue strip instantly outlines an open doorway into Health Dome.

"Did the crystillium shell magically melt away?" I ask.

"We don't need magic here, but I'll admit—zilimite seems to possess magical qualities. Dusting a section of hardened crystillium with zilimite powder allows you to make that section dematerialize and materialize again." He whispers, "Like turning a light bulb on and off."

Vad enters the dome behind me and surprises me by grasping my arm. "Hil is back," he says, staring at the dome's arched ceiling high overhead. Hil was Vad's first dome connection, and they formed a bond. He raises his arms outward. His eyes remain dry, but I sense if he could, he'd be crying. He'll have empathy for Zack when Brita wakes up.

"Hil may be smarter than you now, Vad," Clay says. "She runs Health Dome without the need of human intervention."

"Does Hil have a bot form?" Vad glances from one healthbot to another. Hil is Health Dome's intelligence system, which controls all the healthbots and technical functions of her dome, as do the intelligence systems of all domes. Travis combined our homedome's intelligence with our homebot, giving it a human appearance, and thereby creating Zelfar's first android. Tutorbots have since become androids, appearing human as well. All other bots have hard-shelled bodies of varying colors. Five years ago, Travis programmed Vad to experience emotion, and as an experiment, Hil was given similar programming. If Travis ever has time to give Hil human form, I wonder if he would let Vad help with her design. Poor Travis, everyone will soon want an android and it took him forever to create Vad and clone him to make Einstein.

Clay gives Vad a pat on the back. "Sorry, pal. You'll have to talk to Travis about that." It's as if Clay could read my mind.

Vad remains near the entrance and I stroll with Clay down the large center corridor, which is softly hued in a relaxing pastel blue. We enter a birthing orb where a sconce of fresh white carnations hangs on the curved wall behind a sofa. A clear neotube and a bed for the mother float together near the center of the twelve-foot orb.

Clay grins at my wide eyes and nudges me with his elbow. "There are nineteen more like this one. Only difference is the color of the sofa. Do you want to see them all?"

"I want to see the healing orb."

He leads me farther along the wide center corridor and stops between two potted scotch pines—each six-feet tall. I gently brush the needles on the nearest branch and inhale. With a relaxed smile, I follow Clay through the arched opening.

As if suspended in space and time, a long transparent cylinder floats in the center of the fifteen-foot orb. A few moments inside this tube will rid the human body of physical imperfections, such as broken bones, torn ligaments, and defective organs. Nearly two decades ago, barely finished with health tutoring sessions, I helped Clay design the first healing tube. Why can't we make one to heal brains?

When we exit the healing orb, Clay points to a rainbow-trimmed doorway at the end of the corridor. "Are you hungry?

The new cafeterium is even better than Rainbow Mist Café." Clay knows Rainbow Mist Café, fortunately unharmed in the explosions, is my favorite place to eat in Zelfar.

"Does the cafeterium have a rainbow bigger than the one on the Columbia River?" I whisper. Clay shakes a silencing finger. He leads me toward the seating area where white lights sparkle overhead and pristine white chairs, stuffed for comfort, sit around legless tables.

"Wouldn't Janet love to see this space-age décor?" Clay says softly.

I poke him playfully in the ribs and imitate his gesture for silence as we approach tables with people already seated.

"How's this?" Clay stops at a small table among other open tables.

"Perfect." I sit in the nearest seat, and Clay sits opposite me.

As we sit, a virtual menu scrolls in the air above the surface of the opalescent table.

"Choose your poison," Clay says.

I kick him gently in the shin and lean over the table, moving my face through the virtual text. "You can't talk like that. People will wonder why you're saying weird things."

"Like *rainbow over the Columbia*?" he grins. "At least we can watch out for each other."

Together we say, "Vivacity times two." Laughing softly, we slap one another's palms.

"Let's order." Clay looks up and taps the menu floating in front of him.

Swiping the display to flip pages, I scroll through the menu options and finally choose a spinach casserole and toasted almond bread. We both order iced tea.

"I heard Zack is serving at Energy Dome," Clay says.

"As of today. How'd you know?"

"Emery and I were at the same magna transport station this

morning. He appreciates Zack's brilliance and says the other energy scientists are listening to Zack, too. Apparently, Zack is the expert on zilimite."

I smile and lean back as a servebot places our food and beverages on the table.

Clay drizzles vinegar on his salad greens, followed by a sprinkling of brown sugar. He looks at my toast, taps the menu screen, and soon has a slice of almond bread in front of him. "Speaking of Zack," Clay says, "has he been nagging Owen to look for Rudy?"

"Owen!" I gasp. Why didn't I think of him before? If anyone knows about searching for missing people, Owen would be the one.

Clay lowers his fork and lays his hand on mine. "Is something wrong with Owen?"

"No, I'm sure he's fine. I need to go see him." I'm glad Clay doesn't ask why. I'll share with him what I know about Rudy when I have better information.

Clay leans toward me. "When are you heading back to you-know-where?"

"Maybe tomorrow."

When we finish our meal, a servebot clears our table, and I exit the cafeterium with Clay.

On the platform outside, Clay gives me a hug and says softly, "I'd like to go you-know-where with you when you go, okay?"

I smile and nod. I'm always glad to have Clay with me.

Vad tips his head at Health Dome as if telling Hil to toss pine. When Gram seals the portal and we finally bring Einstein to Zelfar, I wonder if he'll feel the same about Hil, since his brain is paired with Vad's. I swallow a tiny chuckle. A pair of androids in love with the same dome could be interesting.

Vad and I are soon standing in front of Transportation Dome, the tallest dome in Zelfar. A silver band circles the bottom and a translucent silvery hue radiates from the upper shell, both new features.

One hoversphere after another zips high overhead, moving to and from Crystal Lake in obvious test patterns. Zelfar inhabitants live within a short hoverspheres ride to that lake. Only explorers have ventured into the outer regions beyond a hundred-mile radius. I wonder if Owen has a new hoversphere he uses for exploring.

"Vad, please pick up Kayla and take her home. I'll ride a magnadisc back when I'm finished here."

He nods and exits in a blur.

I enter the hub of our hover transport system and follow the words and arrows projected in the air that guide me to the exploration orb where I hope to find Owen. When I get to the orb, I shake out my hands to calm my eagerness. The door to the orb slides open.

"Hi, Zophie." Owen pushes red hair from his forehead. "Please come in."

"Hello, Owen." I look up into Owen's face, towering above me. We tap elbows in greeting, common in my parents' generation.

Owen motions toward a curved bench, but I walk to a large sphere that hovers a foot above the floor in the center of the orb. Maybe Owen can take me exploring in this today.

"You decided to give up on health service and join my crew?" He taps his zelcom, and numbers floating above a miniature sphere on a worktable vanish.

"I wanted to do some exploring and thought maybe you could help."

"Sorry, but my new exploration transport here isn't quite ready." He lifts a hand toward the large sphere.

I sigh and wistfully smooth my fingers on the outside of the clear crystillium shell.

"Didn't take you for an explorer." Owen scratches the thick

hair on his chin. "Think you might find the cure somewhere out there?"

I shrug, more in dismay that his sphere isn't ready than in reply.

"I can give you a virtual tour of the terrain." Owen lifts his zelcom and waits for my cue.

I glance at the open doorway and say softly, "I'm interested in finding a missing person."

He tilts his head, his jaw tight and eyes guarded. After a few seconds, his face softens. "Since you and I are both looking to find things in Zelfar—you the cure for our babies and me the missing people—I'll help you all I can." He points again to the bench. "Have a seat."

Owen seals the door and says, "Opaque." The walls of the orb become solid gray. He rolls a stool toward the bench and sits facing me. "The truth is—and I'm finally glad to say this to someone—I haven't given up on finding our missing people. Your son and his friend were looking for one of the men on my search list—Rudy."

I hope my eyes aren't as wide as they feel. *Owen has a list!* I bite my tongue and force myself to coolly ask one question at a time.

"How many people are on your list?"

"Four. First one has been gone more than thirty years, and April's been missing for six." Owen blinks twice and clears his throat. "Next one was the year after April, and Rudy was the last, close to four years ago."

I squeeze the edge of the bench and force myself to sit still. Four isn't as bad as *list* could have implied, but I was hoping Rudy was our only missing person. "Were they explorers? Male? Female?"

"Two women and two men. None explorers."

"Did they disappear individually?"

"Yep." Owen nods. "One by one."

"And you're still looking for them?"

Owen glances at the sealed doorway. "Yes, to you. No, to everyone else."

"What does that mean?" Seems I'm not the only secret-keeper in Zelfar.

"Quaid insisted I stop looking. These people have families and friends who care about them and miss them." Owen's mouth pinches at the corners. "Quaid said I could ease people's loss by reminding them we're all free to come and go anywhere we want, and their loved one would return if they chose to. But I can tell you, Zophie, there's no easing that kind of loss."

I gaze into Owen's watery eyes and gently lay my hand on his. "Were you close to any of them?"

Owen rubs his large hands on his thighs. "April is my daughter." His voice breaks. "I've been all over these mountains, more than a hundred miles in every direction. I haven't found any sign of her or of any of the others."

"I'm so sorry. If my child were missing, I'd never quit searching, either."

He wipes his face with his sleeve. "With my new exploration sphere," he says, "I'll be able to detect a human presence from miles away. I'll be out searching the day my sphere is ready."

"That sounds encouraging, Owen. I hope you find all four of them. In the meantime," I add, in my best scientific tone, "I'm doing research on family lineage and protizine depletion. Having information on the missing people would be helpful. Does your search record contain more than their names?"

Owen grins. Without hesitation, he taps his zelcom and sends the data to mine. "Names, photographs, ages, when they disappeared, and closest relatives. I'm glad to do anything I can to help you find the cure for our babies."

I push on my knee to keep my foot from bouncing and force

myself to wait to look at the data. "Thank you for the information. I should be going." I rise. "Would you mind if I come back after you've searched with your new sphere?"

"Not at all. Come back anytime." Owen stands and opens the doorway. "Toss pine."

On the way home, I barely notice other magnadisc riders in the homedome loops, or the sun, low on the horizon. My thoughts swirl. Einstein can detect anyone coming through the portal. No one has gone missing in the time my family has been secretly living in both worlds. Coincidence?

And why would Quaid want Owen to stop looking for our missing people?

I lean against a wide maple tree in the center garden next to mine. With keen anticipation about the other three people, I tap my zelcom. Four names—alphabetical, each with a photo, date of disappearance, and family members—scroll onto the screen. I don't actually need family lineage, but knowing their relatives will be helpful if I find any of our missing people.

April, a young woman with long blonde curls that drape her back like a golden shawl, appears first. She was only nineteen when she vanished. Poor Owen. I can't imagine the grief of losing a child. The thought reminds me of Marc's loss, and I put a hand to my chest.

Irene is next, missing five years. Nothing about her is familiar.

Then Rudy's face appears. If he is Johnny Ford, his years in America have aged him. Still, I agree with Zack, they could be the same person. I saw Amber too long ago and too briefly to recognize her features. But if Rudy could be Johnny, perhaps Amber is really April or Irene. The final name is Wyatt, who vanished before I was born.

I plod home with a heavy heart. Now I have more people to be concerned about.

I don't talk much over dinner, and Travis finally asks what's on my mind. I glance at Zack on the other side of the table. I'll tell Travis more when we're in bed.

For now, I merely say, "I'm going to America for a few days."

Zack looks up from his plate, his eyes pleading. "Do I have to go? My team is presenting a new power initiator tomorrow. I need to be here. And I haven't visited Brita in two days."

Before I can come up with a rebuttal, Travis says, "You take Kayla with you, sweetheart, and Zack can stay here with me. I need to start a new field of sput. How about if we join you in a couple of days?"

I nod, and Zack says, "Yes!"

I should be glad Zack is excited to stay in Zelfar, but I can't help wanting to keep a close eye on him. Four Zelfarians are missing . . . and no one knows why.

CHAPTER 19

Kayla and I step from the American cave, and I smile, seeing the sunny day and dry ground. I wish Clay were with us, but I'm sure he'll contact Vad when he's ready to come to America.

"Hi Einstein!" Kayla bounds toward our android, who's standing at the edge of the small pond.

Einstein transports us swiftly through the woods and sets us on our front porch. I grasp the doorknob with an unexpected feeling of "it's good to be home." My skin prickles, and I shake it off. This is not my real home, but I am excited to see Krissie and Gram.

"Mommy!" Krissie yells and runs to me from the living orb. I scoop her up, kissing her soft cheek. Gram smiles from her purple chair.

"No, Princess is mine!" Krissie scoots from my arms and chases after her sister.

"Kayla," I say, sitting on the sofa. "Bring Princess to me."

Kayla ambles to me and slowly extends the doll. I straighten the tiara atop the doll's head. Before giving the doll to Krissie, I say, "Would you help Kayla find her dolly?"

"I know where Frosty is!" Krissie runs to the play area in the corner of the room, reaches into the toy tube, and pulls out a white fluff. "Here, Kayla. Here's Frosty."

Kayla accepts her favorite doll—a stuffed snowman.

While the girls play, I tell Gram what I learned from Owen. When I show her the photographs of Rudy, Irene, April, and Wyatt, Gram merely tilts her head.

"Do you know any of these people?" I ask.

"Yes. I know all of them."

I stare at my grandmother and wait for her to say more. She doesn't. I swallow hard, trying to repress feelings of betrayal. "Did you know they were missing?"

Gram purses her lips and nods. Of course, she knew. I sink into the sofa, confused and disappointed. "Why didn't you tell me Rudy wasn't the only one missing? Please don't keep secrets from me."

She reaches toward my hand, and I jerk my fingers away. Her eyes twitch in surprise.

"Zophie," she says firmly. "I'd rather you let Owen continue his search for our missing people. You're doing enough with shuffling your family and helping Travis with the synthetic honey."

"But Gram, I believe Johnny is Rudy. If he's here, the other three could be, too. Owen can't search in America, but I can."

Gram runs a hand through her hair and meets my gaze. "I know there is no persuading you otherwise. Do you remember the girl on the train from your first trip here?"

"Yes. Her name is Amber."

Gram sighs. "Begin your search with her."

I walk to Gram and give her a hug, glad she's no longer trying to placate me. "Will you watch the girls while I go freshen up?"

"Of course, dear."

On my way to the stairs, I take a detour to the kitchen.

"Einstein, do you know where I can find the Portland telephone book?" I ask.

He opens a drawer under the counter and extends a large paperback book. The stale smell of paper reminds me of my great-grandfather's journal. I think Ozell Farlum's heart would break if he knew his only great-grandchild had a home in the land he fled to found Zelfar.

Alone in my bedroom, I open the thick book and skim the A-section until I see *Amber's Crystal Window*. She's still here!

I scan the address into my zelcom, and a map displays the fifty-mile route to Amber's store, located in Beaverton, on the west side of Portland. I strum my fingers on the open page. Travis isn't here to drive me, so how will I get there? I have a license, courtesy of Hank. Now I wish I'd learned to maneuver our Jeep.

But Einstein knows how to operate a vehicle. I slam the book shut and quickly change into a pair of pedal pushers, white cotton blouse, and green button-down sweater. Tying a thin green scarf around my neck, I chuckle at myself in the mirror, thinking how much I look like Janet in my attire.

After grabbing a stunner from the safe, I leave my bedroom. To my surprise, Einstein awaits at the bottom of the stairs.

"You entered data into your zelcom," he says. "Do you need something?"

"Can you operate our Jeep like you did the motorcycle?"

"Affirmative. Travis gave me a driver's manual. I can operate any vehicle."

"Good," I say. "I'd like you to drive me to Portland." Einstein doesn't have a license, but I don't have time to worry about that now. "Gram?" I call from the hallway.

"Yes, dear?" Gram walks from the living room with the twins at her side.

"I'm going into Beaverton to see Amber and I need Einstein to drive the car. Will you tot-watch the girls for a couple of hours?"

"I wanna go," Krissie and Kayla whine in unison, clinging to my knees.

"I'm sorry this quest has fallen to you, dear," Gram says. "I have something that may help. Wait here." She walks briskly to her bedroom at the end of the hall.

I kneel and hug my daughters. "Mommy will be back real soon. Maybe Gram will let Princess and Frosty eat lunch with you." I rise as the girls run into the living room to retrieve their dolls.

Gram returns carrying a square canvas pouch. "A book on psychiatry that explains hypnotism," she says, extending the bag to me. "And a pendulum in the small zipper pocket."

"But, Gram, I—"

"Your instincts will guide you, dear."

I shove the pouch into my handbag and follow Einstein out the back door to the garage.

Einstein drives us to Beaverton while I read the book's thin section on hypnotism. I look up when our car stops in front of Amber's small store. I move the pendulum from the zipper pocket to my purse, and lay the book on the dashboard.

"Please wait here, Einstein. This meeting may take some time."

"Okay, Zophie."

Multi-faceted prisms dangle in the windows on either side of the entrance. When I open the door, a delicate bell gives a single *ding* as I enter Amber's "portal to peaceful energy."

I rub hard at my nose to ease the intense scents of sandalwood and citrus. Books, crystals, and candles are neatly arranged on clear glass shelves. Soft tinkling sounds chime soothingly in the background. My first instinct is to find a soft mat and reach for a serenity simulator.

A purple curtain parts at the back of the shop. Shiny gold

suns and crescent moons printed on the fabric dance with its movement. A young woman emerges through the veiled doorway.

"Welcome to Amber's Crystal Window. I'm Amber. How may I help you today?"

Her kind voice blends with the ambience of her shop, as does her long, flowing hair and loose-fitting pants and shirt—and a purple armband? In Zelfar, the word *Serenity* would be printed in bold letters. Amber's armband has no lettering.

She resembles the image of April, but her hair is lighter, her face a bit rounder.

"Hi Amber, I'm Zophie." I extend my hand, hoping the scrutiny in my eyes goes unnoticed. "I don't know if you remember me, but we met on the train a couple of years ago. I'm back in the area and thought I'd stop in to see if you were still here."

On my introductory trip to America, I had noticed Amber when she boarded the train and took the seat behind me. She'd been friendly and had given me her business card.

Amber nods. "I remember. You were upset when a mother slapped her child. The mother's action upset me, too."

I glance at an amethyst sphere on the shelf beside her. "Amber, I'm curious about your portal to peaceful energy."

"Of course." She scurries behind a glass case, pulls out a spiral-bound book, and plops it on the counter, spewing pine needles out of a small bowl. I refrain from gasping and help her swish the pine needles back into the dish. "Sorry about that." She opens the book to a page outlined in rainbows and stars.

"No problem," I say. "I like the scent of pine."

"I offer aura readings, chakra cleansing, and energy healing—all designed to rebalance harmony in the body. The first thirty-minute session is free." She lays her hand, adorned with a silver and turquoise ring, on the page, and smiles at me. "I have an opening now if you want it."

"Yes, thank you."

Amber locks the door and hangs a plastic sign in the window, indicating her shop is closed. She leads me behind the curtain into a small room where, thankfully, the scents of sandalwood and citrus are more subtle.

"Have you had a chakra cleansing before?"

"No, but I am familiar with the use of serenity simulation."

Amber's lips part slightly as she lifts her blonde eyebrows. Perhaps I triggered a memory.

"You may hang your bag over there." She points to a brass hook and then to a narrow table-like bed in the center of the room. "Please, lie down and relax."

I hang my purse and jacket and sit on the edge of the thinly-padded table. Amber dims the lights, and I lie back, letting my pumps drop to the floor.

"Will we be able to converse while you're cleaning my chakras?"

"If you like, but it may take a little longer." She places a pillow under my knees.

I inhale deeply, resting my hands at my sides. The faint beat of drums and the soft thrums of harp strings relax my senses. My eyelids drift downward and I barely hear myself ask, "How long have you done this type of service?"

"About six years." Amber's voice seems far away.

"What did you do before that?"

"I don't remember my life before six years ago."

My eyes open. "Do you mean you have amnesia?"

Amber keeps her palms flat and moves them in small circles two inches above my chest. "That's what the doctor calls it. He also told me I gave birth a few months before I lost my memory." She frowns. "I can't believe I have a child out there somewhere. Don't you think if that were true, the father would have found me?"

I try to recall a child without a mother in Zelfar. Motherless children don't exist in my world. I say softly, "Maybe he's still trying to find you."

Amber shrugs. "Maybe." She rubs gentle, soothing hands on my shoulders. "How about you? Are you a professional woman?"

"I'm a psychiatrist." Oh my. One little role-play and I call myself a psychiatrist?

"No wonder you didn't like it when you saw that child being mistreated on the train. You would know about psychological damage to children."

"Are you being treated for your amnesia?" I ask, hoping she'll tell me about her sessions with Filmore.

"Yes, but it isn't working. I don't know why I keep seeing Dr. Filmore. He hypnotizes me and says all I talk about is science fiction, like domes and spaceships. He thinks the things I say might be from a recurring dream."

"That could be a sound theory," I say, trying to sound like I know what I'm talking about.

"Seeing Dr. Filmore drains my energy, but when I try to quit seeing him, he talks me into coming back. Do you have an office here in Beaverton?"

"Uh, no. I'm visiting for a few weeks, doing some research."

Amber's hands leave my shoulders, and I feel an almost imperceptible tug, like a magnetic field above my stomach.

"I feel a connection with your energy," she says. "I don't think Dr. Filmore will ever help me unlock my past. Maybe you could."

My pulse races at the possibility of probing Amber's mind. My eyes look into hers.

"If you're open to it," she says, "maybe you could do a session with me while you're in town. We could meet here in my shop."

"I'd be glad to see if I can help you. Meeting here would be fine." I keep my voice steady, but I can't help wondering if I'm taking my ruse as a psychiatrist too far.

"We'll schedule time before you leave," she says. "We should stop talking now so I can finish harmonizing your energy. Close your eyes and relax."

My eyelids close, but my insides won't relax. When Amber taps my shoulder a few minutes later to tell me our session is complete, I stare at her, wondering if I'm supposed to feel my energy in harmony. I don't. I feel nervous.

Amber waits by the door while I swing my feet to the floor and slip into my shoes. When I take my handbag from the hook, Gram's words course through me: "Your instincts will guide you."

"Amber," I say, touching her arm before she opens the door. "I have time now if you'd like to do a session with me."

CHAPTER 20

"Yes." Amber clasps her hands together. "I would love to do a session with you now. Is this room okay?"

"Yes." I reach into my handbag, retrieve the pendulum Gram gave me, and slip it into my pocket.

Amber pulls a stool from under the table-bed. "Here's a seat. I can turn the background music off if you'd like."

I smile to encourage her to relax as well as to calm my own nerves. "The music is fine."

I perch on the small round seat and mentally review the role of a psychiatrist—ask questions, listen, and take notes. I tap my zelcom to record our session.

Amber lies on her back on the narrow bed. "Are we starting with hypnosis?" she asks.

"I'd prefer to talk first, get to know you better. Perhaps the connection you feel in our energy will open some new memories for you."

"Okay. The power of my amethyst might help, too."

I follow her gaze to the four-foot crystal standing majestically in the corner. A tiny beam of light shines on the facets of deep purple, casting a lavender hue across the tiled floor.

With a deep breath, I put my ruse as a psychiatrist into motion. "I'm sure you've told your story many times, but please share it with me."

She sighs. "Okay Doctor. I'll tell you everything I remember."

For several minutes, Amber relates her first memories. When she comes to the part where she learned about having given birth, she grabs her stomach as if she's been punched, and begins to cry softly.

"I had a baby . . . and my baby died." She sits up, tears streaming down her face. "My baby died. I remember now. My baby died."

I press my hands to my thighs, my heartbeat pulsing in my fingertips. If Amber is April, she and her husband must be fifth generation. Their baby would have succumbed to newborn loss syndrome. Could there have been a case I didn't know about? Owen didn't mention his daughter losing a baby.

I flex my fingers and force myself to breathe. Maybe hypnosis will trigger more of Amber's memories. Calmly, I say, "Remembering your baby is a significant breakthrough. Perhaps we should try hypnosis while your mind is open. How do you feel about that?"

Amber nods, closes her eyes, and relaxes her arms across her abdomen. Unlike me, she's done this before.

I stand and remove the citrine stone from my pocket. At least I'm familiar with the pendulum, thanks to Gram's lessons on the energy-balancing qualities of crystals. Pinching the end of the thin chain, I dangle the clear orange stone above Amber's face.

"Open your eyes and focus on the tip of the crystal."

Amber gazes at the pointed citrine and smiles as if to approve my choice of hypnotherapy device. The pendulum quivers, and I strain to keep my hand steady. Finally, the crystal swings back and forth, gently swaying over one eye and then the other.

"Keep your mind focused on the point. Concentrate only on the pendulum. When your eyelids become heavy, let them close."

After a few seconds, Amber's pupils begin to dilate. Her eyelids vibrate slowly and then drift downward. When her eyes fully close, I clasp the stone with my other hand and put it back in my pocket.

"You will respond honestly to any question I ask," I say firmly.

Now, according to Gram's book, I should offer suggestions to trigger my subject's memories. Suggestions, in this case, only a Zelfarian could make.

"Tell me about coming to America."

"Water, beautiful shiny water." Amber's voice is flat.

"Are you walking through the water?" If she's from my world, she didn't arrive by boat.

"No, through the wall behind the water. Wade opens the wall."

I scour my memory but can't recall anyone by that name. But she came through the portal! Now I have proof. Amber *is* from Zelfar. I want to wake her up and tell her the truth about herself. But what good would that do? She can't remember any of it. Maybe if I take her there. No, not before I understand the repercussions. But how can I not tell Owen I found his daughter?

"How does Wade open the wall?"

"I don't know. It's beautiful, then it's gone."

"What happens after you pass through the wall?"

"Wade and I walk and walk . . . through trees . . . wet, dripping trees. Then we ride. Funny machine rolling along."

"Is Wade your husband?"

"No. Wade is our wise elder. I'm very sad, but I'll follow Wade."

Wait a minute. I grip the edge of the padded table. Does she mean Quaid?

"Where does Quaid take you?" Suggestion. Hypnosis is about suggestion.

"Where I'll be happy. Quaid knows where I'll be happy."

"Are you happy, April? Was Quaid right?"

"I'm serene." Her tone drops and gets softer. "But I'm alone."

Poor April. I wipe a salty teardrop from my upper lip. Quaid brought her to America and left her here. He must have done the same thing to Rudy.

My cheeks flush with anger. Why would Quaid bring them here? Plus why can't they remember? I don't know how I'm going to force answers from Quaid, but somehow, I will.

I swallow hard and say in a level voice, "When you awaken, you will recall this conversation." If she remembers Zelfar, I'll take her home, regardless of the risk of exposing the portal. "You will awaken in three . . . two . . . one." I snap my fingers above her nose.

Amber swings her feet to the side, sits up, and rubs her face. "I feel like I've slept for days. How did you get me so relaxed?"

"You're a great patient. What do you remember from our session?" I bite my lip, waiting for her answer. I wonder how much she told Filmore and wish I had his notes.

"My baby died." Her voice quivers. "I remember my baby died. I must have been married. Maybe we were in a car accident and my husband died, too. That would explain why he isn't looking for me. Maybe the pain of losing them was too much to bear and I blocked out their memory. That's possible, isn't it?"

Amber's teary eyes plead for my agreement. I pat her hand, consoling as Gram would.

"Of course, anything is possible. Is that all you remember?"

"Yes." She wipes her face. "That and your beautiful pendulum. It had such clarity of color. It's perhaps the purest piece of citrine I've ever seen."

The tension in my neck begins to ease. Amber doesn't

remember Zelfar or the portal. I'll return her to Zelfar, but not today. I reach into my pocket and extend the piece of citrine to her. "Here, keep this. A token of your memory breakthrough."

Gram won't mind that I gave the pendulum to Amber. She'd say, "Stones have a way of finding where they belong."

Amber encloses the crystal in her palm and whispers, "Thank you."

When I turn toward the door, she touches my arm. "Aren't you going to tell me what I said? Did I talk about domes and spaceships again?"

I look into her eyes. "You talked about how serene you feel and how you enjoy imparting serenity to others."

She smiles. "Can we do another session before you leave town?"

"Perhaps," I say. "The hypnosis balanced your energy, so you'll feel well rested for a few days. Please call me if you gain any insights throughout the week."

"I'll need your number." Amber hops from the table and leads me back through the curtained doorway. She walks to the counter and gives me a pencil and a small white card.

I write *Zophie Green* and my phone number. I wish Hank had supplied business cards with my fake diploma.

Amber picks up the card, smiles, and says, "Thank you, Dr. Green." Then she slips the card into a small box.

"Toss pine," I say as I leave the store in a jumble of emotions— relieved to know the truth beyond suspicion, but confused and upset. I pull a few pine needles from my jacket pocket and slide into the passenger seat. Einstein starts the engine and says, "Was your meeting productive?"

"Yes," I say, squeezing the prickly needles and fighting back tears.

On the drive home, I envision going back to Zelfar and pummeling Quaid. I need a serenity simulator.

I need my grandmother. She helped me get information from Amber, but I'm sure Gram still has something to share.

CHAPTER 21

After breakfast the next morning, I follow Gram and the twins into the living room. Gram puts Kayla and Krissie in the play area and hands each of them an electronic puzzle toy. The girls sit quietly, tapping their miniature screens. Gram straightens her sweater, sits on the sofa next to me, and peers perceptively into my eyes.

I pull one knee beneath me and lean into the sofa back. "I know you're anxious to hear about my visit to Amber, but I want to know what you're still keeping from me."

"I understand, dear. First, tell me what you and Hank have been up to and what you learned from Amber. Then I'll tell you what I suspect."

I'd rather she tell me first, but I acquiesce and start by sharing Hank's private-eye work and Dr. Filmore's notes. When I tell Gram about my session with Amber and that I know Amber is April, she purses her lips and nods.

I gasp. "You knew, didn't you?"

"I suspected," Gram says softly. "I thought Amber looked

familiar when I saw her on the train four years ago, but discounted the possibility that anyone from Zelfar could be in America. What with Johnny Ford and Owen's list, I realized Amber must be April."

"That's why you gave me the psychiatry book and the pendulum."

"Yes." Gram combs her hair to one side with her fingers. "April's baby was the first to fall to newborn loss syndrome, before you were assigned to oversee all births. I went to console April because I'd heard she was very distraught. Who wouldn't be? A baby transcending had never happened. When I got to her dome, her husband said she was out for a walk. I told him I'd come back another time, but the next day she was reported missing. Owen searched for many weeks, but he never found her. Now, we know why."

My face heats with anger. "Quaid told April he was taking her someplace where she'd be happy. How could he think she'd be happy in America?"

Gram's brow furrows and she places a hand on my knee. "I was unaware and am saddened by Quaid's involvement. I will go with you to see him. He'll account for what he's done."

"Vad will be here soon with Travis and Zack," I say. "Vad can take us to see Quaid today."

The plunking of miniature piano keys turns our attention to the play area. "Gwam. I wanna play the big piano," Kayla says, setting the toy piano aside.

"Of course, dear." Gram stands and motions for Kayla to follow her.

I take Krissie outside and we sit on the porch swing to watch for Travis and Zack. Soon, Travis walks across the lawn and Krissie yells, "Daddy!" She hops from the swing and runs down the steps.

"Krissie!" Travis lifts her above his head, kisses her cheek, and lowers her to the porch. "Hi, sweetheart," he says, smiling at me.

"Hi." I rise to my toes and give him a passionate kiss.

"Mmm," he says. "It's only been one night, but I missed you, too."

I glance toward the lawn. "Where are Zack and Vad?"

"Vad will bring Zack over this evening."

"Gram and I need Vad now and I don't like you and I both leaving Zack." Now that I know the truth about Rudy and Amber, I'm not sure who we can trust.

Travis kisses my crinkled brow. "Zack promised he wouldn't give Vad any trouble. They'll be here soon. Don't worry."

"Is Clay coming with them?"

"Not that I know of."

"Did Vad go check on him?"

"Why would he do that?"

"I told Vad that Clay wanted to come here yesterday. Clay wouldn't change his mind without letting me know."

"Clay can't call you through the portal."

"Which is why I expected he would contact Vad."

"Maybe he'll come over with Vad and Zack this evening."

"You're right. I had an anxious day yesterday. Clay will come over when he can."

Travis pulls me to the wooden swing, and Krissie climbs into his lap.

"What made your day so anxious and why do you and Gram need Vad?" Travis closes his fingers around mine.

"I learned psychiatry and practiced hypnotism."

"What's psychiatry?"

"The science of mental issues, like amnesia."

Travis winces slightly and nods—his sign he knows when my mind is set on something. "So, our son's curiosity about Johnny has infected you. How far are you taking this?"

"As far as needed. I want to learn how to operate our car. Will you teach me while we're waiting for Vad and Zack?"

He laughs out loud and then becomes quiet, studying me. "Are you becoming too integrated here?"

"No! As soon as we can reproduce honey, we are back to Zelfar for good. If I can prove Johnny is Rudy, he should go back with us. Amber, too."

Travis arcs an eyebrow. "Amber?"

"Yes, and two more besides." Gram and I think Quaid is responsible for our missing people. Since the new hoverspheres are still in test mode, we need Vad to take us to Quaid's."

"Quaid? Well, if anyone can get answers from him, it's Gram. I don't know what driving has to do with amnesia, but if you want to drive right now, I'm ready."

"Me, too," Krissie says. "I wanna dive."

"Yes, you, too." Travis moves Krissie from his lap to the porch. "You can ride, but you're too little to drive."

Grinning like a child about to take her first solo hoverdisc ride, I say, "I'll get the keys and meet you in the garage." I pull the keys from the hook in the hallway and hear the faint sounds of the piano. I shout on my way out the door, "Gram, Vad won't be here until later. Travis, Krissie, and I are going for a drive. We'll be back in a little while."

I nervously maneuver the Jeep onto the road and soon realize operating a motor vehicle is merely a physical form of our virtual driving games in Zelfar, so the skill comes easily. Before long, Krissie whines to go home, and I steer in that direction.

"Einstein drove me to Beaverton to see Amber," I say to Travis.

"Easy mastery for him to control a vehicle. But it appears you don't want to depend on Einstein or me to drive you anymore." His forehead wrinkles. "You plan to drive into Portland alone?"

"Only if I have to, and I'll always carry my stunner."

I pull the Jeep into our garage and a familiar silver vehicle pulls up behind me. Travis lifts Krissie from her car seat. He sets her on the ground and says, "I'm glad Hank's here. I have a surprise for him."

"I wanna supise," Krissie says. I pick her up and follow Travis to Hank's car.

Travis gives Hank the traditional handshake. "Would you mind if my brother and I take your car for a quick spin?" Travis asks. "You can watch TV with Zophie and stay for dinner. Okay?"

"Sure, no problem." Hank laughs and tosses his keys to Travis. "But no racing or outrunning the cops, okay?"

Travis chuckles, catching the keys in the air. He raises his wrist to use his zelcom, glances at Hank, and stops.

"Go ahead," Hank says. "Call your brother. I know that thing isn't just a watch."

Travis smirks, calls Einstein, and in a few seconds Travis's "brother" emerges from the back door. Taking the cue to keep our guest occupied, I lead Hank into the house.

Inside, Hank says, "Forget the TV," and extends a large manila envelope to me.

"Mommy, Cindewella is on TV," Kayla shouts, running into the hall from the living room. "Let's watch it."

Gram follows Kayla. "Hello, Hank." She gives him a quick hug. "Would you like to join us for an animated movie?"

"Maybe another time, Lilly. Zophie and I are going to chat in the kitchen. But I am staying for dinner."

"Good," Gram says. "Then we'll see you after the movie." She gives me a half-smile and nudges the girls into the living room. Gram knows I don't like my children to watch television, but she thinks an occasional cartoon is good entertainment.

Seated in the kitchen nook, Hank shakes the contents of the envelope onto the table. A black and white photograph lands in front of me—an image of Amber, an exact likeness of April from

Owen's list.

"Where did you get this photograph?"

"It was taken the day Amber showed up at the hospital six years ago. I thought you said you knew her."

"She . . ." I swallow, "uh . . . reminds me of someone at home."

"Hmm." Hank peers at me, twists his mustache, and picks up three papers. "If you like Amber's photo, you'll like this even better. These are Filmore's notes from his first sessions with her. Talks about how she got her name and why she's into new age stuff."

Setting the photo aside, I take the pages from Hank.

Patient Name: Jane Doe, a.k.a., Amber . . . Retrograde Amnesia . . . Reads and ciphers at college level but lacks understanding of local currency. Is drawn to crystals . . . first word was "amber" referring to a souvenir on my desk and held it for duration of session. I suggested calling her Amber. Patient agreed.

Halfway down the third page, the word "baby" catches my attention.

At mention of her having given birth recently, patient claimed she didn't remember but hugged her abdomen and was distraught that no one had come to take her home.

I look at the other side of the page, expecting to find something about hypnosis, but the other side is blank. "Didn't Filmore give you his notes about doing hypnosis with April, er . . . Amber?"

Hank grins. "Well, Filmore didn't exactly give me the notes. These are all I found."

A car horn startles us. Hank shuffles the papers back into the envelope. "Sounds like your husband wants us outside."

I put the envelope in a drawer and follow Hank out the back door.

"What's all the ruckus?" Hank says. "Did you hurt my Silver Bullet?"

Travis stands outside the driver's door and points to the interior. "Get in and see what's new on the dashboard."

Hank sits behind the steering wheel and scans the dash. "I don't see anything new."

Travis taps his zelcom and says, "Call Hank."

A small silver knob near the steering column illuminates and Hank stiffens. "That's new."

"Pull on the knob," Travis says. Hank pulls, and Travis's voice fills the car. "Hello, Hank."

"How the heck did you do that?" Hank's voice resonates from Travis's wrist.

"Push the knob," Travis says.

Hank does as instructed, and the knob returns to silver, like the others on the dash.

"Zophie mentioned you'd like a car phone. This knob allows you to have one without anyone wondering where you got it."

"But how can a knob be a phone?"

"You saw what happens when someone calls you. To make a call, pull on the knob, and say, 'Call Zophie.'"

Hank's fingers fly to the knob. "Call Zophie."

My zelcom vibrates and I tap it. "Hello, Hank. Can you hear me?"

"Damn straight, I can hear you!"

Travis chuckles. "When you push the knob, the call will end."

"Bye, Zophie." Hank pushes the knob.

"When you want to call Zophie or me, say our names. For anyone else, say the phone number."

"I just say anyone's phone number? The knob knows them all?"

Travis nods.

Hank hops out of his car, wraps his brawny arms around Travis, and thumps him once on the back. "How . . .? Never mind. I don't need to know. Thank you, man. You just made me the happiest darn detective in the business."

"You're welcome, my friend. With all you've done to help us navigate your traditions, I'm glad to be able to help you."

Hank stays for dinner, but no longer. I walk with him to the front door and offer payment for the information about Amber. He refuses the money, pointing to his car in the driveway. "You guys gave me a space-age car phone. I'll *call* you when I have some goods on Filmore's other patients."

I wave goodbye to Hank and glance toward the woods. Vad and Zack should be here by now.

When I step inside and close the door, the twins run up to me with Gram behind them. Krissie rubs her eyes, and Kayla says, "Can we watch Cindewella again?"

I kneel on one knee and pull both girls into a hug. "How would you two like to lie on my bed with me and read *The Magic Slipper*?"

"Yes," they squeal.

Gram rubs my hair. "Good night, dear. We'll talk to Quaid tomorrow."

When the twins are dressed in their pajamas, we snuggle and read on the big bed. Soon their eyelids begin to droop. I dim the lights and cover us with a blanket. I stare blankly at the twinkling lights on the ceiling, wondering why Zack and Vad aren't here yet. I picture Zack's name on Owen's list, and my breath catches. I won't be able to sleep until Zack gets here.

CHAPTER 22

Zack backs away from a snarling bear, one step at a time, closer to the ravine behind him. I'm running to grab him, to reach him in time, but I don't make it. He falls off the cliff—and my eyes fly open.

Kayla and Krissie sleep soundly, nestled together on Travis's side of the bed. It looks like Travis didn't come to bed at all. I ease my feet to the floor and rise. Tiptoeing to the bathroom, I see no sign that Travis has shaved or showered recently.

I grab my robe and leave the bedroom door open so the girls will know to come downstairs when they wake. Down the hallway, I push open Zack's door to see unruffled bedcovers. Panic wells in my throat.

I move quietly downstairs, the cold wood chilling my bare feet. "Travis? Zack?" I call from the bottom of the stairs. No one answers. I scan the hall and glance toward Gram's bedroom. Her closed door means she's probably still sleeping.

When I enter the kitchen, Travis rises from his chair and moves toward me, his face creased with concern. "I heard you calling, but my mouth was full. Are you okay?"

"Did you come to bed last night?" I ask, knowing the answer since I see he's wearing his blue jeans and plaid shirt from yesterday.

Travis shakes his head and kisses my neck. The bristles on his chin prickle my skin.

"Is Zack here?"

Travis nudges me to sit at the counter and takes the stool beside me. Einstein places a plate of muffins in front of us. "While you eat," Travis says, "I'll tell you what I think is delaying Zack and Vad."

"Delay? You said Zack would be here last night." I push the plate away and glare at him.

"I thought he would be." Travis scratches his chin. "I fell asleep in the chair, waiting."

"We should go to Zelfar and make sure he's okay." I start to rise, and Travis takes both my hands in his.

"Sweetheart, I don't think you realize the importance of Zack's role in building the zilimite initiator. He can't leave in the middle of an experiment."

"I know, but—"

He presses a finger to my lips. "I'll go to Zelfar. I promise I'll be back this afternoon with Zack—if he's completed his experiments."

"Promise?"

"I have to check on an experiment in the honey lab today, so I *will* be back this afternoon."

Each new honey experiment could be *the one*. I should run a viability test on Brita's blood sample.

A ray of sunlight peaks through the thin opening in the curtains and glows on my husband's cheek. I smile and meet his lips. We kiss for a long moment and then he touches his forehead to mine. "I'll get cleaned up, zip over to Zelfar, and be back before you miss me."

I give his hand a gentle squeeze of agreement. Birds chirp in a melodious chorus, a sound I've come to enjoy. I wonder if I'll miss the singing birds when I no longer come to America.

"The twins are in our bed," I say. "I'll get them up."

Before Travis and I reach the bottom of the stairway, two giggling little girls patter down the steps. Travis picks up both girls and kisses their cheeks.

"Owie." Kayla winces and rubs the side of her face.

"Sorry, sweetie. Daddy needs to shave." He sets the girls down next to me and strides up the stairs, two at a time.

While Travis showers and shaves, I bathe and feed the girls, then the twins and I join Gram in the living room. Travis's footsteps echo from the hall and he stops in the living room doorway.

"I'll be back soon." He throws kisses to us, and I hear the front door close when he exits.

When the girls take their naps, Gram reads in her favorite chair, and I spend an hour in the lab getting ready to test the next batch of synthetic honey—and to distract myself from worrying about Zack. After removing a small vial of Brita's blood from the preservation chamber, I insert it into the test tube. My shoulders relax when the tube glows green. Her sample is still viable. Using a glass dropper, I put a dab of blood in three indentations on a crystillium tray. Then I return the samples to the preservation chamber.

When I enter the house through the back door, I hear the squeak of the front door. Rushing down the hall, I barely give Zack enough time to throw his jacket on a hook before I circle my arms around him, hugging him like he's been gone for months. Travis smiles at me from behind Zack.

"Mom, come on. I can't breathe." Zack fakes a cough and wiggles free.

"Sorry, son," I say, releasing him. "How did your experiments go?"

"They got complicated. I had to recalculate the water-to-zilimite ratio, but everyone is zapped at how much power the zilimite initiator provides—more than enough to restore transportation and communication simultaneously. Wait 'til you see the initiator."

I'm thrilled everyone appreciates Zack's contribution, but right now, I'm glad we're all together. Except . . . "Where are Vad and Clay?" I ask.

Travis drapes an arm across my shoulders. "Vad said Clay wasn't at Health Dome. After he took Zack and me to the falls, Vad was going to Clay's homedome. I told Vad to hurry because you and Gram need him today. Maybe he's on his way here with Clay right now."

Gram joins us from the living room, about to speak, when my wrist vibrates. "It's Hank," I say.

"Hello, Zophie?" Hank's voice is loud and tense.

"Yes, Hank, it's me. What's wrong?"

"Did you know Clay is in the hospital?"

My knees nearly buckle. I sink onto the bench in the hallway, and Travis crouches next to me. "No." My voice catches. "I didn't know. What happened? What hospital?"

"He's at Providence. And get this: Clay's got amnesia."

"Nooo! That isn't possible!"

"Zophie, are you okay?" Hank's voice booms from my wrist. "Are you going to the hospital?"

"Yes, yes, of course," I say through hitched breaths. "I'm on my way."

"Okay, me too. See you there."

A tap with my trembling fingers ends the call. Adrenalin courses through my body as I reach for my coat. "Travis—," I start, but he's already standing, dangling the car keys.

"I'll drive," he says.

Gram lays a soothing hand on my arm. "Go on, dear. We'll visit Quaid after you help Clay. Einstein and I will tot-watch."

CHAPTER 23

The damp, pungent air annoys me more than usual as we rush down the rain-drenched walkway into the garage. Travis opens the passenger door for me, and I stop short. "I forgot the telephone book. We need the address."

Travis smiles. "We don't need phone books or paper maps anymore. I updated our zelcoms. Now we can find any location on this side of the portal."

I love my husband. He's the smartest man in the whole world—in two whole worlds. I buckle my seatbelt, and Travis steers the Jeep toward Portland. When we get to the hospital, Travis parks in the first space he can find, and we hurry to the entrance.

Hank is waiting inside the large glass doors. "Janet went up to Clay's room. Come on."

My mind whirls with questions, but Travis and I silently follow Hank into the elevator and up to the third floor. I spot Janet, her red hair unmistakable, standing in front of two women wearing white dresses and white shoes. I walk quickly toward her, but before I can ask for Clay's room number, Janet waves her arms at the women and screams, "Where is Clay? Someone needs to tell me right now!"

"I'm sorry, Dr. Murphy," says the short, stout woman. "No one saw him leave. We don't know where he went."

"Well, you better get some people looking."

"I've alerted security," the taller nurse says. "They're already searching for him."

I touch Janet's arm and she flinches.

"Zophie! I'm so sorry. Clay isn't in his room. If he walked out of here, it's all my fault."

I put my hand on her shoulder, and she throws her arms around me.

"How can it be your fault?" I ask, patting her back.

She releases me, pulls a tissue from the box on a nearby counter, and wipes her nose. "Because I wouldn't let them put him in the psych ward where he would have been locked in."

"Take me to his room," I say more calmly than I would have thought possible. "I want to see where he was."

I follow Janet down the corridor, with Travis and Hank behind me, past three open doors and into the fourth. The narrow room has two beds, both empty, one with rumpled sheets. A striped curtain hangs between the two headboards. Beside each bed is a simple chair.

Janet points at the bed by the window. "That one's Clay's."

Hank and Travis stare at the rumpled bed, and I walk to the large glass window. Rain and fog blur the trees and grass below. Where could Clay have gone?

I turn to Janet. "Hank told me on the phone Clay has amnesia. Tell me everything."

"When I came into work this morning, I saw Clay's picture on the counter. They had him listed as a John Doe. They were still processing him, so I made the nurse take me to him. He . . .

he didn't recognize me." Janet pauses to wipe the tears from her cheeks. "He didn't know who he was, where he was, or how he got here. I told him his name was Clay, but he just shook his head. He wouldn't let me touch him."

"I'm so sorry." I pull Janet into another hug, hoping that consoling her will ease my pain, too.

Janet eases herself from my arms. "A nurse said when she was coming into the hospital, someone stopped her and told her she needed to help this guy. The guy—Clay—acted disoriented and couldn't remember his name, so she brought him inside for evaluation." Janet sucks in a sob. "He's gone now, and I don't know how to find him."

"How long has Clay been missing?" Travis asks.

"I was with him an hour ago. I had to run over to my clinic, and when I got back, he was gone."

I wonder where someone with no memory would go in Portland. An hour. He could be anywhere, especially if he got a ride. But Hank knows how to get information.

"Hank," I say. "Can your contacts help us find Clay?"

Hank puts an arm around his daughter. "Don't worry, honey. I'll find him." He looks over Janet's shoulder at me. "I'll find him, Zophie. I promise to let you know as soon as I discover anything."

"Thank you."

After Hank and Janet leave, Travis and I search the closet and bathroom, hoping to find a clue others might not recognize. We find nothing. As soon as we're back to our Jeep, I snap my seat belt, then tap my zelcom.

"Clay? Clay, are you there?"

No answer. My heart feels like lead inside my chest. If Quaid did this, he may have taken Clay's zelcom. I gaze out my window. "Clay is probably wandering out there somewhere."

Travis touches my thigh. "Maybe Clay's instincts took him back to Zelfar."

Through watery eyes, I gaze at Travis. "I need to tell you why Gram and I must talk to Quaid. He's done something terrible."

"Seriously?" Travis wipes my cheek with his finger.

"Quaid brought Owen's daughter, April, to America six years ago, and somehow gave her amnesia. She's been living here as Amber, with no memory of Zelfar. I think he did the same thing to Rudy. Four people are missing from Zelfar, and now I'm afraid Quaid has done the same thing to Clay."

"Missing people and Quaid in the middle of it?" Travis rubs his hands on the steering wheel. "How could a Zelfarian, especially an elder, do something so merciless?"

"That's what Gram and I plan to find out."

"Gram will get answers. Quaid respects her more than anyone. Zack can stay and help me run tests in the honey lab. I'll keep both twins, too. Vad will be all yours."

"Okay," I say weakly.

Travis starts the engine. "Let's search the streets for Clay, working outward from the hospital. Maybe we'll see him."

Drizzle and fog make searching difficult, and soon darkness makes it impossible. I can't imagine being alone here and not knowing anyone.

"Sweetheart." Travis lays his fingers over mine. "We should get home."

"I know." I touch my forehead to the cold glass window. Rain streaks the outside of the pane as tears streak my cheeks. The miles stretch on and on. When I think of life without Clay, my longing turns to rage. Quaid crossed the lines of decency by what he did to April and the others, and now he's attacked someone precious to me.

If he doesn't answer to Gram, he'll have to answer to me.

CHAPTER 24

By ten o'clock the next morning, Gram and I sit in Vad's transformed hands on our way to Quaid's homedome. My pulse races along with Vad's feet as he speeds across Zelfar. The orange juice I drank for breakfast floats unsettled in my stomach. Finally, Vad sets us at Quaid's entrance.

"Wait here," Gram says to Vad.

The door slides open, and Quaid, clad in teal zeltire, unusually pressed for him, stands in front of us. Even his short beard appears recently groomed. He smiles broadly at Gram. "Lilly. Zophie. Thanks for letting me know you were comin'. Nice to have zelcoms again. Come in."

Gram returns his smile and we follow him into his living orb.

"Have a seat," Quaid says, pointing to the dark green sofa facing his overstuffed chair.

Gram and I sit together. I glance at her serene face and wonder how she can look so calm and self-possessed. I clasp my clammy hands on my pants.

"Now, what can I do fer you two ladies?" He folds his hands

in his lap.

Gram squeezes my forearm, a familiar gesture when she wants me to remain silent.

"Quaid, you and I have known each other for many decades, perhaps longer than any two people in Zelfar." Gram's tone is sweet, as if she were talking to me.

"Yep, that we have." He crosses his legs and leans back in his chair. "I'd say best friends fer most of those years, too."

Gram half smiles. "Something has just come to my attention that I'd like you to explain. It involves April. You remember her."

Quaid uncrosses his legs, and his back straightens. "Yeah, I remember her. She was the first one to lose a baby."

Gram's posture matches Quaid's. "Not long after losing her baby, April was taken through the portal to America." Her tone has lost its sweetness. "April says you are the one who took her and left her there. I want to know if that's true and if so, why you would do such a thing."

"Me?" Quaid's voice cracks in a raspy pitch. "Why would I take anyone to America?"

If I were interrogating him, I'd jump up and shout in his face, and probably get us thrown out of Quaid's dome.

My grandmother, however, remains calm. "That was my question, Quaid. Why?"

"Why?" Quaid stands and walks slowly around his chair. "I'll tell ya why. After April lost her baby, she was miserable—cryin' all the time, insistin' she was a freak. Made her husband miserable, too. I felt sorry fer the guy. Said he wished he didn't have to listen to her cryin' every day. I knew she'd be okay in America. She'd fit right in with people always feelin' sorry fer themselves."

My fists tighten on my thighs and I clench my teeth to keep from shouting at him.

He stares at Gram for several seconds before his taut, indignant jaw sags, and he lowers his head. "I didn't know babies were gonna keep dyin'. April might of got over it if she knew it wasn't just her young 'un."

"Then why didn't you bring her back?" I blurt.

"I couldn't."

I open my mouth to say I don't believe him, catch Gram's subtle head shake, and close it again.

Gram gazes at Quaid. "How did you erase April's memory?"

"Look, Lilly, I admit I took April to America, but I didn't have nothin' to do with wiping anyone's memory. That was . . . I mean . . . I think it's time fer you two to go."

"Did you take Rudy through the portal, too?" I jump to my feet, hands clenched, nostrils flared. "And what have you done with Clay?"

Quaid throws a hand in the air. "Rudy was a troublemaker—always complainin'. He belongs in that other world, and I ain't sorry 'bout leavin' him there."

Gram stands and gently touches my elbow. "All right, Quaid. We'll leave now. Thank you for telling us the truth."

I twist and face my grandmother. "Wait a minute, Gram. What about Clay and the other people who are missing?"

I whip my head toward Quaid. "Where is Clay?"

He slouches and mumbles, "Don't know nothin' 'bout Clay."

My grandmother taps my arm. "Come along, Zophie."

I start to resist again, but she grasps my elbow and squeezes.

"Toss pine, Quaid," Gram says and nudges me to the exit. As soon as we step outside, she releases my arm and says to Vad, "Take us to my homedome."

As soon as Vad sets us on the platform in front of her dome, I ask, "Why did you stop interrogating Quaid?" I shouldn't question Gram, but Quaid can't get away with this.

"He explained enough. Be patient, dear. You'll understand." Gram pats my hand, but this time the gesture doesn't console me.

"What will I understand?" I ask, following her into the center corridor. "Why Quaid thinks he can covertly banish people from our world when he thinks they're too unhappy to fit in here?"

Gram waves her hand toward her living orb. "Have some cooiberry juice, dear, and relax for a bit. Feel free to use my serenity orb. I'll be right back."

Watching her walk away, my pulse thumps at my temples. The adrenalin invigorates me, and I ignore the offer to use her serenity simulator. Instead, I plop into an overstuffed chair and strum my fingers on the smooth fabric. Gram's homebot appears with a frosty glass on a small tray.

I slowly sip the cooiberry juice and start formulating a plan to bring April back to Zelfar. Probably Rudy, too. I'll ask Hank to look for the other two as well. But first, I must find Clay. Thinking of Clay, alone and lost, my hand tightens around the glass. Quaid is despicable.

"I see you decided to forego the serenity orb," Gram says, interrupting my thoughts. "Your pensive stare tells me you're still pondering Quaid's behavior."

"I don't see how I can ever understand what he's done."

Gram sits on the ottoman in front of my chair and extends a small flat device. I take the thin white square, wider than my hand, and turn it over. "What is it?"

"An action recorder. Old technology, but still functional. It contains a story you need to see and hear."

"What kind of story?"

"A true story about human nature."

"I don't have time to listen to stories."

"You will take the time," Gram says. "Opinions can change with awareness."

Gram taps the top of the recorder. "Watch the screen."

A three-dimensional picture appears as if I'm gazing through a small window. A young man, maybe age twenty, waves his hand, looking directly at me.

"*Keep the camera on me 'n' my dad,*" he says.

"*I don't want to record you and your father.*" It's Gram's voice. Younger, but still Gram's.

"*Perty please, jist this once? If I can show my dad how he acts, maybe he'll change.*" It's Quaid's voice. I recognize the drawl.

"*How do you know he'll be angry at you?*" Younger Gram asks.

" *'Cause he's always angry. I'm sure I've done somethin' to make him mad. It's the same thing every day. I never talk back, but this time I will. You stay there by the tree and keep recordin'. I'll go inside, and when he starts yellin' at me, I'll run out here. Try not to let him see ya.*"

Quaid enters a dome.

The image quivers, and Gram's younger voice whispers, "*I don't like this.*"

Quaid bursts from the dome and runs a few feet toward the recorder. A large man chases him and grabs Quaid by the shirt, tossing him to the ground.

"*Dad, stop! I didn't do nothin' wrong.*" Quaid's voice is shrill, panicked. *He crosses his arms in front of his face to block his father's fist that's hurling toward him.*

"*I'll teach you to talk back to me,*" his father shouts in an angry voice. "*You can't even use proper English. You're just like your grandfather. I should never have brought him with us. One of you is certain to get us kicked out of this community. We'll be forced to live on our own in the wilderness, or worse yet, get sent back where we came from.*"

Quaid rolls onto his stomach, struggling to get to his knees, but his father knocks him back down, punching him in the ribs. Quaid cringes and cries out.

I feel nauseous. This is so much worse than the woman striking her child on the train in America.

Gram sniffles and gasps. Her hands must have been trembling, because the image of Quaid's dad beating him shakes blurrily on the screen.

Tears sting my eyes, and I turn away, pushing the recorder toward my grandmother.

Gram pushes it back to me. "I know it's difficult to watch, but you must see the rest."

"This is our Garden of Eden," Quaid's father shouts. *"I'll not let the devil in you cause us to be cast from it."*

A small, wrinkled, and stoop-shouldered old man appears on the screen and yells, "Stop it, son! The boy ain't devil-possessed. Stop it, now!"

The old man reaches up to halt the dad's fists from pummeling Quaid. A forceful strike from Quaid's father hits the helpless old man on the side of his head. The camera follows the old man as he flies a few feet through the air and lands with a loud thud, his body crumpled on the ground.

"What's wrong with you, man?" another male voice says loudly.

The camera swerves quickly to a tall man and swerves again to show two men grabbing Quaid's father. They topple Quaid's dad and pin him to the ground.

The screen shows people gathering around. The camera follows someone rushing to the old man. Quaid's grandfather's head lies askew on the ground.

A different man looks up from the body and shakes an angry fist at Quaid's dad. "He's dead! You killed your own father!"

"String him up," someone yells.

"I'll get the rope," another shouts.

I gasp and stare in disbelief at the small screen. This is not at all like the Zelfar where I grew up.

"It was an accident! I didn't mean to hit him." Quaid's father squirms, still pinned under forceful hands.

A smooth male voice says, "But you definitely meant to harm your son. You took an oath of nonviolence when you chose to come to Zelfar. You've broken that oath."

I don't recognize the voice, but the words could have come from my great-grandfather's journal.

More angry voices: *"An eye for an eye,"* and *"We can't have a killer among us."*

The recorder focuses on Quaid, who tugs relentlessly on the old man's lifeless form, wailing, "Grampa! Grampa! I'm so sorry." Heavy sobbing echoes from the recorder, and the screen goes dark.

Tears drip from my cheeks. One lands on the small screen. I wipe my face with the back of my hand and dry the screen with my sleeve.

Gram pats my knee.

I give the recorder to Gram and ask, "Did they hang Quaid's dad?"

"No." Gram puts the recorder on the table next to the chair. "My father restored order by reminding everyone that we left that kind of vengeance in the old world. He said if we were willing to become a lynch mob, we should go back to America and forget about building a peaceful society."

"They didn't let Quaid's dad continue to hurt him, did they?" Minutes earlier, I'd wanted to harm him myself—now I feel sad for him.

"My father proposed that volunteers watch over Quaid's dad, whose name was Jeb. An escort accompanied him everywhere he went for twelve months, and he had to attend daily meditation sessions with my mother." Gram smiles. "My mother was the community counselor."

"That doesn't seem like adequate punishment for killing someone." I might have joined the lynch mob.

"For Quaid's dad, it was. No one trusted or respected him any longer. He wasn't banished, but he was never part of the community again. Jeb knew if he ever yelled at or struck Quaid, or anyone, he would be confined to a small dome. My mother told me Jeb lived in constant paranoia."

I picture Quaid wailing over his grandfather's limp body. "Did Quaid's dad live with him and his mom after that happened?"

"Quaid's mother had transcended while giving birth to him. Quaid was given his own homedome, but he sorely missed his grandfather. I often overheard him pleading with my father to send Jeb back to America. Quaid was convinced America was where his dad belonged."

Gram picks up the recorder and stands. "That incident was the catalyst for creating serenity simulators. You can see why negative impulses had to be controlled. Otherwise, Zelfar could never be the peaceful world my father envisioned."

I stand, too. "Did you show me that story because you think Quaid's past justifies his current behavior?"

"I don't condone Quaid's actions, but I do understand them."

"Well, I don't. He's banished four people from Zelfar. And now Clay. We don't do that to one another."

"And I don't think Quaid, all on his own, would do that either. We need to speak with Bayl."

The pieces fall together in my mind and I gasp. "Bayl! This is why neither of them would talk to me about Rudy."

Gram lays a hand against her breastbone, the corners of her mouth curling down. "And I appointed Bayl to take my place as an elder."

"What would cause Bayl to exile people?"

"I don't know." Gram steps toward the doorway. "Let's go have a discussion with him."

Outside Gram's dome, hoverspheres zoom above our heads, sunlight glinting off their clear shells. The restoration of hover transportation should make me happy. Instead, I have to interrogate elders who banish Zelfarians to America.

We have Vad, so we don't need a hoversphere. I instruct him to take us to History Dome, the likeliest place we'll find Bayl in the early afternoon. Several yards from our destination, Vad slows his pace and informs me that Bayl and Quaid are standing outside the dome, near the back entrance and appear to be arguing.

"Stop," I tell Vad. "Can you hear what they're saying?"

"Yes, I can hear them, and so can you." The android cups his hand over one of my ears and does the same with Gram.

Quaid's voice emanates through Vad's fingers. "I'm tellin' you, Zophie and Lilly know we took Rudy and April to America . . . well, they know I did."

"Do they know why Rudy and April cannot remember Zelfar?" Bayl's voice asks.

"I didn't tell 'em nothin'. And your memory wipin' must wear off, 'cause April told Lilly I was the one who took her to America." Quaid's tone has a slight edge, like he's afraid of Bayl. "What are we gonna do?"

"We do nothing." Bayl's voice is calm. "Let them think you have operated alone."

"What if Rudy starts rememberin' and April remembers more?"

"They will not."

"How can you be sure?" Quaid's voice squeaks.

"Trust me," Bayl replies firmly.

"What about Zophie 'n' her grandmother? What if they keep questionin' me? Or what if they bring April back?"

"You do not need to worry about them." Bayl's tone reflects uncharacteristic impatience. "You have a long history with Lilly. She will not act against you. Zophie has too much at stake with her twin situation to say anything to anyone. Go home and forget about this."

"But Zophie said Clay is missin', too. Did you do somethin'

to him?"

"I said forget about this . . . unless you want to forget *everything.*"

Quaid doesn't respond.

Bayl could threaten to steal my memory and I still wouldn't cast people out of Zelfar. I don't have a lot of patience with Quaid at the moment.

Vad drops his hands from our ears.

"Vad," I say. "Go see if Quaid and Bayl are still there." He leaves in a blur. A moment later, he returns and says, "Quaid walked in the direction of his homedome. Bayl entered History Dome."

"I'm glad we chose Vad instead of a hoversphere," I say to Gram. "Now we know that Bayl is responsible for the memory wiping, and that he, alone, is responsible for Clay's amnesia. In fact, Quaid seems intimidated by Bayl." I start toward the main entrance, determined to confront the devious elder.

Gram grasps my elbow. "Zophie, stop."

"How else are we going to find out how Bayl wipes people's memories?"

Gram asks, "Where in Zelfar could Bayl hide something from everyone else?"

I cover my mouth and whisper, "The archive orb."

"Exactly. Let's hope he isn't there right now."

I grab Vad's arm. "I'm taking Vad with us."

CHAPTER 25

Gram leads Vad and me inside History Dome, directly to the corridor with the secret stairway that descends to the archive orb located beneath the dome. She waves a small aquamarine pyramid at the wall, and when the opening appears, we hurry down the single flight of stairs.

Vad steps into the only three-sided orb in Zelfar. "Extraordinary," he says softly. To my grandmother, he adds, "I applaud the geometrical complexities chosen for the design of this orb."

"Thank you. My father's appreciation of pyramids was my inspiration."

I glance at the small desk that conceals my great-grandfather's journal. Nearly four years have passed since Bayl brought me here to read the journal and prepare me for going to America in search of protizine. Bayl introduced me to the strange world on the other side of the portal. I had trusted him completely.

"What are we looking for?" Vad asks, apparently assuming he is here to help search.

"We need you to stand guard and warn us if you hear Bayl or Quaid approach," I say. Besides Gram, Bayl and Quaid are the only ones able to access this place. Travis and I are the only other people who even know this pyramid exists.

"We can use Vad's help," Gram says. "He can listen while he searches. In answer to your question, Vad, I think we are looking for a small electromagnetic device or a serum and an injection tool. To erase memories, electrical impulses in the brain must be triggered by either a pulse emitted at certain frequencies or specific chemicals injected into the bloodstream."

Gram walks toward a large painting and waves her hand. The painting and the wall behind it slide to the left, revealing shelves, racks, and drawers. "This storage area seems like the best place to start looking." Gram turns from the exposed racks to Vad. "You search the shelves along the back wall while Zophie and I go through the drawers."

I open a drawer and feel like a character in a spy movie, sneaking around to find a hidden object. I hope Bayl doesn't catch us. He might wipe our memories, too. Searching among the handbags that Gram and I have used on our trips to America makes me grateful for Zelfar where handbags aren't needed. I don't have to carry money or fear my things will be snatched from me. We've had no need to steal—until now. If we find whatever Bayl uses to erase memories, I'll be happy to take such a horrible possession from him.

We look in every drawer and on every shelf, twice, and turn up nothing.

"What are we going to do now?" I say, pushing my hair behind one ear.

Gram seals off the storage area, puts her hands on her hips, and gazes at Vad and me. "Okay, think creatively and search to the three corners of this pyramid."

Gram examines two paintings on the walls. Vad searches

every seam in the sofa. I inspect the cedar desk. Sitting in the large swivel chair, my fingers nostalgically open the small drawer containing my great-grandfather's journal. Gently grasping the worn leather cover, I lay the journal on the desk. Touching the first crisp page, I realize the book holds the secrets of Zelfar's origin, not the secrets of Bayl's deception. I doubt Bayl is recording his clandestine acts.

With the care and respect the antique deserves, I slide the journal back into the drawer—except the top edge of the leather binding catches on something. I hear a sharp click and feel a slight pressure across the top of my thighs.

My body goes stiff. "Gram? . . . Vad?"

Vad appears at my side, instantly deduces the situation, and thrusts his hand under the desk. When I no longer feel the pressure on my lap, I roll the chair backward and jump to my feet.

Gram glances excitedly between Vad and me. "What did you find?"

"A hidden shelf," Vad replies. He pulls his hand from under the desk and extends an object toward Gram—a green octagon, about an inch high and slightly wider than Vad's palm. Gram motions for him to lay the item on the desk, and for several seconds, the three of us study the mysterious object.

Unable to figure out what it is, I grasp the flat octagon and turn it over and see the same smooth, hard surface on the underside. My fingers press along the short sides. At the fourth press, two thin rods slide upward, like short straws.

A small screen appears in the center of the device. When I touch the screen, a date materializes—yesterday. I hold my breath, worried I may have activated something.

Vad extends his hand. "May I?"

I gladly place the device on his palm, thankful my memory hasn't been taken away.

Vad holds the octagon and closes his eyes. After a few seconds, he says, "The design and mineral composition enable this device to create electrical pulses, powered by a small green diamond. To activate the pulses, a hexagonal prism must be inserted into this indentation." Vad points to a six-sided impression on one edge of the octagon. "The prism would be unique to this device, likely crafted from clear crystal. With the prism imbedded, the octagon will emit an electrical airwave, allowing access to the hippocampus and basal ganglia within the brain."

Gram taps a finger to her lips. "Vad, can you recreate the prism?"

My mind reels with the possibility of returning Amber's memories of Zelfar. "Will we be able to reverse the memory-altering process?"

"There is a high probability I can recreate the prism," Vad answers. "I cannot yet determine if the device will restore as well as erase memory function."

"Can you also duplicate the device?" Gram asks.

"Yes."

"How long would that take?"

He briefly stares past us and then tells Gram. "Two days."

"Very well." She closes Vad's fingers around the green object. "Keep this device until you're finished. Then I'll put the original back where we found it."

Vad slips the octagon into his oversized shirt pocket.

My jaw drops. "Put it back? No! Bayl might use it again. Shouldn't we inform him we have the device?"

Gram's eyes, calm and focused, meet mine. "We have no proof Bayl made this device. I want to better understand its capabilities before we confront him. More than three years have passed since the last missing person was reported."

"What about Clay?"

"I don't think the community knows Clay is missing yet." When I open my mouth to argue, she says, "Zophie, you're going to have to trust me. I want to solve this as much as you."

I sigh, trying to relax my shoulders. How will I avoid confronting Bayl for two days? "Gram, after I check on Brita today, I'm going to America so I can be with Travis and our children. I should talk with Dr. Filmore again, too. He's our best chance of finding the other two missing people, and he might have an idea where to find Clay. Do you want to come?"

Gram shakes her head. "I want to talk with Bayl. I won't confront him. I'll tell him what Quaid did to April and Rudy, as if he doesn't know, and ask what he thinks we should do about it."

"I don't like that idea. You know how easily he lies. Do you really think you'll learn anything useful?"

"I have to try," she says. "I gave Bayl his elder position, and if I must, I'll take it away. We have his memory-wiping device, so don't worry about me."

I wish I felt as fearless as Gram. Vad and I follow her from the hidden pyramid and out of History Dome. Each step of the way, my stomach flutters with worry about Gram talking to Bayl alone. At the edge of the platform, I tap my zelcom and call for a hoversphere.

I give my grandmother a long hug. "Please take Vad with you when you talk to Bayl."

"I will, dear." She kisses my cheek. "I'll see you soon."

"Do not worry, Zophie," Vad says. "I will duplicate the device and bring Gram to you in two days." He beams at Gram as if pleasing her is the only incentive he needs. I know how he feels.

When I turn toward my sphere, Vad touches my shoulder. "Hil just informed me Brita is to be moved to the new Health Dome in one hour."

"Why did no one tell me they were moving her today?" I ask.

Vad blinks and says, "Hil does not have that information."

I climb into the hoversphere, worried about Brita and wishing Gram were coming with me to America.

I enter the temporary health dome and see no one in the living orb or center corridor. I rush to Brita's orb.

"Zophie?" Elka smiles when I walk through the doorway. My hand goes to my chest at the sight of two unfamiliar neuroscientists standing on either side of the health tube where Brita lies motionless inside. I walk to the taller of the two men.

"Is she okay?" I ask.

"Hello Zophie. My name is Dan. Brita's condition is unchanged." He inserts himself between me and the health tube.

I flinch back slightly and move to the end of the tube, relieved to see its green hue.

"Hello Zophie. I'm Mick." The shorter neurologist stands next to me and taps his zelcom. Brita's stats, close to normal and steady, display above her tube. "We're preparing her for transport to Health Dome where she'll be placed in a neuro-tube." Mick lifts his chin. "We know you're Brita's health expert and we thank you for the care you and the other neurologists have given her."

"Mick and I are her neuro experts now," Dan says. "We'll provide her full care until she awakens."

I should be glad Brita will be constantly attended by brain experts, but I can't help feeling left out.

"Will the neuro-tube awaken her?" I ask

"In addition to maintaining vitals," Dan says, "the neuro-tube will allow us to monitor her brain activity and neurological system, but Mick and I cannot predict when Brita will awaken." He motions toward the door. "Please, let us complete our preparation. Like I told her mother, you may visit Brita once she is settled at Health Dome. Toss pine."

"Toss pine," I say. Nodding for Elka to follow, I trod from Brita's orb, trying to convince myself I'm doing what's best for Brita.

At least I can tell Zack that Brita will be in a new type of healing tube, one that may awaken her. She'll be in the care of dedicated brain experts, too. But I'm Brita's health expert, and I should have been informed that Dan and Mick were replacing the other two neurologists with whom I've been collaborating. As soon as I visit Filmore and find Clay, I'll be back to see this neuro-tube.

CHAPTER 26

Einstein greets me when I step through the falls, and within moments, I walk into the house.

"Hi, Mom." Zack comes into the hall from the living room. "Is Brita awake?"

"Not yet, but I talked with two neurologists who have developed a neuro-tube for her and are now overseeing her care. We can visit Brita at the new Health Dome when we go home again."

"Aren't you still her health expert?"

"I'll be checking on her, but I'm not a brain expert, and that's what she needs."

"Are they going to wake her up?"

"I hope so."

Zack sighs and glances at the stairway. "Kayla and Krissie are taking a nap. I'll be out in the lab with Dad and Einstein." He grabs a handful of candies from the dish on the hall table and walks outside.

I amble into the living room and tap my zelcom.

"Hello, Hank."

"Hi, Zophie. Haven't found him yet, but I've got some leads," he says. "I'll let you know when I find something worth telling."

We end the call, and I sink into my favorite chair, staring at the fire as if it can somehow give me answers. Maybe Dr. Filmore will have insight about where to find Clay.

I tap my zelcom again.

"Dr. Filmore's office," says a pleasant voice.

"Good afternoon. This is Dr. Zophie Green. I would like to schedule a consultation with Dr. Filmore about one of his patients."

"It looks like Dr. Filmore can squeeze you in at eleven o'clock tomorrow. Is that a good time for you?"

"Yes, that would be fine. Thank you."

I hear the back door shut, and a moment later Travis walks into the living room. "There you are." He takes my hand and pulls me to my feet, giving me a welcome-home kiss. "I'm surprised you're back so soon." He sits in the chair, pulling me to perch on his knees. "Did Quaid confess?"

"Quaid admitted to bringing April and Rudy to America, but he isn't the mastermind. And he isn't the one who created a way to erase memories."

"Bayl," Travis says flatly.

I lift an eyebrow.

"He likes control," Travis says. "Shortly after Bayl was appointed an elder, I overheard my dad saying he didn't understand why Lilly would give her position to him. Dad said Bayl had an unhealthy penchant for power."

"I always trusted Bayl, especially when he brought us here, desperate for our help in saving Zelfar." I lean into Travis's shoulder. "How could I be so fooled?"

Travis rubs my hair. "There's no doubt Bayl cares about protecting Zelfar's future."

"Sure, as long as he gets to choose who lives there." I lift my head. "But he won't be able to erase anyone else's memory. Gram and I found his device, and Vad is duplicating it right now."

"What devi—?"

We hear pattering footfalls on the stairs, and our girls enter the living room. I stand and whisk Krissie into my arms. Kayla straddles her dad's shins, urging him to bounce her. If Bayl ever tried to cast one of my children from Zelfar, I'd become his worst nightmare.

* * *

Morning arrives with the usual mist and gray sky. I startle awake from another bad dream: I return to Zelfar to confront Bayl and accidentally wipe out everyone's memory.

After breakfast with my family, I drive alone on Highway 30, frequently peering on either side of the road, hoping to see Clay. By the time I reach the parking lot at the clinic, rain splatters hard against the windshield. I pull the Jeep into an open space near the entrance, grab my umbrella, and sprint through the puddles.

I open the door to the psychiatrist's waiting area. Phew, that smell again. Dr. Filmore stands by the receptionist's desk, probably waiting for me. If that potent, earthy smell is his cologne, and it makes others as uncomfortable as me, he must be a lonely guy.

"Dr. Green, nice to see you again." Filmore graciously takes my umbrella and places it in a brass container by the door. "Please, come in."

"Thank you for working me into your schedule."

Dr. Filmore motions for me to sit in the chair in front of his desk. He sits in a swivel chair on the other side and pushes up his black-rimmed glasses. Clasping his hands in front of him, he narrows his eyes.

I swallow hard and my hand rubs the stunner in my pocket.

"When I learned you treated one of my patients," he says, "I tried to find your number, but there is no listing for a Dr. Zophie Green in the Greater Seattle area."

"Oh, I'm across the border, the Vancouver, B.C. area." More like the portal, but he'll think I mean Canada.

"Hmm, perhaps that explains it." His square little shoulders relax, but his gaze remains steady. "Here in the U.S., treating another doctor's patients is not customary."

Unsure of how to reply, I remain silent, forcing myself to hold his stare.

"I'm willing to overlook your indiscretion, Dr. Green, but only if you'll share what you learned from Amber."

I lean back, mirroring his more relaxed pose, and say, "I understand Amber was referred to you soon after she was found with amnesia. How many other amnesia cases do you have?"

He chuckles. His thick, almost rectangular mustache comically obscures his upper lip, but I don't smile.

"You're bold, Dr. Green, to question me about my patients. Are you looking to treat them, too?"

"No. That was never my intention. Amber's story is similar to those of my own amnesia patients."

He lifts an eyebrow. "How many cases do you have?"

"Two." I'm sure that's the number I gave him before. "My patients also talk of flying spheres and domes, like scenes from the same science fiction movie."

Dr. Filmore doesn't seem surprised. "If you were from the U.S., we wouldn't be having this conversation." He reaches under his desk, and I hear a faint click. He then lays four folders in front of him. I lean forward, straining to read the names on the labels to no avail, wondering if every wooden desk has a hidden compartment.

"These are notes from hypnotherapy sessions with my

amnesia patients." Dr. Filmore places his hand on the folders. "I now have four of them—just got a new one yesterday."

I gaze at the folders, perplexed by the doctor's willingness to show me where he keeps them and even more so that he might share their contents. Janet is always careful what she shares about her patients regardless of where I'm from. Nevertheless, Filmore's new patient could be Clay and I'll take any information he'll give me.

I inhale slowly, hoping Dr. Filmore doesn't sense my excitement. My hand moves slowly toward the folders. "May I see your notes?"

"Not so fast." He slides the folders a little closer to his chest. "What did Amber reveal in her session with you?"

I have to give him something to get something, but I can't jeopardize my people in Zelfar. "She talked about water and a shiny wall."

Filmore grins. "What conclusions have you drawn?"

"I'm not sure. That's why I'm hoping you can help me." Lying is getting too easy.

Dr. Filmore strums his stubby fingers on the desk. "If you're willing to exchange patient secrets, maybe we can help each other with these unusual cases."

I bite my cheek. He'll never get my secrets. But somehow, I will get his.

Dr. Filmore stands, walks around his desk, and leans an elbow on the corner. Pushing the folders out of my reach, he says, "How about if we brainstorm what conclusions we might draw from our amnesia patients?"

"That sounds productive," I say, weighing the risks of snatching the folders and dashing out of the office.

"You said your patients are similar to Amber in that they all relive scenes from the same science fiction movies. What do you make of that?"

I shrug and wrap the edges of my long coat across my lap. The science I know about isn't fiction.

"Well," Dr. Filmore says, "I think they've all been to the same place."

I clench my lips to keep from agreeing. I know where they've all been.

"They may even have known each other."

"Interesting." I tilt my head and cross my arms.

"Two of my patients mentioned a man named Wade, so they have to be connected."

"Wade." I hope I don't slip and say Quaid. It's odd they all call him Wade. I wonder if Quaid told them his name was Wade. "One of my patients said that name as well."

Dr. Filmore leans against his desk and crosses his ankles, studying my face. "They also remember a waterfall and walking through a large glowing rock."

"Well, that can't be real," I blurt.

I take a long breath to regain my composure. Dr. Filmore's gaze is steady, waiting, as if he thinks I'm hiding something. I need to grab those folders, and as Hank would say, "Run like hell."

"Of course, it's not real," Dr. Filmore says. "But anything can *seem* real. What baffles me isn't what they remember, but what they *don't* remember. Did either of your patients lack knowledge of basic things like famous people and well-known landmarks—or fail to recognize one single animal or vehicle?"

"No. It's as if they'd never been to Earth before they showed up with amnesia." The idea of space travel could be a good diversion.

"I don't believe in aliens," he scoffs. "But I do believe in mind tampering. Maybe this Wade person experimented on these people."

"What? Why?" Blatz. I sound less professional every time I

open my mouth.

Dr. Filmore shrugs. "I don't know, but cases of amnesia are never this similar. I intend to find out why someone is altering people's memories."

"Are you looking for this Wade?" Did I just suggest he try to find Quaid?

"I don't have enough information to know where to search." He lifts a bushy brow. "Do you?"

Sighing deeply, looking as dejected as possible, I toss up a hand and say, "I was hoping you'd know where to look."

"If it's experimentation, the government is likely involved."

The government? Another subject I know nothing about. I wish Hank were here. "So, your government will help you search for Wade?"

Dr. Filmore glances at his photo wall, filled with eight-by-ten pictures of him shaking hands with other men. "How much do you know about our government, Dr. Green?"

"Not much." With an involuntary peek at my zelcom, I think how easily I could call Hank.

"Do you have to be somewhere?" Dr. Filmore asks.

"Soon," I say, eyeing the folders on his desk. "If I could study your notes, maybe I could be helpful."

"Did you bring your files with you?"

Dr. Filmore lifts the folders, and I make a desperate grab. My fingertips slip on the heavy paper, and the contents go flying. Dr. Filmore scrambles to collect the documents, but an eight-by-ten image of a man lands face up near my foot.

Faster than a robot, I grab the photo and clutch it to my chest.

"Do you know this man?" Dr. Filmore asks.

I flip over the photograph, hoping for an address. Nothing. I shake the photo at Dr. Filmore and shout, "Clay is my friend! Where is he?"

Dr. Filmore startles and stumbles back a step, gripping the

edge of his desk. "I'm sorry about your friend, but as far as I know, he's still at the hospital. I haven't seen him yet."

"If you haven't seen him, how did you get his picture?"

"It came with his referral paperwork." The doctor straightens his necktie. "If you hadn't been here before, I'd think this man is the reason you came to see me. It's interesting that your friend suddenly has amnesia. Do you know Amber and Johnny, too?"

I take a deep breath and meet his stare. "I didn't know Amber. Let me see your files, and I'll tell you if I recognize anyone else."

He nods pensively, then motions for me to stand at his desk. He opens the folders one at a time.

The labels read: Johnny Ford, Amber Smith, Linda Nelson, and John Doe. Inside John Doe's—Clay's—folder is a single sheet of paper and yesterday's date. I gaze again at Clay's picture. His eyes appear despondent, without the sparkle they'd have if my Clay were behind them.

When Dr. Filmore walks to his chair behind the desk, I slip Clay's photo into my handbag and set my zelcom to scan. I quickly flip through Linda Nelson's file and pause on her picture—Irene's face.

"Well?" Dr. Filmore tilts his square jaw. "Do you recognize Linda Nelson?"

I lay the folders on the desk. "It's curious our patients share a similar story under hypnosis, but I see no other connection. Who would have thought these cases that have been so perplexing would happen to someone I know?" I grip my handbag and sigh. "Where would a person with amnesia go?"

"Normally, to locate a missing person," Dr. Filmore says, "we'd look in places they frequented, but with amnesia, nothing may be familiar, especially if that person is not from here."

I ignore his brow lift and rise to go.

"One more thing," Dr. Filmore says, lifting a gold pen. He scratches over JOHN DOE and writes CLAY on the file tab. With pen poised, he looks up at me. "What is Clay's last name?"

"Um…" Zelfarians don't use surnames, and I don't remember the name Clay gave to Janet.

A trill emits from the bulky black phone on Dr. Filmore's desk. He lifts the handset and says, "I'm busy, Miss Edwards, what do you need? . . . Speak where? Oh, yes, my, yes. Tell them, yes . . ."

I walk quickly to the door, hurry past the receptionist's desk, and don't stop until I'm outside. Water pours in sheets off the awning that covers the entrance. I glance back at the door and wish I'd retrieved my umbrella. Wrapping my coat tightly around me, I rush through the downpour to my car. I'd rather be wet than face Dr. Filmore again.

Shivering, I toss my bag into the Jeep and slide behind the steering wheel. As I turn the ignition, icy water drips from my hair, splattering on my hand. I turn the heat as high as possible and hold my fingers over the vents, wondering what to do next.

"Dr. Green," says Dr. Filmore's voice, muffled by the rain, and I jump. His blurry form appears under the awning. My arms tingle as I quickly shift into reverse, back out of the parking space, shift again, and drive onto the street.

After a few blocks, I slap the steering wheel. "Where are you, Clay?" I shout. "Where are you?" How can I possibly know where to look?

An idea occurs to me, and I steer in the direction of Amber's shop.

CHAPTER 27

I pull my Jeep to the curb in front of Amber's shop and park behind a large black motorcycle. The brass bell dings as I enter, and the door closes with a soft clank. Taking short breaths to ease the strong scent of sandalwood, I walk toward the glass counter. Glancing toward the purple-curtained doorway, I expect to see Amber coming to greet her customer, but the gold moons and suns on the curtain remain motionless.

I swish the pine needles in the metal dish on the counter, waiting for her to emerge. I sigh, thinking she must be giving someone a chakra treatment.

A muffled giggle emits from behind the curtain. I walk around the glass case and pull back the drape.

"Amber?" I call. "It's Zophie, I mean Dr. Green. Are you here?"

Another giggle resounds, this time louder. I step into the narrow hallway and walk past the room where I hypnotized Amber a few days earlier. My heels click on the tile floor as I walk toward the dim light and sounds of laughter coming through an open doorway.

When I peer around the door frame, I see Amber and the back of a husky man in a black leather jacket. Both sit at a square table, barely large enough for two chairs. Directly behind Amber is a short counter with a small sink and a coffee pot. This is the tiniest kitchen I've ever seen.

Amber looks up and grins when she sees me. Dark brown goo covers her teeth and sticks at the corners of her mouth. She licks her lips and wipes them with the back of her hand, making a dark smudge on the end of her sleeve.

"Hi, Dr. Green. I didn't know you were here." Amber speaks each syllable slowly and gets up from her chair to greet me.

"Hi, Amber. I just stopped by to visit for a minute. Is that okay?"

Amber's head bobs up and down, nodding, I assume. She grabs a folded chair from against the wall, opens it facing the tiny table, and waves a hand for me to sit.

I gingerly lower myself into the seat, a little unsure of its sturdiness.

Amber flips her blonde hair over her shoulder and lifts one finger toward the man. "This here's Johnny." She then points to me. "Johnny, meet Dr. Green."

The man turns, and his eyes open wide. "Hey, you're the woman who was with Zack when he saw me outside the doc's office and thought I was Rudy. Is he your kid?"

I nod.

Amber grins again, dark goo still splotching her teeth. "No kidding? What a small world!"

"Yeah, maybe too small," Johnny says, his words slow and deliberate. "You helping your kid follow me around?"

"Uh, no. No. I came to see Amber. But I'm pleased to meet you, Johnny. I apologize for any bad behavior from my son."

Johnny playfully slaps the table. "Well, I'm pleased to meet you, too. Small world indeed. You're the doc Amber's been telling me about, and it's your kid who thinks I'm someone else. Who knows? Maybe I *am* this Rudy fellow. Where's he from?"

Oh, boy. I gaze into the bearded man's eyes. His pupils are dilated, and his personality seems different today. He's friendlier and seems too . . . happy.

Smiling, I say, "My son was mistaken, Johnny. I'm truly sorry for his rudeness."

"I should have offered you a cup of coffee, Dr. Green. And a brownie." Amber slides the plate of fudgy-looking squares toward me and reaches for an empty cup.

"Uh . . . no thank you. I'm fine." The brownies look tasty, but I don't want dark goo on my teeth.

Johnny grins. "You don't know what you're missing, Doc. These are happy brownies. Bet you can't eat just one."

"Happy brownies? What makes them happy?"

Amber and Johnny laugh. Amber swipes her hair from her face, plucks a crumb of brownie from the ends of a long strand, and laughs harder.

"Seriously, what is so funny?" I ask, wondering if they're somehow laughing at me.

Amber picks up a brownie and holds it under her nose, inhaling the scent. "Mmm. I made these brownies with my secret ingredient. Shh." She puts a finger over her lips and whispers, "Don't tell anyone."

Interesting. Her secret ingredient must be the reason for their odd behavior. They seem exceedingly jolly . . . in slow motion. A mind-altering ingredient?

I pick up a brownie and gaze at it—inspect it. Perhaps she talking about the small flecks dotted amid the chocolate. Placing it on the paper napkin in front of me, I glance at Amber and softly say, "What is your special ingredient? I promise not to tell."

Amber reaches behind her and clumsily opens a small drawer

under the counter. Then she lays a palm-sized plastic bag by my napkin and sheepishly whispers, "Weed."

I lift the transparent sack and study the contents—dried crumbles of leaves or herbs. I sniff the sack, and Dr. Filmore's office flashes in my mind.

"What type of weed?" I ask, thinking of dandelions.

"It's not the best," Johnny says, "but it still makes you feel pretty darn good."

Trying not to be too persistent, I ask, "What is it called?"

"Marijuana!" Amber says. "You act like you've never seen weed before, Dr. Green. Dr. Filmore says most psychiatrists use it for hypnosis, or something. I figured you did, too." She looks at me sheepishly.

Filmore? If he uses this plant in hypnosis, maybe its mind-altering effects work on the memory centers in the brain. I need to examine this weed in my lab at home.

I pick up the small bag and look at Amber. "May I keep this?"

"You got cash?" Johnny asks. "Pot isn't free."

"It's my pot," Amber snaps at Johnny. "I can give it to her if I want."

"I don't need a pot." I reach into my purse. "But I can give you money for the weed." I lay a twenty-dollar bill on the table, which seems like a generous amount for a handful of dried plant.

Johnny huffs. "You got two more of those?"

I remove the twenty and replace it with two one-hundred-dollar bills.

Amber gasps. "That's way too much!"

"Hold on." Johnny reaches his long arm across the table and snatches the bills. Squeezing them in his hand, he says, "Amber, we could get a lot of the good stuff."

I nod at Amber. "Yes. You should get the good stuff."

Without waiting for her response, I place the weed in my purse.

Amber giggles and squeezes her slender fingers around Johnny's. He moves the money from his hand to hers, and Amber slips the bills into the pocket of her long shirt.

"Thank you, Dr. Green," she says.

I smile, eager to get to the purpose of my visit. "May I ask you two a question about amnesia?"

"Sure, Doc. Shoot," Johnny says.

"When you first learned you had amnesia, was there any place you wanted to go or thought you should be?"

Amber wrinkles her forehead, shrugs, and takes a bite of brownie.

Johnny scratches his scraggly beard. "Nope. I didn't know one place from another."

"Me neither." Amber licks a chocolaty crumb from her lower lip.

I exhale a hopeless sigh. Between Filmore and these two, I still have nothing to help me find Clay. My only glimmer is perhaps it's different for Clay, since he's familiar with Portland. April and Rudy had never seen a world outside Zelfar—no cars, animals, or square buildings. Clay's subconscious has a broader frame of reference.

I glance at my zelcom. "I better get going. Thank you, Amber. It was nice to meet you, Johnny."

When Johnny and Amber start to rise, I say, "No, please, enjoy your brownies."

"Tell your kid hi for me," Johnny says, reaching for the brownie plate.

"Goodbye." I nod to the pair who playfully slap each other's hands over the plate as if I'm already gone.

I hold my nose and hurry through Amber's shop. The fresh air outside is a relief, but the heavy mist on my hair is as damp as my mood. I step over the dirty water pooling at the curb and get into my car. After starting the engine and turning up the heat, I tap my zelcom.

"Hank? Hi. Any news about Clay?" I know the answer from Hank's heavy sigh.

"Don't worry, Zophie. I've got feelers out. We'll find him."

"Thank you, Hank. I appreciate your help. I'll talk to you soon."

My stomach grumbles. It's midafternoon, and I haven't had lunch. I wave a few pine needles under my nose and put the Jeep in gear. If I had even the slightest inclination where Clay might be, I would drive in that direction. But I don't, so I head toward home. I can wait forty-five minutes to eat.

Traffic flows steadily on Highway 30, and the heavy mist turns to light rain. The wipers squeak back and forth on the foggy windshield. There's no sunshine to warm the chill I feel from my futile search for Clay.

I start through the small community of St. Helens, pondering places that might be familiar in Clay's subconscious. In a blinding flash, I realize he could be at my house! My foot presses hard on the gas pedal, and shops and trees blur.

Red lights flash in my rear-view mirror, and I flinch at the sharp blare of a siren.

CHAPTER 28

I shriek and lift my foot from the gas pedal.

The memory of Travis outrunning a cop three years ago runs through my mind. "Pull over," Hank had told him. But Travis couldn't let us be detained and he easily out-maneuvered the black and white vehicle. We never saw that cop car again.

For a second, I consider trying to outrun this cop, except there are no good escape routes on the single-lane highway. A nervous tremble creeps into my fingers as I ease my car to a stop on the side of the road. Why does this world have so many rules? I strum my fingers on the wheel until a tap on my driver's window signals me to lower the glass.

Trying to appear calm, I smile at the man in a blue uniform and wide-brimmed hat.

"Driver's license and registration, please." His tone is nonthreatening, and he adds, "Please."

"Yes, I have a driver's license," I say cheerfully.

I open my purse, pull out my wallet, and extend my license through the window. Water drips from the brim of the man's hat, and a cold droplet splats on my wrist.

"Registration?" he says.

"Um, this is my husband's car. I'm not sure where he keeps the registration."

He points to the flap above my forehead. "It's probably over the visor or in the glove box."

When I lower the visor, I see a piece of folded paper clipped to the edge. Relieved, I extend the paper to the cop.

"Wait here," he says. "I'll be right back." He walks the few steps to his vehicle, red lights still flashing.

I rub my arms and wait until he returns. He hands me my license and registration, cups the window frame with one hand, and looks at me.

"Did you know you were speeding, ma'am?"

Frantically, I try to recall the correlation between my speedometer and the speed limit signs.

"No," seems like the appropriate answer.

"I clocked you doing sixty going through St. Helens," he says sternly. "Posted speed limit through there is thirty-five. I'm giving you a citation for twenty-five miles over the limit."

I shiver from the cold rain blowing on my arm and hope a citation is something I can handle quickly.

The cop rips a page from a thin tablet and stoops over, extending the page to me. My stomach grumbles at his scent of sweet coffee, and I reach for the slip of paper.

Instead of releasing the paper citation, he suddenly lifts a brow and glares at the seat next to me. I follow his eyes to the bag of weed beside my open purse.

The cop squares his shoulders. "I need you to step out of the car, ma'am."

"I don't want to get out of the car. Just give me the citation so I can go home."

He shifts from one foot to the other and takes a deep breath.

"What's in that little bag there?"

I lift the bag, and as I bring it in front of me, he snatches it from my hand.

"Hey!" I reach out of the window to take it back. "I bought that weed. It's mine!"

The cop's eyes widen. He grasps the handle and yanks open my door. The hinges groan—or maybe that sound came from me.

"Step out of the car," he says, his words as taut as his jaw.

I sigh, unlatch my safety belt, and slide out of the seat. As soon as my feet hit the gravel, the cop takes one of my wrists and says, "Turn around and put your other hand behind you."

Instinctively, I resist—twisting, trying to free my wrist from his grasp. His grip tightens, and in a flash, both of my hands are trapped behind me in cold metal that burns my skin. A metallic click sends waves of panic vibrating up my arms and into my chest. I wiggle fiercely to free my hands, but the frigid metal bites harder into my skin.

"Ow! This isn't funny," I say. "Unlock my wrists!"

"Sorry, ma'am, but you're under arrest for possession of marijuana." He mumbles something about the right to remain silent, but the terror pounding in my head dulls his words. He grasps my upper arm and tries to move me toward his car.

I dig my heels into the wet gravel, but the muscular cop overpowers me, nearly dragging me to the ominous black and white vehicle. Cars zoom past on the highway and not one driver stops to help me.

The cop opens the door behind the driver's seat and says, "Get in!"

Tears of dread flow with the realization he plans to take me somewhere, probably to one of those human cages Hank told me about. "But I can't go with you," I tell him. "I have to find Clay."

"Not unless you can find him from inside a jail cell," he says, pushing me into the back seat.

When he closes the door, I struggle to loosen the metal clamps on my wrists, which only brings more agony. The first thing I would do with a free hand is pinch my nose. Stink is too mild a word for the assaulting, unfamiliar odors in the police car.

The cop walks to the Jeep and returns with my purse and keys. He slides behind the steering wheel and says through the screen behind the front seat, "Your car will be impounded. You can retrieve your car and belongings when, and if, you make bail."

"Why are you taking me and my car? I want to go home!"

He starts the motor. "Just sit back and be quiet."

As the car pulls onto the highway, the movement pushes my shoulders into the seatback. I've never been so physically uncomfortable. My zelcom vibrates, and at first, I flinch. Then hopefulness fills my heart. What if it's Hank? He could make this cop let me go.

If only I could talk to Hank. Scooting forward to relieve the pressure on my wrists, I move my hands in every possible position, attempting to tap my zelcom. One tap and Hank would be able to hear anything I say. Writhe as I might, my fingers can't reach my device.

My mouth goes dry as I comprehend the seriousness of my situation. I'm going to jail. From what Hank has told me, jail is a place with vertical bars for walls and you're locked in until the judge lets you out. I don't know the judge. What if I can't ever see my family again?

The agonizing ride seems to go on forever, and at the same time, only moments. The car stops in front of a large brick building and then the cop half pulls me from the car. He leads me by my upper arm through the door, keeping his tourniquet grip around my bicep until he jerks me to a stop at a small counter, chest high to me, waist high to him. I hold my breath as long as I can from the foul odor of cigarette smoke hanging in the air.

Another man in blue uniform looks at us through a glass window. The thin-faced cop slides the window open and grins, exposing crooked yellow teeth. "Hey, Ted. What you got there?"

I take a step back, and Ted grabs my arm again. "Stand still!"

I freeze, too scared to move.

Ted holds up my bag of weed. "I'm booking this woman for possession. Here's the evidence." Ted lays the bag on the counter and turns toward me.

I sigh with relief, assuming he's about to unlock the metal bracelets. Instead, he grabs the band of my zelcom, tugs on it, twists it, and tugs again. I smile knowing he'll never figure out how to unlatch it.

The cop digs his thick finger between my skin and my zelcom band.

I squirm. "Stop it! You're hurting me."

"I've never seen a watchband like this before. Hand me the scissors," Ted says gruffly to the man at the window.

"No!" I scream.

Both cops ignore my outcry. The cold scissor blades sting my wrist, and with a loud snap, my zelcom springs free. For the first time since I was a teen and got my adult-sized zelcom, my communication device is removed from my wrist.

"You can't take that!" I wail. "I have to call my husband."

Ted scoffs. "You'll get your watch back if you make bail. You'll get your phone call on the way to your cell. Now stand still like I told you to."

My heart beats so hard and fast, I feel dizzy. Ted lays my zelcom, keys, and purse on the counter. He then says to the thin cop, "Log her personal possessions. You'll also need to get the impound number on her vehicle."

"Sure thing."

"Oh, wait," Ted says. "I almost forgot to check her pockets."

My breath stops short.

Ted pats my waist and my hips. He slips his hand into the left hip pocket of my raincoat and withdraws a few pine needles. "You fall into a pine tree?" He replaces the needles and reaches into my right hip pocket. He removes my other Zelfarian device. Ted opens his fingers, exposing my stunner, and says, "What have we got here?"

I clench my teeth, forcing my tongue to stay silent, and give a slight shrug.

"Ever see one of these?" Ted hands my stunner to the cop behind the counter.

The thin man studies the small cylindrical device, slightly longer than his middle finger, and says, "Probably some kind of flashlight." He places my stunner and my other personal items into a large orange envelope. With a black marker, he scribbles Zophie Green and a number across the top of the envelope and then looks up. "Okay, take her on into one of the holding cells."

If I had thought to use my stunner on Ted, I wouldn't be in this predicament.

Ted takes my arm and walks me down a flight of stairs, stopping at a door guarded by another man in uniform. The door opens, and Ted leads me forward to a desk where a black telephone sits next to a large telephone book. Ted removes a small ring of keys from his belt, motions for me to turn, and unlocks the bracelets.

"Ah." I moan and rub my skin.

Ted takes two strides and sits on the other end of the desk, keeping his eyes glued on me. "You get one phone call. Make it quick."

My finger rubs the slight indentation on my wrist where my zelcom has been a part of me forever. I've never made a call without it. Staring at the thick book, my pulse races. I don't know any telephone numbers by memory. Travis's zelcom code won't be in that book.

But Hank's number might be.

Ted scowls and taps the top of the desk. "Do you want your call or not?"

I open the telephone book, quickly flip to the M section, and scan down the list. There are three Henry Murphy listings. I don't recognize the street names in two of them, and the third has no address listed. With trembling fingers, I lift the hand piece and dial the third number. When I raise the earpiece to listen, deafening rings echo from the telephone into my ear, and I forget to breathe.

"Hello?" It's Hank's voice. My knees nearly crumble.

"Hank! It's me, Zophie. I'm in jail! Please help me."

"Holy Moses! Where are you?"

"I said I'm in jail."

"I know, but which one?"

There is more than one? I look at Ted. "Which jail is this?"

"Columbia County Jail," Ted replies.

I repeat this into the mouthpiece.

"Don't worry, Zophie. I'll be right there." I hear a clunk and then the telephone merely hums.

I barely set the hand piece on the base when Ted grasps my arm and barks, "This way."

He leads me out of the room and down a wide hallway with a bare white wall on one side and a wall made of vertical bars on the other. The bars are sectioned into three parts, each forming a square separated by more bars, just like Hank described. Ted stops at the second square, grabs one of the bars, and swings the door outward.

"In," he says gruffly.

I force my feet to shuffle through the opening. He closes the door with a clank.

"Make yourself comfortable. It'll be a while before dinner."

I wince as the loud metal bolt clicks away my freedom.

Watching that awful cop walk down the hall, I feel more alone than when I was a child, after I lost my parents.

CHAPTER 29

A chill colder than icicles on bare hands washes through me. I try to breathe warmth into my fingers, and slowly turn, looking for a heat source. My jail cell is a large box, the only furniture a narrow cot. The one wall without bars is bare stone.

"Hello." A familiar deep voice startles me, and I jump. Whipping around, I grip the barred door, and my eyes dart up and down the dim hallway outside my cell. I don't see him.

"Over here," he says.

I jerk my head and peer toward the cage next to mine, where male hands grip the vertical bars that separate us. I run to him, placing my icy fingers over his. Warmth spreads to my fingertips, not just from his hands, but from the joy in my heart.

"Clay!"

The man's eyes go big and round and he drops his hands.

"Clay, it's me, Zophie. I've been looking for you." Tears well in my eyes, and I cling to the bars.

Clay keeps his distance and shakes his head. "I . . . I don't know you."

"You're my friend, and you have amnesia. I'll help you get your memory back. I'm a psychiatrist." Why did I say that? If Clay could remember me, we'd be laughing so hard right now.

Clay takes a step toward our shared bars. "How can you help me? I don't know much about jail, but it appears we're both trapped here."

"Hank is coming to get me. He's your girlfriend's father and he's good with fixing government stuff. He'll get us out of here."

"I have a girlfriend?"

"Yes, her name is Janet."

Clay crosses his long arms. "If you're talking about the crazy redhead, she tried to lock me up in a hospital. If you're her friend, I don't need your help."

"Clay, please. Even if you don't trust anyone else, you can trust me. Remember? Vivacity times two!" I rub my hands together and insert my palms between the bars.

He stares blankly, keeping his arms crossed.

"Vivacity times two!" I shout, gripping the bars, struggling to shake them. They don't budge. I'm the one shaking. "We've always been best friends, and we always help each other. I need to take you home, so you can remember."

"If you know so much about me," Clay inches closer to the bars between us, "where do I live?"

"Um." Blatz. I can't risk that he'll unknowingly reveal we live in Agate Creek or Zelfar.

"I thought so," he says, turning his back to me. "Seems I can't trust anyone."

"Clay, wait."

He gazes over his shoulder.

"When you can remember again," I say, "you'll understand why I can't tell you where we live. But I can take you there. I do know you. You're a health expert and have been for forty years. So am I. We serve together."

"Forty?" He studies his hands, runs them over his face, and scoffs. "I can't be older than thirty. You seem like someone I could trust, but nothing you've said makes sense."

Blatz, blatz, blatz. I can't make science fiction real to him in this world. I have to get him out of here and take him to Zelfar.

Clay walks to the shadowy corner of his cell and I can barely discern his outline when he lies on his narrow cot.

"Clay," I say, "I love you, and I will take you home."

"Yeah, yeah," his faint voice replies, "that's what Janet said."

I pull a few pine needles from my pocket, hold them under my nose, and try to envision myself at Health Dome with Clay. I wish Hank would hurry. I don't know what he can do to get me out of here, but he said not to worry. I'm sure he'll get Clay out, too.

My thin raincoat and slacks offer little barrier to the cold air in my dank cell. Shivering, I wrap my arms across my chest, hugging myself as tightly as I can, and go sit on the edge of the cot.

Without a clock, I assume hours have passed. Where is Hank? Finally, I hear footsteps, thudding louder as they approach. My heart skips and I rush to my cell door.

"Dinner is served," says a uniformed cop, coming into view holding two trays.

I frown at him. I don't want to eat. I want to leave.

The cop bellows for me to move to the back wall.

I walk backwards until my palms touch the cold stone. He opens my cell door, and I wonder if he thinks I might try to run past him and dash out of here. Is that possible? It doesn't matter. I wouldn't leave Clay.

The cop puts a tray of food on the floor in my cell, relocks my door, and does the same for Clay.

Still pressed against the wall, I glance into the neighboring cell. Clay shows no interest in the food.

The scent of ripe apple makes my stomach rumble. Hungry as I might be, I can't eat.

"Clay, aren't you hungry?" I walk to the bars and gaze toward his cot, but he lies still and silent. "How long have you been here?"

He sits up and lift his face toward me. "Not much longer than you have."

Gripping the bars between us, I press my face into the cold metal. "Don't you want to leave here? Please, Clay, come over here and talk to me."

He rises from his cot and walks the few steps to gaze at me through an opening between two bars. "I don't know what you want me to say. I wish I could remember you, but I don't."

"I can help you remember, if you'll just come with me. Please."

Clay gazes from me to his locked cell door. His jaw softens. "Okay. I'll go with you."

I smile and before I can reply, I hear the sound of footsteps rushing toward us.

"Zophie?"

"Hank! You found me!" I revel in the sweet rush of adrenaline.

Hank stands outside my cell. "I'm sorry it took me so long. I had to borrow money, call the judge, and pull in some favors to get you released prior to your arraignment."

I'm glad Hank knows the judge. "You should have called Travis. You know we have money."

Hank glares at me and gives a quick shake of his head as if sending me a signal. I shrug. Hank steps back, and the same uniformed man who delivered the food trays unlocks my cell door.

"Follow me," the cop says, and I walk out of the cage.

"Wait!" I grab Hank's arm. "We have to take Clay with us."

"Clay? What are you talking about?"

"He's in there." I point to Clay's cell.

"Clay?" Hank peers through the bars, and Clay moves closer.

"Holey Moley! It *is* you. Janet is going to be so happy."

Clay narrows his eyes and steps back.

Hank removes his fedora and scratches his head. "Hmm. I'll have to see why they're holding him."

The cop clears his throat. "Are you two coming with me, or what?"

I grab Hank's arm when he takes a step.

"I'm not leaving without Clay."

Hank leans to my ear. "Look, Zophie, I need to get *you* out of here *now*. I'll come back for Clay as soon I get you to your car and get more funds. You can't help him if they lock you back up."

I glance at my cell and shudder. He's right. I grip the bars in front of Clay. "I'm sorry I can't take you with me right now. My name is Zophie Green. I will come back for you."

Clays sighs and crosses his arms. "Sure." He moves to his cot, and Hank tugs me away.

Hank and I follow the cop past the guard at the door and up the single flight of stairs. We stop to get my possessions at the counter with the small window.

"Here you go," says the thin-faced man who pushes the large envelope toward me.

I quickly remove my purse and grasp my zelcom. Looking at the severed band, I gently rub the face as if making amends to a dear friend. With a huff, I shove my vandalized zelcom into my purse and grab the stunner, fighting the urge to immobilize every cop in the station. I thrust the small device into my pocket, snatch my car keys, and say firmly, "Where is my weed?"

The man behind the window snorts and looks at the cop standing next to me.

"Zophie! Stop talking." I open my mouth to retort, but Hank grabs my arm. "Don't say another word. Let's go get your car." He squeezes my bicep enough to hurt, pulling me toward the exit.

Both cops are laughing when we walk out the door. Hank

rushes me across the parking lot to his long silver car and puts me in the front seat. He scurries to take his place behind the wheel, slams his door shut, and turns to me.

"Where on Earth did you get marijuana?"

"I bought the weed from Amber so I could analyze it. Consuming it has a mind-altering effect and I want to know more about that."

Hank shakes his head as he often does when I don't understand something common to this world. "I'm sorry, Zophie, I should have warned you. I just never thought of you and marijuana in the same sentence. Having marijuana is illegal in this country. But don't worry, I'll get you a good attorney, so you won't have to do more jail time. I still can't believe the cop caught you with the goods and you admitted the marijuana was yours."

"Hank, I'm not worried about me. How do we free Clay?"

"I'll have to make a few calls." Hank starts the engine. "But first, let's get your car."

Hank drives to the impound lot down the road and parks outside the locked gate. I sit with him while the guard retrieves my Jeep.

"Can you make those calls now?" I ask.

Hank points out the side window at the sight of my Jeep. "You get your car and pull over there. I'll make the calls."

I do as Hank says. In a couple of minutes, he parks next to me and hops out of his car. He runs to my window, and I quickly roll the handle.

"Looks like all we need is money," Hank says. "Clay hitched a ride and was dropped at a restaurant. He ordered food and couldn't pay his tab, so the owner called the cops. He tried to run, and they said he pushed one of the officers. Since he didn't have any ID and wouldn't give his name, they took him in for resisting arrest. I can get him out for two-hundred-and-fifty dollars, but, I just drained my resources. Do you have that much cash on you?"

I count the bills in my wallet. "I only have sixty dollars. But we have more at the house." If I hadn't paid so much for the weed, we could take Clay with us right now.

"Okay. I'll follow you home and come back for Clay."

As soon as we're on the highway, I lift my arm to call Travis. Ugh. My zelcom is in my purse, which I tossed in the back. I need a zelcom band that can't be destroyed. When I pull in front of our house, Travis bounds down the steps and runs to the Jeep.

"I've been crazy with worry," he says, practically pulling me from the car before wrapping me in his arms. "Why didn't you answer your zelcom?"

With every muscle in my body, I squeeze Travis, pressing my cheek into the safe contours of his chest, inhaling his spicy lime scent—other than pine, the only scent my nose truly loves.

Travis lifts my chin. "Are you okay?"

"I was in jail!" I thrust my wrist into the air. "The cop cut the band on my zelcom and took it away from me. Then I couldn't get it from my purse once I was driving."

"Jail?" Travis hugs me again. "That's awful. What happened?"

Hank pulls into the driveway, parks behind the Jeep, and gets out of his car. Travis releases me and walks toward our mutual friend.

"I assume I have you to thank for saving Zophie." He shakes Hank's hand.

"Glad I could help. Now we need to get Clay." Hank glances at the front porch.

"You found Clay?" Travis asks.

"Yes," I say, turning toward the house. "He's in the same jail in St. Helens where they held me." Travis and Hank follow me into the house, and I throw my wet raincoat over a wall hook.

"Mommy!" Kayla and Krissie run to me from the living room and hug my legs.

"Would you get some cash for Hank?" I say to Travis as I pat the girls' heads. "He needs two-hundred-fifty dollars to pay for Clay, plus whatever he already paid for me."

"The financial repercussions of your wife's naiveté can wait," Hank says, removing his fedora. "Two-fifty for Clay is enough for now."

Travis trots upstairs, and Hank waits in the hall. I take the girls into the living room, where they go back to coloring pictures with Zack on the floor by the fireplace. When I rejoin Hank in the hall, we hear Travis coming down the stairs. He extends a small white envelope to Hank.

"I'll fetch Clay and bring him here," Hank says, taking the envelope and shoving it into his coat pocket. "Is it okay if Janet comes out to see Clay later?"

"Umm . . . how about we get Clay here first, and let him decide when he wants to see Janet?" I don't want to hurt Janet's feelings, but Clay and I may be in Zelfar later.

I reach for my coat, and Hank lifts his hand to stop me. "Zophie," he says. "I think it's best if you let me go get Clay. I don't want you to be caught hanging around that jail."

"But Clay might not come with you," I say, panic swelling my throat.

Hank gently presses on my shoulder. "He saw I got you out. He'll trust me."

Travis pulls me to him. "You know we can trust Hank. He'll bring Clay to us."

My lips tremble as I thank Hank and close the door behind him.

"Now that you're home," Travis says, "I need to go help Einstein finish up in the lab.".

I glance at our three children happily coloring by the fire. "If you don't need Zack right away, I'd like to take a quick shower."

Travis kisses my forehead. "Send him out when you're done."

Alone in the bedroom, I wish I had a serenity simulator to

slip over my head. I can't stop thinking about my hours in a cold jail cell and leaving Clay behind. The water in the shower washes over my face but doesn't rinse away my anxiety. Why haven't we installed a sonic shower in this house? And a serenity room? Gram should have insisted on it. I wonder how she and Vad are coming with the memory-wiping device. I have to tell them how desperately we need to reverse its effect on Clay. Then I can do the same for April and Rudy.

When I turn off the hair dryer, little-girl giggles reach my ears, and I go downstairs. Kayla and Krissie race into the hall, their pictures in hand, each scrambling to be the first into my arms. My stomach rumbles, and the twins laugh harder.

"Do it again!" Krissie squeals and pats her little hand on my tummy.

"I'll be in the lab with Dad," Zack says, scooting past us.

I take the girls' hands. "Let's go find Mommy something to eat."

Einstein enters through the back door and follows us into the kitchen. "You missed dinner, Zophie," he says. "I assume you're hungry."

"Yes. Mommy's hungwy," Kayla says. "Her tummy said so."

"Banana and a cup of hot tea, please," I say to Einstein.

He soon places my request, along with a bowl of vegetable soup, on the table for me. "You need nourishment."

"I want a banana!" says Krissie.

"Me too!" says Kayla as they both run to their highchairs.

I help the girls into their seats and position my chair between them. With our mouths full of banana, we hear the back door open.

Travis walks up to the counter, and Zack pokes his head into the kitchen doorway. "Hey, mom. I'm going to bed now. I need some *super* sleep for tomorrow. Goodnight." Zack has become enthralled with Superman on the American television. Super is now an overused word in his vocabulary.

"Goodnight, son," I say.

"Night, Zackie," Kayla and Krissie say together.

"What's the big day tomorrow?" I ask, hoping Travis isn't planning another trip to Portland.

"Honey without bees," Travis says, matter-of-factly, like he's done too many times.

I smile, keeping my doubts to myself.

I eat the last spoonful of soup, set the girls on the floor, and tell them to go get into their pajamas. Kayla and Krissie scurry off, and Travis walks with me to the bottom of the stairs.

"Will you wait down here for Hank and Clay?" I ask. "I'll be right down as soon as I put the girls to bed."

"Kiss them twice for me," he says and walks toward the living room.

I lie with Kayla and Krissie on their fluffy pink comforter, read their favorite story, *The Magic Slipper*, a story with similar themes to America's Cinderella, but without horses, mice, or the evil stepmother. I hold my zelcom in my hand and the twins point at the pictures displayed in the air above their bed. They recite most of the words as I read.

"The End," I say, and Krissie whines for another story.

"Not tonight," I say, tucking the blanket under their chins.

I glance longingly at the front door before joining Travis in the living room. Sitting in his favorite recliner, he pats his knee.

"Sit here while we wait," he says. "If you don't mind reliving it, I'd love to hear about your day."

I prop myself comfortably on his lap and begin, "First, I went to see Dr. Filmore . . ." I relate the day's events. When I tell him about Amber and Johnny and the weed brownies, Travis's eyes go wide.

"Mind-altering? A chemical reaction?" he says. "I'd like to study that plant."

"I bought some from Amber so we could analyze it, but the cop took it from me. Amber told me her weed was a secret, but I had no idea it was illegal."

"Do you think we could get more?"

"There is no way I want to repeat today's experience, not even for science."

"If I can prevent it, you'll never have to." He cups my hand in his. "But, I would like to hear what happened at the jail."

After I relate my horrifying experience with the cop and conclude with having to leave Clay in that awful place, Travis pulls me to his chest.

"At least we know Clay is on his way here."

I press my lips to his, grateful he understands. "I adore you, Travis."

"I love you, too, Zophie."

We both chuckle. We don't often call each other by name. I lay my head on his shoulder, inhaling his usually calming scent, but Clay's dejected image when I left him keeps replaying in my mind. My hip vibrates, and I jerk my zelcom from my pocket.

My finger can't tap the screen fast enough. "Hank? Do you have Clay? Are you on your way?"

"Zophie." Hank's voice is too tense, and my chest tightens like a hand gripping my heart.

"Do you have Clay?" My voice rises an octave.

"I'm sorry, but I was too late. He was released to someone else before I got here. And the dang officers won't tell me who."

"You're at the jail?" Travis asks.

"Yes," Hank answers. "But I'm in my car, ready to drive home, unless you want me to bring your money back tonight."

"No," Travis says. "Put it toward what we owe you for getting Zophie out of jail."

"Okay," Hank says. "Zophie?"

"Yes." My breath catches, but I manage to utter the word.

"I'll keep making calls, see if I can find out who Clay is with. I will find him."

"Thank you, Hank," Travis says. "Toss . . . I mean, goodbye."

"Bye." Hank's voice fades, and with a trembling finger, I end the call.

CHAPTER 30

Two days pass with no news about Clay. Saving my world from extinction is the gravest quest I've ever undertaken, but the determination to find my best friend has my head buzzing like the hundreds of bees in the little white boxes behind the barn. Still, I have no sensible ideas. I may have to resort to insensible ones, like sending Einstein to scour every document in the Columbia County Jail. Travis and Zack continue to spend countless hours in the lab, and Travis says their new batch of honey is nearly ready for me to test. I should be excited, but I'm starting to feel like it's going to take more than honey to make my world right again. We can't seal off the portal before we find Clay.

I haven't heard from Gram or Vad either. I expected them to be here by now with Vad's version of Bayl's memory-wiping device. I wish I could tell Gram what's happened to Clay. If she was able to get Bayl to confess, maybe she already knows.

While the twins nap, I sit by the fire with a cup of hot chocolate. The wind whistles outside, and I scoot closer to the hearth. It's already November. Soon, the first snow will fall. I gaze at the tree branches dancing outside the window and hope Clay is somewhere warm and safe. *Where* are *you, my friend*?

I startle with the vibration of my zelcom, nearly spilling my cocoa. Why is everything so intense on this side of the portal?

"Hi, Zophie. This is Hank. I'm calling you from my car." He chuckles. "I sure like saying—"

"Did you find Clay?"

"No, sorry. But I have more of Filmore's notes. There's something you need to see."

I huff. "Forget about Filmore. We need to find Clay."

"I know, but this is urgent. I have to tell you what that shrink's been up to. I'm on my way to your house now."

"Can't you just tell me over the phone?"

"Nope, I'll see you soon. Bye."

My zelcom goes silent just as the large clock by the front door chimes twelve o'clock noon.

Before long, I hear hurried footsteps on the front porch and open the door to find Hank, comically holding his hat on his head with one hand and a wet briefcase with the other. The wind blows in swirls, and the rain seems to fall in waves. Hank hurries inside, shakes water from his hat and coat, and hangs them on hooks by the door.

Stepping beyond the tiled entry, he says, "That's a mighty strong storm brewing. I better make this quick before your creek floods the driveway."

He looks past me, down the hallway. "Are we alone?"

"Yes. The girls are napping."

Hank follows me into the living room and sits next to me on the sofa. He opens his briefcase, slaps four manila folders onto the coffee table, and says, "I think you may be in danger."

"Danger? What do you mean?" Fear is real on this side of the portal.

"I mean Filmore's on to you," Hanks says. "We don't know

what he's capable of."

"How can that tiny man be dangerous?" I scoff, feigning courage.

"I'm telling you, Zophie, Filmore is bad news. You can't trust him." Hank picks up one of the folders and shoves it at me. "Read the last two pages of Johnny's file."

Hank's anxiousness puts knots in my stomach. I take the file and flip to the back.

Patient Name: *John Doe, aka, Johnny Ford*

Remarks: *Patient related interaction with a teenage boy, Zack, who thought he recognized patient as a man named Rudy. Zack tried to jog patient's memory with a small carved figurine. Patient didn't remember the carving. Later, the boy and a man named Einstein went to patient's house to show him the figurine again. Patient and his wife talked with Zack and Einstein. All agreed Johnny was not Rudy.*

NOTE: *Determine Zack's identity. Determine Einstein's identity.*

Zack? My heart thumps in my throat. Johnny will tell Filmore Zack is my son. I flip to the next page, and my eyes stop on the date: *November 4, 1975.*

"This page is from yesterday," I say. "Did you get these files today?"

"Last night. Just keep reading."

Patient Name: *John Doe, aka, Johnny Ford*

Remarks: *Patient visited Amber's shop as I suggested. Dr. Green came in while he was there. He recognized her as Zack's mother. Given Dr. Green's interest in Amber and her son's interest in Johnny, patient wonders if he could possibly be Rudy.*

Hank lays another file in my hands. "This is the most interesting thing of all. You'll know why you can't trust little-bitty Filmore."

I gasp when I see my name on the tab.

Scrawled across the top of the first page is: *Do background check on Dr. Zophie Green.* A bulleted list follows: *What is her address in Canada? Where is she staying in Portland? Who does she work for? What is her connection to amnesia patients—Johnny, Amber, and the one she calls Clay?*

I read the last line of Filmore's notes on me. *I think Dr. Green can lead me to Wade.* The blood drains from my face. Hank is right. Filmore could make being on this side of the portal difficult for me, possibly for our whole family.

I glance at the papers on the table. "Are there notes about Clay?"

Hank shakes his head. "I still can't find Clay, but it crossed my mind Filmore might be the one who bailed him out of jail. That's why I was eager to get Filmore's files, but I didn't find one on Clay."

I sift through the pages, scanning for Clay's name, hoping Hank overlooked something.

Hank touches my hand. "Do you have an address in Canada?"

"No."

The wind whirs into a howl, and the rain beats steadily on the roof. Hank rises and walks to the large living room window.

"This is turning into a serious storm." A loud crack echoes from outside, and Hank jumps. "I don't like the sound of that. In this kind of wind, trees bend and break or get torn up by their roots."

It's curious that a storm has Hank so rattled.

"Your driver's license will lead Filmore to your address here." Hank paces, talking fast. "You can expect him to come poking around and he may not be alone."

I smile warmly at Hank's concern for my well-being. He's a good friend. He doesn't know how safe I am here. I rise and take his hand. With a soft touch, I pat his fingers, comforting like Gram would do. "Don't worry, Hank. Einstein won't let anyone through the gate without our permission."

Hank scowls. "Did Einstein install some kind of lock no one can pick?"

"Something like that."

"Well, regardless, you need to steer clear of Filmore." Hank squeezes my hand between his sturdy palms. "And it's obvious Johnny thinks you and Zack know something. A man desperate for answers is dangerous. Steer clear of him, too."

Johnny will never come roaring up my driveway on his motorcycle, but the fretful lines across Hank's brow tell me his concerns for my safety are justified. I wish I could tell him we have a Zelfarian version of Superman.

Hank drops my hands and wraps me in his arms. Squeezing me too tightly, he whispers in a harsh tone, "If Filmore harms you in any way, I'll kill him."

"Kill?" Could Hank take someone's life? I tug myself away from him.

"Well, make him wish he were dead." Hank clears his throat and places a firm hand on my shoulder. "How much does Travis know?"

"How much do I know about what?" Travis walks into the living room. "About how rain can fall horizontally like it's doing outside right now?"

Hank jerks his hand from my shoulder, like a child caught breaking a dish, and clamps his jaw shut.

I ignore Hank's gesture and smile. "Hi, sweetheart. It seems my investigation of amnesia patients has brought potential danger to us."

Travis shoots a probing glance at Hank. "Like what?"

"More like who," I say. "Johnny Ford and his psychiatrist."

"They're here?" Travis peers at the rain-streaked windows.

"Not yet, but Hank thinks they have our address and might come looking for answers about where Johnny is from."

"Einstein won't let them through the gate," Travis says flatly.

Hank looks quizzically from me to Travis. "Does Einstein have some kind of special forces skills?"

Travis lifts an eyebrow, and I shrug.

"Einstein is adept with security systems," Travis says.

The worried expression on Hank's face doesn't fade. "I can get a police detail to watch your house for a few days."

"That won't be necessary." Travis puts an arm around my shoulder. Neither of us want police in close proximity. I shudder at what they might do to us if they saw an android with passenger seats for arms, racing to and from our front porch, let alone what they would find in our "barn."

"I found you a good lawyer," Hank tells me, thankfully changing the subject. He scoops the documents from the coffee table and stuffs them in his briefcase. "He says he can get you off with a fine. This is one of those times when it's a good thing you're rich."

"We certainly appreciate your help, Hank." Travis says. "How much cash do you need?"

"Nothing yet. I'll let you know how much and when."

Hank turns and Travis and I follow him into the hallway.

The back door bangs open. A gust of cold air chills my arms and brings in the dank odor of wet leaves.

"Dad, we did it!" Zack shouts. "We made honey! Come see!" Zack bursts down the hallway and stops short when he sees Hank. "Oh, hi," he says.

Hank chuckles. "Making honey. You sure say some strange things, kid. You better make sure your hives are battened down, or you'll be looking for them on the coast come morning."

Zack grabs Travis's sleeve. "Come on, Dad."

Does this mean they've done it? We can finally start saving Zelfarian babies? I can barely stifle my excitement. I want to sprint to the lab and test a blood sample.

"Hi and bye, kid. Go on, Travis," Hank says. "The kid seems awful anxious to drag you out to the bee boxes. Just be careful of flying branches. This wind will rip them off the trees like they were twigs for a campfire."

Twigs for a campfire—and Hank thinks Zack says strange things.

"Drive safely, Hank," Travis says and follows Zack out the back door. Another gust of wind chills the house before we hear the door shut.

Hank slips his arms into his coat and removes his hat from the hook. "Promise you'll let me know if Filmore or Johnny give you any trouble?"

"Promise you'll tell me if you find Clay?"

"Deal." Hank opens the door to a strong gust, and with a quick flick of his hand, he barely snatches his hat from the whipping wind. "You better make sure you have flashlights and candles handy," Hank shouts on his way down the porch steps. "There's a good chance this storm's going to take out your power."

If our power came from the local electric company, he might be right. But our energy source won't be affected by the weather.

I raise my arm to keep the rain from stinging my face and shout to Hank. "Is it safe to drive? Maybe you should stay here until the storm passes."

"I'll be careful. Call you tomorrow." Hank sloshes through the water on the cobblestone path and gets into his car. A large branch lands on the graveled driveway, barely missing the back of his silver automobile. Branches on the tall maples lining the drive seem to wave him through the gate.

I slam the door against the brutal wind and hurry to the warmth of the fire. When I start to tap my zelcom to have Einstein come watch the twins, he enters the living room.

"Travis is unsure of the storm and wants me to remain with you and the girls." Einstein stands tall in front of me, awaiting further instructions.

"Good," I say. "Krissie and Kayla will be awake soon. I'm going to the lab."

CHAPTER 31

Has the correct honey formula to cure newborn loss syndrome finally been achieved? Can we all go home? Gram and I still haven't determined how I'll present the twins. She thinks we can avoid the mention of previous dual fetuses. But if I say I kept one of my twins hidden to prevent them from being a scientific study, I don't see how anyone would believe me. Regardless, we both agree they go home with the honey cure.

I grab my coat and race out the back door. Nearly blinded by the thrashing rain, I press hard against the wind to reach the small side door to the barn. A flat board flies from the roof of the barn and crashes across the concrete path where I walked a few seconds ago. The wind pushes as hard as I pull on the door. I manage to open it a few inches when a gust slams the door shut again. Trying again, I shove my elbow and hip into the narrow space. As soon as I slip inside, the door bangs shut behind me. Water drips from my coat, making puddles on the wooden floor. I traverse six feet of slippery planks and wave my hand for the dome to allow entry.

The wind may rattle the wooden structure of the barn, but

it can't impact the clear crystillium dome or its green diamond power source. The wind goes silent when the dome's doorway seals behind me and the storm retreats to the back of my mind. I follow the sweet smell of honey mixed with apple and huckleberry to the far side of the dome, where Travis and Zack work together, their heads bent over a spiral of thin tubes.

"Is it really happening? You made protizine honey?"

"Yes!" Travis moves towards me to lift me and twirl me around. "Of course, you have to test it, but it looks like we can finally go home."

"Do you wanna know how we did it?" Zack's eyes sparkle with enthusiasm, like any scientist eager to share a major breakthrough.

"Absolutely!" I say. Travis releases me, grinning at Zack.

Zack retells the process, pointing to tubes and containers as he talks. "It started with Dad grafting the huckleberry bush and the apple tree. We combined the nectar from the blossoms of the new plant with the glucose oxidase enzyme formula growing in that vat, then we put the mixture into the crystillium honey stomach. It only takes a day to complete the entire regurgitation process, which is faster than the bees do it. We tested our new honey, and it has higher levels of protizine than natural honey."

Travis points to a row of small bushy shrubs. "The process also required Zelfarian power minerals to create an adequate photosynthesis environment. We'd still be waiting for spring if we had to rely on local seasons to grow apple-huck blossoms." Travis winks, pleased with his name for the hybrid plant.

I can't wait to tell our young people their babies will survive. "How long will it take to replicate the honey production in Zelfar?" I envision our birthing orbs in high demand in the coming year.

Travis adjusts the sleeve on his pale blue lab coat. "If your blood test is successful, we can have honey in every Zelfarian cooking orb in about six months. But we can't announce the cure until we've made and tested the honey in our Zelfar lab. You realize that, right?"

"Yes, I understand." I laugh and clap my hands. I haven't felt this much bliss for a long while. "Can I test the honey now?"

Zack hands me a small jar filled with a thick yellow liquid. I rub my fingers across the words: Apple-Huck Honey.

"Give me fifteen minutes."

"Toss pine," Zack and Travis say together.

Hugging the jar to my chest, I walk behind a row of tall shelves and enter my small testing orb. After placing the honey on a half-moon table, I retrieve the tray of blood samples from the preservation chamber. Perching on a stool, I mix two droplets of honey in each of the three indentations containing Brita's blood. I insert the tray into a tube-like machine and initiate the test cycle with a tap on my zelcom which, thanks to Einstein, now boasts an indestructible band.

Eight minutes elapse before my zelcom pulses. I stare at the results displayed on my wrist and forget to breathe. They did it!

I jump from the stool, throw my arms wide, and twirl in Gram's happy dance. For confirmation, I place a sample of blood and honey on a clear slice of glass and validate the results under the microscope—the rate of absorption is higher than necessary to restore protizine balance in the body. I grab the jar and rush out of the orb.

"Travis!" I shout. "You and Zack did it!"

Travis laughs, grabbing me when I leap into his arms.

"Zap the cosmos!" Zack whoops. "Brita and I can have a family!"

Travis lowers my feet to the floor, and I gaze at Zack. Zelfarians can have healthy babies again, but it doesn't mean I can stop using the portal right away. Worry replaces my excitement. I have to find Clay and figure out how to return the other missing people to Zelfar—that is, if they want to return. Surely they wouldn't want to stay in this complicated world where it seems even the weather can kill you. I can't leave them stranded here.

An unexpected light filters into the dome from overhead. I gaze up at the arched ceiling where rain streaks the outer shell of the dome. The wooden roof on the barn appears to be missing a board.

"The dome is impenetrable, right?" I say, unease creeping into my chest.

"Crystillium is a zillion times stronger than wood, Mom," Zack says.

"Don't worry, sweetheart." Travis rubs my neck.

A strong gust rips off more of the roof and exposes the whole top of the dome. I shiver at the sight and look toward the exit. "You don't think the wind will tear the boards off the house, do you?"

"I'm sure the house can withstand more than this wind," Travis says. "Was the wind scaring the girls?"

"It could be now. Are you finished out here for now?" My voice rises as if to yell over the howling wind that we can't even hear through the crystillium shell.

"We'll be in as soon as we fill a few more jars with honey." Travis picks up an empty jar and removes the lid.

"Okay. I'll see you two in the house. I love you both. Toss pine!"

"We love you, too. Toss pine," they say in unison, both holding a beaker of yellow liquid and an empty jar.

I exit the lab and step into the breezeway to whirs and cracks and the hard prattle of rain. With all my strength, I push the barn door and barely manage to squeeze through. Without looking back, I splash through deep puddles on the path to the house. The backdoor swings and bangs against the wall. I step inside and use my body weight to shut the door.

The wall opposite the door flashes bright white, and I jump at the sound of a harsh crack resounding through the air. Slipping on the wet tile, I fall against the door, and slide to the floor. A thunderous boom—an explosion—follows. The small window in the door shatters above my head, and shards of glass spew across the floor in front of me.

In an instant, the light, crackling sound, and boom are replaced by the sounds of wind and rain. The lights go off and screams from Kayla and Krissie bring me to my feet. Thankfully, the ground doesn't tremble.

Before I can take a step, Einstein stands in front of me with both girls in his arms. His fingers and forehead glow, illuminating the hallway. Beams emit from each of the girls' wrists as well, their zelcoms serving as small flashlights in the dimness.

Einstein nods toward the open square in the back door where the window used to be. I swallow a shriek at the sight of the barn to keep from scaring the girls any further. Blackened boards smolder against the gray sky, and most of the roof is gone. Yanking the door, I rush outside, oblivious to puddles up to my ankles. The stench reminds me of the burning forest after our zilimite explosions.

"ZOPHIE! STOP!" Einstein shouts behind me. Heeding the panic in his tone, I stop inches from the barn door, and he thrusts the twins into my arms. "Let me go first," he says. "The walls may be unstable."

The girls hide their faces against my shoulders to shield their eyes from the rain. I'm worried about them out in this weather but too concerned about Zack and Travis to go back into the house.

When Einstein pushes the barn door inward, it lands with a thud on the planks. Kayla holds her wrist high, shining her zelcom beam ahead of us. Instead of seeing a reflection off the dome, her light shines on overturned shelves and cylinders. The crystillium shell is gone.

With a twin locked on each hip, I rush after Einstein, stepping over scattered tubing and beakers until I reach Travis and Zack in the center of the circular lab. They stand amid tree fragments and smashed jars. Honey mixed with water pools at their feet. Both stare, seemingly dazed, with raindrops splattering their upturned faces. The wind subsides as if its mission of destruction is complete.

"Daddy?" Kayla reaches outward.

Krissie buries her face deeper in my shoulder, and Einstein takes Kayla from me. Travis lowers his eyes to mine, his brow shadowed in despair.

"Lightning." Travis splays his arms wide in disbelief. "One bolt disintegrated the dome." He runs a hand over his sodden hair, his gaze traversing the ruined laboratory.

Zack smacks his rain-soaked hands together, splattering us with water. "It was the weirdest thing, Mom. A blade of the brightest light you ever saw came through the hole in the roof and hit the top of the dome. I mean, it was *super* bright. Me and Dad thought it was gonna stab right into us. Then the dome disappeared, and we were standing in the rain. And the stupid wind kept knocking stuff over."

I touch Zack's shoulder. "Are you okay?"

"Yeah." He pushes aside broken glass with his shoe, watery honey oozing at his feet.

"Are *you* okay?" I ask Travis.

He picks up a piece of glass and thrusts it aside. It lands with a crash, adding more shards of glass to the mess. "Everything is destroyed—my equipment, the honey, the enzymes, even the shrubs. I'll have to rebuild everything."

His chest heaves as he kicks an overturned cylinder, sending it skidding across the puddled floor. I feel bad for him—for all of us. We were so close to bringing protizine to Zelfar.

"It'll be all right, dear," I say, attempting to comfort him the way Gram would me. "Let's all go inside and get out of this rain."

Travis flicks water from his fingertips. "The wind seems to be letting up. I better assess the damage and see what I can salvage. Zack and I will be in soon."

"Einstein can stay and help. I'll take the girls inside."

Travis glances toward the dark house, and his eyes go wide. "There's no power?"

"We have our zelcoms." I swing the wide swath of light shining from my wrist. Krissie and Kayla wave their arms, showing their zelcom lights, too.

Travis's lips twitch in a quick smile at our little girls. "Okay, I'll keep Einstein, but be careful. Call if you need anything."

Holding both toddlers tight in my exhausted arms, I carefully make my way to the outer edge of the barn and step around the fallen door. I carry the girls through the back door and past the broken glass in the hallway. Brisk air chills my back, reminding me our clothes are cold and wet.

I put the girls down at the bottom of the stairs and squat to their eye level. "Let's get out of these wet clothes and cuddle on the sofa by the fire. I'll read a story, okay?"

"Magic Slipper," insists Krissie.

"Dry clothes first."

They dash up the stairs to their room and pull warm pants and sweaters from their drawers. After they change, they take turns shining their lights in front of me, escorting me to my room so I can change, too. Soon, the three of us are snuggled on the sofa, wrapped in a blanket, reading.

After one more story, the lights come on. We see Einstein standing in the doorway.

"I was able to restore the power emission from the green diamond. The whole house will be warm momentarily," he says. "I will prepare dinner."

"No, Einstein," I say. "Go back and help Travis. I'll fix the girls something to eat."

I leave the twins under the blanket and walk with Einstein to the back door, intending to clean up the broken glass. I smile at the clean floor.

"Thank you, Einstein." I give our android a hug.

You're welcome," he says softly, patting my back.

Einstein exits, and I gaze through the hole that used to be a window. Jagged silhouettes of what's left of the barn and its high-tech honey lab bring tears to my eyes. The cure for newborn loss syndrome is buried somewhere in that rubble. I'm beginning to feel like we may never get to take our whole family home.

CHAPTER 32

Travis stands in the kitchen doorway, his normally wavy hair hanging in wet strands on his forehead.

"Would you like a sandwich?" I ask.

"I'm not hungry."

The streaks and smudges on his hands and clothes make him look as downtrodden as he sounds. Seeing him disheveled and depressed chills me worse than the icy rain.

"How bad is it?" I say, handing Krissie half a peanut butter and honey sandwich. Kayla, in her highchair next to Krissie's, tries to snatch the sandwich from her sister. Both laugh. I hand the other half to Kayla and glance at Travis, hoping the girls' antics have lightened his mood, but his lips turn down at the corners.

"It's bad," Travis says. "We had it! Zophie, we had it!" He slams his wet hand against the wall, leaving spatters on the floral paper. The twins jump, startled into silence, and look at him.

"I'm so sorry, sweetheart." I reach out my arms, longing to comfort him, but he steps back.

Einstein and Zack enter the kitchen and stop in the doorway, looking at Travis.

"There's nothing more we can do tonight," Travis says to them. "We need more crystillium to rebuild the dome and more cylinders and copper tubing to rebuild the honey processor."

I don't know how to ease his despair, so I focus on the science. "Do you know what happened to the dome?"

"Our crystillium domes have never been exposed to rainfall," Einstein answers as if I had posed the question to him. "The water ionized the air surrounding the dome, producing conductive plasma. The dome emitted an opposite charge, sending an upward leader of current toward the intense electrical field of the thundercloud. The result was a direct lightning strike upon the dome, subsequently dissolving the crystillium shell."

"Another underestimation in mixing Zelfarian technology with the environment on this side of the portal," Travis mutters. "I need to go clean up."

Zack steps aside for Travis to exit, and then ambles over to the table. His jeans and sweatshirt are fresh, but his mood looks as dreary as his father's.

"Bet it feels good to be clean and dry," I say, trying to be positive.

"Yeah. I'm glad we don't have stupid rain storms in Zelfar. Now we have to start all over."

"But you know what to do now. Won't it go faster?"

"Yeah, probably." Zack drops into the chair nearest the twins, and Einstein sets a sandwich in front of him. "Thanks," Zack says. He takes a bite and contorts his face, pretending his mouth and tongue are stuck together. The girls giggle and imitate him.

His levity with the girls lightens the weight on my shoulders a little. "Zack, please bring the girls into the living room when they're done eating," I say.

I walk into the living room and stand by the hearth, gazing

at Gram's waterfall painting above the wooden mantel. Warm air tickles the side of my neck and I flinch. I hadn't heard Travis's footsteps.

He wraps his arms around me and rests his chin on top of my head. "I'm glad Gram missed the storm, but wasn't she supposed to be here by now?"

"Yes. I wish I knew what's keeping her."

"I need to repair and strengthen the roof and do as much as I can in the lab tomorrow, but you can go to Zelfar and check on her."

"I need to go with you, Mom," Zack says as he enters the living room with a chocolate cookie in hand and toddlers on his heels. "Brita's been in that neuro-tube long enough to be awake by now."

"I could use your help here, Zack," Travis says.

"Zack should get back to his tutor sessions." I look up at Travis. "What about Einstein?"

"Einstein will clean up and reassemble shelves, but without Zack, I'll be days, maybe weeks, recreating the breakthrough."

"Sorry, son." I put a hand on his shoulder. "If Brita's awake, I'll send Vad for you."

Zack shoves the cookie into his mouth, folds his arms, and plops into the large chair facing the sofa. "I don't wanna wait to see Brita," he garbles with his mouth full.

Gram's image flashes in my mind, her face taut and confused. This has only happened once in my life, when I saw my parents in my head, terror in their eyes—the day they transcended in that hoversphere crash. My adrenalin spikes, and my hands start to shake. I grab Travis's arm. "I have to go to Gram. Now!"

"What's wrong?"

"I don't know. Gram's face appeared in my awareness, out of nowhere. What if Bayl . . ." I can't even voice that thought.

Travis pulls me to him and whispers, "Bayl better leave

our family alone, or I may become as unpredictable as a bolt of lightning."

He strokes my hair, and I glance at our children huddled in the chair, stone still, staring at us. I smile at Zack and the girls and do my best to relax. "I'll wait until tomorrow to go see Gram," I say. I step toward Zack and start to reach for Krissie.

Einstein rushes into the room and says, "Quaid is here with Gram. I don't know how they got past my detection."

We hear someone on the porch and then loud bangs on the door. The hairs on my arms stand up.

"Please, you have to help us," cries a gravelly voice.

Travis is first at the entryway. With one swift motion, he flips the switch to the outdoor flood lights and flings the door wide.

Quaid stands before us in muddy clothes, gasping for breath.

Zack runs outside. "Is Brita awake?" Before Quaid can answer, Zack stares at the porch steps and says, "What's wrong with Gram?"

"It was an accident!" Quaid cries, rubbing his scraggly beard on a dirty sleeve.

My breath catches, and I run past Quaid to Gram, where she cowers at the bottom of the stairs, one hand on the rail. Her hair hangs in long wet strings and her pants are caked in mud.

"Gram, what happened?" I run down the slippery steps to her.

She flinches and jerks away. "Who are you? Where am I?"

"Nooo!" I cover my mouth as Gram's eyes go wide. "Gram. It's me, Zophie." I force calmness into my voice and ease my hand toward her. "You're cold. Please come inside."

In an instant, Einstein whisks Gram into his arms and carries her inside. I run after them. Einstein gently places my grandmother in her favorite overstuffed chair next to the fire.

"The memory region of Gram's brain has been altered," Einstein says to me, "but her body sustained no injuries."

That despicable Bayl! He wiped Clay's memory and now my grandmother's? I never should have agreed to put his awful device back where he could find it.

"Gwam, G'am." Kayla and Krissie run up to Gram, putting their tiny hands on her muddy knees. I start to snatch them away when Gram unfolds her arms and softly pats the tops of the girls' heads. She looks up, glancing between Travis and me.

"You all seem to know me. Who are you?" As they frequently do, Gram's fingers reach to touch the large pendant of her necklace. Instead, they rub at her bare chest.

I gasp. Gram's necklace, her portal key, is gone.

Travis pulls the girls away as I wrap my arms around Gram's knees. I lay my cheek in her lap, ignoring the pungent dirt, moist and cold against my skin. "I'm your granddaughter. You live here with me and my family. Don't worry. I'll take care of you."

My grandmother touches my hair and rubs my head like I'm her little girl again. "I wish I could remember you, dear. I guess I can stay with you tonight since I don't know where else to go." Her memory may be gone, but she's still Gram.

Quaid's cold hand touches my arm. "Zophie, you gotta believe me. I'm sorry this happened to Lilly. Bayl said to take 'er to Seattle, but I couldn't. I brought 'er to you." His tears and trembling chin elicit no sympathy from me.

Travis grabs Quaid and pulls him aside. "Get away from them."

What's happening to my family? Travis has never been physically aggressive.

I rise, pull Gram to her feet, and say to Travis, "I'm going to get her cleaned up and put her to bed. Keep Quaid here until I get back."

Travis nods and nudges the disheveled elder into a chair.

Gram doesn't resist when I lead her down the hallway. Once she is settled in bed, I return to the living room. When I see

Quaid, my face burns, and I feel like I could breathe fire. This must be rage, another new and horrible emotion.

Quaid holds his head in his hands, his stringy hair hanging over his fingers. I stop in front of him with my fists clenched at my sides, fighting the urge to yank him to his feet.

"Tell me what happened," I say, as steadily as I can.

Quaid looks up. "It was an accident. He didn't mean to do it."

"Just tell me everything." I grit my teeth, struggling to resist grabbing Quaid's throat and shaking the truth from him.

Travis steps between Quaid and me, takes my hand, and eases me onto the sofa next to him. I glance at the girls, wide-eyed and silent. They look from me, to their dad, to the man slumped in the chair. Travis motions for Zack to take the girls to their room.

"But I wanna know, too." Zack crosses his arms and widens his stance in the doorway. "Make Einstein put them to bed."

I agree with Zack. I'm tired of keeping secrets from him. I squeeze Travis's hand and nod toward Einstein.

Einstein picks up the twins and leaves the room. "Let's go read a story," I hear him say.

Zack sits in the chair opposite Quaid, next to the fireplace, and narrows his eyes at the elder.

"Talk," I say to Quaid.

He lifts his scruffy chin. "Well, me and Bayl were bringing Darcy over here. Bayl said he was tired of Darcy's whinin', and he wanted her out of Zelfar."

"No." I look at Travis. "Marc must be sick with worry."

"Lilly musta been followin' us 'cause she came through the portal right after we did. We were still in the cave when Lilly told Bayl she knew what he was doin' and that he better take Darcy back to Zelfar that minute." Quaid rubs his hands on his damp thighs and continues. "Bayl told Lilly he was only doin' what he had to do, to keep Zelfar a harmonious place. He said people like Darcy belonged in a world more suited to their natures, that he was doin' Darcy a favor."

Quaid's voice becomes less gravelly the more he speaks. "Well, Lilly wasn't believin' any of it. She told Bayl she'd have him removed from the council. Then Lilly took a step toward Darcy, and Bayl jumped in front of her. He held his memory device up at Lilly and clicked it on, showing her a finger-sized crystal prism. He said he didn't wanna hurt her, but all he had to do was touch the prism to the base of her skull and she'd lose her memory, wouldn't remember nothin' before that moment."

Quaid's eyes fill with tears. He and Gram have been friends since childhood, but the depth of his concern seems like something more. "I begged Lilly to go back to Zelfar, but she lunged for the crystal and slipped. She fell toward Bayl, and when he grabbed her, the prism musta touched the back of her neck."

Quaid pulls tissues from the box on the coffee table and wipes his nose.

"Lilly went limp," he says. "I let go of Darcy, but I couldn't catch Lilly before her knees hit the ground. Bayl said he didn't mean to, that he wasn't really gonna do it. Lilly, poor Lilly."

Quaid rocks on the edge of the chair with his hands under his armpits, hugging himself. "Darcy screamed and ran out of the cave. Bayl took off after her, and he told me to take Lilly to Seattle. I told him I couldn't do that to Lilly. Bayl yelled at me, told me I better do as he said. But I don't care if he erases my memory 'cause I wouldn't wanna remember takin' Lilly off to Seattle and leavin' her. I couldn't do that. Not to my Lilly. So, I waited 'til she woke up and brought her here."

I reach a hand to Quaid's shoulder. "Thank you for bringing Gram to me. I may have done something regretful if Gram had disappeared." I pause to swallow the lump forming in my throat, and ask, "Where is her portal key?"

"Here." Quaid pulls Gram's pendant and chain from his pocket.

I take the necklace and ask, "Do you have Clay's portal key, too?"

Quaid shakes his head. "I told ya, I don't know nothin' about Clay."

My eyes narrow, and Travis puts a hand on my thigh. "Hon," he says, "Quaid has no reason to lie after admitting what happened to Gram."

"At least Gram is awake," Zack says, leaning forward and putting his elbows on his knees. "I wish Brita would wake up, even if she doesn't remember me."

I manage a weak smile for Zack and turn back to Quaid. "When did Bayl start banishing Zelfarians to America, and how did he get you to go along with him?"

Quaid clears his throat and stares at his feet. "Wyatt was the first. You probably don't know him. He was the same age as me and Bayl and Lilly, but we didn't like Wyatt. Nobody did 'cause he was a bully. Bayl said, more 'n once, Wyatt reminded him of my dad. My dad was mean and violent, too—killed his own father—'cause Grampa was protecting me." His voice breaks, and my heart softens with the realization Quaid blames himself for his grandfather's death.

"After we grew up," Quaid continues, "Lilly created serenity orbs, and everyone started usin' 'em. Everyone except Wyatt. He said he didn't want some machine takin' his anger away. There wasn't much we could do but try to stay out of his way. Then about thirty-five years ago, after Lilly gave her elder position to Bayl and told him about the portal, Bayl started thinking how we could send Wyatt to America and rid Zelfar of such a menace. We couldn't risk Wyatt tellin' anyone about the portal, so Bayl decided he'd invent a device that would make Wyatt forget everything."

Quaid squirms in his chair. "I ain't proud of it, but I agreed Wyatt didn't belong in our world, so I helped Bayl. I didn't know he was gonna do the same thing to more people. He said if I didn't keep helpin' him, I'd be next, and I'd never see Lilly again."

I stomp the floor, and Zack gasps. "So, to save yourself," I shout at Quaid, "you banished more and more people from Zelfar?"

"I'm sorry." He cowers. "I shoulda been stronger and tried to stop him."

"Who did you banish, and where did you take them?" I demand.

"There's Wyatt and April," Quaid ticks off on his fingers. "And Irene and Rudy. We took 'em all to Portland." The names match the ones Owen gave me.

Zack slaps his leg. "I knew it! Johnny Ford is Rudy."

"Why did Bayl tell you to take Gram to Seattle?" Travis asks.

"Probably 'cause he didn't want you to run into her like you did Rudy." Quaid grabs another handful of tissues and blows his nose.

I get up from the sofa and stand over Quaid. "Why did you banish Clay? He wasn't a menace!"

Quaid looks up at me and splays his hands. "Honest, Zophie. I don't know nothin' 'bout Clay."

Travis stands behind me, pressing gently on my shoulders to calm me.

I glance at Zack, wondering if I was right to burden him with another secret.

"Son—"

"I know, Mom. I won't say anything to anyone."

I turn back to Quaid. "Could Bayl have taken Clay through the portal and erased his memory without your help?"

"I guess so. If he did, he probably left him on the hospital steps—hospital or police station."

My fingernails cut into my palms. I must stop Bayl.

Travis gently unclenches my fists and takes my hands in his.

"That's enough for tonight."

I don't know if he's talking to me or Quaid, but I don't argue.

Despite my anger, I look at Quaid's puffy face and mud-splotched clothes and can't help but reach out and lay a gentle hand on his back. "For now, stay here and help me find these people, okay?"

Quaid sighs. "Thank you. I'll do anything. I hafta stay away from Bayl, and I wanna help Lilly."

"Zack," Travis says, "take Quaid upstairs to the guestroom and show him where he can find clean clothes . . . and a shower."

As soon as they leave, Travis steers me to our bedroom. Exhausted, I sit on the edge of the bed and stare at my empty hands. "Clay is lost, and Gram doesn't know me. What am I going to do?"

Travis pulls me to him, his muscular arms a warm shield around me. "You're going to be strong, like you always are. Gram is here. The honey lab cleanup can wait a day. I'll go to Zelfar in the morning and talk to Vad. Maybe he's already learned how to reverse the effects of the memory device."

Vad. In all the turmoil, I had forgotten about Vad.

CHAPTER 33

Sunshine coming through the window wakes me and I dress quickly in black slacks and a gray sweater. In the kitchen, I'm surprised to find Gram, Zack, and Quaid already sitting at the counter, eating banana-nut waffles. My stomach rumbles at the scent of fresh maple syrup, but food is not my first concern.

"Good morning, dear." Gram sounds so normal. Could she have regained her memory overnight?

"Good morning, Gram. How did you sleep?"

"Quite well, for not knowing where I am. I'm grateful for being with family. I just wish I could remember you." Gram's calmness seems odd to me. I'd be panicked if I didn't know who I was or know anyone around me.

I sigh inwardly and hug Gram's shoulders, breathing in her strawberry scent, same as always. "I love you, Gram, and I'm going to do everything I can to help you remember."

"Would you like a waffle?" Einstein asks. Before I answer, he straightens and says, "Travis and Vad are on their way from Agate Falls. I want to ask why Einstein didn't sense Gram and

Quaid last night, but that question can wait.

"I'll eat later." I hurry out of the kitchen, grab my coat, and go out the front door in time to see Vad set Travis on the cobblestone path.

"Vad! I'm so glad to see you." I run down the porch steps and throw my arms around the android.

"I am pleased to see you, too." He pats me twice on the back, his routine display of physical affection.

"Vad was already on his way here," Travis says. "We showed up in the cave at the same time. He has the device."

After a quick glance at the house, I say, "Let's talk in the . . ." I glance toward the demolished honey lab. "I mean, let's talk out here."

Vad's eyes follow mine to the rubble, which I expect him to question, but he doesn't.

"Don't you want to know what happened?"

Vad taps a finger to his temple.

"Of course, your link to Einstein. Did Travis tell you about Gram?

Vad's head droops as he nods. "I'm sorry I wasn't with Gram. She and I met with Bayl early yesterday. He didn't reveal anything to us, but Gram insisted we put his device back where we found it. I must have been working on my copy of the device when Gram followed Bayl and Quaid to the falls. Since hoverspheres are working again, she didn't need me. I didn't want to wake her last night, but when I was unable to locate her in Zelfar today, I came here. I should never have left her alone."

"You're right, Vad, you should have been with her." His head droops lower and I add, "But I know you were instructed to complete your copy of the device. Can it restore Gram's memory?"

Vad removes a green octagon, exactly like Bayl's, from his hip pocket, and a hexagonal prism, about the size of his little finger, from his shirt pocket. "Using these together will *erase* memories, as will Bayl's original, but neither device can *restore* memories."

"Then both your device and Bayl's must be destroyed."

"I disagree," Vad says flatly, slipping the octagon and prism back into his pockets.

"That device took Gram's and Clay's memories." My fingers clench. "Without a way to reverse the memory loss, those devices are dangerous. And you are not your own person, Vad. You are my android, and you will do as I say."

Travis takes my hands and massages my fingers, loosening my fists. "Vad is a member of our family, not a zelcom waiting for commands. I know you're upset, but please listen to him. He hasn't given up on reversing the effects of the device. You need to let him help."

I close my eyes and pull pine needles from my pocket, using the scent to help me refocus. "Okay, Vad, but make sure you keep that device and prism hidden. And maybe you should steal Bayl's device again. I could stop him from making another one by exposing his actions to the community."

"But that would mean divulging the portal, which would jeopardize Zelfar's future," Vad replies.

I sigh and drop my hands to my sides. "You're right. I'm sorry for the way I spoke to you. I just . . ." I peer at Travis. "What are we going to do?"

Travis puts a hand on my waist. "First thing I'm going to do is see why Bayl's device interferes with my androids' abilities to sense human presence near the portal. Vad told me that's why Einstein didn't know when Gram, Bayl, Quaid, and Darcy were at Agate Falls yesterday. In the meantime, you and Vad can focus on restoring Gram's memory."

Vad turns toward the porch. "May I go see Gram now?"

My eyes lock on our android's hands. "Vad, can you heal minds like you heal bodies?"

"Perhaps."

One word, but it's enough.

Excited over the possibility, I hurry into the house with Vad and Travis behind me. We find Gram and Quaid sitting on the sofa in the living room, and Zack coloring with the girls in front of the fireplace.

"Quite a family you got here, Zophie," Quaid says when he sees me. "Twin kids 'n' twin robots. Can't tell neither apart if they ain't dressed different."

Gram stands, extending her hand to Vad. "You must be Einstein's twin brother. I'm sure Quaid is teasing about you being a robot. They call me Gram. It's nice to meet you."

Vad takes Gram's hand and pulls her to him, engulfing her petite body in his long human-like arms. He silently hugs her to his chest, holding her for the longest moment. His back-patting, stiff embrace doesn't apply to Gram.

He finally relaxes his arms and smiles down at her. "I am Vad, and I am glad you are safe."

"Gram," I say, "would you come upstairs with me, please? I'd like to show you our healing room." I flick my eyebrow at Vad to go ahead of us.

"Of course, dear. A healing room sounds quite interesting."

I lead Gram upstairs, and once inside the room, I shut the door and motion for her to sit on the narrow floating bed. She doesn't seem shocked by the space-age appearance, as Americans would say. With no point of reference, maybe Gram just accepts what she sees.

Vad eases Gram into a lying position and explains he is going to do a scan of her body.

"Will it hurt?" she asks.

"You won't feel a thing," he replies.

She relaxes, letting her eyelids close, and the image of her form appears in the air over the bed. Vad moves his hands above her physical body from her head to her feet. After the initial scan, his hands linger over Gram's forehead. His eyes lock on her scalp as if his vision can penetrate her skull.

The minutes pass slowly. My fingers grip the fabric of my pants, pinching and releasing. What's taking so long? I want my grandmother back.

Finally, Vad lowers his hands, and Gram's virtual image disappears.

"Vad," I whisper, "did you succeed?"

He gives a hint of a shrug, touches my grandmother's arm, and says, "Gram, you can sit up now."

She opens her eyes and raises up. "Are we all done?" Vad nods, and Gram adds, "You're right, Vad. I didn't feel a thing."

I take Gram's hand as she stands. "Do you remember anything before last night?"

"I wish I could tell you I did, dear."

Tears burn in my eyes, and I turn, doing my best to blink them away. Vad couldn't heal Brita's mind. I don't know why I thought he could help Gram.

Vad's lower lip quivers, and he gazes at Gram. "Bayl will pay for what he has done to you." I've never heard this sharp edge in his tone.

Would Vad harm Bayl? I know his brain and emotions are evolving, and I empathize with his desire for vengeance, but I don't like thinking our android could hurt someone out of anger. I'll discuss Vad's behavior later with Travis.

I give Gram a hug. "I'll find another way to restore your memories."

"It'll be all right, dear."

Gram and I go downstairs to the living room where Travis and Zack each bounce a twin on their knees. The girls giggle, their long hair flopping with each bounce. I want to be as happy and carefree as our daughters.

Gram smiles at Quaid, who moves from his spot by the fire

and walks toward her.

She says to me, "Would you mind if I take the little ones for a walk? It's beautiful outside."

"Not at all. Einstein can go with you so you don't get lost." At least Gram seems content. But I don't want to ever leave her alone again.

"I'll go with 'em," Quaid says. "Can I borrow a jacket?" Without waiting for a reply, he takes one of Travis's from a hook and slips it on. The black coat hangs loosely on his gangly arms.

I walk out to the porch to watch Gram take each twin by a hand. The girls happily hop down the steps onto the cobblestone path. Einstein and Quaid join them, and the group crosses the front lawn to the trail along Agate Creek.

Travis stands next to me at the porch railing. "It *is* a beautiful day."

"You'd never know last night's storm ever happened."

"Well, I wouldn't say that." He scowls at the yard. "Look at all the broken limbs on the lawn and driveway. And there's the mess in the honey lab. I'd better go see what I can salvage."

"I'm sorry I sent Einstein with Gram. You need him to help you."

Travis shrugs and glances at Vad and Zack standing in the doorway. "I have these two," he says. "Einstein can help when he gets back if you don't have something else for him to do."

"No, of course not. I'll send him right out to you."

Travis trudges down the steps and around the side of the house with Vad and Zack behind him.

I tie the belt on my long sweater, ease myself onto the porch swing, and lean my head against the hard wooden slats. I feel like crying, but that won't fix Gram, find Clay, or undo the storm. Thinking of the storm makes me wonder about Hank and I tap my zelcom.

"Hello?" Hank responds.

"Hi, Hank. I just wanted to make sure you got home safely last night."

"It was a dicey drive all right, like playing dodge ball with tree branches. But still not as bad as Hurricane Rita in '62. How about you? Any trees fall on the house?"

"No, but we had some damage to the barn. Travis is making repairs now."

"You're lucky then," Hank says. "A lot of folks are going to be without power for a while."

"How about Janet? Is she okay?" What I really want to know is if he's heard anything about Clay.

"Yep, she's fine. She was on emergency call at the hospital all night. I know you want an update on Clay, but I have to tell you, I'm stymied on this one. My contact at the station says there's no record of who bailed him out, or that he was even at Columbia County Jail."

"We saw him!"

"Yeah, yeah, I know. Don't worry. I'll track him down. Someone has to know something."

I stare helplessly at my zelcom.

"Zophie? You still there?"

I nod, still forgetting he can't see my image. "Yes. I'm here. I feel terrible for Clay. Thank you for not giving up."

"Just so you know, I'm keeping tabs on Filmore in case Clay becomes his patient again. Janet's been buddying up to him at the clinic, too. Thinks he might share things with her, one professional to another."

"That's good." I certainly don't want to be Dr. Filmore's buddy.

"I'll give you a call as soon as I know anything. Keep your chin up."

"Thanks, Hank." I tap my zelcom to end the call and picture Clay eating a weed brownie in Dr. Filmore's office on that ugly sofa, getting ready to be hypnotized.

Hypnotherapy! I can hypnotize Gram . . . in a quiet place—her room with her crystals and aromatic oils. I jump up and lean over the rail, gazing expectantly at the edge of the yard, anxious for Gram to emerge from the woods. Finally, I see Einstein step from the path and onto the grass. His hands are passenger seats, on which Gram and Quaid perch, each holding a toddler.

Gram steps onto the ground and says to me, "I don't know how this young man did it, but he whipped up those chairs and carried us the last half mile as if his muscles never tire."

"That's normal for an android." I see no reason to hide anything about Zelfar from her. "Gram. I have an idea that could help you remember your past."

"Oh my, that would be wonderful, dear. Come along, little ones." Gram swooshes Kayla and Krissie through the door in front of her. The girls kick off their wet shoes in the tiled entry.

"Einstein, please feed the girls and read them a story so Gram and I can have some time alone." He nods and starts toward the kitchen when I remember my promise. "Wait! I told Travis I would send you outside to help him."

Quaid hangs Travis's jacket back on the hook, and I ask, "Would you mind tot-watching the girls?"

He gives me an unexpected smile. "I'll be glad to tend to the young 'uns while you go fix Lilly."

Einstein walks toward the back door, and Quaid directs the twins to the kitchen.

Gram hangs her sweater, removes her shoes, and slides her feet into her furry slippers. Imagining Gram with her memory back, I smile into her beautiful hazel eyes.

"What's your idea, dear?" she asks.

"I'm going to use a technique called hypnosis. Does that word sound familiar to you?"

She shakes her head. "How does it work?"

"Let's go to your room and I'll show you."

Once inside her bedroom, I gently close the door and say, "Lie on your bed, facing the ceiling. I'll help you relax, ask you a few questions, and you'll answer whatever you can."

Gram takes her position on the bed, her fingers rubbing her necklace pendant. Hopefully, in a few minutes, she'll remember the necklace is her portal key to her real home. I walk to Gram's dresser and look at the six pendulums dangling from her mirror. I choose the small pointed amethyst stone on a thin silver chain—her favorite—hoping that since Gram's memory wipe is so recent, hypnosis will work better on her than with Amber and Johnny. Or at least she'll say something that will spark another idea for me to try.

I hold the purple crystal above Gram's face. When the stone begins to sway in short rhythmic strokes, I repeat in a soft, steady voice, "Focus on the pendulum. Let your eyes follow the point."

When Gram's pupils dilate, I wrap the stone in my fingers. "You will respond to any question I ask."

Gram's eyelids vibrate slightly and close. I wet my lips and carefully lay the pendulum on the nightstand.

"Let's go to Zelfar, where you live," I say. "What do you see?"

Gram's face lights up with a grin. "Flowers and trees and lots of domes. And hoverspheres, with people inside them, gliding through the air."

Excellent! Her mind remembers our world. "Where are you?"

"I'm in my beautiful homedome that's colored like a rainbow." Gram sounds like herself, unlike the flat monotone of Amber's voice.

I touch the pine needles in my pocket and will my voice to sound calm. "Are you with anyone?"

"I'm . . ." She pauses.

"It's okay, Gram, take your time." Oops, maybe I shouldn't have called her by name.

"Zophie, I told you I have to go see Bayl."

What? Is she awake? She can't be—her eyelids are still quivering.

"Is Bayl with you now?"

"He doesn't see me, but I hear him telling Quaid to go get Darcy and meet him at the falls. Bayl is doing it again. I have to stop him." Gram squirms and her jaw tightens.

My stomach knots as if her anxiety is mine. After a few seconds, she seems to relax, and I continue. "How will you stop Bayl?"

"Rush home, get my necklace, and hurry to Paradise Falls. Bayl slips behind the water. I run through the portal and find him and Quaid in the cave. They have Darcy!" Gram's voice rises an octave, and her legs twitch on the bed.

Maybe I should wake her. I already know what happens next.

"Bayl, you have no right to banish people. Take Darcy back to Zelfar this instant!"

I flinch and look over my shoulder, half-expecting to see Bayl behind me.

Gram's legs twitch again, and I hold my breath, hoping she doesn't try to get up. When they go still, I exhale with relief.

"Does Bayl do as you say?" I ask tentatively.

"No. He is ridding our world of misfits, like Darcy. Says she refuses to serve, and she's telling everyone the scientists are making robots out of our babies."

Darcy's mind must be seriously ill. Is that what happens when someone goes for months without using a serenity orb?

"I misjudged you, Bayl. I'm going to take back my position on the council," she declares as if he's in the room with us. "Bayl! How dare you threaten me? Give me that device. You're never using it again . . . Eeee! Ouch!"

My temples throb. I have to bring Gram out of this mental torture. I force my voice to sound mechanical, suggestive. "You are calm," I tell her. "When you awaken you will remember everything you have told me."

I release Gram from her hypnotic state and stand anxiously by her bed. She doesn't move. Is she still in trance? Did I do something wrong? "Gram, are you awake?" I whisper.

Her eyelids open slowly, and she lifts her head. "Have I been asleep?"

"Yes, for a little while. What do you remember after you laid down?"

She yawns and smiles. "You waved a pendulum over my eyes and made me sleepy. Have I been napping long?"

"Not long." I swallow hard. "How do you feel?"

"Relaxed." She sits up and rubs her eyes.

I love Gram so much. I wish she knew how much she loves me, too.

I glance at Gram's necklace and realize that since the memory wiping device was made in Zelfar, any clues to reversing the effects would likely be found there. "Gram, I'm going to be gone overnight. Do you think you'll be all right here until I return tomorrow?"

"You're leaving? What about the hypnosis technique? I'm sorry I fell asleep, dear. I'll stay awake. I promise."

I sit next to her on the bed and wrap her in my arms. "The hypnosis didn't work, but it's all right, Gram. When I get home tomorrow, I'll tell you all about your past, okay?"

She kisses my cheek. "Of course, dear. Perhaps hearing about my past will help me remember."

"I love you, Gram. I'll have Einstein wake you later." I pull a soft blanket over her and leave the room, closing the door with a soft click.

When I enter the living room, Quaid rises from the sofa. "Did you find out . . .?" My sullen face must give him the answer because his head drops, and he stares at the floor.

"She's napping. And the girls?"

"They are, too."

"I'm going to Zelfar," I say. "There has to be a clue there for how to get her memory back. I'll let Travis know I'm taking Krissie with me."

"Good luck to ya, Zophie." He plops in Gram's favorite chair. "I'll sit here 'til Lilly or Kayla wake up."

"Thank you, Quaid."

I walk to my room and change into zeltire. Sitting on the edge of the bed, I pull pine needles from my pocket and immerse myself in the calming scent to mentally prepare for Travis's foreseeable reaction to my plan. I hate to interrupt him, but I need to go now.

"Hi, hon." Travis's voice resounds through my zelcom, with rustling and clanking in the background.

"I'm taking Krissie to Zelfar. We'll be back tomorrow. I'm leaving Vad with you to help rebuild the lab."

"No!" Travis shouts over the din. "You need protection from Bayl. I'm tense enough with this project. I don't want to worry about you, too."

"Sweetheart, I appreciate your concern, but you need Vad. Krissie and I will be fine in Zelfar. I promise to stay away from Bayl."

Travis is silent for several seconds before he says, "Zophie, please, take Vad with you."

"No. Please don't send him after me."

A loud sigh comes from my zelcom. "Please be vigilant. I love you."

"I promise. I love you, too. See you tomorrow."

I silently gather toddler zeltire, ease Krissie from the bed, and slip out the door, careful not to wake Kayla. Always having to abandon one of the girls is torture—for them and for me. I dress Krissie in the living room and carry her out the front door.

She stirs as we near the falls.

"I wanna walk, Mommy."

As soon as her feet touch the ground, she runs ahead on the trail. I dash after her, wondering if I inadvertently brought Kayla. Snatching her up from behind, I run into the cave at Agate Falls.

"Let's go to Zelfar," I say. With an unexpected tremble to my fingers, I pull on the tiny pyramids of my earrings, attaching them under my chin. Staring at the glowing rock, I wonder if I've made a mistake by not bringing Vad.

I close my eyes, and for a second Gram's radiant smile glows inside my head. I have to find a way to fix her memory. With renewed conviction, I lift Krissie.

She tries to wiggle away. "I wanna walk."

"Kayla?"

She narrows her little brow. "I'm not Kayla."

I chuckle for doubting myself. "Of course, you're not, Krissie. You have to hold onto the little pyramids under my chin, remember?"

She nods. "Can we stay in Zelfar this time? I like it better there."

Without giving her an answer, I step through the shimmer.

CHAPTER 34

Standing in the cave behind Paradise Falls, I enjoy the momentary sense of peace and say, "I like it better here, too."

"I wanna ride in the glass ball." Krissie wiggles from my grasp and runs out of the cave.

"It's a hoversphere," I say, chasing after her. "And it's *want to,* not *wanna.*"

"I *want to* ride in the *huvasphere.*"

I chuckle and tap my zelcom. Krissie mimics me. Soon she'll ask to call for the transport, but thankfully, today isn't that day. Our little girls are growing up so fast.

When our hoversphere arrives, Krissie hops in and claps when her child-size seat appears. I sit on the adult seat that materializes opposite hers.

"Loop Four, Circle Elm, Dome Purple," I say.

"Dome Purple?" Krissie looks up at me. "That's our house, Mommy."

"Homedome, Krissie. Homedome, not house." Travis *must* get the honey lab rebuilt soon.

Soaring over the forest, we see several acres of new growth beginning to sprout. The forest gives way to circles of multicolored domes, like clusters of cul-de-sacs in America. Krissie scoots to the edge of her seat and presses her finger against the clear shell of the sphere.

"The purple one," she says. "That's our *homedome.*"

"Yes, it is. It feels good to be home, doesn't it?"

Her eyes twinkle when she smiles. "Can we stay here?"

"For a while." I pat her hand.

When the hoversphere stops in front of our dome, Krissie jumps out and runs to the entrance, which slides open as she approaches. I send the hoversphere away and hurry after her. She stops in the center corridor and shouts, "Kayla? Where are you?"

I kneel and take her hands in mine. "Sweetheart, why do you think Kayla is here?"

Her lips twitch, and her eyes shine with tears. "Before you carried me to the waterfall, we were playing here together."

"You were dreaming, sweetie." I stroke her fingers. "I woke you from your nap before I carried you to the falls."

Krissie whimpers. "How come Kayla couldn't come with us?"

"I'll explain when you're a little older. Right now, let's go choose a pretty outfit for you to wear today."

We walk in silence to her sleeping orb. Without Vad's voice to greet us, the dome feels unnervingly quiet and impersonal—like a house. At least the mechanical functions don't rely on Vad's presence.

"I want purple," Krissie says, pulling a short-sleeved tunic from a shelf. Dressed all in purple, she runs ahead of me to my unity orb. "Match me." She pinches the fabric of her shirt and points at my clothing shelf. "We love purple, like G'am."

"Yes, we do." I don a deep purple tunic and long pants. When our hoversphere arrives, we climb inside, and I say, "Toddler Tutor Dome."

"No, Mommy. I wanna go with you."

"Krissie," I say, curling her fingers in mine, "you need to go to your tutor sessions to learn how to read and create so you can be a scientist like Daddy and me."

When we exit the hoversphere, a tutorbot awaits, wearing the customary bright yellow pantsuit of all bots that serve in that dome. The bot has a light brown skin tone and dark brown hair, shoulder length, to personify a female.

Krissie clutches my hand, pressing herself into my legs. How could I have thought she was Kayla? I let her cling, knowing the tutorbot will soon woo her away with paints or coloring wands.

"K," the bot says, kneeling in front of Krissie. "We are floor painting today with our feet."

Krissie doesn't move.

"Patty chose green paint socks. What color would you like?"

"I want purple." Krissie releases my hand and walks with the tutorbot into the dome.

I start to turn toward the hoversphere and stop when I hear my name in a robotic tone. "Zophie." A tutorbot walks toward me. "I'd like to speak with you." The bot's request is unusual. Feedback regarding our children is usually communicated through our zelcoms.

"We are concerned about your child," the bot says. "She draws with great detail."

My motherly defenses send a surge up the back of my neck. "She's a budding artist."

"She drew this." A surprisingly discernable depiction of Peanut, Janet's dog, appears in the air above the tutorbot's palm, including the tiny purple bow on Peanut's fluffy head.

I hope this tutorbot can't detect the rapid rise in my pulse, or she might send an alert to Health Dome. "I'm happy to see my daughter has such a wonderful imagination. Why is this image a concern?"

"K insists this is a real peanut. She confuses the other children with talk of invisible friends she calls Kayla and Krissie." The bot stares at me with unfeeling eyes. "We recommend neural testing and focused serenity orb treatments. May we start the process?"

"No, you may not!" I inhale and say calmly, "I'm a health expert, and I will see to her needs. Do I make myself clear?"

"As you wish, Zophie." The tutorbot turns and walks toward the dome.

Reentering my hoversphere, I feel shaky all over. I can't make Gram remember Zelfar, and I can't make my twins forget America. At least the musings of young children can be explained as imagination. Soon, we'll be making honey here, and I won't have to worry about juggling the twins between worlds. Otherwise, it's only a matter of time before one of my daughters reveals something I can't explain.

Before I can tell the hoversphere where to take me, a slight pulse on my wrist signals an incoming call. Soon I see Owen's virtual face. "Hi. Zophie. Did you get my messages?"

"Sorry, Owen. I haven't had a chance to check for messages."

"I've been trying to let you know we have another missing person. Darcy. You know her, right?"

"Oh, no." I put my hand to my mouth, hoping my surprise is convincing.

"Her husband is mighty upset."

"Poor Marc. He must be so worried." I wish I could tell Marc I plan to locate his wife and bring her back.

"He wants me to take him out to look for her. My new exploring sphere is ready, so I told him we could search for her today. Do you want to come?"

"Thanks, Owen, but I'm on my way to see Brita. Please let me know if you locate Darcy. If I see her, I'll let you know, too."

"Toss pine." Owen's image vanishes.

"Health Dome," I say to my transport. Besides checking on

Brita, it's the logical place to look for memory cures.

Health Dome emerges as a giant bubble amid brightly colored foliage, and the outer shell reflects the gentle ripples from nearby Crystal Lake. When I step onto the platform, the blue-rimmed opening appears, welcoming me inside.

The corridors sparkle with large crystal vases filled with red and yellow flowers. The sky casts soft blue hues, making the hall appear as a soothing underwater tunnel. I'll be glad when life becomes simple again, and I can go back to serving as a health expert. I desperately wish Clay were here.

"Zophie." A woman wearing a red armband walks toward me from the corridor that leads to the cafeterium. "I've been trying to contact Clay for several days, but he hasn't responded. Have you seen him?"

"Um, I . . . no, I haven't. Is there something I can do for you?"

"An expectant mother is due to give birth next week, and Clay asked if I would like to perform the delivery. He's waiting for my answer, and I need to tell him yes."

"That's wonderful. I'll let Clay know you will be the health expert in the birthing orb."

"Okay. Thanks, Zophie. Toss pine." She walks back toward the cafeterium, and I continue down the center corridor. I should get used to people asking about Clay. I swallow the lump in my throat.

A few paces from Brita's orb, I grasp the pine needles inside my pocket, hoping to find the neuro-tube empty, hoping to give Zack good news. My eyes fall on Brita lying motionless inside the orb, and my hand crushes the pine needles.

The ends of her neuro-tube glow green, but the thin beams of white light on Brita's scalp are new. Dan and Mick stand on either side of her. I step quickly to the entrance. The door remains sealed, and Dan, a foot taller than his colleague, walks toward me.

His voice emanates from my zelcom. "Hello, Zophie. We are preparing for an experiment and must control the environment. No visitors for the rest of today."

"What kind of experiment?"

"Impulse manipulation of the corticospinal and corticobulbar tracts."

"Brain signal to motor function," I interpret aloud. "Interesting."

"If she awakens, I will alert you." Dan taps his zelcom, and the clear shell between us becomes an opaque blue.

I've never been denied access to anywhere in Zelfar. I could insist they let me in, but I don't want to jeopardize their experiment. I lift my hands and lay my arms and forehead on the shell, which is cool to my skin.

"Brita," I say softly, "we really need you to wake up. Zack misses you, we all miss you. Please come back to us. You're like a daughter to me, and if Zack has his way, you'll be my daughter-in-law." She can't hear me, but somehow talking to her is comforting. I tap my zelcom and raise my eyes to the high arched ceiling. "Hil?"

"Yes, Zophie. How may I help you?"

"Please transfer all data related to neurological and memory function to my zelcom." Perhaps there's a way to manipulate brain signals to restore memory.

"Done. Is that all?"

"Yes, Hil. Thank you."

"Please say hello to Vad for me. I haven't felt his connection yet today."

Blatz. I wonder if the other service domes notice Vad's absence. "I will."

Almost to the exit, I stop short when I see Bayl getting out of a hoversphere. I leap behind a large planter. The impulse for vengeance threatens to consume me. I want to squeeze Bayl's neck, feel him collapse with the pressure on his windpipe, but my promise to Travis holds me back.

I crouch behind the pot, peeking through a narrow space between leaves. Holding my breath as Bayl walks past, I wonder if the bulge in the side pocket of his tunic is the memory-wiping device. I'm glad I didn't confront him.

As soon as Bayl enters a corridor out of my view, I dash around the planter and hurry to my hoversphere. My heart still thumps when I rush into my homedome a few moments later. The doorway slides closed, and I press myself against the cool shell, glad to be safe at home.

No one should feel such nauseating fear here in Zelfar. I wish I had a serenity orb. Maybe I'll go use the one at Gram's.

"Serenity simulators heal the mind," I hear her say in my head, and her words ease the tension in my stomach. Maybe serenity simulators can heal memory, too!

Without waiting for her tutor sessions to end, I retrieve Krissie from Toddler Tutor Dome. When she's seated, I say to our hoversphere, "Paradise Falls."

"We're going to go tell Gram about Zelfar and bring her back here to a serenity orb."

"And see Kayla!" Krissie claps when I nod. She seems to have forgotten she'd wanted to stay in Zelfar.

CHAPTER 35

With Krissie on my back, I jog through the woods, which are dim with approaching dusk. I smile, seeing Vad on the path.

"When I told Travis you were coming through the portal," Vad says, "he sent me to check on you." Vad transports us the rest of the way, and when he sets us on our porch a familiar earthy pungency takes me by surprise.

"Is Dr. Filmore here?" I look for a car in the driveway.

"He left recently," Vad says.

Krissie opens the door and scurries inside. I remain on the porch with Vad.

"Did he get into the house?"

"No," Vad says. "I stopped him before he reached the front door. He said he came to visit you. I told him you were out of town and escorted him to his car on the other side of the gate."

"He climbed the gate?"

"That is correct."

Imagining the short man scrambling over the wrought iron almost makes me chuckle; the fact that he did makes me fume.

But how can I condemn his clandestine behavior when I sent Hank to snoop in his office? "Was he alone?"

"Yes."

Well, that's a relief at least. "Did Travis or Zack see Filmore?"

"No. They and Einstein were in Portland."

"Portland? Are they home now?"

"The three of them are in the lab."

I'm not sure what I find more reassuring—Zack wasn't here for Dr. Filmore to question, or Zack made it safely home from Portland.

"Thank you for checking on me and for sending Filmore away. Hopefully, he won't be back." My nervous stomach tells me he will. I pull the last of my pine needles from my pocket and toss them onto the steps.

Vad and I walk inside, and I close the door, gladly leaving thoughts of Filmore and his lingering odor outside.

"Mommy!" Kayla runs from the living room with Gram behind her.

"Zophie, dear." Gram gives me a hug. "How was your trip?"

I hold her in my arms, inhaling her scent. "Zelfar isn't the same without you."

"Vad," I say, releasing Gram. "Will you entertain the girls for a few minutes?"

He lifts an eyebrow, and I get the weird impression he doesn't think I should assume he's the tot-watcher. Einstein would never hesitate when it comes to the twins.

I ignore my assumption and ask, "Is Travis expecting you back in the lab?"

Vad nods. "I will inform him of your safe arrival." He walks briskly toward the back door.

I stare after him, thinking I liked it better when our android was more predictable. I'm tempted to follow him to the lab, to see how the salvage is coming, but Gram's sleeve brushes my arm.

"Come sit down, dear. I think you wanted to tell me something."

I follow her into the living room. Quaid stands next to the fireplace. He tips his head in an unspoken hello. Instead of sitting in her favorite overstuffed chair, Gram sits on the sofa, and softly pats the seat for me to sit next to her.

Sitting on the edge of the cushion, I face her and say, "Are you ready to hear about your life?"

She sweeps her silvery-blonde hair behind one ear. "Oh my, yes, dear. I want to know everything."

Krissie climbs onto Gram's lap. "I wanna know, too."

Kayla pulls her toddler-sized chair up close, pressing her knees against my shins. I catch a glimpse of a smile from Quaid, who settles into the chair by the fire, and know he's listening, too.

"The place where you were born, Gram, where you grew up, and where you belong, is very different from this house and what you've seen here." I smile at her. "Our world has crystillium domes instead of wooden houses. We get from one place to another in hoverspheres, not loud and smoky cars. The weather is always sunny and mild. Everyone has plenty of everything."

"This place sounds lovely, dear. Why are we here instead?"

"Complexities."

Gram places her dainty hand on my knee, and I wrap her warm fingers in mine. With the same softness I've heard since childhood, she says, "It'll be all right, dear. Complexities often untangle themselves. Now tell me more about that wonderful world."

I feel like I'm spilling my heart to a close friend, like I'm telling Janet all about my real world instead of telling my grandmother about hers. Gram smiles when I describe her homedome, grinning widely as she takes in my version of her life story. Sometimes she asks for more detail, like when I talk about the serenity orbs. I know she feels a connection.

When she smiles, I notice a new wrinkle at the corner of her mouth, and a pang of guilt hits me. I often forget how much faster people age on this side of the portal. It's my fault Gram spends so much time here. She needs to be in Zelfar.

"One big complexity, Gram, is that people from America, like Hank and Janet, don't know about our world, and we can't tell them."

Her head nods, but her narrowed brow tells me she doesn't understand. She looks to Quaid as if remembering he's a trusted friend.

"They wouldn't believe ya, Lilly. And you can't take 'em there to prove it."

"Do I know Hank and Janet?" Gram asks. I forgot Gram doesn't remember them. I shouldn't have used them as examples.

"You did," Quaid answers. "You were friends with Hank's mother."

"All right. I won't tell them." Gram squares her shoulders, repositions Krissie on her lap, and turns to me. "I would like to see this other world for myself."

"And you will, soon." As soon as I determine who will tot-watch one of the girls.

"You will take me there now." Gram sets Krissie on the sofa beside her. "I'll get my sweater."

I stand and try to catch Gram by the arm, but she pulls back.

"Zophie, you will take me to my world."

I've never seen her agitated like this. "Okay, Gram. We'll go now."

Quaid's face turns ashen. "I . . . I have to stay here."

I glare at the cowardly elder. "A serenity orb might heal Gram. If you care so much about her, why aren't you willing to stand up to Bayl to protect her?"

"I *do* care about Lilly. More than anything." He gets up from his chair and goes to Gram. "I . . . I love you."

Gram stands, touches Quaid's hand, and the tightness in her jaw softens. "You love me?"

"Yeah, Lilly. And I ain't gonna let Bayl hurt you again." Quaid places a gentle hand on her cheek and kisses her forehead. "I'll go with ya to Zelfar."

I smile inwardly and give a small, fake cough. "While you two change into zeltire, I'll let Travis know our plans."

Gram and Quaid walk out of the living room holding hands.

"Let's go visit Daddy in the lab," I say to the twins.

We hurry down the walkway. I'm amazed to see the barn has already been repaired with fresh lumber to replace the boards that flew off in the storm. Inside the barn, a new dome, smaller than the old one, fills me with renewed hope. How did Travis get the crystillium already?

Travis is surprised but pleased to see us. He wipes his hands on a rag hanging from his pocket before he hugs and kisses me. The girls run to his legs and swing around his calves.

"Did you have a reserve of crystillium here?" I ask. "How did you do all this in one day?"

"Vad made a fast trek to Zelfar for crystillium." Travis winks. "Hil told him you were fine, too." Travis splays his hand toward the neatly arranged jars on a row of upright shelves atop a spotless floor. "I wouldn't be making this kind of progress without the help of Zack and both of our androids. Thank the cosmos we were able to salvage three of the apple-huck shrubs and a canister of the new honey."

"This is impressive, sweetheart. I have to take Gram to Zelfar. Now. So . . . I'll take the twins with me." I look down at the girls still clinging to his legs.

"Have you lost your mind, too?"

"Gram hasn't lost her mind—just her memory. I think a serenity simulator will heal her. I know taking both girls is a risk, but you need our androids. I won't let anyone see the twins together."

Travis rubs the back of his neck. "Zophie, you're zapping the cosmos." He strokes Kayla's hair and gazes at Krissie. "I'll keep one of them here. The honey can wait."

"No! The honey cannot wait. If you don't re-create the honey process, Zelfar will fall apart anyway." I take his hand and hope my gaze is reassuring. "I'll heal Gram. You make the honey."

He lets out an exasperated sigh. "What about Quaid? Does he have to go with you?"

I stare blankly. "Um. I guess I assumed we needed him in case we encountered Bayl, but Gram and I can take a hoversphere to her homedome and back to the falls." I give Travis a kiss. "I'll ask Quaid to tot-watch."

"I love you," he says. "I can spare Vad long enough to transport you and Gram to Agate Falls. Please hurry back. It'll be dark soon."

"I will." I take the girls to the house, where Gram and Quaid wait by the front door.

I glance at Quaid's dark blue zeltire. "Quaid, I'm sorry for trying to shame you into going with us, but would you mind tot-watching the girls here while I zip over to Zelfar with Gram?"

"But I have to protect her from Bayl." He drapes an arm around Gram's shoulders.

"We'll go straight to Gram's and back here."

"It'll be all right, Quaid." Gram moves from his arm and touches his cheek.

"Okay," he says to her. "Hurry back."

Gram grabs her sweater from the hook, something she won't need in Zelfar. When she opens the door, Vad stands on the porch.

I sit in one of Vad's hand-chairs, glad I'm not risking the twins being discovered. I doubt the council will admit they've performed unauthorized abortions on dual fetuses all these years. They aborted one to save one, but without the mothers' knowledge or consent. When we can make honey in Zelfar, Gram wants me to introduce the twins as an anomaly. She thinks I can say I've shuffled their whereabouts in Zelfar so they would be perceived as one child because I wasn't willing for them to be test subjects. Gram is sure the next set of twins will be conceived soon enough.

When Vad deposits us at Agate Falls, Gram clicks her necklace, activating the portal.

"Gram, what else do you remember?" I hold my breath on the faint hope her portal key triggered her memory.

She fumbles with her pendant and says, "Doesn't this turn on the light at every waterfall?"

"No, Gram," I say, trying to keep the disappointment out of my voice. "Just this one."

CHAPTER 36

I follow Gram through the glow and walk with her out of the cave.

"Is this what magic feels like?" Gram asks. "Are we truly in another world?"

I put a hand gently on her shoulder. "We're in Zelfar, and you mustn't react to anything that appears strange to you. No one can suspect your memory is impaired. And please, please, don't mention the portal."

Gram pats my hand. "It'll be fine, dear."

I give her a half-smile as I call for our hoversphere. When we soar over the homedome loops, I nervously watch for familiar faces in nearby hoverspheres. No one seems to notice us. Most stare at their zelcoms or talk to other passengers.

Gram's homedome finally comes into view. I touch her knee and say, "That dome with the rainbow hue is your home."

Gram presses her forehead to the sphere. "Ooh. It's truly beautiful."

Seeing happiness on Gram's face settles my jitters a little. The hoversphere sets down on her platform, and she exits the sphere, opening her arms as if to embrace her dome.

A male neighbor shouts, "Hi, Lilly."

"Wave, Gram," I say out of the corner of my mouth. She raises an unsure hand, and I wave at him, too. We enter her dome, and the door slides closed.

"Welcome home, Lilly," her dome says.

"Who is here?" She looks up at the arched ceiling and peers from side to side. Her lavender-colored homebot walks toward her.

Gram starts to back away, and I gently take her arm. "The voice you heard is your dome, and this is your robot, called a homebot. You instruct your dome, and your dome instructs your homebot."

"Why do I have a robot?"

"It cooks and cleans for you."

Gram scoots around the bot and walks to her favorite chair in the living orb.

"Do things feel familiar?" I ask as I sit on the end of the sofa nearest her.

"Only this chair in this room." She rubs the purple fabric. "It's like the one at your house."

I hide a chuckle, thinking how much Gram sounds like one of the toddlers. "The sections of our homedomes," I say, "are called orbs instead of rooms. They're named for their function, like sleeping orb or cooking orb. There's a special orb I want you to see. Maybe you'll remember designing it." I'm glad Gram's dome is one of the few with a serenity orb so I don't have to take her to a public one.

With a smile of encouragement, I rise and extend my hand to Gram. "Let's go to your serenity orb."

She walks with me to a small orb off the central corridor. Gram steps inside and puts a hand over her gaping mouth. "I have palm trees . . . and all these orchids inside my home? Are we in Hawaii, that place I saw on your TV yesterday?" She touches the palm fronds as if to ensure they're real.

"No. Hawaii is a place on the other side of the portal." The subtle scent of freesia subdues my anxiety as I lead her to the lounge chair next to a tall orchid.

"Lie down and relax. I'll position the serenity simulator for you."

"What is its purpose?"

"It calms your mind and helps you focus your intentions."

"But I already feel calm, dear. I'd like to go see what's inside the big domes I noticed when we were flying here."

I sit on the lounge, gently tugging her hand until she lowers herself beside me. I pull her fingers to my thumping heart and look into her eyes. "You created serenity simulators, and you once told me they heal the mind like our instant healing tubes heal the body. That means a few minutes of serenity simulation might restore your memories."

"Okay, dear. I understand."

I stand, making room for Gram to fully recline. Her floral zeltire blends with the fabric, bringing out the gold in her hair and the pink in her cheeks.

I move the serenity simulator into position an inch above Gram's face. She raises her hand as if to push it away.

"It's all right, Gram. The simulator will mold around your face, but it won't touch you. You'll be able to breathe normally, and you won't feel a thing."

She gives me a little nod and relaxes. I release the simulator and it molds to her features in an almost transparent shield from her chin to the top of her head. Within seconds, her eyes close in quiet peace.

I tap my zelcom, setting a ten-minute timer, and sit on a small bench next to the lounge. The minutes pass slowly. Feeling more anxious than should be possible inside a serenity orb, I jerk when my zelcom pulses.

I stand over Gram. She looks like the same petite woman who has loved me since I was born. I want so desperately for her to remember. Slowly, carefully, I nudge the simulator to return to its original position in the air above the lounge.

"Gram?" I whisper, waiting for her to look at me, hoping for that soul-to-soul connection we've always shared.

"Zophie?" She opens her eyes and blinks once, twice. Her head and torso rise enough to prop herself on her elbows. She glances around the orb until her gaze meets mine.

Tears well inside me. There's no spark of recognition.

With a deep sigh, Gram lets her head plop back onto the pillow. "It didn't work, dear. Why did you think it would?"

"Because you told me serenity simulators heal the mind. Maybe we didn't give it long enough." I grasp the floating simulator again and say, "May I?" She nods, and I let the clear mask mold again to her face. Tears blur my vision, and I tap my zelcom to alert me in twenty minutes. The seconds crawl endlessly. I stare at her, hoping she'll suddenly call out and say she remembers me.

The timer finally pulses. I remove the simulator and hold my breath. When Gram sits up and looks at me, her stare tells me she still doesn't remember how important we've always been to one another.

I smack the serenity simulator, hard, envisioning it crashing against the shell of the orb, but the device simply bobs a little and remains in place.

"You're upset, dear. Do you need this lounge for a while?" Gram swings her legs to the side and stands.

I shake my head. The serenity simulator would ease my turmoil, but it wouldn't give me answers. I don't know what else to try that might help her, but I know we can't stay here. I won't let Bayl get near Gram again. I never thought the safest place for my family would be America.

I put an arm around Gram and lead her toward the exit. "Let's go back to our house while I try to think of another way to restore your memory."

Gram nods and walks with me to our hoversphere. Soaring toward Paradise Falls, my shoulders begin to relax . . . until we pass over History Dome, and I see Bayl and Marc on the platform, hurrying toward the entrance. Why is Marc with Bayl? Does Bayl plan to banish Marc, too? I start to tell the hoversphere to go back to History Dome. Then I notice Gram's reflection in the shell.

"I'm sorry again, Marc," I mumble to myself. "I couldn't save your baby, and now I can't save you."

CHAPTER 37

I breathe easier when Gram and I pass through the portal. Yet here, in America, Clay is alone somewhere and probably afraid. I don't understand how Bayl can feel justified in doing such horrendous things that, in his mind, protect Zelfar.

The cave behind Agate Falls is dark enough that we need our zelcom lights. "Einstein!" I say with a jolt of joy when my light shines on our android entering the cave. He carries us swiftly through the darkening woods and sets us on the front porch. "Thank you," I say, giving him a hug.

He follows us into the house and says, "Dinner will be ready soon."

I leave the girls with Gram and go out to the lab. Inside the small dome, I inhale the faint scents of honey, huckleberry, and apple. One small shelf, now stacked with full jars of honey, stands between two bushy trees in large pots. Vad and Zack pour a clear liquid through a narrow tube into a round canister. It's almost as if the storm never happened. But I won't say that to Travis.

Travis's eyes sparkle when he sees me. He points to an

apparatus, which looks like a short fat robot with tubes for arms and a green crystal hat. Travis tosses a short tool onto a table and picks up a clean towel from the bench.

"We made honey again," he says.

Grinning widely, I ask, "Now we can have honey in every cooking orb?"

Zack looks up. "Dad says you have to test it again."

"Then we can start replicating the process in Zelfar," Travis says. He wipes his hands, tosses the towel into a bin, and pulls me to him. "Tell me about Gram and the serenity orb."

I rest my cheek against his flannel shirt. "It didn't work."

Travis releases me and rubs his chin, glancing pensively from the bushy trees to the robotic apparatus, to the round canister filled with clear liquid.

"Zack, Vad," he says loudly, "we're going to Zelfar tomorrow to set up the honey lab there." Travis looks wide-eyed at me. "We have the formula. Six months. In six months, there'll be golden honey everywhere in Zelfar."

"Thank the cosmos." I press my face into his chest, clutching his shirt.

He rubs a hand over my hair. "I think maybe it's time I confront Bayl. He should know how to reverse the effect of his own device."

"No!" I lift my head. "Stay away from him. If Vad can't undo the effects, I don't see how anyone can. If Bayl were to use that horrible memory eraser on you, it scares me to think what I might do."

Travis kisses the top of my head. "Okay, sweetheart. You're right. I'll focus on the honey."

"And I'll find Clay and a way to restore memories."

* * *

Shortly after dawn the next morning, Travis and Zack sit on Vad's hand-chairs, and I watch as Vad zooms across the lawn and disappears down the path to Agate Falls. My zip-up sweatshirt provides little warmth in the winter air, but I ignore the chill as I sit alone on the porch swing. I tap my zelcom.

"Hello?"

"Hi Hank. It's Zophie. Hope I didn't wake you."

"Hi there, Zoph. I was already up. How are you?"

Zoph? That's new. "I miss Clay. Have you found him?"

"Sorry, no. But I may have a new lead. I'll let you know if it turns into something useful."

"Well, Dr. Filmore showed up at my house yesterday."

"Ha! I knew that weasel would come sneaking around. Did you throw him out?"

"I wasn't home, but Vad caught Filmore and escorted him away."

"Good. I'm checking the shrink's office again—see if he has any notes on Clay."

"Yes, please do. I'll pay you when I see you again."

"You don't owe me anything for searching for Clay. This is personal. Besides being my daughter's boyfriend, Clay is my friend, too. I *will* find him."

"Thank you, Hank. I'll talk to you soon."

"Bye, Zoph," he says, and the line disconnects. I'm not sure I like my new nickname.

Knowing I can't do anything else to help Clay right now, I tap my zelcom to bring up the neuroscience data I got from Hil. Diagrams, charts, and technical details scroll in the air in a wide swath above my wrist, immersing me in information about brain and nerve function. I pay closest attention to corticospinal and hypothalamic material.

Rain patters against the porch rail, and a few drops spatter onto my pants. I look beyond the images and data, surprised to see the sun high overhead. Einstein opens the screen door and says, "Lunch is ready."

"Thank you. I'll be right there."

I tap my zelcom, feeling certain I've absorbed enough knowledge to prove myself useful in the neuroscience research for Brita. Hopefully, working with Dan and Mick will not only help Brita regain consciousness, but I'll learn something to help reverse amnesia.

I spend the afternoon and evening laughing and playing with the girls. Gram sits on the sofa with Quaid while he shows her how to use her zelcom and all the tasks it can do.

I go to bed early, thinking about tomorrow. Somehow, I must convince two brain experts, who seem to want nothing to do with me, to let me serve with them to revive Brita.

CHAPTER 38

Kayla and I step through the portal and into Zelfar. As we do, my zelcom vibrates with two messages. The first, from Elka, was sent an hour ago. "Zophie! Brita is awake. Please hurry."

The second message is from Zack. "Mom, Brita's awake and they won't let me see her!"

I tap my zelcom once more to summon a hoversphere. When it arrives, Kayla and I hop inside, and I say, "Health Dome."

The sphere barely stops on the platform before I grab Kayla and jump out. I sprint through the open entrance and on to Brita's healing orb where Elka, Emery, Zack, and Sheldon stand in the corridor outside, staring within. Each strums the shell, taps a foot, or stands stoop shouldered.

"Zophie." Elka reaches for me, and her fingers tremble around my arm. "I'm so glad you're here."

"They won't let us in." Zack points to the sealed doorway.

I lower Kayla, and she runs to Zack's side. "Is Bwita awake? I wanna see her." She presses her face against the crystillium shell.

In the center of the orb, Brita sits with her legs dangling off the side of her thin bed. Dan and Mick stand on either side of her. Dan touches his long fingers to Brita's shoulders, encouraging her to lie down. Mick, clad in green, stares in the air above Brita's bed. From the corridor, I can't see the information Hil is projecting.

I wave my hand at the doorway, but it doesn't open. I wave again. After waving a third time, I tap the crystillium shell.

Brita's lips form my name. "Zophie!" She hops from the bed, and Dan grabs her forearm, stopping her.

Mick walks toward me and taps his zelcom. "We need to run tests," his flat voice says at my wrist.

"I'm Brita's health expert," I reply. "Let me help."

Brita squirms, trying to free herself from Dan's grip.

"They have to let you in, don't they?" Zack slaps the clear shell. "We have to get to Brita."

Emery bangs one loud thump on the shell. "Open this door and let my daughter's health expert tend to her." When neither neurologist moves, he yells, "NOW!"

My hands ball into fists at my sides, and I narrow my eyes at Mick, ready to get Vad to override their sensors and let me in.

Mick turns to Dan who shakes his head. I can't hear them, but their stilted movements appear as if they're arguing. Apparently, Mick won the exchange because Dan flicks his hand and releases Brita. Mick looks at us in the corridor, taps his zelcom, and the door slides open. Zack runs past me and embraces Brita, lifting and swinging her the way Travis does with me.

Dan and Mick move slowly to stand at the foot of Brita's bed.

Elka and Emery wait patiently while Brita and Zack hold each other for several moments. Sheldon finally throws his gangly arms around his two friends. Soon, the three release their embrace with awkward chuckles.

Kayla whispers. "I wanna hug Bwita, too."

Kayla's innocent little voice says my own thoughts aloud. I lift Kayla, and hold her close, stroking her curls to console myself as much her.

Brita moves into her mother's arms. They cling, sobbing on each other's shoulders. Emery stands tall above them, soothingly rubbing the backs of their necks. "Toss pine," he says, the relief in his voice almost painful, and he kisses the top of his daughter's head.

Brita smiles when she sees me. "Hi, Zophie."

Kayla squirms to get down. When her feet touch the floor, she walks up to Brita. "I miss you!" she says, and everyone chuckles, breaking the tension in the orb a little.

Emery and Elka step back and I move closer to Brita, giving my patient a quick scan.

"I'm so happy you're awake," I say, smiling at her and her appearance of good health. "How do you feel?"

Brita glances right and left. "Well, I feel fine, except I'm confused about how I got here and why I'm wearing *this*." She tugs on the front of her rose-print gown. "Why is everyone so glad I'm awake?"

Mick walks toward Brita, and I step between them.

"Brita," I say, "what is the last thing you remember?"

"I was on my way to the clearing when a green flash knocked me off my hoverdisc." She looks at her hands and arms, turning them over. "I'm lucky I didn't get hurt. Did I miss the energy demonstration?"

"The demonstration caused an explosion." Zack takes Brita's fingers in his. "You hit your head when you fell. You've been asleep for a while." His voice cracks, and he swallows hard.

"Asleep?" What are you talking about? Why am I not at home?" Brita's face reddens, and her breath starts to come in short gasps.

"You've been in what we call a coma," Mick says, stepping closer. "We've been trying to wake you."

"What's a coma?" Brita asks, her voice trembling.

"You were in a deep state of unconsciousness for quite some time," Mick replies.

"For how long?"

"Almost six months," Zack says softly, attempting to take her hand.

"That's not possible!" Brita gasps and covers her mouth.

I pull the frightened girl into my arms and sweep her long hair from her cheeks. "You're awake now, sweetheart. It's going to be okay."

Clearing his throat, Dan glances at Zack and Sheldon. "Brita needs to undergo further testing. Her parents and her health expert may have a few more minutes, but everyone else, please exit the orb now."

I look at Zack and tip my head toward Kayla. He picks up his little sister and says, "Brita will be fine, right, Mom?"

"Yes. She just needs time to adjust." I put my arm around his waist and walk with him to the door. Zack's life has changed in the months Brita has been unconscious, in a way he can't share. "Don't tell her our secret," I whisper in his ear.

Zack yanks away from me and frowns. "I'll see ya later, Brita," he says and nudges Sheldon to follow him out of the orb.

"I'll come over as soon as I get home," Brita yells to Zack.

Why did I have to ruin the thrill of Brita waking for him?

"Zophie," Dan says, glancing at the doorway, "you and Brita's parents need to leave while we run some tests. Please move into the corridor, so I can seal the orb."

"Why does Brita need more tests?" Elka grabs my forearm. "You're her health expert. Isn't she all right now?"

Emery widens his stance. "Our daughter is awake now. We want to take her home."

I glance from Emery to Dan and notice the flat octagonal device in the neurologist's hand. If Dan's sleeve were any longer, I might have missed how oddly similar his device is to Bayl's memory-wiping device. I don't know why Brita needs more tests, but I want to know if Dan's blue octagon caused Brita to regain consciousness.

"Your daughter appears to be doing well." I smile reassuringly at Elka and Emery. "I'll stay for the tests and let you know when she can come home."

Elka gives me a shallow smile, takes her husband's hand, and they exit the orb.

When I start toward Brita, Mick stands with his stocky body between her and me. I square my shoulders and take a step to walk around him.

"Zophie, you *don't* need to be here." He lifts his short arms outward, using his baggy sleeves as a barrier, but it's his emphasis on the word "don't" that annoys me most.

"I'm staying," I say firmly, meeting his glare. "I let you refuse entry to me before, but you have no reason to exclude me now. I'm Brita's health expert, and I possess considerable knowledge of neuroscience."

Tightening his jaw, Dan stands on the opposite side of Brita's bed and glowers at me.

I purse my lips, dig my fingernails into my palms, and stare back.

"Please, don't make her leave," Brita says, looking from Mick to Dan.

"Brita, we know—" Mick starts.

"She can stay," Dan interrupts. Lowering his eyes, he taps his zelcom, sealing the orb.

I don't understand their behavior. Sharing knowledge is what we do in Zelfar. I set my zelcom to record.

Dan positions the blue octagonal device three inches above Brita's face. As the octagon hovers, transparent walls protrude downward until they form a shield around Brita's head and neck. Her eyelids drift downward, and she appears unconscious again.

My pulse rises. "Please explain what you're doing."

After exhaling an irritated breath, Dan says, "We are comparing the neuron receptors in her corticospinal and corticobulbar tracts before and after she awoke."

I nod, thankful I understood him. The data is important.

Red and blue beams flash inside the clear shield, like arrows shooting into Brita's hair. My scalp tingles with empathy as if the lasers prick her skin.

"What caused her to wake up?" I gaze at Brita's expressionless face.

"Her awareness returned when we stimulated her neurons with this new tool," Mick answers in a friendlier tone. "Its power source emits a much higher pulse than our old method." He points a stubby finger at the blue device in Dan's hand. "We call it a neuropulsator."

"Can she feel those lasers?" I see no sign indicating she does, but I want to know before I try this on Gram.

Brita's fingers touch my leg, and I flinch. I gasp as her hands twitch and her chest heaves.

Mick moves quickly to join his colleague on the opposite side of the bed. They turn their backs to me and lower their heads.

"What's happening?" I ask.

Neither neurologist answers.

My ears aren't as sharp as my nose, but they're good enough to overhear Dan. "But Bayl said to—"

"Bayl said to what?" I reach for the octagon. "Brita is not a guinea pig."

"What's a guinea pig?" Mick asks.

Dan grabs my hand. "I don't know what you mean by guinea pig, but we aren't finished."

I jerk from Dan's grasp, ready to call Vad.

"Dan, we have to stop." Mick rubs his forehead, wiping a bead of sweat, staring at Brita's quivering legs.

Dan huffs and touches his zelcom. The laser lights cease, and the transparent shield retracts. Dan grasps the neuropulsator and places the flat octagon in the side pocket of his long shirt.

Brita becomes still and her breathing returns to normal. I expect her to open her eyes. Instead, she appears lifeless—again—and the neuroscientists scurry from the orb. They must be getting their instructions from Bayl. That could explain why Dan and Mick tried to exclude me and why I wasn't informed when they replaced the neurologists with whom I'd previously been working.

"Hil," I say, "please do a health scan on Brita and display the results." The stats glow in blue text above her, and they look good. Brita should be awake.

"Brita? Brita can you hear me?" I shake her gently, trying not to panic. Brita's eyes flutter, and I grip the edge of her bed. "Brita, please, come back to us."

She blinks and, thank the cosmos, her lids stay open. She sits up with a jolt and jumps from the bed, shrinking to the outer wall of the orb. "Was I in a coma again?" she cries. "What's wrong with me?"

I hurry to her and fold her in my arms, patting her gently as she clutches me and presses her face into my shoulder. "Shh, you're okay, Brita. No more tests."

"I wanna go home."

"Hil, I'm taking Brita home," I announce to the orb. "Please send zeltire for her."

"Yes, Zophie."

When the healthbot arrives, I take the bundle of clothing and send the bot away. Brita dresses herself quicker than I expect. The scan reported her muscles and motor skills as sound, but I thought lying still for so long would have made her less stable.

Looking like the familiar girl next door in her white shirt and red knee-length shorts, Brita walks briskly beside me out of

Health Dome and to our hoversphere.

"Is this a new kind of transport?" She places her hands on the sphere and pokes her head inside. With the same infectious curiosity I remember, she asks, "Where are the seats?"

I chuckle, feeling lighter than I have in a long time. "The seats form to the size of the passengers. Get in and you'll see."

When Brita steps into the sphere, a thin clear slab slides from the outer shell at the right height and size for her to sit comfortably. When I step in, another seat appears for me.

My gaze follows Brita's as she stares up at Health Dome.

"I don't remember Health Dome being so big—or so beautiful. Has everything changed while I've been asleep?"

"The explosions from the energy demonstration caused a lot of damage, and we've had to rebuild some service domes."

"Loop Four, Circle Elm, Dome Green," I tell the hoversphere.

Brita grins. "I'm glad the instructions are the same."

I call Elka and tell her I'm bringing her daughter home.

"How different are hoverdiscs?" Brita asks when she sees one zip by.

"Have Zack take you to Transport Dome so you can see all of the new transports."

Brita waves at a girlfriend in a passing hoversphere. The friend waves her arm excitedly when she realizes it's Brita's.

Elka and Emery run toward us when we stop on their platform.

"Dad!" Brita springs from the sphere and jumps into her father's arms. They hug and kiss cheeks, and he cries tears of joy.

Elka hugs me, wetting my cheek with her grateful kisses. "Thank you, Zophie. Toss pine to the cosmos."

Brita moves from Emery's arms into Elka's.

"Would you like to come inside and have some juice?" Emery asks.

"Thank you, but I'll let you and your daughter have some

time together." I smile, toss a handful of pine needles, and walk next door to my purple homedome.

I enter my dome to the joyful sounds of Kayla's giggle and hear Zack say, "I got you, and you can't get away."

When Zack sees me, he hops up from the floor, releasing the playful hold on his sister. "Where's Brita? Is she okay?"

"Brita's at home," I say and sit in the rocking chair. "Unless Brita calls you, you need to give her this evening with her parents, okay?"

Zack sinks into the sofa. "Okay." He crosses his arms, and the corners of his mouth turn down. "At least she's not in that stupid coma."

Kayla runs out of the living orb, returns shortly, and lays Brita's doll on Zack's lap. "Bwita needs her dolly."

Zack sets the doll beside him. "We'll take it to her tomorrow." He crosses his legs and bounces Kayla on his foot. She squeals with delight. I watch them, but my mind is on the neuropulsator that could heal Gram.

"Vad, are you here?" I ask. He appears in front of my rocking chair. How is he so quick?

"Hello, Zophie. I am pleased Brita is conscious," he says. "How is Gram?"

"The same. I want to tell you about the device that was used to awaken Brita's brain. Maybe you can make something similar to awaken Gram's memory."

Zack's eyes widen, and he shushes Kayla.

I tap my zelcom, and Vad studies the three-dimensional image displayed above my wrist.

"The neuroscientists," I explain, "said the power source in this device, which they call a neuropulsator, emitted lasers that stimulated Brita's neurons.

Vad reaches into his pocket, removes the copy of Bayl's device, and holds his green octagon in the air next to the blue virtual image. Other than color, they appear the same—flat octagons about an inch deep and five inches wide. The devices are similar. Bayl is likely the inventor of both.

Zack sets Kayla on the sofa and edges up to the image for a closer look. "If they had used zilimite as the power source, Brita would probably have been awake months ago."

"Zilimite," Vad repeats, like something clicked in his synthetic brain. He thrusts the green device into his pocket. In a blur, his hand forms a passenger seat, which he extends to Zack.

Zack scrunches his eyebrows and takes a step back. Vad's movement takes me by surprise, too. He has always gone outside before transforming his hands into transport chairs.

"I need your help." When Zack doesn't move, Vad adds, "Please."

"Uh . . . okay." Zack moves cautiously, and when he's seated in Vad's hand-chair, Vad streaks out of the dome.

"Where did Vad take Zackie?" Kayla asks, climbing onto my lap.

"I don't know, sweetheart, but I think it's somewhere good."

CHAPTER 39

I stare blankly at the doorway. Kayla runs to her toy tube, pulls out a set of stackable bells, and spreads them onto the floor. "Let's play, Mommy."

I lift my zelcom to let Travis know about Brita, but decide not to interrupt him while he's setting up his Zelfarian honey lab. Instead, I sit on the floor with Kayla, stacking one bell atop another, wondering how long before Vad and Zack will return.

In less than two hours, Zack bursts into the living orb with Vad behind him. The excitement in his eyes makes me jump to my feet. "Can the device make Gram remember?"

Kayla hops up from her toys and points at the device in Vad's hand. "Can I do it?"

"Not now, sweetie," I say and look inquisitively at Vad.

A smile spreads across his face. He reaches into his pocket and withdraws a new device—octagonal, like the neuropulsator and the original memory-wiping device, but this one has a translucent orange shell instead of blue or green, and dots of darker orange sparkle from within it—zilimite.

Unsure about touching the device, I gaze up at Vad. "Are you sure this will bring back Gram's memories?"

Vad holds the new device at his side and lays his other hand on Zack's shoulder. Instead of flinching at Vad's touch, Zack stands tall, his eyes bright with confidence.

"Vad wants me to run the final test with Gram."

My knees go strangely weak, and I lean on the arm of the sofa. "Gram's at the house."

"We should not expose the device to the portal," Vad says. "We have not tested how zilimite will react in America's atmosphere."

"Gram has to come here," Zack says, as if I don't understand.

"Of course," I say, hoping this won't be another crushing disappointment.

Kayla claps her hands. "I wanna see Gwam!"

Vad extends the device to Zack and tips his head. Zack hesitates at first. Then he takes the orange octagon, presses it to his chest, and gazes at Vad. "Hurry back."

Vad speeds away. He doesn't need me to tell him to fetch Gram.

"Where did you and Vad go?" I ask.

"Energy Dome," Zack replies and walks to the edge of the doorway. His back slides down the curved wall, and he sits on the floor, knees bent, clutching the device.

"Mommy, come help me." Kayla picks up a red bell and stacks it with the others on her rainbow tower. I sit on the floor next to her, but my mind is with Gram and Vad. Kayla nudges me to stack another bell, so I distractedly put a yellow one atop the others.

Three multi-colored towers later, Vad walks into the living orb, followed by Gram and Quaid. Zack and I scramble to our feet. Kayla follows, staying at my heels.

Gram rushes to me and grasps my arm. "Zophie, are you all right? Vad said you needed to see me immediately."

"I'm fine, Gram." I gently pat her hand like she's done to mine so many times. "We think we can restore your memory. That's why Vad brought you here."

Gram glances around her. "Where am I?"

"You're in Zelfar, in my homedome."

Zack walks up to Vad. "Now?"

"Yes." Vad starts toward my grandmother. "I'll hold Gram."

Gram sinks backward and puts a hand to her cheek.

Quaid jumps between her and Vad. "I ain't lettin' you hurt her, robot."

Quaid's protection is misplaced, but earnest—and sweet. A smile tugs at my lips. This is a side of him I haven't seen before.

I say softly to Quaid, "Vad and Zack have created a new device that we hope will undo the effects of Bayl's atrocious device."

Quaid keeps Gram behind him. "Will it hurt her?"

"No," I say. "Well, the one they used to wake Brita didn't seem to hurt."

"Brita's awake?" Quaid grins at Zack. "That hasta make ya happy, huh, Zackie boy? Sure tickles me."

Zack grins. "We think we can heal Gram, too."

I gaze into Gram's gentle face. "You have to know, even in the short time since you lost your memory, that I would never do anything to hurt you."

Quaid nods and faces Gram. "Lilly, I think you should give it a try. I trust yer granddaughter."

Gram smiles weakly. Vad transforms one hand into a chair, contoured for relaxing, not riding, and extends it to her. She shrinks away, curling her arms to her chest. Seeing her in such anguish makes me hate Bayl.

What is Bayl doing to our world? Travis and I have been trying to save Zelfar from extinction. Now that the cure for newborn loss syndrome is almost here, we have to focus on saving our community from Bayl.

"Zophie?" Gram reaches a hand to me.

"Yes, Gram." I take her fingers in mine. "It's going to be okay."

She sighs, and her face softens. "I'll try for you, dear." She sits on the chair Vad offered and pats my hand. "Please don't be disappointed if it doesn't work. I can be happy without all those memories. I want you to be happy, too."

When my grandmother knows how precious she's always been to me, then I'll be happy. When I find Clay, and he knows who I am, I'll be happy. When Rudy and Amber and the other outcasts can choose to come home, I'll be happy. When my whole family is in Zelfar, together, and the portal is no longer a potential passageway for exploiters . . . then I'll be happy.

I hug Kayla to my legs and watch Zack move next to Gram. He taps one edge of the octagon, and a slender prism, the size of his little finger, drops into his hand. Next, he positions the orange octagon about four inches from the tip of Gram's nose and releases the device. As the octagon floats above her face, a thin, transparent sheath forms around Gram's head, like the neuropulsator with Brita, except Gram's neck is exposed, and her eyes remain open.

Zack grips the prism with the ends of his fingers and meets Vad's gaze.

"Thalamus," Zack says.

"Thalamus," Vad echoes.

In one swift motion, Vad places his free hand against Gram's throat while Zack touches the tip of the prism to the base of her skull. Inside the sheath, threads of tiny dart-like shafts of orange and yellow light penetrate Gram's scalp.

Her eyes close, but her head stays erect.

I can't breathe. My stomach spasms and I swallow back the urge to be sick. What have I done? If Gram starts to twitch, this test is over.

I look from Vad to Zack and catch a glimpse of Quaid on the

floor with his arms wrapped around his shins. He taps his chin in a steady rhythm on his knees.

Kayla starts toward Zack and I pick her up.

"Harmony," Vad says.

"Harmony," Zack echoes.

Zack holds the prism above the device and opens his fingers. The prism descends slowly until it touches the top of the orange octagon. The sheath around Gram's head vanishes, and the prism continues downward, merging with the octagon. Zack takes the device and puts it into his pocket.

Gram goes limp and Vad's hand-chair instantly contours around her, allowing her to recline.

I set Kayla on the floor behind me. "Vad? Zack?" I loom over Gram, my hands too shaky to touch her. "Is she supposed to be awake now?"

"Um . . ."

Zack's response sends tremors to my hands and fingers.

"Yes." Vad's voice cracks.

I drop to my knees in front of my grandmother. "Gram? Gram! Please wake up." I pat her cheek and touch my forehead to hers. A coma is worse than no memories. "I'm so sorry, Gram. I'm so—"

"Zophie?"

I jolt and stare at my grandmother. Her eyes brighten and her soul shines through, the confusion gone from her face. I laugh and shout with joy, "Gram! You're back!"

With the agility of a teenager, she scoots from Vad's cradling arm, straightens every inch of her five-foot frame, and looks curiously at me.

"Back from where, dear?"

CHAPTER 40

"Gwam!" Kayla jumps toward her and slams into Gram's legs. Gram pats Kayla's head.

Zack and I hug Gram, too, but Quaid hangs back. It occurs to me he may never have told her how he felt before she lost her memory.

Gram looks at Quaid and wrinkles her brow. "What are you doing here? And where is Darcy?"

Quaid's eyes go wide, and he freezes in place.

"Gram," I say, gently turning her to face me. "What is the last thing you remember?"

"I was in the cave with Quaid and Bayl. They were about to banish Darcy. Then I fell and . . ." She touches the back of her neck. "Did Bayl use the device on me?"

"Yes. You fell against him and the prism touched your neck. Quaid went against Bayl to bring you to me. That was a few days ago. We've been trying everything to restore your memory. Today, from what we learned when Brita awoke, Vad and Zack were able to alter the octagon device and reverse the memory-loss effect."

"I'm glad to hear Brita is awake." Gram moves her gaze from me to Quaid. "You protected me?"

Quaid nods. "I . . . I love you, Lilly. I won't let Bayl hurt you again."

"Come here." She holds her arms out to Quaid and he moves into her arms. "We'll talk later," she tells him as she releases him. Gram smiles at Vad and Zack. "Thank you for bringing my memory back."

Vad drapes an arm over Zack's shoulder. They're both beaming.

Gram gives a quick tug to the bottom of her short purple tunic. "I need to see Bayl. Right now." She turns, taps her zelcom, and marches out of the living orb.

"Zack, stay here and tot-watch Kayla," I shout, hurrying after Gram.

Quaid sprints at my heels, and we reach Gram's hoversphere in time to climb in with her.

"History Dome," Gram tells the sphere.

"Gram," I say as we lift into the air. "What are you going to say to Bayl? What are you going to do?"

"Zophie, dear," Gram pats my hand, "perhaps you should return to your homedome."

"No," I say. "I want to see Bayl atone for banishing people from Zelfar. He has to tell me how to find Clay, too."

Quaid's feet jitter and he strums his fingertips on his knees, staring blankly at the sky. I hope his nerves settle by the time we confront Bayl.

"Vad!" I thank the cosmos when I see our android waiting on the platform in front of History Dome.

"Bayl is in conference orb two," Vad says when Gram steps out of the hoversphere.

Quaid and I walk a brisk pace behind them into History Dome and down the large center corridor. We stop when Vad says, "In here."

Gram waves her hand at the door. When it doesn't slide, she taps her zelcom.

"Open the door," Gram says to Bayl's image above her wrist.

The door slides and is barely half open when Oak and Marc dash through it, bumping me aside. My mouth gapes as I watch them streak around a curve in the corridor and out of sight. I'm glad to see Bayl didn't banish Marc, but I don't like the way Marc and Oak ran away as if they're guilty of something.

"Lilly." Bayl stands in front of his chair at the large round table, his chin held high.

"Sit," she says and presses her hand on the wall adjacent the doorway, changing the command from Bayl's cue to hers, and the door slides closed.

Gram sits opposite Bayl and rests her clasped hands on the table. Quaid and I sit on either side of her, and Vad walks around the table to stand behind Bayl.

"I apologize, Lilly," Bayl says, leaning forward. "I didn't mean to hurt you."

I open my mouth to speak, then close it when Gram places her hand on my forearm.

"I believe you, Bayl," Gram says in an even tone. "Your intention was to intimidate me with your memory-wiping device. I'll assume its use on me was an accident." Gram's lips tighten. "However, your actions were deliberate with Wyatt . . . April . . . Irene . . . Rudy . . . Clay . . . and Darcy." She says each name slowly as if hoping to sting Bayl's mind with each despicable banishment.

The mention of Clay sends a renewed surge of rage through me. I clench my fists and grit my teeth, forcing myself to stay silent . . . for the moment.

Bayl clears his throat and folds his arms on the table. "I did what had to be done to preserve the harmony we enjoy in Zelfar."

Gram gives a small nod. "I understand your motivation. But I won't condone your method. I am withdrawing your appointment as elder and relieving you of your seat on the council." She lays an open palm on the table. "Give me your memory-wiping device and your portal key."

Bayl swipes a hand across his forehead and glares at me. His eyes move from me to Quaid and stop on Gram. "There is no need to withdraw my appointment," he says in his usual monotone. "I will not use my device again."

"My decision is final." Gram stands and holds her palm toward Bayl. "Your device and the portal key."

Bayl springs up, and Vad steps quickly beside him.

"No," Bayl says. "I am an elder. You alone cannot relieve me of my position. You have been away so often, Lilly, you do not realize how little influence you now have. There are many who believe Zelfar is a better place without petulant whiners who impair our serenity."

Rage overtakes me, and I rise from my chair, slapping the table. "Clay doesn't whine. Where is he?" I fight the urge to crawl across the table and choke Bayl.

"Clay was unfortunate," Bayl says dryly. "I left him at the hospital for his girlfriend to find."

"Why Clay?" I lean forward, ready to shake the answers out of him, but Gram grips my arm.

"Zophie, calm yourself." Her eyes are steady on mine, and she sets her jaw.

My anger wants to ignore her, but I acquiesce.

"Bayl," Gram says loudly, "This is your last opportunity to comply. Give me your device and portal key."

"I said NO!" Bayl starts toward the door. Vad steps in front of him.

Gram tips her head to Vad. "Silence his awareness."

Vad places a palm on Bayl's forehead, and Bayl sags into Vad's hand-chair, which instantly contours around Bayl's limp body.

"Bring him to the archive orb." Gram waves her hand at the door and exits first.

She leads us down one corridor and stops before entering the next. I peer with her around the corner to see a man standing in the corridor, tapping his zelcom, not far from where the wall opens to the hidden stairwell. Gram motions for Vad to stay where he is, out of the man's sight. Gram walks toward the man. From the intersection of the corridors, I glance from Bayl, crumpled in Vad's hand-chair, to Gram and nervously wait until the man ambles away before Gram reaches him. Gram turns and nods to me.

"Let's go," I say to Vad and Quaid.

Gram waves a small stone at the wall, an opening appears, and we follow her down the steps and into the pyramid beneath History Dome. Vad lays Bayl on the sofa and removes the green octagon device from Bayl's pocket, along with the linked prism.

"His portal key is not on his person," Vad says to Gram.

"I'll get it fer ya." Quaid retrieves Bayl's portal key from the storage area and hands it to Vad.

"Gram," I say. "What are you going to do with Bayl?" I bite my lip at the urge to banish him to America.

"I have to protect Zelfar from him. He will remain in this orb . . . alone . . . for a time. Vad and I will change the access cues before he awakens Bayl."

"I can bring Bayl's food 'n' water," Quaid says, leaning against the stair rail.

"Thank you," Gram says, "but I prefer Vad be the only one to interact with Bayl for now."

"Zophie, dear," Gram takes my hands and gazes warmly into my eyes, "you have the device to cure amnesia. While Travis is working on the honey cure, try to find our banished citizens and see if they want to come home."

"Oh, Gram, you don't know yet." I squeeze her fingertips.

"We finally have the correct formula, and Travis has already started to build his honey lab here. Travis says in six months we'll be able to test the first Zelfarian batch and announce the cure for newborn loss syndrome."

Gram laughs. "We'll have a huge celebration." She takes my hands and we twirl in her happy dance. Then her face turns somber and she releases me. "You better hurry and find Clay, dear. I want to seal off the portal as soon as we announce the cure. Thank the cosmos, your double life will soon be over."

Quaid steps close to Gram and touches her waist. "Do ya want me to relinquish my elder position, too, Lilly?"

She kisses his cheek. "No, but I hope you'll help Zophie find our missing people."

Quaid winks at me and says, "Be glad to bring 'em home." He looks back at Gram. "Even Wyatt?"

"Even Wyatt," she replies.

I glance at my zelcom, anxious to talk to Travis. He's going to zap when I tell him about everything that's happened today.

Gram takes my arm. "You can go, dear. I'll let you out." She leads me to the top of the stairs and opens the door into the corridor. "I'll see you later." She turns and vanishes behind the curved wall.

I walk quickly to the exit, hurry outside, and find a private spot on the side of the dome. I tap my zelcom, eager for Travis's image to appear. I know he can't go with me today, but for the first time, I'm anxious to go to Portland. I'll find Clay, reverse his memory loss, and get my best friend back.

But, like Gram said, our other missing Zelfarians may want to come home—or not. I gently bite my lower lip, wondering what we'll do about their memories of Zelfar and the portal if their choice is to stay in America. I guess we'll let those pine needles fall where they may. For now, I'm excited to bring my whole family home to Zelfar.

PLEASE LEAVE A REVIEW!

WOULD YOU BE SO KIND as to leave a book review? Authors' books have a much better chance at being successful when the readers share that they've enjoyed reading the book . . . which I hope you did. Doing so will mean that you'll help the book be more visible where it's sold. That makes a huge difference to us lesser-known authors. If you could take those few minutes to leave a review, I'd appreciate it ever so much.

ABOUT THE AUTHOR

I'VE ALWAYS KNOWN I would be an author . . . someday. Someday came when I was caring for my older sister, Janet, as she went through chemo-therapy. To keep her focused on living, I suggested we write a book. Her eyes lit up and we began to build our perfect world—a utopian society with androids, hoverspheres, and homedomes—hidden through a secret portal behind a majestic waterfall.

I wrote the story and Janet gave big-sister advice. Our story-building pastime soon worked its magic on both of us. It made her good days better and I had found my passion. It wasn't long before I was encouraged to turn our project into a book series. Janet passed away shortly before the first book was completed, but I made a promise to her and myself that I would finish our Zelfar series and share it for all to enjoy.

The Zelfar Series includes a bit of Pacific Northwest history, areas familiar to me, having lived in SW Washington most of my life. I retired from Intel Corporation in 2007 and live in Central Oregon with my husband.

I love to hear from my readers. Contact me at http://www.ruthcolter.com.

BONUS

Subscribe to my free newsletter for peeks behind-the-scenes,
fun facts, discounts, short stories and more,
plus chances to win Amazon gift cards and free books.
http://www.ruthcolter.com/contact.html#newsletter

Stay in the loop on release dates of future books
in the Zelfar Series.
http://www.ruthcolter.com/contact.html#newsletter

CHAPTER 1

I gaze expectantly at the front door. The tall clock in the hall chimes twice, and the afternoon sun beams a yellow swath across the polished wood floor. I glance at the stairs. Kayla and Krissie, my three-year-old twins, will be waking from their naps soon, and Quaid still isn't here.

When I walk into the kitchen, our android, a six-foot male dressed in plaid shirt and blue jeans, looks up from chopping salad greens by the sink.

"Einstein," I ask, "has Quaid passed through the portal yet?"

"No, Zophie," he replies. "The cave behind Agate Falls has had no activity since you and Krissie arrived yesterday. I will alert you when Quaid steps into the cave, as I'm sure you'll want me to transport him to the house."

"Of course." With a heavy sigh, I plop onto a stool, wishing I hadn't promised Gram and my husband, Travis, that I wouldn't go to Portland alone. They're afraid I might get shot by thugs or land in jail—both experiences as raw in my mind as if they occurred yesterday.

Gram assured me Quaid would be here by nine this morning. I don't like waiting. Quaid knows how important it is that I find Clay and the other five missing Zelfarians. But Clay first. Like the others, he was stripped of his memories and left to fend for himself in Portland. He needs me, and I want my best friend back.

Einstein rinses the salad greens and puts them in the cooling cupboard. If I didn't need our android to tot-watch the twins, I'd have him accompany me to Portland. I'm stuck with Quaid . . . if he ever arrives.

My zelcom vibrates, making me flinch. I tap the small round screen on my wrist.

"Zophie!" Hank's voice emanates from my communication device. His image doesn't portray like it would in Zelfar, but at least I can talk to him. Hank has been my closest American friend since we met four years ago when I came through the portal for the first time. He's a private investigator, and through his ability to navigate this world's intricate laws, Travis and I have licenses to drive, diplomas in science and medicine, and ownership of a ten-acre estate that includes Agate Falls. The cave behind Agate Falls hides the portal to Zelfar, a secret paradise discovered by my great-grandfather. He left his 1850 America, along with other scientists, and founded a new society in a new world, still unknown to today's Americans.

"Hank! Did you find Clay?"

"Almost. My sources tell me Clay left the jailhouse with a short guy who wore black-framed glasses. Who does that sound like to you?"

"Filmore." I gulp. Dr. Filmore is a psychiatrist who specializes in treating amnesia. Three of our six missing Zelfarians, now four with Clay, are his patients, and Filmore's relentless determination to uncover their secrets makes me cringe. Filmore must never learn these patients are from another world—my world. I won't risk exposing the portal and allow exploiters to destroy the harmony of Zelfar.

"Exactly," Hank replies, "and I think Filmore has Clay

stashed at a hotel in downtown Portland. I put a tail on Filmore, and he's been in and out of the same hotel every day. The gal at the registration desk didn't recognize a photo of Clay, but she did recognize the doc."

"Did you go to his room to see if Clay is there?"

"Not yet. I'm on my way to the hotel now. I'm calling because I figured you'd want to be there when we find Clay."

"Yes! Of course I do." I can't wait for Quaid. "What hotel?"

I recognize the name: Brooks Hotel. I stayed there with Gram on one of my first trips through the portal. I tap the name into my zelcom and the directions appear.

"It'll take me almost an hour to get there, Hank. Maybe you shouldn't wait for me."

"I'm a good thirty minutes out myself. I'll meet you in the lobby. Bye, Zoph."

"Okay. Bye." With trembling fingers, I end the call.

Einstein dries his hands on a towel and says, "I'll listen for the girls to wake from their naps."

"Thank you." I hop from the stool. "I'll be back with Clay as soon as possible."

I dash to the master suite and retrieve the neuro-reviver—a memory restoring device—as well as my stunner from our bedroom safe. Zelfarian stunners can immobilize a person or animal for a full sixty seconds. I've never had to use mine, but to save Clay, I'll do anything.

Tiptoeing past the girl's bedroom, I rush downstairs to the back door. I grab my purse and coat from the wall hook and shove my arms into the coat sleeves on the way to the garage.

The winter chill bites at my skin for most of the drive along Highway 30. My 1971 Jeep Wagoneer, now four years old, finally blows warm air through the tiny vent slots as I drive slowly through the small town of St. Helens. I can't risk getting stopped by a cop again. When I arrive in Portland, I park around the corner from the hotel, knowing the curb in front is reserved for valet and taxi services.

I jam a quarter into the parking meter and walk briskly toward the entrance. Still a few feet away, I see Clay run out of the hotel with Doctor Filmore at his heels. I gasp as Filmore nudges Clay toward a yellow cab parked at the curb.

"Clay," I scream, running toward him, nearly dropping my purse. Hank sprints from the hotel, shouting for Filmore to stop. Why is Clay going with Filmore?

I think I see Clay hesitate, but before Hank or I can reach the curb, Filmore opens the cab door, shoves Clay inside, and jumps in after him, slamming the door shut. Hank's fingertips barely scrape the rear of the taxicab as it zooms away.

"Nooo!"

The cab driver can't hear my plea. The yellow car turns the corner. My heart thrashes wildly as my friend vanishes.

Hank, panting from exertion, grabs my arm. "I know where Filmore lives. Come on, I'll drive."

I barely have time to buckle my seatbelt before Hank pulls his long silver Pontiac away from the curb and into heavy traffic. He glances at me, his bushy mustache curling downward. "You were right, Zophie. I should have been here sooner."

"No, it's my fault, Hank. I was worried about the speed limit."

Hank rubs a hand on my shoulder. "I guess it's no one's fault."

Hank's wrong. I shouldn't have let my fear of cops keep me from getting to Clay as fast as possible. We missed bailing Clay out of jail because I didn't carry enough cash, and now we've missed getting Clay from Filmore's clutches because I didn't drive fast enough.

Hank doesn't know that the reason Filmore wants to keep Clay to himself is to probe his mind to learn about the world of homedomes and flying hoverspheres beyond the waterfall. Hank doesn't know where I'm truly from. I can't tell him, just like I can't tell Filmore.

Hank swerves from one lane to another, slowing as we approach a neighborhood with sloped yards and tall houses. He stops at the curb and points across the street. "That's Filmore's place."

A three-story white house with a single-car garage sits atop a verdant green lawn surrounded by a low concrete wall. Wide gray steps lead to the porch and front door.

"I don't see anyone, Hank. Are you sure they were coming here?"

"Pretty sure." Hank rubs his mustache and glances up and down the street.

I reach for my door handle. "Maybe they're already inside."

"Wait!" Hank reaches for me. "They ran from us at the hotel. Do you think Filmore is going to answer his doorbell and invite us in?"

I let out a deep sigh. "I don't know what to think. I just know I have to get Clay."

Hank relaxes a little and turns to me. "Let's wait a couple of minutes to give Filmore long enough to think he got away from us. Then we'll scout around the house and maybe get a peek in the windows."

"I don't like waiting, Hank. Why can't we bang on the door until Filmore opens it?"

"Zophie." Hank shakes his head as he always does at my naiveté. "Filmore would probably call the cops. We don't want that, do we?"

"No." I swallow hard. "No, we don't."

I stare at Filmore's house and intermittently glance at the small clock on the dash. The minute hand moves from one number to the next. Hank starts the engine and pulls away from the curb.

"Where are—"

"Just parking on Filmore's side of the street, out of sight," Hank says.

We step onto the sidewalk, and Hank leads me across the sloped lawn. He motions for me to crouch as we approach a large window near the front side of Filmore's house. I step between two azaleas and stoop under the window, inching my head up far enough to gaze inside. The room is lit with an overhead light clearly showing the sofa and chairs are empty. I peer through the living room and into the hall, but see no sign of Filmore or Clay.

Hank taps my arm and waves his hand for me to follow him toward the back of the house. We creep to a bay window and peek inside. Filmore and Clay sit on opposite ends of an oval table, with Clay facing me. I can barely see the back of Filmore's head as he leans forward, seemingly deep in conversation with Clay.

Clay's eyes remain focused on Filmore. Why is Clay so calm? Hank tugs my sleeve and we duck below the window. When I open my mouth to speak, he holds a silencing finger to his lips and has me follow him around the back corner of the house.

"Clay appears to trust Filmore," Hank whispers. "He may not want to leave with us."

I whisper as loud as I dare. "He has to come with us. I'm going in there right now."

Before Hank can stop me, I grab the knob on the back door. It turns, and I step inside.

ACKNOWLEDGMENTS

I HAVE SO MANY PEOPLE TO THANK who continue to support me in this amazing journey:

My husband, LaDell, not just for his love and support, but for making life so easy for me and encouraging me every step of the way. Our daughter, Leanne, and her husband, Mike Skeie, for their legal and professorship advice as beta readers, our daughter, Candi Linnell and our son, Nolan Colter, for their high-tech inspiration and encouragement. My sister Carol Sessions for her great ideas as a beta reader. All five of my brothers, Archie, Jim, Ed, Will, and Don for their encouragement and belief in Zelfar.

My Life Coach, and wonderful friend, Dorothy Tannahill-Moran, for keeping me on task and for loving me and believing in me even when I doubted myself.

My author friends, critique partners, and all the members of Central Oregon Writers Guild for sharing their knowledge and experience.

My webmaster, Rae Monet, for my stunning website and her ongoing support; Trish Wilkinson, writing coach, for her story structure. My publisher, editor, and spiritual sister, Linda Stirling, for her spin and polish on the manuscript and her professional publishing and marketing guidance.

They say it takes a village; and I'd like to thank this one for helping me bring my Zelfar Series to life.

OTHER BOOKS IN THE ZELFAR SERIES

Zelfar — Discovery
BOOK ONE